EARTHLY VESSELS

EARTHLY VESSELS

THE ISAAK COLLECTION

DAVID T. ISAAK

Dedicated to Raymond Obstfeld and his writing cohort: Anna, Brie, Britt, Cathy, Chris, Denise, Hannah, Jacob, JD, John, Judy, Ken, Kimberly, Mark, Midge, Mike, Nancy and Nancy, Phyllis, Rufi, Steve, Terry, Tiffany, Toyette, and Vickie.

David's favorite event of the year was Ray's annual writing retreat. Please raise a glass to him as you sit writing and reading and basking by the pool—and know that he loved you all.

A Man and a Satyr met in the woods, and became friends.

One cold winter's day, as they talked, the Man put his
fingers to his mouth and blew on them. When the Satyr
asked the reason for this, the man explained he did it
to warm his hands because they were so cold.

Later on in the day they sat down to eat, and the Man discovered
that the food was quite scalding. The Man raised one of
the dishes a little towards his mouth and blew onto it.

When the Satyr again inquired the reason, the Man
replied he did it to cool the meat, which was too hot.

"I can no longer consider you as a friend," said the Satyr, "a
fellow who with the same breath blows both hot and cold."

Aesop's Fables

INTRODUCTION TO
THE ISAAK COLLECTION

My husband, David Isaak, and I first met in January of 1969, in ninth grade world history class. When I saw him walk into class, I immediately decided we needed to be the best of friends. He had similar feelings. Our first date was to an Iron Butterfly concert in February of that same year.

David and I were together for over fifty years, ever since that first concert, and I thought we'd have lots more time together. That was not to be. He was only sixty-seven when he died—he turned sixty-seven laying in a hospital bed after a massive stroke. He died three weeks later, and did not come home to me. However, he left behind a treasure: five glorious novels. I won't judge you if you feel like I may be biased. I am. His novels *are* great, though. Here is what fellow author and creative writing professor, Raymond Obstfeld, says about David's writing:

> "In my over 40 years of teaching creative writing, I've had the pleasure of witnessing many writers flourish, whether as amazing artists or successful authors, or both. David Isaak was that rare writer who was both. He wrote with wit and charm that entertained, but he also gave us sophisticated insights worthy of our best writers. I envy the readers who are about to experience David's writing for the first time because they are entering David's world, a world that is filled with compelling characters, poetic style, laugh-aloud humor, and a way of looking at the world like no other. Congratulations. Reading is about to get a lot more fun."

> —Raymond Obstfeld, co-author of *Becoming Kareem: Growing Up On and Off the Court*

My mission in life now is to ensure that this literary treasure is David's legacy. We did not have children, but David encapsulated some of his fine mind in the form of these thought-provoking, amusing, diverse, passionate stories.

These five books form *The Isaak Collection*. In addition to the magical realism of *Earthly Vessels* (with the forces of light and dark battling on Earth), the collection includes: *Tomorrowville* (dystopian science fiction), *A Map of the Edge* (a coming-of-age story with some dark elements), *Things Unseen* (a murder mystery with metaphysical underpinnings), and *Smite the Waters* (a political thriller with a twist).

Here, in David's writing, you can hear the voice of a man who is now silent, but whose words will live on—reaching across time. Words that speak loudly of David's passions, of his sense of social justice, and of his appreciation for other humans and the complex relationships we have with one another. Please join him—and me—as he continues his journey.

Thank you.

David's wife, Pamela Blake
Huntington Beach, CA
July 2022

1

East Coast People Are Weird

The guardians of the traditional religions might not admit it, but the key to the meaning of life, to the *Mysterium Tremendum*, is real estate. Location, location, location. Everything that exists has to have somewhere to be. Even space takes up space.

Yet any realtor can tell you that the value of real estate changes with time. In 2031 BC, for example, the most coveted property on Earth was the huge flint mine in Britain, the mounds and tunnels now known as Grimes Graves. Jump forward to 1348 AD, and the most jealously guarded holding on the planet was the island of Murano in Venice, home to the fabled Venetian glass industry.

A little time changes everything. By 1969, despite the fact the farmland had been covered by concrete and the oyster beds ruined by pollution, despite the lack of any deposits of valuable minerals, despite the absence of any strategic industries, despite the distinct proximity of New Jersey, the most prized piece of land anywhere on Earth was the island of Manhattan.

A puzzle, but not one that concerned most people. Nor did they much care it was 1969. "The Sixties" was a misnomer: the period where America came unglued, when anything seemed possible, when bones bent and walls flexed, began with the release of *Sgt. Pepper's* in 1967, and ended with Nixon's resignation in 1973.

Hendrix, Morrison, and Joplin were still alive and going strong. The Beatles' album *Abbey Road* swamped the airwaves, individual tracks taking all the top slots. Despite the scorn of the critics, all over America people in highly altered states lined up to see *2001: A Space Odyssey*. When Armstrong walked on the Moon, the main reaction was, *Hey, what took so long?*

1969 wasn't the end of the sixties. It was the crest of the wave.

If 1969 had been awarded a coat of arms, Crystal Keeling would have been engraved upon it. Glossy straight black hair and radiant skin: at the end of a decade of perms, flips, bangs, and Dippity-Doo, she was a vigorous seedling pushing her way through a crack in the concrete to stand upright in the sun, glowing with natural health. Her only concession to makeup was a daily touch of Slicker gloss, leaving her lips wet as though she'd just taken the first bite of the forbidden fruit.

With her friend Sheila, she'd hitched from San Diego to the Big Apple by way of New Orleans: a six-month-long detour where they'd lived in a garage with three musicians as the trio groped toward the jazz-rock blend that would become Fusion.

Sheila's friend Skazz had promised them a place to stay in the Village, but by the time they finally arrived in New York he was in the process of getting evicted. They spent a couple of nights in sleeping bags on his floor—he'd already sold his furniture—and then Sheila and Skazz piled into his van to head for a commune in Vermont. Crystal was invited along, of course; but she decided to hang around the big city for a while.

Spring had just touched the Village, but you could smell Washington Square Park for a mile in any direction, the blend of pot and patchouli overwhelming even the leaded-gasoline fumes of the Yellow Cabs. With her good looks and California Love Child attitude, Crystal was welcome in every cluster of guitar-players, pot-puffers, or wide-eyed acidheads; she'd been passed so many bomber joints of low-potency Iowa ditchweed that her throat was getting raw before noon.

She bought a hot chocolate from a street vendor and sat down on a bench, trying to sense the rays of the struggling Manhattan Sun. The flap pocket of her pack held a secondhand paperback copy of *Cat's Cradle*. She opened it to the latest dog-ear and tried to get back into it.

"So you believe in Sexual Liberation?" a voice asked.

She looked up. The speaker was a middle-aged man, portly, wearing clothes that suggested the aliens had landed at last: a wide-lapeled three-piece suit in light blue, with a paisley Apache tie.

Things sure were different Back East.

She smiled. "Sure."

"Well, howabout sharing some of it with me?" He flushed as he said it, and then added, "There's fifty bucks for you in it."

Crystal shook her head. It was insulting, sure, but the desperation in his eyes ran so deep that, for a brief moment, she considered going somewhere with him and giving him a decent charity fuck.

At least until he said, "A hundred, then."

She stood up and slung her backpack over one shoulder. "Man," she asked, "what is your *trip*, anyway?"

Crystal stalked away, and found a place on the steps by the Arch where she could lean against her backpack and read. She was pondering the pronouncements of the Books of Bokonon when she realized that her butt was freezing off against the cold concrete.

Her eyes sought the Sun with an accusative squint. She'd read that the Aztecs had torn out the hearts of hundreds of sacrificial victims each year when the Sun was at its weakest, using the blood to feed the Sun, to encourage it to bloom again.

Hell, that was in Mexico City, not far from the tropics.

Good thing the Aztecs didn't live in New York. They would've needed millions of sacrificial victims each winter solstice, an assembly-line of heart-gougers, a regular Detroit of cardiac surgeons.

A handful of antiwar protestors marched through chanting, "Ho, Ho, Ho Chi Minh," the ones in front carrying a banner that she couldn't read. Around the park fists rose in solidarity, and there were whistles and hoots of support.

"A *granfaloon*, I fear," a male voice behind her said.

She turned to look up at the speaker. It was impossible to tell his age—he might have been thirty, he might have been fifty. His black hair was slicked down; his dark beard was trimmed in a neat goatee. Despite the hint of a Midwest twang, Crystal thought there was something European about him.

He sat down beside her and gestured at her paperback with an elegant hand. "I couldn't help noticing…" A heavy lace cuff dangled from the sleeve of his Victorian jacket.

"You're right," she said. "I was just reading about it. They're a *granfaloon*—even if I'm on their side." She chewed her lip for a moment. "But, I guess all organizations are *granfaloons*, aren't they?"

He gave a sardonic smile. "No, though one might be forgiven for thinking so. No, for those who can see a little deeper than the common run of man, the real connections become clear. And you, my dear…" He interlaced his fingers with hers and sat her hand down in his lap, patting it with his free hand. "You, my dear, just might be part of something very real indeed."

That was how Crystal came to Anton Reginald LaMarr and The Children of Pan.

The Children lived together in a soaring townhouse off Abingdon Square. And, although most of them dwelt four or even five to a room, Anton gave Crystal—a Guest, rather than a Child—a room of her own, high up against the gabled roof.

Crystal was never initiated into The Children, and her understanding of their theology remained fuzzy. What she understood was that, like her, they were launched on a spiritual quest, and that they shunned traditional, husband-wife, ownership relations. There seemed to be a deep undercurrent of nature worship in their ceremonies, and Crystal wondered at this; New York City seemed a strange venue for a nature cult.

For their part, The Children treated her sweetly, with an attitude that verged on deference. They understood she too was a seeker, and though their code forbade drugs, they didn't judge her; when she came home from parties with her pupils wide, smelling of pot and wine, they merely smiled. The strangest feature of life with The Children was that no one, neither male nor female, approached her sexually; and when she made overtures toward a few of them, they retreated like dogs shying from being petted.

She tried to help in the kitchen, but someone always eased her out, taking over whatever chore she attempted. She offered to clean up around the house, or even get a job and chip in some rent, but she gradually came to understand that her help wasn't wanted. So she read—*Cat's Cradle* (wonderful), *The Glass Bead Game* (curious), *The Harrad Experiment* (laughable)—partied at other Village houses, and deepened her meditation practice.

When Anton finally asked if she'd be willing to play a lead role in The Children's fertility rites, she felt she owed them something; and when she discovered it involved no more than a little friendly semipublic sex, she was happy to oblige. As the old world crumbled around her, Crystal was clear on the trends: By the year 2000, men and women would be equal in every way, race would matter no more than eye color, and sex would be something that happened all the time between friends.

Sort of like a decent back rub.

"I agreed I'd ball him, not that I'd shed all my fur," she said as they shaved her legs. The attention was fun: she'd been massaged, bathed, wrapped in hot towels, cleaned, and polished down to the tiniest crevice. But she had no desire to lose her leg hair—never plentiful, in any case—or the meager bushes under her arms. "It itches when it starts growing back…"

The three female Children attending her laughed like—well, *children*…and went right on trimming, soaping, and shaving. By the time they started on her pubic hair, the sensation had become intriguing. What the hell: sure, she'd spend a week scratching, but in the meantime why not enjoy it for what it was worth?

By the time they were done she was hairless from the neck down, and the very molecules of the air were tiny Ben-Wa balls, dinging against her skin. Talk about naked…

"Far out," Crystal said.

When they started painting symbols atop her chakras, it began to seem ludicrous. Crystal had done body painting before—had even made love with a San Diego artist whose canvases were nothing more than the trysting sheets where he and his lover of the moment writhed, coated in poster paints. But The Children were so damn serious about the whole thing…and the sigil they inscribed around her belly button tickled.

As for the indigo sickle of Saturn on her perineum—well, come on.

The Children's communal dining room—undoubtedly a ballroom in the heyday of the townhouse—had been cleared of furniture. The walls were festooned with fresh-cut pine boughs that wafted their resinous scent through the room, and a pentagonal platform eight feet across had been erected at the end of the hall, opposite the great double doors.

By the time two strong Children carried Crystal into the room, their arms crossed beneath her buttocks to form a chair, the room was lit by the flames of a half-dozen oil lamps suspended from the stamped-tin ceiling by long chains. To either side of the impromptu aisleway, The Children stood—a greater crowd than lived in the house, a hundred or more. Their shapes were wreathed in muslin shrouds, men and women indistinguishable in the shadows.

An insistent drumming started somewhere. Crystal's bearers carried her to the platform, turned to face the crowd, and then lifted her, standing her upright to look out across them.

In the next moment, they whisked away her robe.

Her first sensation was the cold of air on her naked, shaved body.

The next was one of heat, as she felt hundreds of eyes upon her.

Kind of a turn-on, really.

The drums stopped. Then, like a wave passing across the crowd, the onlookers peeled back their muslin shrouds. A hundred bodies stood there, naked to the waist—black or white, breasted or hairy, every chest rising and falling with arousal.

Maybe these Children know how to party after all, Crystal thought. And then the crowd sprouted a forest of a hundred upraised arms, each fist clutching a short whip, and in unison The Children lashed them down upon their own backs, a soft hiss ending in an ugly, reverberating smack.

Way too weird. Crystal stood and watched the self-flagellation as the flails rose and fell, rose and fell, and she found herself counting in sick fascination.

Thirty-two. Thirty-two, or maybe thirty-three.

A palate-tickling smell of blood fingered its way through the room.

Then the drums started up again, and there was a sigh of anticipation as the Hornéd One entered through the double doors and strode down the hall.

Halfway to the altar he threw aside his robes and lifted his arms high into the air, and the crowd roared approval.

The maneuver reminded Crystal of pro wrestling on TV, but she knew what was expected. She lowered herself to the top of the altar and lay on her back, waiting.

The goat-head mask loomed over her as the god clambered onto the altar.

The audience quieted as he positioned himself atop her.

Without pause, he thrust himself easily into Crystal's waiting body.

When she responded with a yummy sound, it seemed to disconcert the Hornéd One, who'd perhaps expected more amazement from her.

She was sorry to disappoint; but if he'd wanted her to be less prepared, he should have jumped her about three hours before. And maybe skipped all the massages, and the whole shaving scene.

Whatever the Hornéd One was thinking, he decided to make the best of it, and, supporting himself on his arms, he drew back and thrust deep once more. Crystal hummed, lifted her legs wider, and, as he drew back, reached around to grab onto his buttocks to pull him down harder.

The goat-headed man survived this treatment for a half-dozen thrusts before he groaned and pumped his sperm deep inside her, making a dying sound with each spasm.

The crowd roared its approval.

Crystal had learned to be philosophical about premature ejaculation; there must have been a dozen over the years who hadn't even gotten all the way in before they came. It was easy enough to get them up again, usually…though she hadn't tried it in front of an audience.

She was wondering what to do next when the Hornéd One slid out of her with a grunt. Strong hands seized her, and four men hoisted her up to shoulder level and carried her away from the platform.

For a moment this was both scary and exciting—she didn't know what they had planned, and in her state of mind, she might have gone along with just about anything…

But they just carried her back to her room and left her there.

Hours of preparation, and then no orgy?

For a moment, she thought about just doing herself and then going to sleep; but the more she thought about it, the more pissed off she became.

Popping off prematurely: hey, it could happen to anybody.

Popping off prematurely and not giving a shit: bad manners.

Popping off prematurely and having her carted off to her bed when it happened in front of a roomful of aroused people, male and female, any number of whom would probably have been happy to leap into the breach: now that was just plain fucking selfish.

Talk about feeling used.

Come to think of it, she wasn't sure she'd had anybody bang her in a decent, considerate, hot, nasty way since she'd crossed the Mississippi.

She paused, trying to figure out which side of the Mississippi New Orleans sat on. She shrugged, rooted through the wad of clothes in her backpack, and pulled on an Indian print top and a pair of elephant bellbottoms. She hoisted the backpack over one shoulder and pushed open the door.

One of The Children, the guy called Will, stood outside.

"I'm sorry, Mother," he said, "but I can't allow you to leave."

"*Mother?*" she said.

"You will be the Mother to the god; and then, you will be Mother to us all."

"I'm not going to be 'Mother' to anyone," she said.

He shook his head, smiling. "The seed entered you tonight. Didn't you feel it?"

"I didn't feel much, actually. But maybe I stopped paying attention for the, oh, *ten seconds or so* that it took."

He refused to acknowledge her tone. "I am honored to be the one sent to watch over you, as you grow heavy with his seed."

Crystal dropped her backpack to the floor. "Are you saying I can't leave?"

"Not until the Promised One comes, Mother. I am here to serve you. But I cannot let you leave."

She leaned close. "Listen. I'm not pregnant, if that's what you think you mean. I'm on the fucking *Pill*. So there's no way that I got knocked up tonight by Mister Speedster. No way."

Will tilted his head back, smiling beatifically. "Still. It has happened. Nothing anyone does now can interfere with it."

"Nothing can interfere with it?"

Will shook his head, a wide, happy grin on his face.

"And, other than letting me go, you're here to serve me?"

He nodded, still smiling.

Crystal reached out and grabbed him by his collar. "Then I'm sure you won't mind," she whispered, "coming in here and fucking me until my nose bleeds."

In point of fact, her nose never bled. And, in point of fact, on his first pass, he didn't manage to stay with her any longer than the Hornéd One.

The second time around, he stayed with her long enough that she started to have some fun.

The third time took forever—long enough that Crystal started to worry that Will's shift might end, and he'd be replaced.

They worked through a good third of the extended version of the Kama Sutra before he gave out, but Striking With the Flat of Hand While Sitting on Hams did him in.

He snored as she dressed. She had just lifted her backpack by one strap when he spoke.

"Crystal?"

"Yeah, Will?"

There was a long pause, as if he'd fallen completely asleep again; and then he said, "I love you…"

"I love you too, Will," she whispered.

She stepped into the hallway and, with all the stealth she could muster, raised the window in front of the fire escape.

When her feet hit the bottom flight, where the last stairs of the escape needed to swing downward to allow egress, there was a horrendous screeching of iron as hinges rusted in place broke free.

She ran to the street, her thumb out.

Her first ride only intended to go crosstown, but instead he drove her as far as an onramp in Brooklyn in exchange for her phone number.

Well, for *a* phone number.

It took her two more rides to get out of New York City.

Larry, the third one who picked her up, was headed back to the Rockies. "You ever been to Boulder?" he asked.

"No. Is it cool?"

"Mindblowing. There's these *huge* rocks, and they're just…well, *huge*." He shook his head as if clearing it. "Spent too long here. Need to get back home."

"Tell me," Crystal said. "East Coast people are weird."

When it happens at all, conception typically comes between twelve and forty-eight hours after the Greek Fleet of ejaculate sets sail toward Troy.

Twelve hours is about the minimum swim time; and forty-eight hours is about the maximum survival time for sperm, intrepid little sailors who set forth on their journeys without packing a lunch.

Several variables affect the length of this voyage, not least of which is Helen's smile itself: during a woman's orgasm the cervix comes alive, dipping its head down into the pooling semen and dilating slightly, swallowing hundreds of thousands of sperm at each gulp. A few decent contractions can cut the needed swim time by more than half.

The woman's cycle also affects the trip; as estrus approaches, the mucus in the cervical channel thins to a watery consistency. Earlier or later in the month, traveling through the cervical canal can be like struggling through a bowl of congealing oatmeal…but time it just right, and it can be like diving into the pool at the Tropicana on a hot summer day.

Then, of course, they say sperm motility is critical. Fertility researchers place great weight on sperm motility, like fishermen searching through the bait tray for the liveliest worms. The fact is that, until recently, almost all fertility researchers were men, and men just had to believe their manly vigor has something to do with the whole thing, that sperm had to be, if you will, spunky.

The real truth is, it doesn't matter whether the sperm charge out with all the enthusiasm of a high-school production of *Oklahoma!* or sulk in their tents like Achilles. The process is like swimming the Pacific, and success has more to do with the condition of the ocean than with the conditioning of the swimmer.

Forget about sperm motility. Just get over it.

A final factor, which all women instinctively understand, is the cussedness of the universe.

If pregnancy is unsought, inconvenient, preferably even disastrous, then it happens readily and almost instantaneously. If the woman is only thirteen, or is having a secret affair, or has finally received a long-desired promotion to a high-pressure job, or has just won the 400-meter race in the Olympic qualifying trials—under any of these conditions, the woman in question can become pregnant even while menstruating, despite using six different forms of FDA-approved contraception simultaneously.

The cussedness factor—known to researchers as OSNNS (Oh-Shit-Not-Now Syndrome) or the OSNWHC (Oh-Shit-Not-With-Him Conundrum)—continues to baffle scientists.

The cussedness factor may account for the fact that, snoozing in the passenger seat on Interstate 80, Crystal conceived, a mere six hours after the ceremony in Greenwich Village. Had she known at the time, she would have been righteously pissed: How can you get pregnant on the Pill?

The Children wouldn't have been surprised.

The lucky single sperm adhering to the oocytic cell membrane dropped its tail, saying farewell to everything but its packet of DNA. Once it began to fuse with the cell membrane, the egg's thick coat of the zona pellucida suddenly began to granulate and swell, straightarming all other suitors back into the waters of the womb. *Closed, Cerrado, Out of Business. Try one of our other fine locations.*

Textbooks love to say we acquire half our biological traits from our father, half from our mother. This is usually described in two words: *Equal Inheritance.*

Here's two better words: *Phallocentric bullshit.*

From our fathers, we inherit half of the DNA in the cell nucleus.

From our mothers, we inherit our mitochondria, our ribosomes, the cell spindles, the nuclear walls, the Golgi bodies, all of the transport structures built into the cell walls, and our entire Starter Set of metabolic proteins and enzymes.

And, oh yeah, the other half of the nuclear DNA.

You can't even say we inherit half our DNA from our fathers. Just the *nuclear* DNA. Mitochondria, the powerhouses of the cell, have their own DNA, and reproduce like independent little organisms inside the enormous cells of our body.

Dad contributes some mitochondria to the reproductive process at first: they sit there in the tail of the sperm, running the waving flagellum like the motor of a powerboat.

But these are discarded like used Band-Aids when the sperm drops its tail: *Nuclear DNA Only Past This Point.*

So what was growing now in Crystal's belly was mostly Crystal. Mostly Crystal, but with something special added.

As the nuclei of egg and sperm fused, occultists all over the Northeast of the US felt a trembling pass through them, and those that were abed came suddenly awake.

In the Olympic Mountains of western Washington a dozen mountain goats, hunkered down in a snow drift, rose suddenly and peered about, their shaggy white coats bright against the night sky…

In a radio studio, rehearsing for the next day's broadcast, a famous evangelist was afflicted with such a sudden and rampant erection that he threw down his headphones and ran for the bathroom…

In a basement of an Alphabet City tenement on the island of Manhattan, Gary Masello decided not to kill himself, and put the revolver down on the floor beside his mattress. There was something he was supposed to do…

In the house of The Children of Pan near Abingdon Square, Anton Reginald LaMarr raged and threw things, and ordered The Children out into the night to search for The Mother…

…but Crystal snoozed her way across Pennsylvania. She ate pancakes at an IHOP outside Akron, Ohio; bought four fingers of decent pot at a truck stop near Chicago; and she kept on heading west when Jerry, her ride, dropped her in Boulder.

She was in San Francisco when Gary Masello made the papers by breaking into The Children's townhouse and shooting everyone he could find in the top-floor bedrooms.

She was at a concert in Ashland, Oregon, when an arsonist set a fire that raged through The Children's townhouse in the night, killing a dozen of them, and gutting the building.

She was living in a treehouse near Mount Angel, Oregon, by the time that Anton Reginald LaMarr disbanded The Children and went into hiding.

Treehouses were awesomely cool, living up among the leaves. When Crystal found she was pregnant, she was more than a little irritated; but she couldn't imagine a better place to have a baby.

She wasn't sure whose baby it was—maybe Will's? Larry's?—but the whole fatherhood thing was so property-based anyway.

She was confident that, by the year 2000, nobody would care about the paternity thing anymore.

2

Inside the Red Line

By 2005 AD, the most valuable piece of real estate in the world was the city of Dhahran in Saudi Arabia.

Everyone in Dhahran knew it read 2005 on the wall calendars distributed by Schlumberger, Hughes Tool, Halliburton, and Mitsubishi Heavy Industries, but the local calendars all showed it was The Year of the Prophet 1425. Which looks like a simple difference of 580 years; but, based on a lunar technology that the Mayans or Aztecs would have thought the work of schoolchildren, the Islamic calendar had only 354 days, so the months skidded across the seasons like a camel on rollerskates.

The value of Dhahran lay not in the city, but beneath the sands, down in the supergiant Ghawar structure, the world's largest oil field.

Prior to 1948, Dhahran had little to recommend it. Owned at times by the Baghdad Caliphate, the Ottoman Empire, and a whole series of squabbling nomadic tribes, it had been claimed by the tribal leader Abdul-Aziz al-Saud in 1902, when he seized the town of Riyadh as part of his campaign to unify the Arabian Peninsula. He never managed to grab all of Arabia, but in 1933 he decided to hell with it and declared what he'd conquered to be the Kingdom of Saudi Arabia—the only modern nation named after its proprietors.

No one cared at the time. The whole province surrounding Ghawar was a barren stretch of dirt that existed mainly to keep Kuwait in the north from bump-assing against the peninsula of Qatar in the south.

Not many people would have noticed if Kuwait had bumped into Qatar anyway. A few Kuwaitis and Qataris would have stared at their new neighbors in amazement, but most others would have accounted it a big plus, bringing real countries—meaning Iran and Iraq—closer to the Straits of Hormuz. The so-called Kingdom of Saudi Arabia was made up of unwanted miles of sand.

After World War I (called The Great War at the time, folks not having the foresight to know it needed a number), the French and British set about carving up the remnants of the Ottoman Empire, creating their Spheres of Influence. Those were franker days; nobody sensible wanted the hassle of real colonies anymore, but friendly puppet regimes were always worth having.

So, taking a red pen and a map of the Middle East, the Brits and the French drew a big wobbly red circle around the region and gave themselves exclusive trading and exploration concessions inside the line.

There was only one minor hitch: They'd forgotten about their allies, the Americans. You had to give the Yanks *something*…

So they gave them the hugest expanse of worthless, uninhabitable, desolate land in the region, Saudi Arabia, which as a bonus included along the western fringe the potentially pain-in-the-ass holy cities of Mecca and Medina. Look, they said to the Americans, we saved you the biggest piece.

And the dumb, affable Americans, still suffering from locker-room embarrassment at having tiny Spheres of Influence (Cuba? The Philippines? American Samoa?) reported back to a satisfied Congress that although the Yanks were excluded from Iran and Iraq and Egypt and Lebanon and Syria and Palestine and Aden and Muscat, that they were welcome to an exclusive opportunity to trade and do business and even drill for oil in the biggest area of them all.

And damned if the Americans didn't even find themselves some oil out there, round about 1938. Had to pay them Saudis near $5,000 for the right to explore, though.

Things might have moved faster if it weren't for the blockbuster sequel to the Great War, World War II. With the same all-star cast as the original (with the tragic exception of the late Ottoman Empire), and featuring all the major players in all the same roles, this lavish production left neither time nor money for anything else.

After the war, though, BP and Shell and Total and Elf Aquitaine all went back to work in Iraq, pumping out new-found oil. At the same time, the fresh-faced Americans, deluded but ever-optimistic, banded Chevron, Exxon, Mobil, and Texaco into ARAMCO, the Arabian-American Oil Company, and yee-hawed their way out into the Saudi desert to make some holes.

To the Americans, the wasteland looked promising. Hell, strip those fairy-assed bedsheets off the Bedouins, slap some sombreros on 'em, and you could be right back in Texas…

The first major hole ARAMCO made found the largest oil field on the planet.

Most of Dhahran was a compound city, surrounded by fences. Until recently, passing through the gates into Dhahran took you directly from the Saudi desert to 1962 America. Lawns, ranch-style homes, happy housewives watching children ride their trikes up and down the smooth sidewalks. With the exception that both booze and Christianity had to keep a low profile—and what's an American city without an equal number of churches and liquor stores?—inside the city of Dhahran it was always Howdy-Doody Time.

In the 90s, Dhahran changed as ARAMCO was gradually "Saudi-ized." Fewer ex-pats were hired, and a greater percentage of those that were came from other Muslim countries. The Kingdom continued to pump out its hundred-and-fifty-billion gallons of oil each year, but with a steady decrease in the number of Americans doing the pumping.

Miles outside Dhahran, Arby sat on the sand under the twilit sky and let his thoughts feel their way down through the caprock, his imagination reaching into the porous sediments like roots groping for moisture, his mind relaxing at last when he sensed the oil, the viscous, inert product of millions of years of slow, soft pressure.

Millions of years, his own thirty-five years a trifle by comparison. So much life buried beneath these sands—so much undoubted strife and pain and energy, all now at peace, all converted to the calm black-green of lustrous Arab Light crude.

By comparison, missing Liz was a tiny thing, the quiver of an ant's knee, the shift of one grain of sand in a dune, and the more of the evening he spent there, the calmer he became, the easier he could return to his dorm room, the sooner he could sleep, the less his mind would be dominated by the compulsion to work out the time difference and dial her number.

He knew his ARAMCO employers thought him peculiar: eighteen months in Dhahran without asking for leave; no weekends in Bahrain; his turn-down of the offer to move from the short-term workers' dorm to real housing. His only demand had been for the use of a Jeep, and ARAMCO was happy to give him one, gasoline included.

Without these nights in the desert, he wouldn't sleep—not that sleep was a cure. More than once his fingers had fumbled their way onto the nightstand and dialed her number. He'd awaken to her voice on the answering machine and find the receiver pressed to his ear, his body curled on the bed.

After the third time he called her in his sleep, he unplugged his phone each night and stashed it in a dresser drawer far across the dorm room. But still he roused it out and plugged it back in each morning.

Just in case she decided to call.

The dream that night involved being trapped in an oil barrel. No matter how hard Arby hammered at the sides, no one heard him, and the drumming of his fists on the sides boomed hollowly in his ears.

He sat up. Someone was banging on the door. The knocking continued as he tripped over his clothes and stumbled through the dark. He turned the handle, pulled, and stuck his face into the hallway. "Wha…?"

Josh, who lived a few doors down, stood in the hall. "You got a call at the front desk. Couldn't get through to your room, and they said it's important."

Arby let the door swing open and retreated inside to grope for his clothes where they lay tangled on the chair.

"The clerk handed me the phone. It's a girl. Somebody named Crystal, and her voice is *sexxx-eeee…*"

Arby froze with his T-shirt over his head, and then pulled his head through the stretchy neck like a turtle reluctant to look outside. "It's my mom," he said, and stepped out into the hall beside Josh.

"Your *mom?*" Josh said. "Oh. Sorry, man, I didn't mean—"

"It's okay," Arby said. "I've been hearing stuff like that my whole life."

"Do you know what time it is?" he asked.

The phone connection was so clear he could hear Crystal readjust the receiver on her shoulder as she looked around the room. "Well, just a second, I'll see…"

"No, Mom. Do you know what time it is *here?*" He'd never been able to sort out whether Crystal didn't understand about time zones, or just didn't believe in them.

"Oh. Late, I suppose."

"It's two in the morning."

"Sorry," she said, without a note of apology in her voice.

"They said it was important."

A long pause on the line. "I just wondered when you were coming home. You said a few months, and now it's more than a year. All that hatred and killing—"

"I'm in Saudi Arabia, Mom, not Iraq."

"—with all of that negative energy. I've had a really bad premonition. Something awful is going to happen."

Arby sighed, not bothering to hide the sound from the phone, and hitched his butt up onto a corner of the reception desk. "I'm still real busy over here, and I like the job."

"There's lots of jobs, Arby. And lots of other girls, too."

"This isn't about Liz."

"Nobody thought her vibe was good for you, you know."

"The opinions of your friends are about as important to me as the message inside a fortune cookie."

"Oh, Arb…" She fell silent for a moment. "You know, this sounds silly, but when you were little I actually learned something important from a fortune cookie. We'd just moved out of Don's place—not the Don you remember but another one, and I didn't have money for a place of our own, and I was at dinner at this place called the Ruby Palace, you were there too, in a booster seat, and—"

"Mom. I'm sorry. I've got a big day tomorrow. I can call you back, but unless you have something else on your mind…"

He heard her breathing across the line. "I do. I went to the doctor the other day—I'm not really into the whole allopathic scene, but whenever Saturn squares my natal Neptune…well. He told me some things."

Arby's throat tightened and he slid off the desk to stand on his feet. Across the linoleum-floored lobby the Pakistani desk clerk looked up from his seat on the couch to see if the phone call was ending. Arby shook his head and held up a finger, and the man returned to his magazine. "What is it?"

"I…" Crystal exhaled and waited a moment. "I'd really rather talk about it face to face."

He looked down at the desk. The clerk had left his laptop open in the middle of a game of solitaire, and as Arby studied it the screen went blank, probably slipping into powersaver mode. "Can you at least…?" was all he could manage.

"It's a life-threatening situation," she said, and her voice was no different than if she'd been discussing her garden.

"I'll come. I'll get a flight tomorrow morning."

"You don't need to drop everything this second—"

"Mom. I'm coming."

He listened to her chatter for a few more moments, then made his goodbyes and hung up the phone. Impossible. Crystal had always seemed immortal to him, more a force of nature than a living being.

He knew it was the normal state of things that children should outlive their parents, but, still… He stared down at the blank screen of the computer as if an explanatory message might appear.

"Mr. Keeling? You okay?" The desk clerk had returned and seated himself behind the desk.

Arby rubbed his eyes. "Yeah. Just sleepy. But thanks—it *was* important." He headed across the lobby to the stairwell. He had his hand on the doorknob of the heavy door when the clerk made an angry sound in what must have been Urdu.

"Hey! What you do to my computer?"

Arby turned, blinking. "I didn't touch it. I think it went into sleep mode."

The man tapped at keys, rapped on the touchpad, stabbed the power button with his index finger. "It's not sleeping, it's dead!"

Great. On top of everything else, the episodes were starting again. "I didn't touch it," he said, feeling a familiar tickle of guilt, and he opened the door and headed up to his room to pack.

3

The Pauli Effect

Dhahran has its own airport, but the best connections for Arby's purposes departed from Bahrain, the tiny island nation just off the Saudi coast. And though you could fly from Dhahran to Bahrain, with the time spent on check-in and security it was faster to drive across the twenty-mile causeway that bridged that shallow bit of the Gulf.

There were longer bridges here and there in the world, but surely none so popular. In Bahrain you could drink; in Bahrain, you could see belly dancing; in Bahrain the Saudis could do all those things they couldn't do at home, which is why the Saudis had happily paid for the giant four-lane road across the water.

All of which made it possible for the car Arby rode in to break down halfway to Bahrain.

The ARAMCO driver insisted on poking around under the hood, and Arby climbed out of the car and stood by the railing, looking south over the smooth waters. At seven in the morning the temperature was just about perfect for short sleeves, but he could feel the moist exhalations of the Gulf starting to rise; in another hour, the air would be intolerable. A rainbow iridescence shimmered on the oily surface of the sea, as though rosy-fingered Dawn had touched the East and then stumbled over Iran, breaking her fall by plunging her hands into the waters of the Gulf.

He hoped the driver would find something simple, but his heart knew what was happening. He'd need another car, maybe two, to get to Bahrain. With any luck, this episode would be short.

In principle, he could walk. All his possessions fit in one roll-along suitcase and his old red leather pack, the latter now supple with wear.

"I radio," the driver said. "When you need to be at airport?"

"Not until noon," Arby said.

"Left plenty time, eh?" the driver said, following his words with a salacious wink. Bahrain was considerably less wild than, say, Wichita, Kansas, but viewed from Dhahran it seemed like Sin City.

"Yep," Arby said, staring at the lifeless car, "who wouldn't?"

As it turned out, one more car was sufficient, and just past noon Arby lounged in a first-class aisle seat on one of Gulf Air's new Boeing 777s. Passengers were still boarding, but first class did have its perks, and one was the constant supply of orange juice, champagne, or mimosas while waiting on the ground.

These were delivered by stewardesses—not flight attendants, but stewardesses, young Brits every one. Their pillbox hats sported wispy scarves, sort of down-market *I Dream of Jeannie* couture, and there was no pretense that they weren't selected for their age and looks. Like the city of Dhahran, Gulf Air was a trip to 1962.

When the woman boarded, everyone in first class stared. A model? Actress? Whoever she might be, she radiated the sense she was someone famous, someone every passenger ought to recognize. The air of mystery was enhanced by the large wraparound sunglasses atop her high cheekbones, and by the way she simply stood at the head of the aisle, not bothering to move toward her seat.

She tugged off her black headscarf and shook out her luminous blond pageboy, but then waited as though surveying the cabin. Arby was entranced—any woman was entrancing after eighteen months in Saudi Arabia, and this one was something special—but also irritated. What was she expecting, applause?

Then a stewardess put her arm around the woman's shoulders and started steering her down the aisle, and Arby saw the white cane and felt ashamed.

They stopped beside him. "It's the window seat here…" the stewardess said.

Arby cleared his throat. "Umm, she could—rather, you could have the aisle, if that would be easier."

He would have happily sat out on the wing for the smile the blind woman gave him. "Oh, if you wouldn't mind—it's so much more convenient—" Her voice was so unaccented it seemed like all accents at once, vaguely foreign in its precision, but belonging to no nation. "But I *couldn't*—you must have booked it far in advance, and—"

Her full, wide lips tilted and then wobbled themselves into an apologetic squiggle. Arby's heart was wrenched with a memory of Liz and her crooked grins; but all women reminded him of Liz now. He jumped to his feet. "No, no, I only booked it this morning, and I'd rather sit by the window really, I'm a geologist and I like to watch the ground when we fly and—"

He realized he was babbling, and simply flopped into the window seat. "Please," he said. God, what a dope.

"Thank you." She began folding her cane into sections. "I can manage from here," she said to the stewardess.

She wore nondescript business gray with a crisp white blouse, but she managed to make the outfit look both sexy and smart. How did she dress herself, anyway, how did she put on that precision lipstick? Maybe she wasn't blind blind. Maybe she was just legally blind.

Sighing as all airline passengers do nowadays when, after the gauntlet of ground transport and check-in and baggage and customs and security, they finally lower themselves into their seats, she touched down with a graceful waggle of her hips and then leaned forward and stuffed her purse and folded cane into the oversized pocket on the seatback ahead of her.

"It was very kind," she said. "And you're right, of course: a window would be wasted on me."

He shook his head. "I didn't mean it that way."

"No, no, I am sincere. What do I do with a window? Everyone nowadays tries to pretend there is no elephant, when the elephant is right in the room with them, crowding them against the walls."

Arby was still trying to parse this observation when the flight attendant announced they should buckle up.

Ah, Gulf Air. British and American pilots, for the most part. He far preferred it to Saudia, where the copilot chanted prayers across the loudspeakers as the plane began hurtling down the runway.

Pilots praying aloud during takeoff was just plain unnerving: it made the whole process seem feckless, as though even the folks flying the plane harbored deep reservations about leaving the ground.

Once the plane leveled off, the woman loosened her seatbelt, leaned forward with a magnificent arch of her lower back, and felt through her purse. Arby glanced at her, almost unwillingly; if she had some degree of vision he didn't want to be caught staring, while watching someone who couldn't see at all made him feel like a voyeur.

She ripped open a packet of pre-moistened towelettes, and a clean citrus smell invaded his nostrils. Then she pulled off the sunglasses and dropped them onto her lap.

What did he expect? Sightless, watery orbs? Hollow eyesockets? Perhaps some fierce scar that lashed across her otherwise-flawless face?

What he saw, as she luxuriated in the touch of the cool evaporation, were long-closed eyes, the eyes of Sleeping Beauty, eyes that had perhaps never opened.

She rubbed the towelette down her bare forearms and exhaled her pleasure.

Her face turned to him, though her eyes remained closed. Her eyelashes were long and thick, but there was something odd about them, and he realized the top lashes were entangled with the bottom, as though they had interlinked arms. "You'll feel better," she said.

He realized she was offering him the remaining towelette. He started to demur, but she cut him off: "It's already open."

She was right. Once the cool citrus hit his skin, he did feel better.

He gathered up the packet and the used towelettes from her hands, crumpled them into a ball, and she murmured her thanks.

"Elaina," she said, offering her hand.

Arby had been raised in communes, extended families, and living arrangements that defied labels. Nakedness, touch, an ease with physical human contact were all part of his birthright…but when he had ventured out into the straight world he learned in immediate, savage ways that touch was freakishly complex for most people, that even a simple hug was weighted with meaning, and the result was that he, who as a child had clambered up into the arms of any adult who was handy, who had lain naked in bed with dozens of people without any overtone of sex, found male-female handshaking to be like conning a fogbound ship through a sea filled with ice floes. *Should I just give her the masculine shake-and-pump? Hold her hand for a moment? Do we turn side-to-side, or do I accept her descending palm in mine as though she were the Queen of England? A squeeze or a shake?*

To hell with it. He let her hand rest in his—weren't blind people more sensitive, wouldn't she feel what he meant rather than what he did?—and wrapped his fingers around hers and gave a long, delicate pressure. "Elaina," he said. "I'm Arby."

With her free hand she slid the glasses back onto her face and smiled. She waited for him to release her hand, but seemed in no hurry for him to do so.

"Arby…" she said. "A strange name to me. Is it short for something? Though—is it not a sandwich in your country?"

As if he hadn't lived with *that* his whole life. He released her hand with a cautious motion, as though he were letting a butterfly escape. "Yeah. But it's really my initials. RB. *R* as in Robert, *B* as in Bob."

"It stands for Robert Bob?"

"No. It's just the initials."

"Initials for what?"

"Just initials, okay?" The edge in his words hadn't been planned, but there it was, like a bug splattered on the windshield of their conversation. He sat back in his seat, thoroughly discontented with himself and the universe.

He hadn't realized her body had been turned toward him until she steered herself straight ahead. "Just initials." Her tone wasn't frosty; more like the empty chill of interstellar space. "I understand." She leaned forward and felt through the seat pocket, probably searching for headphones. Her posture was impeccable, her shoulders still thrown back, her stiff tilt accentuating the vault from her lower back onto the sudden, unjustified ski-jump of her ass, and he knew that beneath the starchy business clothes the small of her back would have those thumb-deep dimples.

Just like Liz.

"rrchd btty m'srry," he mumbled.

"Excuse me?" She sat up and turned to him, the bowls of those sightless sunglasses pointed at his face like ceiling cameras in a Vegas casino.

"Rainchild Bounty. I'm sorry. It's such a stupid name."

"It's beautiful."

"My mom was a hippie. Is. Sorry I got mean."

"What did they call you at home?"

"RB. Arby." He paused and took in a breath. "At any rate, once I got old enough, and started insisting." He waited. Why did he care, anyway, and why did it seem like this blind woman was staring at him? "Rain. Mostly, they called me Rain."

"Rain." She seemed to taste the name, and then she nodded. "Rain. It's a good name."

Arby thought it was a humiliating, absurd name, but if Elaina liked it he didn't want to argue. He was sorting through possible responses when a giant fist punched the belly of the plane.

Her hand sought his and clutched, first as a crude grasp, and then interwove her fingers with his.

Arby hadn't been trained in self-awareness, so his conscious mind noticed little of what happened then. He felt the contact with her skin and the tightening grip of her hand as a jolt of excitement, but it was mixed up with the adrenaline release from the blow that had seemingly hit the airplane. Yet his pupils dilated with pleasure, rather than contracting with fear, and his brain poured transmitters into the synapses that drove the parasympathetic spinal nerves. In response the sweat glands in his armpits and groin opened slightly, and the cells lining those glands oozed out their loads of goaty alpha-androstenol.

The brain's insistent twanging on the parasympathetic nerves at last found a clear line down into his genitals, and the nerve endings answered the phone and dumped the enzyme NNOS into his bloodstream. The enzyme snagged onto molecules of L-arginine still circulating in his bloodstream, broken down from the protein in his scrambled eggs at breakfast. The enzymes clutched the arginine, snipped and clipped, and released a dollop of nitric oxide into the blood.

The smooth muscles of the corpi cavernosum and spongiosum in the penis are normally as uptight as the guards at Buckingham Palace, holding themselves rigidly open so blood can leave. But give them a little snort of nitric oxide and they sigh and relax; give them a strong dose, and they fall over and block the gateway, turning the penis into a one-way trip for most blood cells—they flood in like the crowd at a Stones concert, but the exit develops a line like the queue at the Women's Restroom.

Arby wasn't going fully erect—more in the nature of an Orange Alert—but every drop of blood that stays in the penis is a drop that isn't available to the brain, and his thinking became just a bit clouded, though he didn't mind. According to best estimates, this happens to most men about thirty-five times a day. (Less often in the Middle East, of course, owing to lack of stimulus, which may explain some things about the tone of political discourse in the region.)

Parasympathetic arousal was far from the full story, though. Something new happened, far below the level of Arby's consciousness, below the level of science's best molecular monitoring. When Elaina squeezed his hand, for the first time in his adult life Old Kundalini, the serpent coiled at the base of his spine, raised its head and peered around, its unblinking eyes surveying the energy field of Arby's world.

Had he looked around the cabin, he would have seen colored auras flaring out from other passengers' bodies, with assorted dark blotches: smoky black beneath the right armpit of the female stockbroker in 3A, where a malignant lymphoma was growing; dark purple behind the neck of the male engineer in 2B, where two of his cervical vertebrae had fused after the disc was crushed in a rear-ender; and stormy coal-black above the head of the male lobbyist in 4D, who had just been startled awake from an erotic dream about the seven-year-old boy who lived next door.

But Arby missed all of this, because he was looking at Elaina. And, true, she seemed to glow, but it was a uniform light, the green of springtime, and he saw it not as an aura but as sheer health.

"Ladies and gentlemen," the captain said across the speakers, "I'm sure you all felt that. There's no cause for alarm, but for some reason our landing gear deployed, and it won't retract." Murmurs ran through the cabin, and Elaina's hand squeezed his tighter. "We don't see that there's any real danger, but we're going to have to turn her around and set down back in Bahrain until we understand what's going on here—"

"I'm sorry," Arby said, patting her hand with his free palm, "things go wrong when I'm around. It's the Pauli Effect. But it'll be okay, it always is…"

"What are you talking about?"

"Wolfgang Pauli. He—"

"The friend of Carl Jung?" she asked.

"Umm…no, I don't think so."

"The quantum physicist?"

"Yeah." This was disconcerting: people seldom knew who Pauli was, but this woman seemed to know more about him than Arby did. "I learned about it in college, from a roommate." The plane shifted beneath them as the pilot banked in a wide turn to head them back to Bahrain. "It's not important…" he said, waving the topic away.

"No, please. Tell me this story."

She seemed nervous—the whole cabin seemed nervous—and it might be a good distraction for the two of them. "Pauli was a great scientist, on the chalkboard, but if he even entered a lab, everything went wrong…"

He told her the tale, including the famous case where an experiment in Professor Franck's lab went awry simply because Pauli had passed by in a train; and the case where a group of students had rigged a booby trap to set off a Rube-Goldberg series of calamities when Pauli walked onstage to lecture…only to have the booby trap itself fail.

"And I do the same thing," he said.

"You believe this?" she asked. "Even though you are a scientist?"

"Pauli was a scientist, too. And, yeah—that's why I ended up in geology. I don't seem to affect rocks much. Whole labs of chemical equipment, on the other hand…"

She seemed to be staring at him, and he reminded himself that she was blind.

The captain announced they'd been cleared for a special landing back at Bahrain International, and the stewardesses began hustling through the aisles, gathering up glasses and trash.

After they'd brought their seatbacks to the full and upright locked position and ensured that their tray tables were stowed, Elaina asked, "And this Pauli effect happens to you all the time?"

"No. More when I'm upset."

"And you're upset now?"

He shrugged. "A little, I guess. I'm flying home because my mother is sick. But she won't tell me what's wrong."

"Mothers," she said, as though that summed up everything. "Have you asked your siblings, your father?"

Arby laughed, but not entirely with amusement. "I have no idea who my father is. And I've never had any real brothers or sisters."

She cinched her seat belt tighter around her trim waist. "That's sad," she said, though her voice sounded more thoughtful than sympathetic.

The plane touched down perfectly, but as it turned to taxi back to the terminal, from the front of the plane to the rear, running back like a wave, all of the overhead storage bins fell open.

As you know, many of the articles stowed there, which had shifted during the flight, were heavy or awkward, and there were cries of surprise, anger, and pain as the contents tumbled into the aisles.

4

The Back Forty

Everything in the universe, on every plane, is the same. Only different.

The templates, the patterns, the underlying dynamics of the Inner Planes are identical to those in the world around us.

The ancients said it like this: As Above, So Below.

Look closely at nature. Creatures do what they do to preserve themselves, either in the immediate sense or by passing on their genes. One species preys upon another, not as the result of moral imperatives, but to continue to exist. Listen carefully, and, beneath the harmony of the spheres, behind the great symphony of creation, you'll hear a mindless disco beat: "Stayin' Alive."

Religions prefer everything to be different on the Other Side: a war between good and evil, or an ideal city counterpoised by a place of endless torment, or even a numinous infinity where all is one. A place where actions during a mortal span are rewarded or punished; a place where all existence is purer, better, finer…

Horse patootie. The Other Side is an ecosystem, a struggle for survival, just like the Amazon jungle, or Newark, New Jersey.

An economist once claimed you only had to study two principles to understand Wall Street: greed and fear.

As Below, So Above.

Or, as the journalists put it, let's follow the money.

The Sun beams down. A tiny fraction of that energy is captured by plants. That transformed energy is consumed by other lifeforms, many of whom also consume one another.

As Above, So Below. The pneuma, the prana, the Kundalini, streams down into the physical world. A tiny fraction is captured by living things. That transformed energy is released upward in emotion, vibrancy, struggle, aspiration, despair…and is consumed by other lifeforms, many of whom also consume one another.

It's an ecosystem. There are entities who feed exclusively on love, entities who feed exclusively on war, even rarefied entities who feed on intellectual excitement. There are others with more catholic tastes, feeding on an array of emotions. Any of them, of course, thrive on worship, for these entities, when encountered by humans, are called gods.

All of them exert their very limited powers to steer events on our plane. But they do this not out of devotion to principles, not to advance the cause of some cosmic moral code. They do it because they are hungry.

And because unless they remain powerful, another entity will eat them.

Greed and fear. Sure, Venus is the Goddess of Love, and anyone will tell you she's easy on the eyes. Worshipping at her shrine is intoxicating.

Don't be fooled. Your doctor and your shrink are both your good friends, too—but they don't give it away for free, do they?

On the lower etheric, the world of Yetzirah, the plane of existence just above the physical, power equals real estate. The more power an entity accumulates, the greater the etheric territory they mold to their liking. An entity and its kingdom are one and the same.

By the twentieth century, the biggest property holder on the Other Side was an entity who fled a lower level of the Dark Tree, who fled the Qliphoth; an entity who lived in both worlds, the etheric and the physical.

On the Inner Planes he was known by his ancient Hebrew name: Tanagrim, the Flayer.

On Earth, he adopted the name von Fleischer. Many Germans smirked at the ennobling "von" he added, for that family name was far from noble: Fleischer was a tradesman's name.

It meant "the Butcher."

Benedikt von Fleischer's lanky body sat in the library of his club near Mayfair—cherrywood bookcases, dark oak paneling, oxblood leather chairs, burgundy carpet—but his consciousness was in Yetzirah, very low on the etheric.

An observer on that plane would have seen a vast expanse of level ground surrounded by distant mountain peaks. Here and there, head-high clumps of fat tendrils protruded through the soil, their translucent purple-black flesh undulating as though they were sea anemones tasting the ocean currents.

His Aspect in this part of his kingdom—for he called this area the Back Forty—was a perfect replica of the dour-faced farmer from Grant Wood's painting *American Gothic*. At the moment, the farmer leaned forward and peered through his spectacles at an especially active clump of tendrils. Their flesh swelled as he watched, pumping up like water balloons.

A bit more fun being piped in from northern Liberia. He'd foreseen the Liberian mess decades ago, far ahead of any of his competitors, and he had helped it along: a little money here, a few arms shipments there, and even a few personal visits to Nudge a handful of key players.

He could take credit for his foresight, but not for the creative way the Liberians implemented their little rebellion. Mutilations far outnumbered killings, and there was a kind of genius in amputating villagers' hands, both hands, and then letting them live.

Though none of them knew they were worshipping at his temple, nothing could have served von Fleischer's purpose better. The flood of emotion from a murder lasted only moments; the despair, horror, and hatred that the mutilations spawned were like a fat annuity, pumping up into the Back Forty year after year.

You had to hand it—well, perhaps that wasn't the best verb—to the Africans: they knew how to get serious mileage out of limited resources. What did they call that back in the Small-is-Beautiful era, *appropriate technology*? Chopping off appendages; the South African "necklaces" of burning tires; all the fascinating things that could be done with a little time and a hungry rat…

The farmer squeezed one of the tendrils with his callused hand. Time to harvest soon.

"Boss?" A whisper in a vulgar American accent interrupted his scrying.

Von Fleischer sighed in irritation and opened his eyes back in his London club.

Rooker's muscular bulk bent down over his chair. The man's lumpish proletarian face hid a keen mind, and von Fleischer knew Rooker wouldn't disturb him if it weren't a matter of consequence.

Blinking, he stood, and followed Rooker into the visitor's room, where they could talk. He didn't bother to make for the chairs, but instead slouched against the wall as soon as they passed the doorway. "Mister Rooker?"

"A source of ours spotted the blind bitch on a flight to the Middle East."

Von Fleischer straightened. Something had been twanging the threads in that part of the world for months now. "She knows something, then." He considered. "Knock over everything we have in the area. Don't just Nudge, Push. I'll join in as soon as I can."

"Boss…is that wise?"

Von Fleischer fixed him with a stare that would have cowed most men, but Rooker merely shrugged his monstrous shoulders. "Thing is," Rooker said, "she must think she's found an avatar down there—but we don't know who or what."

"I don't care who or what. I'd rather have a dead potential ally than a live potential enemy. Find out everything you can—but Push everything you can, too."

"Gotcha." Rooker hesitated. "You want to come back to the house while I get things rolling?"

"I'm working. Have Richardson bring the car around at"—he consulted his watch— "half past three."

The man turned to go, but von Fleischer said, "Rooker?"

Rooker's massive body halted and half-turned. "Boss?"

"If she's found an avatar and there's anything…*heroic* involved, then give it an opportunity to don its full Aspect." He smiled at Rooker's raised eyebrow. "In other words, don't be subtle. Kill some people."

5

But Dogs Like Me

When the phone rang in Arby's room at the Sheraton Bahrain, he assumed it was Gulf Air telling him that the flight had been delayed yet again. In typical airline fashion, they'd kept everyone waiting on the plane for an hour after touchdown while the mechanics had tinkered; had herded them off the plane into a holding area for another two hours; and then finally, grudgingly, had admitted they would have to "relocate equipment," and that those passengers who did not wish to be rebooked on another flight would be put up in a hotel until the new expected departure time of 6 a.m.

He lost Elaina early in the process—an airline representative had led her off, presumably for special help because of her handicap, leaving Arby standing in a line. Yes, he wished to be rebooked on another flight, but after endless, inscrutable tapping at a keyboard, the Gulf Air rep couldn't come up with a connection that would get Arby back to Oregon any quicker than waiting for the rescheduled Gulf Air flight.

All in all, waiting twelve hours in a hotel room was more appealing than spending the same amount of time in transit lounges that ran Athens-Frankfort-New York-Salt Lake City-Portland.

On the other hand, if they were calling to push off the flight time yet again…

He picked up the phone. "Yes?"

"Arby? Elaina." A pause. "I had a difficult time locating you, since I didn't know your last name."

"Oh." He realized he was smiling like a fool. "Where are you?"

"Here. In the hotel. Are you busy?"

He laughed. "I've got nothing but time."

"Would you take me for a walk, then, or perhaps a drink?"

"Why not both?" He stood and slung his backpack over his shoulder.

The Sheraton wasn't far north of the Old Town of Manama, and after a few frightening crossings through the Bahraini traffic, they wandered through the old city gates onto smaller, more pedestrian-friendly streets, and the spice smells of the market hung heavy in the warm evening air.

Elaina had linked her arm through his as if that were the most natural thing in the world, and it felt good, but for a time it made him nervous. It wasn't uncommon to see Arab men holding hands as they walked—usually by interlinking their pinky fingers—but promenading with the opposite sex was frowned on, and some of the passersby gave him glances of deep disapprobation until they noticed Elaina's cane.

As they strolled she continued to ask him about himself, and he found himself describing his childhood, the whole series of communes, co-ops, and living arrangements that defied labels. He'd seen a children's book once—one the religious right wanted banned—entitled *Heather Has Two Mommies*. Big deal. *Arby Has Two Mommies and a Daddy. Arby Has Two Daddies and a Mommy.*

"And this Pauli effect?" she asked. "Was it apparent then, back in your communes? Did you make the cows give bad milk and all the cornstalks fall down?"

"No," he said, "nothing like that. Although I don't have much of a green thumb, either. One of the times I planted corn, the corn came up okay—but so did a couple of watermelons, some turnips, and a half-dozen marijuana plants." She smiled, and he continued.

Even back at the Salmon Creek Farm Commune, when he was only five, they'd banned him from the woodshop and the equipment sheds. "Him and technology don't agree," Uncle Hawk had said, grinning through his long gray whiskers.

"That's my boy," Crystal had said, pride in her voice.

It had only gotten worse as he'd grown older, and the week Liz left him it had reached epic proportions: his refrigerator had conked out, the ignition on his gas stove had shorted, his water heater had burst, and his CD player had actually caught fire, melting his copy of Max Lasser's *Earthwalk*. A bus had died after he boarded, and a day later another had wheezed its way up to his bus stop and expired right in front of him, belching smoke. Two cars had stalled at crosswalks when he'd walked by, and he'd spent five days using stairways, not wanting to spend hours stuck in an elevator.

He told it all in a humorous tone, but she seemed to receive it all with a calm seriousness. "Your Uncle Hawk, you said. I thought you said you had no relatives." She put her hand to her mouth. "I'm sorry. I have no right to pose questions as accusations. It's just my nature, my training."

"Your training?" He glanced at her as they passed the light of a shop selling kebabs, and the smell of the overcooked meat made her nose wrinkle in disgust. "What is it you do, then—you're a lawyer?"

"Almost. I work for the Department of Justice in Sweden. Weights and measures. Ensuring scales and pumps are set correctly." She let that squiggly smile appear for a moment on those full lips. "Very boring to most people. But it is why I am visiting Bahrain, a technical assistance program."

"You're Swedish, then? You accent isn't very strong."

She shrugged her thrown-back, posture-perfect shoulders. "I was raised far from home. A diplomatic family."

Even with the sunburst gold of her hair covered once more by a dark scarf, Elaina was a stunning woman, and a man strolling by gave Arby a look that was frank in its envy. He could understand that appraisal, but Arby felt drawn to this woman by more than mere appearances. Slim, erect, she moved with a surety and centeredness that somehow gave him the same sense of timelessness and gravity—and hidden possibilities—that he found in grand geological features.

They walked in silence for a while, and at last he said, "I have dozens of uncles. In fact, the way I was raised, pretty much any adult was either my aunt or my uncle." He laughed. "Hey, even one who started as my uncle and ended up as my aunt. But Hawk was the one that came closest to being a father." He stopped walking. "I want to show you something."

She nodded. He unlinked his arm from hers and unslung his backpack. He held it out to her. "Hawk made this. I know you can't see it, but you might like to touch it."

Elaina held up her hands, her cane slung from one wrist by a loop of fabric, and Arby lowered the backpack into her grasp, slowly so she could adjust to the weight.

She gathered it to her breast like an infant and let her fingers run across it. She smiled at the complexity of what she found there, and Arby in turn found himself smiling at her pleasure.

"What is it made of?" she asked.

"Leather."

"Yet very soft." Her fingertips traced the surface as though she were reading Braille. "There are symbols. The biggest here is an eye. And this is—this is the Pisces symbol, also very large."

"I'm a Pisces," he said, "for whatever that's worth. Hawk put a lot of faith in such things. If you could see it, you'd see that every square inch has been hammered and embossed with symbols and glyphs and—"

"I know. I can probably feel more here than you can see. It's beautiful. What do you carry in it?"

Hard to describe. The usual that came to hand—a bottle of water, whatever book he was reading at the moment, airline tickets, passport, toothbrush and toothpaste, the detritus of everyday life. Those came and went. But also: the spinning toy top Uncle Jaz had carved for him. The eagle feather from the bald eagle that had lived above their cabin. Three beautiful river-rounded rocks, agate, serpentine, and olivine-laden basalt, that had set him off down the road of science at age eight. The watch Liz had given him, which had, of course, stopped working within a week of the gift.

"You know, stuff," he said. Her face showed no expression, as though he'd said nothing. "Memories, mostly."

She nodded to herself and offered him the backpack. "It's a magnificent thing."

Across town, well to the east, an alarm sounded, and then a series of sirens formed a chorus. He stepped out into the empty street and looked in that direction. A thin cloud of smoke rose into the night sky, its underbelly illuminated by the city lights. "A fire," he said.

Then from the west came the unmistakable thud of a large explosion.

"What is it?" Elaina asked.

More sirens from the other side of town.

"I don't know what it is," he said, hooking her arm into his, "but I think maybe we should get back to the hotel."

Arby had a fine sense of direction, honed by years of geology fieldwork, and he guided them back toward the Sheraton on as many deserted back streets as he could find. Something felt wrong, and having a woman clutching his arm would only make them more conspicuous, and more conspicuously foreign, in a situation he didn't understand. The squat dun-colored buildings of Old Town that seemed so charming as the sun set now hunkered along the narrow streets, hemming them into a maze.

His back tingled as he heard tapping footsteps hurrying to catch them. He risked a glance back over his shoulder, feeling as though he were signing a full confession of guilt.

"What?" Elaina asked.

"A dog. Just a little dog." Pale, knee-high, probably some kind of spaniel mutt, it looked too healthy to be a stray, and too clean to be on the streets at all.

Arby started moving again, and the dog trotted up beside him and paced them, wagging its tail and leaping up alongside him as though they were heading to the park to play fetch. He leaned down and patted it with his free hand, but continued walking. "Good boy," he said, "good boy, but I'm guessing they won't want you at the hotel."

"It's friendly?" Elaina asked.

"Very. But dogs like me." He made a shooing gesture. "Go on."

"What does it look like?"

"Just a dog. Medium. White." He sighed. Next thing you knew, he'd be saying something like *don't you see?* "Sorry. Guess 'white' doesn't mean much."

"I understand 'white.' It is the color I sense when I feel light on my face, yes? And black, that is its absence. Black and white I understand."

They rounded a corner, and Arby saw the towers of the Sheraton across a broad street. Traffic had been shut down, and half a dozen military vehicles ringed the building. "They've called out the army, and they're around the hotel. But whatever's going on, I assume we'd be safer inside than out here."

"I agree."

"Then we'll head that way. Slowly." He stepped down off the curb. "Go on," he said to the dog.

"Dogs love you, then?"

"Sure, but this one should clear out."

"Then tell it so. Speak as if you mean it, not as though you don't expect him to understand."

She said this with such assurance that Arby decided it was better to comply than protest. He looked down at the dog, which promptly sat and cocked its head, studying him. "Look, boy. Or girl. We're going into that hotel, and they won't let you in. And it isn't safe out here tonight. So you go on home. Go someplace safe. Okay?"

The dog gave one little affirmative yap, jumped to its feet, and then trotted back down the street as though it were on a mission.

"What the hell was that?" Arby asked.

"I guess you have a way with dogs."

Bahraini soldiers had formed two large *V*s of men, one inside the other like the stripes of a chevron, with the entrance doors to the Sheraton lobby at the tip of the inner *V*. A crowd had gathered inside the wings of the outer *V*, and moved gradually forward as an official examined passports and let a few through. After a few minutes in the throng, Arby understood that most of the people weren't trying to get into the hotel; they had simply gathered to gawk, to collect rumors, or to feel safer under the shelter of the army's weaponry.

Arby squeezed his way through the crowd, one hand leading Elaina, the other clutching his passport. When they had worked their way to the tip of the *V*, a man stood there, examining faces and checking passports. He waved Arby and Elaina through with an impatient gesture, as though they were impeding his search, and the two of them stepped past the first line of soldiers.

In the empty ten-foot gap between the two lines, a second official stood, his hand out for their passports. Arby put his arm around Elaina and guided her toward the man.

An uproar of voices. A wild-eyed man, clearly a local, had burst through the line of soldiers only a few feet away. Despite the warmth of the night, the man wore a heavy jacket, and he yanked it open to reveal a torso strapped with even rows of dynamite sticks, neat and overlapped like lacquered samurai armor.

The man reached for some kind of dangling handle, and screams rose from the crowd. Without any conscious thought, Arby spun on his heel, spread his arms wide, and jumped between the bomber and Elaina.

He saw a cloud of darkness swirl out around the man's head. Inexplicable.

The man yanked down on the handle.

From behind, Elaina shoved Arby with the force of a rear-end collision.

Arby flew forward, arms still wide, and embraced the bomber. Together they fell to the pavement, Arby atop the struggling man.

And then…nothing.

Soldiers leapt on them, and Arby felt himself lifted away and placed on his feet, men still gripping him, unsure of what they ought to do.

He looked to the side and saw Elaina.

"You pushed me!" he said.

She took a pair of faltering steps in his direction. "I'm sorry!"

"But, but…you *pushed* me!"

More soldiers closed in, blocking his view of her. They began to usher him away from the doors, and he found himself beside a trio of soldiers that were moving Elaina in the same direction. "Why?" he asked. "Why?"

"It's okay!" she said, raising her voice over the tramp of booted feet and the sounds of the crowd. She sounded excited, as though he ought to be happy. "I think I know who you are now!"

6

Clouds

The soldiers whisked both of them away in separate personnel carriers, and refused to answer Arby's questions. But when they arrived at their command center—a flattish nondescript building that must have been designed by an architect who specialized in pre-fab high schools—they took him into a narrow office that, if the high-school analogy held, might have been the Career Guidance Center, and there they had plenty of questions for him. Why was he in Bahrain? What had happened? Did he know the bomber? Why had he jumped? Who was the woman? Why didn't the bomb explode?

His chief interrogator was friendly enough, despite his disconcerting resemblance to a young Saddam Hussein, and the questions were more curious than hostile: the authorities were puzzled. Arby explained why he was in Bahrain, but he couldn't help them out with their other issues—he didn't know the answers. Well, he guessed that the bomb hadn't gone off because the Pauli effect was running strong, but bringing up this topic, even couched in the most scientific terms, would instantly confirm him as a liar, a nutcase, or both.

A discomfited guard opened the door and asked a quick question in Arabic. The interrogator sighed and threw up one hand.

The guard stepped aside and a harried young American in a suit pushed through the door. "Mr. Keeling, I'm Karl Devoe, the deputy ambassador. I'm here to take you back to our embassy." He turned his attention to the Saddam look-alike. "The United States government is extremely concerned about this incident. From what I've heard, you should be giving this young man a medal, not the third degree. And I assure you, we plan on demanding a full explanation."

Saddam let out a long breath. "We have had more than a dozen terrorist incidents here in one night. This young man was closely involved in one, and we needed to interview him. We have done nothing like your so-called third degree." He looked to Arby, his upturned palms beseeching. "Tell this man. Have I threatened you? Mistreated you in any way?"

Arby shook his head. "No. Although I still wish you'd tell me what happened to my friend."

"Miss, uh…" The interrogator scanned the papers on the desk before him. "Miss Suh…Suh-vuh—"

"Elaina Svärdfors," Devoe said.

"As he says. We released her over an hour ago—"

"And she came to us. Mr. Keeling, if you're ready to go?"

Arby rose, and Devoe stepped aside to let him through the door. As he passed, Devoe said to Saddam, "Diplomatic protocol and just plain common courtesy demand that you let us know when you pick up one of ours. We *do* plan to follow up on this."

From the rear seat of the limo, Arby watched the driver and the guard scan the streets as they drove toward the embassy. Whatever had happened in Bahrain that night had the men spooked. They crawled the big car up to each intersection, peered right and left, and then accelerated across the empty street as though they expected rocket fire.

"You're quite a hero," Devoe said.

"I didn't do anything."

"The heck you didn't."

"I fell on a guy. His bomb malfunctioned. It was all an accident."

Devoe waggled a finger, coyly admonishing. "Nope. Jumped right in front of that girl, your arms spread to shield her. And then tackled that sonofabitch—"

"That's not what happened."

"Listen, Mr. Modesty, I saw the whole thing on tape."

"Videotape?"

"Sure. Hell, half the world saw what you did—there was a CNN guy there rolling tape, and Fox picked it up. Both of them want interviews."

"Oh, Christ." He imagined trying to explain to Crystal why he was appearing on Fox News Network—*Fairly Unbalanced*, as she called it—and groaned. "No way."

"Mr. Keeling. You have to understand. Your country needs heroes right now. Why, I bet the President himself would like to shake your hand."

"Also on Fox, I suppose."

"Sure, whatever you like."

"Mr. Devoe, with all due respect, I'd rather get up every morning and have a high colonic. Now get this straight. I'm not a hero, and no matter what it looked like, what happened out there tonight was an accident, and all I intend to do is go home. My mother is sick and she needs me."

Devoe sank back into the leather seats and seemed to sulk. Then he brightened. "Say, that's a pretty good story right there. Saves the woman he loves and a whole crowd of onlookers, and then, avoiding publicity, flies home to be with his ailing mother. Can we do the story that way?"

"I don't want a story, not any story! Will you get that clear?"

Devoe waited. "You're already a story. Nothing I can do about that."

"Fine. Just get me the hell out of town, okay?"

"We can facilitate that. Where to?"

"Oregon. Portland, if you can manage it."

The man pulled out his PDA and poked at it with his stylus. "Adjacent seats, I suppose?"

"Huh?"

"For Ms. Svärdfors." He took in Arby's confusion. "She gave us to understand that you were traveling together." Arby felt the man watching him. "If there's some complication, of course, we can be discreet."

Arby rubbed his forehead and tried to sort this out. Elaina told them she was coming with him to the US? That made no sense—though, when he thought about it, he couldn't recall that she'd said where she was headed. And perhaps the embassy people had simply misunderstood.

"An extraordinary woman," Devoe said, "if you don't mind my saying so. Smart, decisive, and, lordy—no one in the embassy can remember the last time a stunner like that walked through the door, not at this posting. It's so unfortunate that—"

That she's blind? Arby grinned to himself as Devoe realized he'd ventured out onto slippery ground and was about to fall.

"—that the two of you were separated like that," Devoe continued in a rush.

Nice save.

Devoe pursed his lips, warming to his new theme. "It's not like the movies, is it? You save the girl, then you're supposed to have this great movie moment. She owes you her life."

"I think I owe her a few things, too," Arby said, and leaned back against the plush seat cushions.

He kept his mouth shut until they were through security and immigration.

"What the hell were you thinking?" he asked. "I could have been killed."

She shouldered her purse and scanned the floor in front of her with the tip of her cane. "I can tell the way is clear for me to walk," she said, "but not which direction to find our gate."

He readjusted his backpack and steered her to the right. "Oh, I understand your thinking, I suppose—the Pauli effect and all. But you can't count on it."

Her expression remained so serene that he wasn't sure she'd even heard him until she said, "We were only a few feet away. If the bomber had been successful, we would both have died, whether you were embracing him, or standing in front of me. Which was very noble, very beautiful, by the way. But I was already certain by then."

"Of what?"

She asked, "Are you aware there are no rivers in this country?"

"It's a flat little island surrounded by countries full of sand. Of course there aren't any rivers." He exhaled an exasperated breath. "Elaina, why are you still here, and what the hell is going on?"

She stopped, and he waited. "Give me your hand."

He reached over to her outstretched palm, and she interlaced her fingers with his. She squeezed his hand tight. "Now look around carefully," she said, "and tell me what you see."

He let his gaze roam around the terminal. Except for the fact that many of the travelers were in Arab dress, it could have been any modern airport in almost any country. There were more guards than usual, dressed in sand camo, cradling stubby automatics… He shook his head to clear it. His vision seemed blurry, and the people passing by were silhouetted by clear watery lines like the heat waves rising from a baking asphalt road. Tired. Too long on the road with too little sleep.

"More guards than usual," he said. "Everything else looks normal."

Elaina gave a snort of impatience. "Why do you have to be so difficult?" She pulled her hand from his, unbuttoned the cuffs of her white blouse, and rolled up the sleeves. She slid the loop on her cane up to her elbow and let it dangle. Holding her forearms up like a freshly scrubbed surgeon waiting to be robed and gloved, she turned to face him. "Embrace me," she said.

"Huh?"

"Hug me. It that so repellant?"

"No, but…" But it was the Middle East, and although the prospect of wrapping his arms around Elaina was pleasing enough, this wasn't the ideal situation. "You know," he said, as he opened his arms, "I'm starting to think you're crazy."

"Shut up," she said. Her slim shoulders were surprisingly strong in his arms, and she reached her own arms around his waist and eased her body up against him, which felt just fine.

Then she slid both of her forearms up the back of his shirt and pressed her arms and open palms against his bare back. "Hey!" he said. A tingling started where her skin touched his, and then heat began coursing into him. "Look, Elaina—"

"Shut up and look around!" she said in a fierce whisper, her lips near his ear.

"Holy shit," he said.

The world had changed. Every living thing in the terminal, including the potted palm trees, had blossomed shifting auras that glowed and slithered like the Northern Lights.

"*Now* tell me what you see."

"People—people are glowing. Greens and reds and golds…"

"Yes, yes, but what else? Study them."

He looked at a middle-aged woman who stared back at him as though her privacy had been invaded. Around the center of her stomach, an inky black pool interrupted the green of her aura, and something about the sight made Arby's stomach clench. "A black thing, solid black—"

"That's an illness, ignore those. Look for storm clouds."

After a moment, he saw what she meant. Within the auras surrounding the heads of several people were swirling, moving masses of dark matter, and in a few cases these clouds gathered into a widening funnel that sprouted far above the aura, like a tornado punching through a rainbow. His mouth felt dry, and he fought to swallow before speaking. "Clouds. I see them."

"That's evil. Cultivated evil, an obsession that has come to dominate someone. What else? Study the clouds."

A guard paced by, the cloud in his aura towering a few feet above his head. The man's hands clutched at his automatic, and Arby knew, somehow knew with perfect certainty, that the man would like nothing better than to open fire and mow down everyone in the terminal, and that this fantasy was riding atop the man's consciousness like a warrior on a stallion.

The guard locked gazes with Arby for only a moment, and Arby felt a rush of hatred from the man, and then sensed something…

Arby glanced at the cloud above the guard's head. There, off-center, at one side of the tornado, a fist-sized knot of dark purple and blue throbbed, like a bruise on the cloud.

Arby turned his head to the far end of the terminal, sure that if he stared in the guard's direction for one more moment the man would give in to his urge and open fire.

"Some of the clouds are—are injured. Bruised or something." His voice sounded trembly in his own ears. "I thought that one of the guards was going to shoot us."

Elaina slid her arms from under his shirt, eased out of Arby's embrace, and smoothed down her cuffs. "He might," she said. "Lead us away from him."

Though he was no longer touching Elaina, Arby still saw auras as they walked, though the effect had diminished by half. He found himself fighting the urge to swerve away from the auras of others as though to touch them would be to bump into their physical bodies.

The auras were misshapen, unruly things, and he saw more storm clouds, and in the cloud above a brooding man sitting on a suitcase he saw another bruise. The instant he noticed it, the man noticed him, and glared.

"What is all this?" Arby whispered to Elaina.

"How the world really is, but worse than usual," she said. "Are you frightened yet?"

"Yes."

"Good. Now if you want to live, you must stop being difficult and let me help you."

A big part of Arby wanted to deny that any of this was happening. But the auras were all too real; he strode past a parade of distorted essences that pawed at him like the inmates of a Victorian madhouse. "We're coming to our gate," he said.

"Good." She stopped, and turned to take both of his hands in hers, as though they were bride and groom. It was only then that he saw Elaina's own aura. Perfectly symmetrical, it was almost invisible unless he focused on it, but when he studied it, it shone out from her like a beacon. Russian dolls of burnished colors nestling one within another: starting at her core, a dark indigo, then red around her skin, green beyond that, and finally a gold and gold-white nimbus that encapsulated all. Unlike the other auras he'd seen, there were no distortions, no bulges, and no real movement other than a slight tidal surge that he suddenly knew must be her pulse.

"Stand with your feet together," she said. "Heel-to-heel, toe-to-toe."

He obeyed, but teetered. "I feel off-balance," he said.

"You are. Now listen. One long inhale, gather all of it in to you, and then surrender. Breathe out and let me take it all."

He drew in breath until his chest hurt, paused, and then exhaled. Something gathered within him and flooded out through his hands, and as he watched, Elaina's prefect aura quivered and twisted, blotching with gray in uneven spots.

Elaina shuddered, and then stood still again, and her aura pulled into her body and then bloomed out again, its perfection restored. Then it faded from view.

She sucked at her teeth for a moment. "You have an interesting aftertaste," she said. "Better now?"

He realized his shoulders were hanging, all tension gone. His backpack swung loose, ready to drop from his shoulder. Around the terminal passengers lugged suitcases, sprawled in chairs, waited in lines. Not a single aura anywhere, much less any clouds.

"Much better," he said. In fact, he was now so relaxed he could have curled up on the marble floor and slept. "Thank you."

She released his hands. "I didn't do it just for you. To be frank, I'd prefer the plane keep working properly on this next flight."

7

Minor Indiscretions

The plush crimson runner that arced its way down the stairs absorbed any sound his footfalls might have made, but von Fleischer took delicate steps as he ascended to the second story of the guest wing. Already morning light streamed through the high bullseye-paned windows onto the landing above; he didn't want to awaken the man before his arrival.

He paused at the second door down the hall, the one whose windows faced the gloomy north of Scotland. A country estate: no gentleman should be without one. After holding his breath and listening, he let his mind rise on the planes. The watery surge of dreamstuff pressed at him from beyond the door, but only one little lake of it, not two. Good. The boy must already be awake.

He rapped on the door, sudden and hard. He heard the rustling of bedthings, a groan, and then feet hitting the floor, running lightly over toward the door. Then Armbruster's nasal American voice, still dazed with sleep: "Hey. No, wait a minute there—!"

Liam opened the door, still pulling a silky robe around his shoulders.

Von Fleischer feigned mild surprise. "Why, Liam! I didn't know you'd stayed over…"

"Hadn't planned it," the boy said. "One thing led to another, y'know." He didn't bother to close the robe, but cocked one slim hip as though inviting the older man to examine the goods. Von Fleischer was unimpressed—his tastes ran more toward women—but he favored Liam with an inscrutable smile, and Liam blushed in a way that lit up his blue eyes.

Von Fleischer paid no obvious attention to Armbruster in the canopied bed. The man first began climbing out, and then panicked and flopped back against the pillows, jerking the covers up to his chin. "I'd think," von Fleischer said, "that you ought to be going on home in any case. Ask Sellars to take you in the car."

Liam gathered up his clothes from the floor, clambered onto the bed and whispered something to Armbruster, and then scampered from the room, letting the robe flow behind him like a cape.

"I *do* apologize," von Fleischer said to Armbruster, "but you asked me to knock you up early enough for breakfast before your tee time." He began pulling the door shut. "Join me in the conservatory in, say, twenty minutes?"

The sunlight had come on strong, which was never to be counted on of a March in the British Isles, and von Fleischer said as much—a banal comment, but something he hoped would reassure Armbruster that all was normal in the world. "Clear and windless," he added, "the gods must favor you."

Armbruster fidgeted, his big football-player fingers toying with the delicate china coffee cup. The man tossed a glance at Rooker, who stood silhouetted against the diffuse light of a greenhouse window, and then looked over his shoulder at the glass doors where McMahon waited, playing butler. Armbruster shook his ponderous head as though clearing it. He leaned forward in a confiding manner, but the man's whisper was big enough to be heard for blocks. "I don't know what happened last night," he said. "I don't seem to remember."

You liar, von Fleischer thought. He tilted his head, a polite, questioning, nonjudgmental posture.

"It's just—well, you gotta believe me. I've never done—I mean, I'm not a guy who—"

The hell you aren't. Settling on Liam had taken hours of consultation, and von Fleischer and Rooker had agreed that he fit Armbruster's tastes to perfection. "I'm sure you aren't, Senator," von Fleischer said. "To many of our young boys, America is such a…*virile* culture by comparison. Liam is young and a little foolish, and, if I may say so, looks to be as much a girl as a boy." He gave an elaborate stage shrug that would have served for an audience of two thousand. "We view these things differently in Europe, perhaps. Minor indiscretions are nothing more than…minor indiscretions."

Armbruster gulped his coffee. McMahon hastened over to refill it and then withdrew just as quickly. "Well it ain't like that in the States," Armbruster said. "It could ruin me. Plus, what you must think of me now…"

"On the contrary." Von Fleischer slid his hand inside his jacket and pulled the envelope from the inner pocket. "In fact, I have more confidence in you than ever. And so do my associates." He placed the envelope on the table near Armbruster's saucer. "Checks from more than a dozen organizations." He tapped it with his finger. "Little nonprofit affairs, all—what's the phrase?—below the radar."

Armbruster nodded. "Thing is—I need to know that last night stays below the radar, too. I don't think you understand that—"

Von Fleischer raised his palm and waved it side-to-side, as though wiping away the other man's words. "I am a great keeper of secrets. And I will share one of mine with you. I too have made love to a boy. And not just once. Many times, over many months."

Indeed I did, he thought, *and more than one boy; every new body I live in requires one.* Von Fleischer let a fond expression appear on his face, an easy mask for him to don: after more than four hundred years on this plane, he had accumulated plenty of material for genuine nostalgia.

He flicked his fingers in a lazy throw-aside gesture. "I am not a homosexual. It is my passion for the fair sex in all its variety that has kept me a bachelor these many years. Yet I don't regret that boy. Why should you regret yours?"

Insofar as someone can seem genuinely touched at the same moment they are engaged in scooping up an envelope filled with campaign contributions, Armbruster seemed moved. He pocketed the envelope, his eyes a little wet, and said, "You know, Benedikt, sometimes I think you understand me better than anybody."

"I can't express," von Fleischer said, putting on his most aristocratic smile, "how much pleasure it gives me to hear you say that."

Over by the ancient, root-bound orange tree, Rooker cleared his throat.

Von Fleischer raised his eyebrow. "Yes? Ah." He turned his attention back to Armbruster. "If you're to make your eleven o'clock tee time, you'll have to be heading out soon."

"Sure you won't join me?"

"Alas, as your Mr. Twain had it, for me the sport of golf is little more than a good walk spoiled."

Armbruster stood, his knees pushing back the chair before McMahon could hurry over to ease it back. "We still need to talk about quite a few things."

"There's this evening, of course." McMahon pulled back von Fleischer's chair as he rose. He glanced at his wristwatch. "Or, if you prefer, you could change to an afternoon tee time—I'm sure it can be arranged." He put on a false brightness, as though a thought had just occurred to him. "In fact, if you prefer to go in late afternoon, Liam could caddy for you."

A sequence of uninterpretable emotions emerged on Armbruster's face, each taking one glance at the world outside and then diving for cover.

Von Fleischer did his best not to notice. "The boy's supposed to be quite good," he said, "a rising star. All of the pros think he ought to go on full time at the links. But he's still required by law to attend school most of the day. He's only—how old, McMahon?"

"Just coming on fifteen, I believe, sir."

Armbruster's eyes acquired a hunted look, but von Fleischer crossed the greenhouse and steered the man out by an affectionate grip on his elbow. "We'll have plenty of time this evening," he said. "Party doesn't begin until after eight."

At times, von Fleischer thought Rooker might be the ugliest man he'd ever seen. The man's thickset, muscular body was ill-proportioned, with stumpy forearms and shins. His oversized forehead was lumpy, and von Fleischer wished that phrenology were still in fashion: its enthusiasts would have lined up to fondle Rooker's skull.

By the time von Fleischer returned from escorting Senator Armbruster to the car, Rooker already lounged at the table, feet up on a neighboring chair, a cup of coffee clutched in his big paw. "So I should have the kid there again tonight?" Rooker asked.

"Once the party is well underway. Not too early. Let the senator imbibe a good quantity of decent scotch first." Von Fleischer plucked a slice of quartered orange from the platter, fit it into his mouth and bit down, neatly carving the flesh from the peel. Acid sunny brightness poured into his mouth. Oranges in Europe in March—when he'd been a child in Bavaria in the late 1500s, a lettuce in March, even an unrotted cabbage, would have been a miracle. Oranges. He'd never stop marveling.

As though stirred by example, Rooker snagged himself an orange quarter and imitated his master. The man's features were vulgar and bulbous, von Fleischer noted, but his lips were full and almost feminine, with a perfect Cupid's bow pointing down beneath his potato nose. A sensual mouth that warred with the man's essence.

Rooker licked the juice from his lips. "You think he'll cash 'em all?"

"Has he failed us before?" Von Fleischer folded his long frame into the chair Armbruster had abandoned. "Let's just ensure that he has another night or two of bliss before he flies on home."

"Yeah. But half of town saw him almost banging the kid after cocktails last night." Rooker laughed and reached for another orange quarter. "You own him now."

Von Fleischer considered. "In America they have a story about a farmer who captures a wild pig by feeding him every day as he gradually constructs a fence around the feeding area."

Rooker tilted his thumbs upward from where his hands sprawled on his lap, a gesture that said *…and…?*

"You said I owned Armbruster now. Like that farmer, I'm afraid I must correct you: I owned him the first minute he ever ate my corn."

Von Fleischer watched the waiters circulating through the chattering, elegant guests in the great room of his country estate and reflected that money made it possible to be gracious and yet spend almost no effort attending to the needs of guests. Social intercourse had many lubricants, but none so slick as cash.

Earning a fortune over a working life of, say, forty years was a chancy proposition, but anyone who couldn't become wealthy given a couple of centuries was a fool. In the long term, land always increases in value; wait long enough and your cheap furniture matures into priceless antiques. Above all, there is nothing like hanging about for a dozen generations to demonstrate the inexorable power of compound interest.

At the age of 425, von Fleischer had acquired not one fortune but many, stashed away in a dozen different countries; the history of Europe since 1580 had taught him not to take anything for granted.

He surveyed the room with a critical frown on his face, as though appraising the performance of his catering staff, but in fact he was assessing the guests. In the midst of the crowd, Lorelei Fitzhugh-Roberts tossed her golden curls off her bare shoulders and flashed a smile. A second wife. All of, what, twenty-three, married no more than a year, and already on the prowl? He gave her a pleasant, noncommittal, lord-of-the-manor nod and let his gaze drift elsewhere.

Not that she wasn't sexy enough by objective standards. Lorelei was magazine-pretty, and von Fleischer was certain she would cheerfully sign up for anything that didn't leave marks.

And therein lay the problem. He sighed, remembering the fine, repressed days of the nineteenth century, when sexual quirks and desires were hidden from view, so that over time they sank their roots deep into the psyche and twisted the very soul.

To be sure, kink, however defined, was far more plentiful in the modern times…but it meant less. On his last trip to America, one soccer mom he'd seduced had brought along her own handcuffs. What had happened to those lovely Victorian girls who'd thrown themselves from bridges because they'd been plagued with impure thoughts? Or to those charming young men whose furtive masturbation to their memories of boarding school drove them mad?

People in those days had real character.

Not that it really mattered. The twentieth century, for all its faults, had fed him well, and the twenty-first was looking very promising indeed. Fear, horror, hatred and cruelty abounded. But the shortage of shame and self-loathing was appalling. All small matters, he admitted: a real man couldn't get by on a diet of shame even when Victoria was on the throne. But these little things were the spices to the Big Four, and now they were vanishing, along with decent table manners.

Armbruster stood near the fireplace, regaling a handful of guests with some loud anecdote. The scotch had already bloomed in his cheeks, and it would be time to ease Liam back into the picture soon.

Miklos entered the room from the far hallway, slinking in with his usual languor, and a buzz of conversation ran through the guests in that region of the great room. Only five months ago, von Fleischer had formally adopted Miklos as his son and heir, and many of society's eyebrows remained raised. Despite von Fleischer's insistence that the twenty-year-old was his closest living relative, Miklos's caramel Greek skin and sultry brown eyes made it hard to link him with northern European nobility.

Whatever his antecedents, no one would deny the boy's beauty, and his looks and his coming inheritance made him a spectacular prize. His only drawback lay in the fact that he was so obviously gay, and many a mother with unmarried daughters tried to tell themselves that he was simply going through a phase, or, at the worst, that he was quite probably only bisexual. The psychologists said that everyone was, really, didn't they?

At the end of the room, Margot Southbrook—now the young *Lady* Southbrook, he recalled—leaned laughing against the French doors, attended by a circle of admiring men. Odd that she was in the neighborhood; her husband had lately been called down to London, amidst rumors he was to be something in the new Cabinet.

She caught von Fleischer's eye and gave him what started as a smile and stopped just short of lip-licking, an expression so vivid that a pair of the men glanced over their shoulders to find the object of her attention. Von Fleischer assessed her aura, and the evening became much more interesting.

He sensed bulk looming at his elbow. Rooker, in evening wear. Von Fleischer stood six foot two, but Rooker had to lean down to whisper to him. "News," he said. "An incident in Bahrain. A man—we still don't have all the details on him—defended the blind one from a bomber. A Hero type, it seems."

"But *who*?" Von Fleischer rubbed his temple. "It makes no sense. Every Hero has been taken before they reached the cradle."

"So maybe he's not a Hero. Maybe he's just heroic. But we've got a name and some details."

"And? Get on with it, man."

"Arby Keeling. Nothing important about him we've found. Studies rocks. The US embassy booked him out of Bahrain via Rome and Atlanta to Portland, Oregon." Rooker twisted his mouth. "They're packing some juice, too—twanged every thread we had before they left Bahrain."

"Documentation?"

"Plenty of pictures of him on TV."

Von Fleischer knitted his fingers behind his back and resisted the urge to pace. "Oregon. Why Oregon? Not that Moonie lot, is it?"

"Not them. I'm coming up empty, boss."

"The Green Ray. It must be. A Nature Hero, maybe an elemental."

"Showed no signs of it in Bahrain, or anywhere else we can trace. Just a regular guy. Except he jumps on bombs."

He saw that Margot was in the process of disengaging from her group and would probably make her way over to him in a matter of moments. "Find what you can, and get any information on his cult or worshippers…or family. See what he is. But if you get a suitable opportunity, kill him."

"And the bitch?"

"Is there some question, Rooker?"

"I've seen her. Twice now. And I wouldn't mind keeping her around for…well, a few days of questioning."

Von Fleischer groaned. "If I might propose an alternative, why not just stick your little John Thomas in a guillotine and lop it off? It would be faster, certainly more pleasurable, and you'd have a better chance of surviving. So what am I saying?"

Rooker looked unhappy. "Kill the bitch."

"That's right. And it worries me that there was ever any confusion on the topic."

8

Taking Time Out for the Dark Ages, Of Course

In the year 1 AD, the most valuable piece of real estate on the planet lay at the end of the Via Sacra in the heart of the Empire of Rome. Of course, the residents weren't aware that it was 1 AD; the more scholarly thought it was 754 *Ab Urbe Condita*, while the common people named the year after the current consuls, *The Year of Consuls Gaius Iulius Caesar and Lucius Aemilius Paullus*, which was not only a mouthful, but also made calculations a little tricky—you not only had to remember two Latinate names for each and every year, but had to remember their sequence. Let's see, Bobby was born in *Lucius Cornelius Lentulus and Marcus Valerius Messalla Messallinus*, and since then we've had *Imperator Caesar Divi filius Augustus XIII and Marcus Plautus Silvanus*, and then *Cossus Cornelius Lentulus and Lucius Calpurnius Piso*, and then…gosh, the little tyke must be almost three already!

The citizens of Rome considered themselves, for no apparent reason, to be the most virtuous people on the planet—for, after all, had they not been born at the center of power? And did they not elect the Senate, the body that ruled the most powerful empire the West had known?

The confusion of luck and virtue is a long-standing human trait, especially among the lucky.

Yet many of the residents of the city of Rome were not among the lucky, because Rome's economy was based on slavery. With the ever-increasing need for slaves, and the ever-present possibility of slave revolts, wars of conquest and gratuitous slaughter and cruelty were the fuel that made daily life possible.

As time went on, Rome's rich became richer and the poor became poorer and the middle class began to vanish. Farming and manufacturing moved overseas. The election of senators was increasingly rigged, and the Senate in any case quailed before the growing might and arbitrary power of the emperor. Even the military was gradually contracted out, with foreigners serving Rome to obtain citizenship.

Learning and engineering expanded as never before, but most citizens were more than content to remain ignorant—ignorant of the world they lived in, ignorant of any skills or trades, ignorant even of the basic infrastructure that supplied them with the means of life. Massive aqueducts moved water into Rome; ships brought in grain from overseas farms. The Romans ate the grain and drank the water and shit and pissed the results into the Cloaca Maxima, the giant sewer system that carried away Rome's waste and dumped it into polluted rivers and ultimately poisoned the sea.

People sensed that something had gone awry with their world, and that they sat far out on a limb they were busily sawing off, but those in power profited mightily from this unstable structure. Those citizens not in power were encouraged to blame their problems on the breakdown of traditional values: refusing to honor the Roman gods; the weakening of the patriarchal family; uppity women who tried to have lives independent of their husbands; children who were disrespectful. And, of course, on evil outside forces, such as Christianity, intent on undermining Roman traditions and the faith of their fathers.

But most of this discontent was no more than grousing over goblets at the wineshop. The only real concerns of most Roman citizens (read: men) were watching sports, and ensuring that the Empire kept taxes low.

Sports were bloody affairs, and in some cases they were little more than spectacles of organized murder. But great, lucky athletes— charioteers or gladiators—could not only fight their way out of slavery, but could become rich and famous, and return to their villas to find the daughters of Rome's elite sprawling on their beds.

Those were the few. Most of the slaves who died for the amusement of the Romans never had a chance—they were fed to animals or executed in horribly imaginative ways. The best of these, such as the brass bull, were reserved for private affairs: a slave or two would be locked inside the hollow bull and a fire would be built beneath it, and the slaves' screams as they roasted to death would make the bull bellow, much to the amusement of the dinner party.

From cruelty as an artform to cruelty as a fact of daily existence: viewed from on high, the glory that was Rome sounded like one centuries-long cry of anguish.

The conversion of Rome to Christianity eliminated some of the more gratuitous bloodsports, but the system was still founded on slavery, war, and oppression, and once the Christians were in power, they themselves proved to be quite adept at the business of persecution.

For a thousand years, an assortment of Powers and Principalities on the Other Side grew fat on the energy that emanated from Rome. It was a common joke on the Inner Planes, though, that no matter how many folks the Christians slaughtered in His name, Jesus never seemed to gain an ounce.

Rome was a long time a-falling, but when it fell it fell hard. By the time the Papacy moved back to Rome in the Renaissance, the Coliseum and the Forum were buried deep, and Michelangelo could sketch shepherds taking their ease on fragments of marble columns while their goats grazed in the lush grass.

From the air in 2005, Rome was an architectural hodgepodge covering two-and-a-half millennia—taking time out for the Dark Ages, of course, when the town lay deserted. Excavated classic Roman ruins stood between Renaissance domes and twentieth-century townhouses. Across the Tiber, Vatican City stood in gleaming perfection.

To those who had eyes to see, of course, the etheric plane presented a very different picture. The grainy, dark purple-greens of magnetic forces looped and twisted their way through the ground like a den of sluggish snakes, the earth itself permanently charged from the forces wielded there during the Empire.

Across the river, Saint Peter's presented a more lively scene. The center of Catholicism glowed with the gold-white of the genuine devotion of millions of worshippers, but the blue-black of raw power politics webbed its way through the whole like veins through flesh, and beneath it all the dark burdens of the Inquisition and slavery and the South American genocide throbbed like a well-fed tumor.

Arby saw none of this from the airplane, however, because he was immersed in a deep, dreamless sleep that began before they left the ground in Bahrain and didn't end until the pilot banked the plane and announced that they were approaching Fiumicino International Airport, the main gateway to Rome.

He sat up, blinking, unsure where he was, or even who, until he saw Elaina sitting in the aisle seat beside him. "Feeling better after your nap?" she asked.

He yawned and stretched, nodding. He glanced around the cabin. "Things look normal again." He shuddered. "I've spent most of my adult life trying to get away from that new-agey stuff."

"Ever wonder why that might be?" she asked.

It might or might not have been intended as a rhetorical question, but Arby ignored it by digging into his backpack and finding their itinerary. "Two-hour layover and a plane change," he said. "I wonder if there's anywhere in the airport to grab a shower."

Elaina leaned near to him and whispered, "We won't be making that connection. But as compensation, I believe I can promise you a bath of sorts."

"I'm not going to do this," he said again as they herded off the plane.

"Not so loudly, please." Elaina edged them out of the flow of disembarking passengers. "Listen to me." She dropped her voice to an urgent whisper. "These people are powerful. It's your luck alone that I found you before they did. They want to kill you, they want to kill me, and I am sure they have had no trouble finding out where we are headed and on what flights."

"I need to get back to the States. I don't know what's wrong, but my mother needs me."

"And to the United States we are headed. But not on this flight, and not today. And we can't go to Oregon."

He set his mouth. "I need to."

As the door swung shut, Elaina said, "Call your mother. See how urgent her condition is. She will be in danger, too. Have her go somewhere, to some place where we can find her later."

"You *lied* to me," Arby said into the telephone.

"No," Crystal said. "Misled, maybe. I *did* go to the doctor, baby-boy. And something life-threatening *was* happening. I never *said* it was *my* life being threatened…"

"Mom—"

"—and now you can see that I was right, in fact the whole world saw someone trying to blow you up, and—"

"And if I hadn't left Dhahran, I would have stayed perfectly safe!"

There was a silence on the line for a moment before Crystal said, "You haven't been looking at the news, have you? Not that I blame you, I mean, *I* never did until you decided to go live in the Middle East. That same night you were in Bahrain, there were a dozen bombings in Dhahran, too. Including some of those dormitories you were staying in."

Where was the point in arguing? He didn't know what was happening, but he believed Elaina when she said that Crystal might be in danger. "Okay, Mom. You were right, okay? And now something's going on that might be dangerous for you, too. Can you go somewhere safe for a few days? Maybe go down to Jilly's place in Napa?"

"I'm busy with quite a few things right now, Rain. I—"

"This is important."

"Okay, I can do it, but there's things to take care of at the shop first…"

"No, no 'things to take care of.' Leave right away. Go to Jilly's, and don't tell anyone where you're headed."

"Fine, but—"

"No 'but.' Just trust me and go. Do you promise, Mom?"

She sighed. "Sure, Rain. I'll go." Crystal's voice rattled on with more details, but Arby barely heard them. As best he could he steered the conversation toward farewell, but steering Crystal had always been like trying to steer a breeze.

When he finally said goodbye, she said, "I'm so glad you're getting out of there. I know you never pay attention to me, but the energy of that place was just bad for you."

"You know, Mom," he said, "maybe next time I'll listen, all right?"

The cab headed toward Rome proper. Arby adjusted himself on the cracked leather of the back seat. In a mere two turns of the earth on its axis he had been dragged away from his job by his mother, pinned down in Bahrain by the weird effects that emotional upsets always had on him, nearly blown up by a suicide bomber, and pushed into a world of glowing auras and creepy innuendoes by a blind woman with strange powers. He was willing to go with her, because he indeed did sense something terrible hovering over him, but his patience and credibility were wearing thin. "I think it's time you gave me some explanations."

"Lower your voice, please. Explanations of?"

Arby scooted closer to her. "Everything."

"You took physics and chemistry in college, yes?"

"Yeah. Except I had problems with the labs."

"No doubt. Understand this, then. When you ask me to explain 'everything,' you are asking me to teach quantum chemistry to someone who never troubled to learn simple arithmetic, a child who has not yet learned that there are such entities as atoms." She settled back in the seat and folded her hands over the gray shoulder bag that sat on her lap. "It's not as if you never had opportunities. You ought to have paid more attention to the communities in which you were raised."

"Well I didn't!" he said, and then realized his voice had risen to the point where the cab driver glanced at him in the mirror. Arby dropped his voice to a whisper. "But now don't you think I need to know?"

"No. And at the moment, you have other tasks to perform. You need to be watching—behind us especially, but all around—to see if anything is following us yet."

"*Yet?*" He leaned an arm on the back of the seat and scanned the highway behind them. Given the nature of highways, there were indeed hundreds of cars following them. "I thought the whole point of getting off in Rome was to lose everybody."

"It was. But there will come a point where they realize we did not make our connection. Then they will attempt to find if we have boarded another flight, but unless they are very unwise, they will also consider that we may have left the airport."

Arby backed up and hitched himself sideways on the seat, leaning his back against the door of the cab. In this position he could keep watch on the road behind them, but he could also let his gaze linger on Elaina. She sat in perfect symmetry, her knees touching just below the hem of her skirt, the heels and toes of her low pumps pressed together on the floor, her hands folded just so. Arby was rumpled and felt vaguely sweaty from the long flight, but Elaina sat there calm and clear-skinned in her sharply creased skirt and blouse, posed like some model advertising a deodorant spray, and he felt infuriated by the woman's poise, seized by an urge to yell, to grab her and shake her, to do something to throw her off-balance and make her join him in his confusion.

Then he noticed the driver. The man was studying Elaina in the mirror, spending as much time watching her as the road ahead of him, and the man's face radiated a simple joy at having this beautiful woman riding in his cab. Around the man's head a halo of green and yellow light began to spread.

"I'm capable of watching the road and listening to explanations at the same time," he said.

"You are not capable of keeping your thoughts to yourself, though," she said in a low voice. "In the state you are in you are like a loudspeaker shouting out 'here we are!' and I don't want to make it even worse. Wait until I've covered our tracks." She held a hand by her temple and made waving motions as though shooing thoughts away. "Think about something else."

"Like what?"

"The Hindus would say to hurl your thoughts at Arjuna, but many people use daydreams of fame, guilt about dead pets, childhood trauma, or lost love." She smiled. "And sexual fantasy is always a good way to blend into the mass mind as well."

He caught the taxi driver staring in the mirror again, the green-yellow glow around the man's head brightening. Was that what a sexual fantasy looked like? But there was something innocent and bright about it; a good sexual fantasy would probably have been darker, with more red and purple…

Arby snorted to himself, irritated by Elaina and the driver both, and even more by himself. He turned his head to inspect the stream of cars behind them. He was surprised to find himself annoyed enough that no good fantasies came to mind, so he searched his memory for dead pets.

Closer to the heart of Rome, the driver turned onto a boulevard that wound along the Tiber. The brown waters were visible between the trunks of spring-budded trees that lined the steep banks. "Trastevere," the driver said, announcing it as though he had accomplished a miracle.

Elaina ran off a long sentence in Italian, and the driver asked a question. She responded at length, and the driver laughed and said, "Okay."

"I wonder," she said to Arby, "if there is anywhere in the world where they do not use the American word 'okay.'"

"You seem to speak good Italian."

"Not so good, in fact. But my Latin is more than passable, and that is a great help with vocabulary."

The driver turned the car away from the Tiber and steered it down the narrow streets of Trastevere, nosing the cab at last into a parking spot so small that the rear stuck out into the roadway. He said something in a joking tone to Elaina and jumped out of the car, leaving the door open and the motor running.

The man still glowed green and yellow in Arby's eyes. "I'm seeing auras again," he said.

"You can see them any time. Just pay attention."

"I don't like it."

"No doubt that is why you trained yourself to stop seeing them as a child." She gave a smile that might have been sad, but without any signals from her eyes it remained inscrutable. "I fear that you may be forced to grow up now…Rain."

9

Talent

Arby clambered out of the river and onto one of the dark boulders piled on the steep bank. Water poured from his sopping clothes.

He turned to grasp Elaina's outstretched hand and half-guided, half-hauled her up beside him. She had left her sunglasses with their other gear, and it was surreal to watch her feel her way onto the boulder with her eyes closed.

"This is insane," he said. "And even if it isn't insane, it's going to look insane to anyone who sees us."

"Time to go," she said.

It had been a chore working down the boulder-reinforced bank with Elaina; it was worse helping her back up. In a few spots he had no choice but to lift her, and their combined weight forced the sharp contours of the rock into his bare feet. He was grateful to reach the stone steps that led up to the grounds of the church and hospital.

At last they stood on the level path that encircled the grounds of Isola Tiberina, the island in the center of the Tiber. The Church of St. Bartholomew's shaded them from the late-afternoon light, and Arby shivered as a breeze touched him. "It's cold," he said.

Elaina stood there and wrung the water from her short hair. "And a very good thing, I think. On a warm day, this island throngs with people." Her clothes were plastered to her body, her blouse now translucent, yet Arby found himself strangely unmoved by her flawless figure. Flawless it surely was, but her posture and self-control made her less a living thing and more akin to a marble sculpture.

She stood shaking and rubbing her hands in the breeze to dry them. "Where are the things we left, Rain?" she asked.

"Over here." He placed his hands on her shoulders from behind and guided her to stand next to the pile. "Are you going to keep calling me that?"

She squatted, her skirt taut, and felt across the pile, acquainting herself with the dimensions and positions of the items: their pairs of shoes and socks; Arby's backpack and her purse; her sunglasses and cane; his wristwatch and wallet. Well to the right sat the bag the cabdriver had brought her from the market. She reached into the bag and withdrew a half-pound cardboard canister of salt.

Arby wouldn't have said there was such a thing as a delicate grunt, but that was the sound she made as she stood. "Salt," she said. "Pour it into my palm." As he dug his fingernail into the packaging to open the spout, she asked, "Does it bother you? If I call you Rain, I mean?" She held out her right hand, her palm cupped.

"I suppose not. How much do you need?"

"A good handful." He poured a white volcano of salt into her hand, and she closed her hand into a fist, turned her fist thumb-up, and then led her hand in a wide clockwise circle around their pile of goods, letting a stream of salt trickle from her hand.

"Both hands, now," she said. Arby filled both of her cupped palms. She made fists, murmured some words under her breath, and then bent down, touching her paired fists first to her feet, and then, as she straightened, to her groin, her belly, her diaphragm, her throat, and her forehead. Last of all she held them above her head, her lips moving silently, and then she leaned forward and let the salt trickle from her fists onto the items in the pile. As she did so she weaved her hands right and left and back toward her body, as though she were drawing intertwined snakes in the air.

She opened her hands, fingers splayed wide, letting the last of the salt fall. Then she slapped her hands together with a crack that resounded across the Tiber.

Far at the other end of the island, a handful of tourists looked up in surprise. A woman pointed.

"I think we're attracting attention," he said.

Elaina squatted and felt her way through the pile, touching every object with her open hands. "It is good," she said. "Water is better than salt—water is the only thing that will work for living beings—but there is nothing to be found here now."

"If salt clears inanimate objects, then why did we soak our clothes?" he asked, and then said, "Oh…"

"No, I am not shy, if that is what you're thinking." She shook the salt crystals from her sunglasses and slid them onto her face. "Possibly insane, as you put it, and wet, is one sort of thing. But insane, wet, and naked: now there is a way to draw attention."

They crossed the short Ponte Fabricio onto the true Roman side of the river, and began a long crosstown walk. "No discussions until we get to the heart of the city," she said, "we are trying to disappear. Street directions only."

Arby was grateful for the exercise; by the time they left the island his teeth had started chattering. Elaina seemed less affected by the cold, but did clasp her arms together over her chest while they walked.

He recited the names of the intersections as they arrived, and she told him which way to turn—she carried an impeccable map of the city in her head.

By the time they reached the base of the Spanish Steps their clothes had dried. Dusk was descending on the city, and Arby was glad to rest on a stair amongst the passing crowds.

Elaina opened her purse and took out a lipstick. He stared, fascinated, as she touched the top of her upper lip with the fingernail of her left pinky finger. With her right hand she touched the lipstick to her lip just below that fingernail, and then drew them together along the contour of her lip, laying down a pure, confident line.

"So now we're—what?" he asked. "Cleansed? Invisible?"

"Demagnetized is probably the best way for you to think about it. We are far from invisible, and our very presence here will be noted." She stopped long enough to do her bottom lip, and Arby wondered how he could have thought of her as cold and unerotic back on the island; her mouth alone was hypnotic. "When people of our kind move through a Power Center, our presence can be felt from afar. But now we at least are not leaving footprints, so to speak."

"And what kind of people are those—'people of our kind?'"

"Talents. Powers. That's how we found you. The Middle East has become a Power Center, and everyone could sense that someone had arrived there."

"A Power Center? Because of the oil, I suppose?"

"Not because of the oil. Because of how people feel about the oil. Power is about emotion, and you were in a place that draws much of the world's greed and envy." She capped her lipstick and slid it back into her purse. "You are lucky I found you first."

"So you say. But why should I believe it?"

She smiled. "I would like to say, because your heart tells you that it is true." Her smile grew wider, and slightly cockeyed. "But instead I will say because the other one who searches for you has put forth all his power to kill you. Who knows how many innocents died in the last few days, in all those bombings that were meant to destroy you or flush you out?"

Arby had tasted many flavors of guilt before, but never the responsibility for the death of another—much less the deaths of tens, or even hundreds. He felt sickened and dizzy. "Perhaps you should have let him find me."

"Do not blame yourself. It is right that this pains you, but do not take up these deaths as a burden. To him, the deaths of a thousand, even tens of thousands, are small matters. Blame him."

"And who is 'he,' the one who doesn't care, the one who wants me dead?"

"Of this, we will not speak, not now. Not here. Naming a thing calls it." Elaina lifted her face as if she were gazing out into the crowd.

Arby crossed his forearms on his knees and rested his chin there. Madness. Every bit of it was crazy...and yet he knew it was true, knew it in the way that only one who had lived among the believers could know it. His whole childhood had been soaked in spirituality and occult beliefs and transcendental practices—tarot and yoga and runes and nature worship and religions running from Christianity to the Norse gods—perhaps every variation had passed through his life, and he had staunchly ignored them, preferring to hike or watch birds or build treehouses.

"What is a Talent, or a Power, or whatever? What you did back at the Tiber, with the salt and all? You're a magician?"

She laughed, and he saw gold shimmer around her head. "No, that was simple technology. I'm not a magician, and 'magic' as you conceive of it does not exist. My Talent is a small one, a minor thing, and the most important thing in the universe." She lowered her head for a moment in concentration. "Are you seeing auras? Go ahead, let yourself…"

He sat up, and then swallowed hard. Even though the milling crowd was already glowing, he found it frightening to go further, as though he might be overwhelmed.

And that was exactly what happened. The auras of the crowd blossomed into a riot of leaping, pulsing colored plasmas. He must have made a sound of alarm, because Elaina said, "Let it roll past you, like traffic on a busy street. Pay attention to what you want to find, and ignore the rest."

"And what do I want to find?" he asked, surprised at how thin his voice sounded in his own ears.

"There is a couple walking together. In love. But angry with one another."

At first all he saw was a smear of colors, as though an artist had wiped a towel across a painting that had not yet dried. But then he saw them: a young man and woman, and once he focused on the pair of them he no longer understood the auras as colors but as love, with protrusions of sadness and anger bulging out like fat hanging over a waistband. "I think I see them."

"Here is my Talent, the smallest of all."

Elaina stilled herself. The couple continued walking through the crowd, even twisting aside to avoid touching one another, and Arby said, "I'm not sure I'm watching the right—"

"Shhh!"

The woman's hand reached out, grudging, unsure, and touched the man's fingers. He clasped her hand, and then dropped it and instead reached his arm around her shoulder and hugged her up against his side. The bulges and protrusions shrank and red and yellow bloomed around them and blended.

Arby found that his throat was so tight he could barely speak, and he saw Liz in his mind, laughing, pushing him in response to some stupid comment he'd made. "Love," he managed to say. "You—you make people love each other."

Elaina snorted. "No power in the universe can do that." She patted his arm. "No. Now find the brat in the crowd, his long-suffering mother…"

This time it was easier. A child, five or six years old, filled with erratic, jagged energy that swiped at the crowd as he trampled his way back and forth. His mother, worn down, her aura almost drooping under the weight of sad blue-grays. She called after the child, and he ran farther away, then turned and ran back at her, his energies leaping like a brushfire.

Something flickered in the mother's aura, and then she knelt, seized the child by the shoulders, and spoke long and hard into his astonished face. The child burst into tears, and she gathered him into her arms and lifted him, and his energies calmed and quelled, but at the same time they seemed to invade and illuminate hers, lifting her up, straightening her back.

"You make people reconcile?" Arby asked.

"Again, no. And no one can ever make anyone do anything. Even those like our enemy, who pushed those people in Bahrain to do great evil—all he did was encourage them to follow a path they already desired. My gift"—she took off her sunglasses and ran her hand down her face—"is to allow people to return to themselves, to ease their way, to let them to return to balance. If they choose."

"That seems like—like a powerful thing. And a good thing."

She slipped her sunglasses back onto her face. "Most people can return to themselves with only the smallest amount of help. I could do much good in the world, it is true…if I weren't hunted like an animal."

"How long has this been going on?"

"Longer than you can imagine." Her hand sought his. "I'm sorry it is your fate to join me in this."

Arby stared at the shifting, swirling colors on the street below. "And what is my Talent?" he asked. "I break things?"

"No, though breaking things is certainly sometimes a side effect."

"Elaina: back in front of the hotel in Bahrain, when the bomb didn't go off, you said something weird. You said, 'I think I know who you are now!' What did you mean?"

"I'm sorry. I was excited. I don't know, not with certainty."

"Fine. Who do you *think* I am?"

She shook her head. "I can't tell you."

Arby let out a sigh of exasperation. "Why not?"

There was just a hint of a smile when she said, "I can't tell you why not, either."

"This is ridiculous. How long are we going to play this game?"

"It is not a game, and I have my reasons for what I withhold. We are on our way to the Adeptus Exemptus, the greatest of his kind still on this plane. He will tell you who and what you are."

"This…Adeptus guy? He's in Rome?"

"No, more's the pity. Tonight we will stay in the house of a Magus, but not one of the great ones." She squeezed his hand and lowered her voice. "He will shelter us for the night—but he is not to be trusted. In the morning we will travel south to Naples. There is a ferry to Palermo, and there I know people who can get us onto a safe boat to Algiers."

Naples, Palermo, Algiers. America seemed farther away by the moment. "Great. Can we stop off in Casablanca for a drink at Rick's?"

"I don't understand you, but your voice sounds as if you are making a joke." Her hand shook his to underline her words. "You must put some faith in my tactics, Rain. Strategy is not in my nature. But I am very adept in matters of tactics."

Whatever the hell that meant. Arby gazed at the colors of the shifting crowd, and then down the street that ended at the Spanish

Steps, and his eyes saw the lights of auras fading into the distance in the darkened street, and in his mind he saw lights spreading out across all of Rome, and lights in every house and apartment, and concert halls filled with lights, and restrooms and soccer stadiums and bars filled with lights, and an Italy and a Europe and a planet glowing with lights, a swirling boreal display surrounding every one of the eight billion humans on the planet, and he tried to shut it all out and then was astonished when it all faded at his command, and all he felt was Elaina's hand in his.

10

Evil and Empathy

Modern thinkers have oft asserted that no person chooses what they truly believe to be evil. Even the most vicious criminal, they say, thinks his actions are somehow justified; every man believes he is the hero of his own story.

Von Fleischer knew this was wishful thinking. Some people just didn't care to see human nature in its totality. He wouldn't deny that people were inclined to rationalize evil acts after the fact, dress up their behaviors and send them to town masquerading as upstanding citizens, but the truth was there for anyone to see: a pig in evening wear is a pig for all that.

Some psychologists argue that sociopaths and psychopaths are lacking in empathy, and von Fleischer admitted that might be true. But real evil wasn't committed by the insane. Real evil demanded empathy. The sweaty-palmed excitement of a professional torturer as he went about his state-sanctioned work, the agitated arousal of a gang rape, the smug pleasure of armed guards forcing prisoners to dig their own graves—these all demanded an understanding of what the helpless victims were experiencing, and it was this knowledge that gave these acts their special, inimitable flavor. As surely as it has receptors for sweet, sour, and salt, the human tongue has taste buds for deliberate cruelty.

Von Fleischer had met Reggie and the boys in Texas, on his last little trip through America. The Lone Star Bar and Grill—as far as he could tell, half of the dining establishments in Texas had this name—was a dive on Interstate 10 not far from El Paso. Twangy, whiny-voiced songs from a jukebox filled a room floored with sawdust and peanut shells. Von Fleischer winced at what passed for music in this region, and then made himself as conspicuous as possible, sitting alone and aloof at a table with a mixed drink, dressed in his cream-colored silk suit.

It wasn't long before Reggie and three other boys swaggered over to his table. All four appeared to be in their twenties, and all were dressed alike in Levis, boots, and T-shirts with the sleeves ripped off. Was this some sort of gang? Von Fleischer couldn't recall if white southerners had gangs or not.

"So," Reggie said, "guess you ain't from around here."

"No," von Fleischer said, "a traveler passing through. Wanted to see the real America."

He could see inside Reggie without much effort. Angry, bored, insecure, mean as a ghetto rat and ten times more stupid—though not as stupid as his companions. Von Fleischer probed, tapped, and Nudged, not bothering with the other three.

Reggie narrowed his eyes with suspicion and then brightened as von Fleischer found the boy's sweet spot. "Well, you come to the right place."

"Might I buy you drinks?"

One of Reggie's crew said, "What are you, some kinda—" but Reggie cut him off with a sharp backhand to the shoulder.

"Back off, Jimmy. Show some Texan hospitality." He looked back to von Fleischer. "Love a beer, if you're serious."

They pulled up chairs and von Fleischer flagged down the waitress and ordered four beers, though he himself stuck to gin and water.

"Gin and water?" Reggie asked.

"Once a very popular drink in Europe," von Fleischer said. True enough: about two hundred years ago.

"Europe, huh?" he asked, pronouncing it *Yurp*. "Whereabouts?"

"Germany, originally." Back when it was Prussia, that is.

"Germany," Jimmy said. "Germany's cool."

"Oh? You've been there?"

Jimmy frowned. "No. I mean, no, I never been—but the Nazis and all that shit."

Reggie glared at Jimmy, clearly worried that their guest would be offended, and von Fleischer smiled and said, "Yes, those were glory days for my country—days when we might have ruled the world. But those times are gone, alas. There's only one real power left in the world, and that's this country." He paused, and lifted his glass. "A salute, gentlemen, to the United States of America."

They lifted their bottles, pious cow-eyed expressions on their faces, and drank to the US of A.

Von Fleischer bought round after round, explaining that he was "in sales" and "on expenses." As their drunkenness increased, he reached down into his bag and pulled out a camcorder, and filmed the boys as they mugged and waved into the lens.

Jimmy was watching the playback when he said, "Man, these things are totally fucked up." He said this in what sounded like a positive tone, but it took von Fleischer a moment's reflection to conclude that the boy's words indeed indicated approval.

"You find these toys attractive?" he asked. "I own a spare you may have as a gift." He pulled up a slightly smaller unit from the bag and pushed it over to Jimmy. "This one didn't have all the features I wanted."

"Naw, man—!" Reggie said.

"Hell, I couldn't take that," Jimmy said, "must have cost a bundle."

Von Fleischer nodded. This was the tenth camcorder he'd given away in a week, and he now had the story down. "You see, though, I will have to leave one behind when I return home. When I go through customs, if I have two of these, they will charge me import duties, expenses many times the value of the unit."

"You're *giving* this to us?" Jimmy asked.

"Certainly. It's no money out of my pocket; the company pays for everything."

"Man," Reggie said, "I want to work for a company like that."

There was a period of hilarity, and this was followed by increasing moroseness, and half an hour later, Reggie was slurring, "Fuckin' great company you work for. We ain't got companies like that." Von Fleischer arched his eyebrow, waiting. "Between the coons and the spics, ain't no jobs for hard-working guys like us. Half the niggers are on welfare, and the other half take all the jobs. By law, man, *by law* they get all the jobs first." Reggie glowered at the beer bottle in his fist. "Bet you ain't got problems like that back in Germany."

"Oh, but you're wrong. Immigrants, so-called guest workers. Turks, North Africans, people of every color except white. We are flooded with them, swamped, and it has destroyed what was once a great nation." He Nudged Reggie, then Nudged the other three.

"Isn't bad enough the government lets in everybody from everywhere," Reggie said, "fuckin' wetbacks coming into the country. No stopping them. Government doesn't even try. A million of 'em"— Reggie pointed his finger at von Fleischer—"a million of 'em every day, and the government doesn't do a goddamn thing."

Von Fleischer had his doubts about Reggie's statistics, but said, "Someone should do something."

"Damn right. Make a fucking example of somebody, is what they ought to do."

He kept them talking until the bar closed and the boys staggered out to their pickup trucks, shouting drunken farewells and waving the camcorder.

Weeks later he'd forgotten the boys in the Lone Star, and the dozens of others he'd met on his little American tour, but he had attuned himself enough to Reggie that even in his London townhouse he felt the frisson of the act when it finally began. His book—Crowley's *Book of Thoth*, with all of its amusing misinformation—dropped to his lap and he opened himself to the flow, drinking in the victim's pain and despair, and absorbing every drop of the gloating anger of the boys. Too far away to tell what they had done, but he tasted just a hint of something…chemical? A solvent?

As he'd hoped, a few days later he learned the full story from television news. A group of young men had attacked a Mexican illegal in the desert, beaten him, and then doused him in gasoline and burned him to death. And, most appalling of all, they had taped the entire thing, and copies of that videotape had found their way to the news stations, and although it was too graphic to broadcast, and although the networks were hand-wringingly horrified, just horrified by it all, they couldn't help but show the first few seconds of footage, while the man pleaded for his life...

Of course, within hours the whole tape was available on the Internet.

Undirected rage, fear, horror, despair...and on the part of many, titillation, gloating, or a head-shaking satisfaction. And yet another wedge in race relations, a deeper division between right and left, even a brewing diplomatic rift between Mexico and the US.

On the Other Side, von Fleischer could sense the scrambling of some of his lesser competitors, but it was too late for them. He sent his consciousness hurtling to the Back Forty—which in fact was closer to the Back Forty Thousand—and inhabited his Grant Wood farmer avatar, leaning on his pitchfork beside a patch of barren brown hardpan.

The soil began to crack, and bushes of fat tendrils wormed their way out of the soil to stand six feet tall, pulsing as black-purple emotion pumped in from the lower plane. The farmer raised his eyes toward the horizon. For miles, new growths burst through the ground and filled, swelling heavy as nursing breasts.

Elsewhere, von Fleischer knew, in kingdoms ruled by others, tendrils of purer light would be appearing, mostly in whites and golds, but a few in purples or blues; these were prayers addressed to specific entities—though not always to the entities the prayerful thought they were addressing. Those were already owned, and there was no nourishment for him there.

Ah, but these... Black-purples streaky with angry reds, the tendrils probed high into the night, seeking some unnamed higher power. Aimless cries into the Inner Planes, these were his for the taking.

Small entities scurried onto the plain, seen through von Fleischer's eyes as deformed rodents. He dropped his farmer avatar and rose to his full height as the Flayer, thousands of feet tall, and his shadow fell across the plain, sending many of the rodents skittering away. He crossed his arms over his chest and then let them fall forward palms upward, and as his hands reached out they split apart into myriad rubbery tentacles, reaching out across the miles to seize the tendrils that had sprouted from the soil.

He opened his mouth and it expanded into a toothy red maw that dominated the horizon like a crimson moon.

Down below, one of the fatter rodents glanced up at him, and there was something familiar there. He thought of sending a tentacle down for it, but something tapped at his consciousness, gentle but urgent.

It had to be Rooker, back in Malkuth. Who else would dare?

Rooker swiveled his chair around from the roll-top desk. "They're in Rome," he said. "The whole place is vibrating."

Von Fleischer slid into an antique armchair and rubbed his neck. This body was growing old. "Are you tracking them?"

"She wiped the traces."

"Hmm." Rome. He glanced up at the clock. Late evening in London, even later in Rome. "Makes more sense than Portland, Oregon, at least."

"The man might have been heading for Portland for real. Turns out his mom lives there."

Von Fleischer sat up. "And who is she? Who is the father?"

"Can't trace the father. The mom's a nobody named Crystal Keeling."

"This can't be right. Talents don't appear out of nowhere."

"Sure. But I didn't tell you the best part. Our guy's birthday is in March of 1970." Rooker smiled, clearly proud to be one step ahead of his boss, and von Fleischer gnawed back his impatience. "Back it up nine months, I get June of 1969—"

"LaMarr and the damned Children. I thought I'd eliminated all the possibilities there."

"Hey, boss, even Herod missed one or two."

Sometimes Rooker's manner grew too cheeky by half. But the man was right—New York, 1969, a loose end that was never tied up to anyone's satisfaction. "And my intuition was right—he Children would try to embody some manner of Nature Hero, some servant of the Green…"

"Still no sign of that," Rooker said. "We get no read on this guy at all. You still sure dead is how you want him? He might be a neutral. The bitch is."

"No she isn't. Anyone who isn't on my side is an enemy. Whatever resources we have in Rome, start them running."

"We've got a trio of the Tall Boys."

"That's all?"

"They've got a Beastie."

"Ah." That more than evened the odds, but von Fleischer didn't care for playing fields that lay even close to level. "No one else?"

"Everybody's still down in the Mideast, or chasing that bogus trip to Oregon."

"Oregon." Von Fleischer stood. "Set things in order in Rome, but then book the two of us a flight to Oregon. I think it's time we found out what really happened in 1969." He began to stride from the room, but paused. "And, Rooker? Give the boys a little incentive. A million euros to the man who brings me the bitch's head. That much plus an unattached Portal, free and clear, to anyone who erases her." He waited. "And the same to whoever does in our uninvited guest."

He turned to go, but Rooker's voice stopped him. "Boss." Von Fleischer half-turned and inclined his head, impatient but listening. "Let me go," Rooker said. "Let me get them."

Von Fleischer let the man wait, hoping Rooker was reflecting on the foolishness of his words. "Do you want it so soon?" he asked, at length. "And haven't I promised you a Portal of your own, in due time? Don't you trust me, Mister Rooker?"

As much as I trust a warm day in January was the obvious and truthful answer, but while Rooker had gotten cheeky in the last few years, von Fleischer doubted that the man was suicidal.

"I just want to see that it's done right, that's all," Rooker said. "Boss."

The man folded his thick, knuckly hands on his lap in contrition, and von Fleischer wondered what it would feel like to be Rooker—one life to live with this persona, and a body as hard and ugly as a lightning-blasted oak. "I value your loyalty, Rooker," he said, "you can't imagine how I do."

11

Warded, Blocked, and Sealed

For a time in the dark of the café, over pasta and chianti, Arby almost felt as though the world had returned to normal. The candlelight made Elaina even more beautiful, warming those austere Swedish features, and her sunglasses in the dimness gave the scene the feel of a glossy movie, logic and practicality sacrificed to visual impact. Watching her eat was entrancing. With deft, unobtrusive movements of her hands, she had located every item before her, and she then ate with precision, even twining angel-hair pasta onto her fork and gauging its weight with a subtle relaxation of her wrist.

She was easy to talk to. Her interest in him seemed genuine yet disinterested, far beyond typical male-female interactions, and he found himself telling her things he hadn't even voiced to Liz.

"So what was it that you wanted?" she asked. "What gives you happiness?"

"New things. Finding out what's around that bend, or under the ground, or beyond that mountain. Or inside nature's own laws. Hiking. Traveling. Science. The ocean. *Seeing* things."

He winced as he heard his last two words, but Elaina seemed unperturbed. "Why, then, did you choose a woman who valued none of that? What did this Liz want? From what you tell me, a partnership in her law firm, and eventually children, timed just right, and fine cars and fine clothes."

He pulled the basket to his side of the table and broke off a crusty piece of bread. On his bread plate the pool of golden olive oil encircling a purple oval of balsamic vinegar looked like a fried egg from another galaxy, and he relished the way the vinegar shattered into a thousand little moons when he crushed the bread into the liquid. "You don't understand. I loved her. It wasn't a matter of logic."

"Obviously not. Though, if I might say so without giving offense, I often hear such sentiments from those who are in love with the idea of someone rather than in love with a person." She forked pasta into her mouth and chewed, placing her fork alongside her plate. "Would you be so good as to put the bread basket back where it was when you are finished?"

He pushed the basket back to her side of the table. Where exactly had it been before? "No. I loved her. But she always thought I was strange, even in the early days, back when she seemed to *like* strange. She said I wasn't like other people. Said at times I seemed almost inhuman."

"She was correct on both counts. Your nature is different than hers."

"Great." He leaned on one elbow. "Oh, hell, it didn't make any sense, somebody like her and somebody like me. It was a fluke we slept together in the first place."

At this Elaina's lips moved into a slow, ever-widening smile.

"Enough about Liz and me," Arby said, "what about you? Husband, boyfriend, lover? Kids? Dogs?"

"Despite your joking tone, I will answer this. No children, ever. Lovers? It has been some time. Though when I was younger, and often in other bodies…"

"Oh, good," he said. "Now we get down to it. Reincarnation. And who were you before, Cleopatra? And was I Caesar, or was I Marc Antony?"

"Were I to choose an eternal lover, there is a distinct possibility that it might not be you." She touched her fork as though ensuring it still lay where she had left it. "I am joking, of course. I am always I, and you are always you. People—the normal people, like your Liz—they come and go. And except for Cleopatra, no one was once Cleopatra—or rather, many people were, but only partly. It's a matter of congruence."

"Huh?"

She shook her head in irritation. "It can't really be understood when we are in Malkuth, in the time-bound plane of dense matter. But perform the mathematics. If every one of those people out there has lived many lives, how can there be eight billion of them? Souls are not liquid, to be dumped from bottle to bottle."

"You're always you? What does that mean?"

"They evolve in their way, and we evolve in ours. I have maintained consciousness now through three lifecycles, without having to relearn."

"And I'm relearning? Why do you know everything and I don't know anything?"

"Do you know the fable of the grasshopper and the ant?" She waited for him to make an affirmative sound. "You are the grasshopper. I am the ant. I made special preparations. You…well, you have not been back for some time."

On the long walk through the nighttime streets of Rome, she made him rehearse it again and again: turning on his senses, flooding his awareness with auras and the grainy vision of the physical world that accompanied it; and then closing it off, returning to everyday perception.

"It is very much like—" she said.

"What?" he asked. She dismissed it with a wave of her hand. "No, c'mon, what were you going to say?"

"It is very much like toilet training. You learn how to hold it in, how to let it out, but there is no real way to describe it to a child. It is a matter of practice with the muscles involved." She stopped, and tapped the tip of her cane on a curb, as though she had foreseen it coming. "What you must learn quickest is to shut it all out. When you are open on the etheric plane, there are new ways you can be hurt."

Midnight was near when they reached the townhouse east of Trajan's Market, and Arby felt dubious as he led Elaina up the steps of the grimy three-story building. "Isn't it a little late to drop in on somebody?"

"I assure you, for this one the night is still young."

Arby rapped the lion-head knocker against its platen three times, and waited.

He wasn't sure what to expect—Gandalf, perhaps?—but a dark-eyed young woman in a maid's uniform was a surprise.

"Elaina Svärdfors to see Master Canetti." She repeated herself in Italian.

"Master works," the maid said, not moving from the doorway.

A strong voice rang out from a distance behind her. "*Permettali di entrare*, Concetta."

The maid bobbed her head and stepped aside, drawing the door open.

The building might have seemed rundown from the outside, but the interior was that of a palace—marble floors, a sweeping staircase with gilt banisters, and ornate baroque paneling on every wall.

Except for the bushy arched eyebrows, the black-eyed man in the broad entryway didn't resemble Gandalf, though he made Arby feel hobbit-sized. Master Canetti must have stood almost seven feet tall, and it wasn't the stretched-out length of a basketball player. His shoulders were wide and his head sat atop his thick neck like the oversized bust of an ancient emperor. That red smoking jacket used enough velvet for a bedspread.

The maid closed the door behind them. "Why are we speaking English, Elaina?" Canetti asked, crossing the floor toward her, his arms open. He leaned down to embrace her and she lifted her cheek to be kissed, but Arby sensed no great warmth in their greeting.

"My companion is American," she said, easing out of the man's gargantuan hands, "and my English is still far better than my Italian." She turned and gestured toward Arby. "This is a man called Arby by his friends. We need shelter for the night."

"I felt that some power had arrived in the city. Every skein is trembling, but not, I think, from you alone." He stared down at her, and her unseeing eyes seemed to gaze straight ahead at his diaphragm. "Are you pursued?"

"Yes."

"And you come to me? Why should I help?"

"I believe you owe me a favor. Perhaps more than one. This night is all we ask. In the morning we will leave for Venezia."

In the plush drawing room, all of the furniture had been scaled up to Canetti's size. Elaina perched in her chair like a porcelain miniature. Canetti had Concetta bring them "brandy all'albicocca," which despite the imposing name turned out not to be some concoction, but rather a smooth apricot brandy.

Canetti ventured a few pleasantries in Arby's direction, clearly probing to find out more about his unsolicited guest, and Arby ducked the man's questions with noncommittal but polite answers.

"Perhaps, as I am offering you refuge," Canetti said to Elaina, "you might tell me the name of your pursuer?"

"I am sure you will be able to discover that on your own," she said. "All we ask is lodging. And, at the moment, I could do with a shower."

Canetti shambled from the room, ducking his head at the doorframe, and called for Concetta.

When Canetti was beyond earshot, Elaina asked, "Have you been seeing auras?"

"Not so far. Though something about that man feels strange. Apart from the fact that he's a giant."

"Yes, I could tell he was much bigger than the last time I saw him."

"When did you see him last, in preschool?" This seemed odd: Canetti appeared to be about sixty.

"Of course not. But it is one of several strategies for the prolongation of life: never stop growing. As do the giant turtles of the Galapagos." She sniffed at her untouched brandy. "It is quite painful to the bones and joints, I understand, continuing to grow after adulthood."

She sat back in her chair and frowned as if listening for a sound in the distance.

Arby stood and wandered the room. It was like a museum: two suits of battle armor mounted on the wall, complete with pointed helmets; crossbows, pikes, and morningstars held to the paneling by hooks; crossed swords above the marble mantelpiece.

Canetti ducked his way into the room, trailed by Concetta. "You may have that shower right now, if you like."

Elaina thanked him and rose, and Concetta met her and led her from the room.

Canetti stepped over to stand by Arby at the fireplace. He clapped one enormous hand down on Arby's shoulder and rested it there, and Arby reflected that Elaina could easily have sat in the man's palm. "Admiring the collection, eh?" Canetti asked. "Perhaps you, too, prize antiquities?"

"I like them," Arby said. "Don't know much about them."

"You don't?" The giant lifted his heavy hand from Arby's shoulder. "Hmph. What about this, then?" He lifted a large crystal of rose quartz from the mantel. "Don't suppose you see the flaw deep in the center here?"

Arby gazed at the crystal and frowned. If there was a flaw in the heart of the crystal, he couldn't see it. But green-purple colors began to swirl, and Arby realized with a jolt that he was seeing the aura around Canetti's fingers. "No," he said, concentrating on shutting down his contact with the etheric, "I don't see anything."

He tried to turn his head and discovered that his neck was frozen.

"I thought that might be the case," Canetti said. The man added a few more words in a language Arby could not understand, and then placed the crystal back on the mantel. "I think you and I should have a little chat."

Arby sat in an armchair, a pleasant smile on his face, his inner person revolting with every word, and answered Canetti's questions. *Who are you?* Arby Keeling. *No, you idiot, what Power, what Talent?* I don't know.

Elaina won't tell me. *Why not?* I don't know. She wouldn't tell me why not, either. *Who is pursuing you, and why?* I don't know.

Where are you truly traveling tomorrow? He tried to say "Venice" to match with Elaina's earlier lie, but despite the building fury within him he found himself answering as though he were describing a planned vacation to a friend: Naples. By ferry to Palermo. By boat to Algiers. Then to somewhere, perhaps to find some Adept…

"Are you telling me the truth?" Canetti asked. He leaned down, lifted Arby's chin with a thumb and forefinger, and stared into his eyes. "Open up, now, little boy. Here I come."

The discomfort that followed was enormous, and hurt in places he couldn't identify.

At length, Canetti said, "Whoever you may be, you are a genuine idiot. Unfortunate that I did not find you first." He held up a small copper figurine, perhaps an inch long, that seemed to portray a hound. "A present for you." Canetti went to Arby's backpack where it lay next to the chair and slid the little statue under the flap. "Don't lose it."

Canetti straightened and then strode to what had been Elaina's chair and lifted her abandoned brandy. "You will say nothing of our conversation, not by any means. You will evade. You will tell plausible lies. This time is apart, do you understand? Warded, blocked, and sealed."

Arby smiled and nodded while his inner self screamed and beat at the walls of its new prison.

Elaina came into the room, guided by Concetta. Her hair was still wet, and she wore a red silk robe many sizes too large; the excess fabric dragged along behind her like the train of a gown. The sleeves of the robe had been rolled a dozen times, and the maladroit, gamine effect of her little hands protruding from the impromptu cuffs was heart-achingly beautiful. Arby wanted to cry out to her, to confess that he had betrayed them both, but instead he smiled and nodded, smiled and nodded, and crossed his legs, displaying a picture of affability for a woman who couldn't see.

Beneath one arm she carried her own clothes, rolled into a tight, perfect bundle. "Arby, can you stow these in your pack?"

Arby stepped over and took them, and tried to whisper something to her, but found himself speaking in his normal voice. "Happy to, of course, no problem…"

"Not the best fit," Canetti said, "but I believe my dressing gown becomes you."

"It is serviceable. Arby, do you want a shower now?"

What he wanted was to tell her what had happened while she was gone from the room. "No thanks," he said, and then, not wanting to sound like a complete pig, added, "I'm so tired. Maybe in the morning?"

"As you wish." Canetti rubbed those massive hands together. "Now. Perhaps we should discuss sleeping arrangements? Concetta, I think the blue room for Miss Svärdfors, and—"

"One room will be sufficient," Elaina said.

"Oh?" Those bushy eyebrows rose. "And one bed too, then?"

"Of course."

Canetti shot Arby a glance that in any language said *you've got to be kidding*. Arby smiled and nodded, smiled and nodded.

"Fine," Canetti said. He rattled off something in Italian to Concetta, and said, "The Angel Room. Old, but trustworthy. A bed even I couldn't break."

"You are not telling me that you are going to retire so soon, Nicolo?" Elaina asked. "In the old days, you traded jobs with the birds each morning. Do you even know how to sleep in the dark?"

"I am bigger now, Elaina," he said, "and much older, too. Already it is past my usual bedtime."

"Ah." Elaina readjusted the way the huge robe hung on her shoulders. "May you have the dreams you deserve, then."

The Angel Room was well-named, the moldings festooned with fat-bottomed cherubs gilt in gold. Arby wanted to scream with frustration, but instead his body, despite his will, assumed a sedate pace with his hands clasped behind his back, studying the chubby, winged babies as though preparing for an oral exam in architectural ornamentation of the Baroque period.

Elaina sat on the edge of the giant canopied bed. Had they really been lovers, they would have had plenty of room—enough room for them, a dozen friends, and a high-school marching band. "Rain, come here," she said. "Sit."

He wandered toward her, hands still clasped at the base of his spine, and sat down beside her. He smiled and nodded, the most affable of companions.

"Listen," she said. "He made you tell him, didn't he?"

"No, not at all," Arby said. Part of him watched in horror as the speaking part of him lied, his body casual and relaxed. "We talked about Rome, about the weather…"

"I understand. Don't fight it. I know it hurts." She touched his hair. "This will be lifted from you. Do you see now why I couldn't answer your questions? I'm sorry you had to be used like this."

He felt his face assume a puzzled expression and his mouth said, "Elaina—I don't have the slightest idea what you're talking about," but the tension in his inner self eased by half.

She petted his head. "Lie down and wait, Rain. Here. Rest here a while." She drew him down until his head rested on her lap. "Sleep if you can, for a moment. And don't worry about what you cannot say. It is all as it should be. Do you understand? All as it should be." Her hand stroked his shoulder. "*Pioggia*," she said, "that is *Rain* in Italian, though the Romans would have said *Imber*… In my country, we say *Regna*, or even *Regn*, almost the same word that you use… "

With the side of his face pressed against her thigh, Arby nodded. He felt as though he wanted to cry.

"*Pioggia*." Elaina stroked his cheek, and he came awake with no idea of how much time had passed. Elaina stood beside the bed, dressed once again in her skirt and blouse. "It is time to wake up, Rain."

Rain. For a moment it almost seemed as though Crystal was waking him for breakfast in some decade long past.

"Rain. You need to sit up now."

He groaned and pushed himself upright.

"Wake up now. Do you hear me?"

He nodded.

"What time is it?"

He rubbed his fists into his eyes and glanced around. Near the door hung a preposterous golden clock supported by two insipid cherubs. "Three fifteen."

"Are there weapons in this room?"

"No. Just fat-butted babies with wings."

"Listen. Canetti has retreated to his rooms, placed wards. I had hoped he wouldn't betray us until well after we'd left—that he would try to sell us, but to stay in my good graces as well." She sighed, and held up the little hound figurine. "The market value of my good graces seems to have declined."

Arby pointed at the statuette, but when he tried to ask about it, all he could do was stammer.

"Something to trace us. We'll leave it here, for the moment. Listen: someone is coming. Do you remember weapons down on the lower floors?"

"In the drawing room. Crossbows, swords, all kinds of things… but old stuff, probably medieval."

"At the risk of quibbling, I'd imagine it's Renaissance." She held out her hand toward him, groping for support. "Do you mind stowing my purse and shoes in your pack? We need to go downstairs and arm ourselves. And then we need to find the basement and hope for morning."

12

Above Fifteen Watts

After finding Elaina a dagger, Arby grabbed one of the drawing-room armchairs, dragged it to the hearth, and climbed up onto the seat. "Why morning? What is this, some kind of vampire movie?" The first of the swords came off its hooks easily into his hands. It was far weightier than he'd expected, and he laid it carefully on the mantel.

"I would have thought that even you would have some inkling of the Sun's power over the etheric plane," Elaina said. "The darkness and the sunlight are as different as—shall we say night and day?"

The second sword put up a struggle. He tugged and twisted and there was a scream of wrenching metal.

Sword in hand, he paused for the universe to react to this ear-slicing sound. There was nothing. "Sorry," he said. He placed the points of both of the heavy swords on the floor and held the hilts in one hand while he stepped down from the chair.

Elaina ignored his apology and reached out her right arm, palm upward. "The handle, please," she said, with a suggestion of a smile, "not the blade."

He leaned one sword against the chair, and rested the grip of the other in her palm. Her hand clenched it, and he saw the cords of muscles in her slim forearm as she hefted and tested its weight. "This is good. Now pick up yours and we will go."

"Elaina—I don't know how to use a sword."

"There are subtleties, but the basics would be obvious to a child." She rotated her wrist, waggling the sword, and a fearful competence surged from her arm. "Jab with the point, chop with the edge."

He led her to the entryway and at her instruction tested the front door. It stood unlocked. "Lock it and bolt it," she said.

He obeyed, but as they turned and he guided her down the hallway, he asked, "Can't they—I don't know, just 'magic' it open or something?"

"What you call 'magic' is a very subtle force down here on the physical. It would take a tremendous amount of power to do such a thing. Why do it, when an axe or a lockpick would serve better?"

Ahead of them in the hallway one of the doors glowed, as though it were translucent and the sun shone through. "What's that light?"

She stopped. "It's Canetti's warding, and you shouldn't be able to see it. Shut down your higher senses, now, and keep them down!"

He concentrated on closing himself off as she'd taught and the light dwindled and finally disappeared. It became much harder to navigate the shadows that stretched before him.

Where the hallway reached a T-intersection, she said, "Turn right, here." He led her around the corner and she said, "This door. Open it."

He obeyed. He sensed rather than saw a long passageway plunging down, and darkness seemed to flow up from it like a fog. "I can't see anything."

She removed her sunglasses and folded them into the pocket of her blouse. She rubbed her eyes with her knuckles and then ground her eyelashes back and forth between thumbs and forefingers. After a long sigh, she said, "I hate this more than almost anything," and opened her eyes.

Her pupils were dilated wide, and the irises surrounding them coruscated with brilliant, hot reds and greens, glowing and moving like a psychedelic Christmas pageant.

Arby found himself recoiling. "You can see?"

"Not as you can. But down there…"

There was something terrible in her sightless, luminous gaze, and Arby shivered.

Elaina gave a sad laugh. "I won't hurt you, Rain. Myself, perhaps. But now it is my turn to lead you."

With the door closed behind them the darkness was intergalactic: uncompromising and uncaring. Yet it was not empty. Arby felt, or thought he felt, currents of air parting before him as Elaina led him down the steps. Her voice murmured reassurance at his side. "The steps are not all level. Nor are they the same distance down or forward. But there is nothing to fear if you move slowly." Nothing to fear. It was the nothingness that was most fearsome. He clung to Elaina's elbow with his left arm, and with his right he used the point of his sword as a cane, testing before him.

It must be like this for her every day, he realized, even on a sunny afternoon in the park. The utter isolation of blindness became more real for him than the stone steps beneath his feet.

After an endless descent he shuffled his feet a few steps across a cobblestone floor. "Wait here a moment," Elaina said, and removed her arm from his grasp.

The soft pad of her bare feet against the stones disappeared in the darkness to his left. Without the surety of sight, he felt afraid to move, and the longer he stood there the more it seemed he was balanced atop a pinnacle with vast emptiness to all sides. He closed his eyes, tried to calm his breath, and when he opened his eyes again he could see.

A faint glow, like the light from a television set seen through the curtains of a nighttime window. The basement was high-ceilinged, and a sparse forest of brick pillars supported the roof. Perhaps thirty feet ahead Arby saw a stone wall with a doorless opening.

He took a few steps forward and peered right and left. That far wall seemed to be a sequence of open doorways, and hanging open from a few he saw rusting iron grates.

A prison. A prison or a dungeon. A sickening feeling began to leak up from the floor and invade him, forcing itself into his awareness as surely as a smell of raw sewage. Terrible things had happened here.

The human brain burns glucose at a rate of about fifteen watts, and at moments of intense concentration, such as an engineer's calculation of stress analysis, or a dancer's pirouette, this can jump as high as twenty watts.

Arby's brain was working at thirty-two watts. A Qabalist would point out that this corresponds to the Thirty-two Paths of Wisdom upon the Tree of Life. An anatomist would note that it corresponds to the thirty-two human teeth and the thirty-two human vertebrae. (Thirty-three human vertebrae if one includes the tiny vestigial tail. But, then, there are really thirty-three Paths on the Tree if one includes Da'ath, the absent Sephiroth that inhabits the Abyss—though Qabalists assert that there are not thirty-three Paths, but rather thirty-two plus one.)

Of the extra seventeen watts Arby burned above his fifteen-watt baseline, four were in his pineal gland, the third eye, centered between his eyebrows.

In so-called lower creatures, such as the Tuatara lizard of New Zealand, the pineal is still a functioning eye, seeing light, shadow, and motion.

From Asclepius onward for thousands of years, scholars believed that the pineal was a vital organ of the brain. Descartes went further, calling it the Seat of the Soul.

Yet for many years, modern scientists asserted that the pineal was a vestigial organ, like the appendix, about as useful as nipples on men…until they discovered that the pineal is still literally a third eye. Although the little gland is hidden behind the thick bone of the brow ridge, in humans it is so exquisitely sensitive to radiation of all forms that it can sense the tiny amount of light that penetrates the skull.

The pineal monitors the day-night cycle and adjusts the body's clock accordingly, secreting the hormone melatonin to initiate sleep, sending out a dozen transmitters to increase awareness during the day. Jet lag? You've confused your third eye.

Of course, as any occultist who has reached even the rank of Zelator—the kindergarten of the occult lodges—can report, it is the pineal that receives the illumination of the etheric planes. And the dungeon was full of etheric light.

Fifteen watts baseline plus four in Arby's pineal left thirteen watts of the Glorious thirty-two unaccounted for. All that extra glucose was busily being oxidated by the mitochondria in the neurons at the PFT juncture, the place where the parietal, frontal, and temporal lobes meet.

A few neuroscientists called this the God-center. Occultists call it the Crown Nexus. Stimulation of that portion of the brain invariably caused mystical experiences in research subjects.

The religious cited this as proof of God's existence: the very human brain had been designed to communicate with the All High.

Atheists cited this as proof that God was no more than a construction of the brain.

But babies know what the Crown Nexus is: a window to the Inner Planes.

If unattached, spirit and mind will invade any highly organized energetic systems, and more often than not a crying baby has seen some etheric presence stalking it, seeking a host. Clutched in a parent's arms, their auras intermingled, the baby is defended.

Eventually the fontanelle, the soft spot, closes, and for most untrained humans the window closes with it.

Arby's skull sutures had sealed and calcified long ago, but over the previous days his Crown Nexus had opened wide, and the more he looked the more he saw. Translucent tubes of force, thick as treetrunks, moved and twisted in purple-green knots between the brick pillars, the tubes stacked atop one another to a height above his head. As he watched he understood that these snaking pipes were everywhere, even slithering around his own body, as though he'd been buried in a titan's intestines.

Elaina strode through the pipes of force without effort, and they burst and reformed in her wake. "I've found his *fornaio*—" she began. She stopped short when she saw Arby, her eyes whirling red and green. "I told you to stay closed off. Shut it down, now!"

"I can't…" He concentrated. Nothing changed.

Elaina gave an impatient snort, laid her sword on the floor, and grasped his wrists. The lights and the serpentine pipes dimmed for a moment and then brightened again. "Oh, this is not good," she said, "not good at all." She knelt and seized her sword from the cobbles. "Well. At least you can see now. Follow me."

At the far end of the dungeon, a short stairway led down farther to an old arched doorway. The door swung open without a squeak. Beyond it a long tunnel ran off to the left and right, supported every so often by brick arches. Here, too, the long tubes of force wrapped around one another, flowing and flexing.

"A feed drain to the Cloaca Maxima," Elaina said. "A good thing it isn't raining."

She turned to the right and padded ahead.

Arby followed her, sniffing the air. It smelt of hidden waters and mildew. "Does this lead out?"

"Undoubtedly. But until sunrise, we're safer down here."

She stepped up her pace, weaving between piles of rubble that had fallen from the ceiling. After the third archway she stopped. "There it is."

Her head was turned to the right, and for a moment Arby saw nothing but blank wall.

Then, as though he had stepped from a lighted house and his eyes grew accustomed to the dark, the wall began to glow with that same golden filtered light he'd seen shining through the door of Canetti's bedroom.

"If it can protect him, it can protect us," she said. "Hold my sword."

Arby stood there with his backpack over his shoulder and a sword in either hand, feeling useless. "What are you doing?"

"Shh! This takes some concentration."

Elaina approached the glowing wall with her arms straight in front of her. She bent her elbows so her forearms lay one above the other, and then began spinning one forearm over the other, like a bad 1960s dance move.

Sheets of light began to pour from the wall and wrapped themselves around her forearms as though she were reeling cloth into a thick bolt.

When her arms were afire with this strange light, she ran back the way they had come, to the door leading up from the culvert into the dungeon. Her motions were hidden from Arby, but the sudden light from the doorway cast a distorted shadow of Elaina across the floor of the tunnel and up the wall opposite.

That light persisted when she came hustling back. At the second archway she stopped, and performed a maneuver he found it hard to understand—a bend to the left side, bringing her elbow down onto her bent knee, and then jerking her whole body upright, flinging her arms above her head as though snapping a bedsheet at the ceiling. Yellow light sprayed out and clung to the archway, and she dashed forward and tugged the light downward toward the floor, Saran-Wrapping the whole opening of the archway in transparent yellow.

Elaina worked her way around the edges of the seal, performing some inscrutable small motions with her hands, but Arby sensed something behind him.

He turned, both swords lifted. A dozen figures, perhaps more, stood there. Ghostly figures, he might have said, but that wasn't right. There was nothing white or filmy about these. They were grainy, like a newspaper photograph viewed through a magnifying glass. "Elaina…" he said.

"Just a minute!" she said from afar.

The figures were male and female, in rags, and their faces were contorted with rage and pain. Their hatred was a thing he felt he needed to push away with open palms, but he had swords in both hands.

In unison, they took one step forward, and Arby took one step back.

"Elaina!" he shouted.

Her replying voice was exasperated, as though she were answering a fourth phone call after three wrong numbers. "*What?*"

The figures stepped forward again, and Arby fell back. For some reason, his tongue no longer worked. When he tried, he found he couldn't even swallow.

"*Them?*" Elaina's voice said, from just behind his shoulder. "Shoo! Go on, get away from here!" She stepped past him and waved her hand,

and the figures grew dim and vanished. "Now, one more I think, just in case they decide to come in from a storm drain…"

He followed her to an archway far down the culvert behind them. She performed the same maneuver there, stretching light across the whole of the tunnel. She surveyed her work, and, with a satisfied nod, waved her forearms in front of her body as though shaking off water. The light on her arms vanished. "My sword?" she asked.

He handed it to her. "Is this stuff dangerous to touch?"

"No." She poked her hand through the sheet of light. "Go ahead."

He did the same. He felt, or fancied he felt, only the slightest touch. "What is it?"

"A ward. Similar to the one Canetti has cast around his bedroom. A protective shield."

"Some shield. I just stuck my hand through it."

"Most things can pass through it. But not beings who wish us harm."

Arby's mind could encompass the idea of force-fields or invisible shields, either of which could be accommodated by science or by TV-quality science fiction, but he had no model for this. "Oh, really? And how does that work—the ward asks them twenty questions?"

Her eyes narrowed to red-green slivers. "I'll tell you how it works, Rain. It works the same way as the seal Canetti placed on you after you told him we were headed for Naples."

Arby shook his head in a display of disappointed affability, like Ronald Reagan preparing to answer a difficult question from the press corps. To his horror, he smiled and said, "I don't know why you keep harping on that. I've already explained that he didn't even ask where we were headed." In his most earnest, almost whiny voice, he added, "I don't know *why* you don't *believe me*."

"Quod erat demonstrandum. Understand now?"

He did, and wished that he didn't. He breathed, trying to quell the imprisoned, panicky part of him that had been cut off from his voice. The scientist part of him took over. "Okay. So no one can come through. What about inanimate objects? What about bullets, and hand grenades?"

"They won't come with guns or bombs."

"They did in Bahrain."

"Those were—how do I say?—unwitting volunteers, fanatics believing they were serving some higher purpose. Those who come now will destroy your physical body, but only as a side effect." Her face turned toward him and the wattage of her eyes surged. "These wish to slay us on the higher planes—to obliterate us forever, to destroy what you might call our souls." She sighed. "Let's go sit down."

She turned and walked back toward the section of the tunnel where Canetti's *fornaio* glowed in the wall. Arby stood still for a moment, and then hurried after her. He'd never before been sure he had a soul, but in an instant it seemed like his most valuable possession. "With what? How can they do that?"

"Kill our etheric bodies while our consciousness is elevated onto this plane. Why do you think I tried to keep your mind down on the physical?" She stopped and turned to face him, her sword out. "This is what they seek." Her body remained upright, but a transparent double leaned out of it to the right, holding a transparent sword. Then the whole double stepped to the side and stood, cobwebby lines stretching between them and then vanishing. Two Elainas, one a faint replica.

"Now watch," she said, her mouths moving in synchrony. The Elainas bent forward, laid their swords on the floor, and then straightened. The Elainas pointed down. The physical sword lay on the bricks. Its transparent double shimmered and vanished.

She stepped sideways and merged her two forms, and retrieved her sword. "A weapon must be held by the etheric body to be effective on the etheric plane," she said. "No arrows, no bullets, no spears. *Mano a mano*, as the Spaniards have it." She smiled, and her teeth seemed to gleam as bright as her eyes. "Of course, that means that your enemy must be as exposed as you are. There's a justice in that, don't you think?"

Arby found himself open-mouthed. Questions philosophers had debated for millennia, matters that transcended the boundaries of modern science, all seemed revealed in a matter of moments. "Did I just see your—your *soul?*"

Elaina laughed. "You say that as though I showed you, I don't know, my ovaries. I *was* still dressed, you noticed. That was my lower etheric body, and inside that is my higher etheric body, and inside that is an astral body, and so on. Four bodies, by some reckonings, and ten by others, or thirty-two, or one hundred twenty-eight. Thousands, in some systems." Her voice lost its mirth. "Tonight they hope to slay all of them, for all time. So if you value all these bodies you didn't realize you have, you will do as I say and skip all the questions."

Some large cubes of stone had fallen from the roof in past ages, and they used these as stools and sat in the green-and-purple shadows. Elaina closed her eyes and leaned her face into her palms, massaging as though her head ached.

Arby gazed at the light of the *fornaio*. At first the glow seemed smooth and undifferentiated, but as he watched it seemed to him that lines of brighter light showed here and there, and, as he gazed, these began to organize themselves into mechanisms of dazzling complexity, like a vast clockwork made of organic forms, one turning another like misshapen gears. "It's like a big machine..." he said.

Elaina didn't bother to raise her head from her hands. "What is?"

"The *fornaio*."

"It's a powerplant of sorts. It harnesses all the forces you see flowing around us—all the horror and the glory that was Rome, permanently imprinted on the etheric plane of this city."

"Like a... I don't know, like a waterwheel?"

"After a fashion. But the flows are tidal, governed by the Moon. And this is just one of thousands of places you could tap this energy in Rome." She sighed. "The place is sick with it."

Arby felt a wobbling in his body, a moment of dizziness, and then heard a scream inside his head. The yellow glow in the wall and the sheet of light sealing the archway dimmed and then brightened, and the chilly tubes of force slipping past him seemed to contract in a moment's peristalsis.

"Something's attacking Canetti's ward upstairs," she said. "I don't know what they have brought..."

Elaina stood and Arby rose with her. The perfect rainbow of her aura billowed out from her, and the reds and greens of her irises seemed to dance through it all. He heard a ripping noise, and saw that she had used her dagger to rip the right side-seam of her skirt, opening it from hem to mid-hip.

Down the tunnel, a beam of light shone into the tunnel from the dungeon. A pale figure clutching a flashlight ran down the steps from the dungeon, bursting through the ward without resistance. As the figure turned and ran toward them, Arby saw it was Concetta, clad in a white nightdress. As she neared the second ward, Arby could read the terror on her face. She screamed in Italian as she ran, and he saw Elaina tense.

"You will have to go now," Elaina said. "Take the girl."

"And do what?"

Concetta passed through the second ward as though it weren't there, gasping. Elaina snapped out something at her in Italian and pointed at Arby. Concetta stumbled to his side and clung to his arm, crying.

"There will be a way to the street," Elaina said, "many ways, down this tunnel. Run, get out, and keep going. One of ours will find you." She looked at Concetta. "*Corette!*" Arby felt Concetta tug on his arm, but when Elaina yelled, "*Volate via, sciocchi!*" the woman released her grip and began running.

"Elaina—"

The sheet of yellow light in the archway flamed and dimmed.

Elaina braced herself in a crouch and lifted her sword with both hands on the hilt. "Don't make me go through this for nothing," she said, "go." She glared at him and her eyes blazed green and red in the darkness. "Run, damn you!" she shouted. "*Run now!*"

Her command was irresistible as a hurricane. It spun him on his heel and sent him flying down the tunnel after Concetta, his gait unbalanced by his pack and by the heavy sword he still gripped in his hand.

13

Further Than Body Deep

Even though the privacy window of the limousine was closed, von Fleischer still heard the slither of the wiperblades in the endless Oregon drizzle. Rooker hulked in the seat across from him, facing the rear of the limo, no doubt keeping an eye on the van they had brought along.

Von Fleischer checked messages on his cell phone, deleted all but one, and speed-dialed that number. A male voice answered with nothing but a cautious, "American Expediting."

"This is a return customer calling to see if my new order has been shipped."

"Can you wait while I confirm the phone number?" A pause. "I'm happy to report that our delivery service picked it up last night, and you ought to be getting it ahead of schedule. Can I help you with anything else?"

Von Fleischer signed off and dialed Armbruster's number in the Senate Office Building. When the receptionist answered he identified himself, and found himself transferred to a nervous young man who identified himself as Justin. "We've got standing orders to put you through to the senator direct, sir, but he's in committee at the moment. I can have him return your call just as soon as the session is over, but I—"

"No, no, it's nothing urgent, just a friendly hello. Just tell the senator that I rang to thank him for the little gift, and remind him that we'd like to see him at our estate any time. Oh, and say hello from Liam?"

"Liam, sir?" He sounded baffled by the name. "Is there a last name, or…?"

"Just an old, fond friend. Bob'll know the fellow."

After he said goodbye he snapped the phone shut and grinned at Rooker. "The OCX is on the water. More of it than we can use, honestly. Want to keep a barrel or two for those nights you can't sleep?"

"I'll pass."

"You ought to reconsider. All in all, it might be the ultimate date-rape drug."

Rooker rotated those powerful shoulders to release tension and sat up straighter, his short-cropped hair nearly touching the roof of the limo. "Where's the fun in that? I like 'em conscious."

Any woman who found herself at Rooker's tender mercies would probably beg to suck a big lungful of OCX-27 first, but he decided not to share that opinion with the big ugly man who sat across from him.

People misunderstand the military view of technology. The pursuit of bigger, faster, and more powerful, although they have an allure of their own, are only means to an end. It is easy to caricature the Joint Chiefs of Staff as pawns of the Strangeloves, drawn to the biggest explosion of them all by a sexual force, but the real goal, the true desideratum, is one thing only: Control.

Control isn't solely concerned with the projection of force; control also requires invulnerability, and the regulation of timing. It is the old desire of kings and the politicians who have followed in their footsteps: just hand me all the power, and I promise to do what's best.

The police thought they'd found it in the Taser, the little gun that shocked people into unconsciousness without causing pain or damage. Perfect. When in doubt, Tase everyone in sight and sort it out later. Unfortunately, Tasers turned out to be painful and often deadly, but they embodied the basic desires: unconditional power, self-protection, and the control of timing.

For the military, the Holy Grail has long been the Magic Gas—the substance that can render whole populations immobile or unconscious or ineffectual without causing death or injury. Secret billions have been spent on the Magic Gas. Anesthetics, nauseogenics, even hallucinogenics—aerosol compounds based on LSD and tryptamines enjoyed a vogue in the sixties, until they were found to be wildly unpredictable—every kind of approach was tried, including comedy concepts like inhaled superlaxatives and airborne marijuana derivatives.

Superlaxatives? Airborne dope dens? No real statistics are available, but a conservative estimate suggests that fifteen percent of secret information is so classified for true national security reasons, another fifteen percent to cover up malfeasance by government officials, and a full forty percent to prevent government officials from looking like the Marx Brothers. (The remainder, of course, is to prevent taxpayers from seeing where their money is going.)

No Magic Gas was both effective and non-lethal, but for a time in the late 1990s, it seemed like the problem had been solved by OCX-27, the twenty-seventh Organic-Cage Xenon compound investigated.

The inert gas Xenon, a cousin of the more flamboyant Neon, is the anesthetic of choice in most modern hospitals—side effects are few, interactions are rare, and anesthesia hangovers are minimal. But dosing with Xenon requires constant monitoring and an artful hand. Too little and the patient wakes, but too much and the patient slips into the sleep without end.

The OCX series solved the problem of automatic dosage. The "Organic Cages" were derivatives of the Fullerenes, carbon ovoids latticed like a geodesic dome. Each caged a cargo of Xenon atoms, and when they were inhaled and carried into the bloodstream, they set up their own balance, opening like clams to release more Xenon when its partial pressure fell, capturing more Xenon when the partial pressure rose. OCX-27 seemed perfect, keeping blood levels at concentrations that ensured anesthesia ranging from extreme lassitude to unconsciousness.

Hours after the original exposure, as the last of the Xenon was exhaled, the Organic Cages collapsed and were excreted in the urine—a perfect, elegant, non-lethal way of pacifying a city, a state, a country. Of course, there would be *some* casualties—those who inhaled the gas while driving, or in the bath, or when their mother was lugging them down the stairs. But it was a beautiful weapon: gas everyone and sort enemy from friend later.

The human trials began with healthy male volunteers, and then moved on to mixed-gender groups, elderly groups, and finally—in another country—to children and infants. There were no deaths and no real side effects apart from a few cases of nausea, and so a strategic stockpile of three hundred tons was synthesized, enough OCX-27 to send the entire population of India off to slumberland.

It was a few years before disquieting reports began to filter back from the volunteers. They themselves experienced no apparent ill-health, but the rate of birth defects among their children seemed disturbing at first, and then shocking. Miscarriages and spontaneous abortions more than tripled, but of the live births, one hundred percent of them were hideously deformed in unpredictable ways, and they carried damaged DNA so that none of their descendants, if they had them, would ever be normal. Somehow the fullerene derivatives degraded into breakdown products that attacked egg and sperm alike.

The volunteers were bought off with a combination of large stipends and threats, and the reluctant decision was taken to incinerate the entire stockpile.

Normally this would have been done at considerable expense and with immense caution at one of the Army's disposal sites, but Senator Armbruster's influence in various secret committees, where he made speeches touting the benefits of privatization and the dangers of rail transport of hazardous materials inside the United States, especially in an age of terrorism, had resulted in a new policy, where materials classified as having "no practicable military uses" could be shipped overseas for disposal.

Once OCX-27 had been so classified, it was no more than another load of toxic crap slated for incineration—though most cargoes scheduled for incineration were in fact simply buried—in some Third World dump. The bulk of the world supply of OCX-27 had been moved to the largely defunct Aberdeen Proving Grounds on the Chesapeake Bay, where they waited to be loaded onto a freighter; another, smaller load, had been dispatched to Mexico.

Americans in general had stopped throwing trash from the windows of their cars, but by the end of the twentieth century the nation's most noxious garbage was tossed into other countries while the US economy sped down the highway. Integrated Logistics Management, Ltd.—which von Fleischer owned through an untraceable tangle of dummy corporations in a dozen countries—had profited mightily from unwanted American rubbish: not only toxic wastes, but also goods that could be sold overseas where regulations were weak, such as outlawed pesticides, dangerous solvents, or childhood vaccines preserved with methyl-mercury.

It had been a profitable business over the years, though it was one in which von Fleischer seldom took much interest. But the contract to dispose of the OCX-27 stockpile was about more than money.

Though he'd gladly take their money, too.

The eclecticism—or to be less charitable, the total lack of discrimination—of the American mind never ceased to amaze von Fleischer. Crystal Keeling's spiritual gift shop in Northeast Portland, *Ancient Days*, was an utter mishmash, but he had to admit it was an Equal Opportunity mishmash. A Wiccan section, a Buddhist section, an Egyptian section, a Christian section, ten different flavors of New World indigenous religions, an Australo-Pacific section...

Where else could you go to purchase a three-foot-high wooden penis statue from the New Guinea Highlands, and also pick up a Tibetan gong, a string of rosary beads, and a nosepipe for inhaling pulverized *Anadenathera* seeds? One-stop shopping for multiple lifetimes.

But Crystal Keeling herself was of even more interest. Fifty-five years old, Rooker's network had found, but she looked...

She didn't look any particular age. Crystal had spent the time since he and Rooker had come into the shop dealing with a young, very fussy man in a teal turtleneck; a man searching for Oaxacan yarn paintings with very specific characteristics—had to be quadrant-based, had to show deer gods, had to highlight energy flows, but couldn't have too much orange and yellow in the composition.

At odd moments, she looked up from showing the man photo samples in notebooks and flashed them an apologetic smile as they pretended to browse. She had smile lines, and laugh lines, and what von Fleischer could only think of as ecstasy lines—it was easy to picture that mouth dropping open into a luscious moan. The silver sprinkled through her dark hair seemed like a style rather than a sign of aging. Her body beneath the Indian print dress was lithe and looked fine. Maybe better than fine.

He let his consciousness drift upward, and what he saw there was even more intriguing. Her aura was drenched in sub-indigo and green and red, the green fire of the Venusian love force blended with the cock-heavy Martian red, and beneath it all the grinding, powerful, transformative Plutonian, a red-purple so dark it approached blackness. In a trio of contemporary words, she was hot—and it went much further than skin-deep. It went further than body-deep.

All very titillating, he granted. But what piqued his interest was the fine structure of her aura—flowing, detailed, yet incredibly balanced. In fact, apart from the blind bitch in her many incarnations, it might be the most balanced aura he'd ever seen; but unlike the bitch's simplistic rainbow, this was balanced and complex at the same time.

Was her soul human? And if not, what was she?

When she disappeared to the back room of the store—most likely to gather up another armful of notebooks to display to the man in the turtleneck—von Fleischer stepped to the display cabinet at the rear of the store. "I say," he said, "I'm afraid I don't know your name— mine's Richardson—but we've come quite some distance to talk to the proprietress, and if we could have her alone for even fifteen minutes…"

He Nudged the man, but the man responded with a prissy push back to center. "My name's *Jared*, and *I've* come in all the way from *Beaver*ton, and set aside most of the day for this, and it's *al*most closing time, and I *am* sorry, but you'll just have to get in line like everyone else."

Von Fleischer glanced over at Rooker in the Christianity section and raised one eyebrow.

A foot-long metal crucifix sliced through the air and hit the wall in front of Jared's nose. It stuck there, embedded by the corner of one crosspiece, humming like a tuning fork.

Rooker crossed the floor in a few quick steps and clamped his arm over Jared's shoulders. "We need to have a talk, pal," Rooker said.

Von Fleischer smiled as he watched the man blanch. In close proximity, Rooker simply repelled women, but he terrified men.

With one arm still over Jared's shoulder, Rooker steered the man around toward the front door, opened it to the ding-a-ling of a bell, and edged the two of them out onto the sidewalk as a unit.

Crystal rushed out from the back, a stack of notebooks clutched to her breast, and frowned as she saw von Fleischer where Jared had stood before. She glanced around the vacant shop, and said, "Where did he go?"

"Excitable young man. He remembered something urgent and had to leave."

"Oh, great. Far fucking out. He only made me get half the catalogue out first." She dumped the notebooks on the counter and then saw the crucifix stuck into the wall. Her eyes narrowed. "Did *he* do this? Because I have to tell you—we respect all paths here, and every one of these items is sacred—"

Crystal stood on tiptoe—a lovely sight in itself—and tried to wrestle the crucifix from the wood.

"Allow me," von Fleischer said. He gentled her hands away and then wrenched it out of the wall. He sat it down atop her notebooks and patted it. "Poor boy clearly hasn't had enough to eat, and then's been hung up on a cross to boot."

The ding-a-ling announced Rooker's return. He nodded to von Fleischer and then shambled across the room. Von Fleischer observed Crystal, waiting for the usual recoil from Rooker's presence, but she only smiled at the two of them. "Well," she said, waving her hands in front of her face as though shooing flies, "let it go out in the universe, right? No point in dwelling on the negative…" She closed her eyes, and he saw the slight disturbances in her aura rebalance themselves. When her eyes opened again, he was struck by their beauty. Were they dark blue, or green, or hazel, or even brown, or all colors at once?

Who the hell was she?

"So," she said, "I'm sorry I had to keep you waiting. How can I help you?"

Von Fleischer steepled his fingers in front of his mouth and tapped his fingertips together. "You might call us spiritual seekers. And I'm sure you see seekers all day. Why am I here? What is my purpose? Where is my path?" He dropped his hands and spread them wide before his chest. "As it happens, we have already answered those questions, but there are other issues…"

Rooker stepped up close to her, and she showed no reaction. "What my boss means is," he said, "we got some real specific stuff. Stuff only you can help us with."

Her laughter sang in the room. "I'm no guru…but I'll help both of you in absolutely any way that I can."

Von Fleischer nodded his head. If there were one atom of guile in her, he couldn't find it. "I can't tell you," he said, "how happy I am to hear you say that. Because it means you won't mind being our guest for a while. I'll have Elliott bring the van around back. Rooker?"

He inclined his head toward Crystal, and Rooker clapped his hand over her mouth and grabbed her wrists.

14

Tall Boys

Ahead of him, Arby saw Concetta fall on the rubble-strewn floor. The flashlight skidded out of her hand and he heard her sobbing as she crawled after it.

Somehow this broke the spell that Elaina's command seemed to have cast upon him. What was he doing? Running away to leave Elaina facing whatever was coming—and running to what? He knew nothing of those who pursued him, nothing of those who might aid him. Hell, he didn't even know who he was.

Echoing footfalls came from far behind him. Many footfalls, and a strange huffing sound.

He had to go back.

His tailbone tingled and fear twined up his spine.

Once someone had told him that courage was the ability to act in spite of fear; that fearlessness was not courage, but foolhardiness.

As he turned to face what lay behind him, he prayed for a good dose of foolhardiness, as courage seemed ready to desert him.

Thirty yards back, he saw Elaina from behind, still poised for action with her sword lifted. Beyond her, he saw three human figures through the glow of the ward she had stretched across the tunnel. Beside one of the trio squatted a huge, translucent beast shaped like a bulldog, but closer in size to a hippo. This creature opened a wide, froglike mouth and began chewing at the light of the ward, ripping it and swallowing it in sheets as though it were eating curtains.

Two men stepped through the hole the beast was enlarging. Both wore well-tailored business suits, one in gray, one in black. Both held bludgeons in their left hand and swords in their right. They paused only a moment, and then ran toward Elaina at a trot. Aside from the weapons, they could have been two junior executives late for a meeting.

Arby felt a dizzy urge to laugh, and hefted the sword in his hand. Jab with the point and chop with the blade, was it? That might be enough to deal with The Attack of the Twin Accountants.

He dropped his pack to the floor of the tunnel. Just as he began to jog back to join Elaina, pale flares blossomed from the heads of the men. He stopped, staring. Long lines of shadowy substance reared up toward the ceiling and widened, as though the men had sprouted treetrunk-thick cobras from their shoulders.

The tops of the serpentine trunks bore faces—huge caricatures of human faces with giant eyes and cruel, thick-lipped smiles, like terrible primitive masks.

Elaina gave some wordless cry and charged. As she closed with them, both protruding heads opened their jaws and struck down at her.

Elaina leapt back even as she slashed her sword at the snapping faces. The snake-like necks arched upward, away from her blade, but the human bodies beneath used the moment to move closer, and she parried the slash of the gray man's sword, and continued the move to glance her blade against the black man's bludgeon and steer it toward the floor.

It was as if she battled four foes at once, and Arby knew she wouldn't survive a moment more. "*No!*" he shouted, and ran toward them.

Four heads—two human faces and two horrific masks—stared at Arby in shock.

Elaina dove between the two men, skidding across the rough floor on her side. From behind, with all the force of both arms, she swung her blade at the leg of the man in the black suit.

An ugly thunk, then a cracking sound. The man stared down in amazement for a moment and then screamed as her blade came free from his leg. Where before there had been a knee, now there was only a strip of flesh connecting his thigh to his shin, and he toppled. In agony, he flung aside his sword and clutched at his thigh with both hands. Dark blood spouted, and around it Arby saw clouds of life-force fountaining out.

The swordsman's etheric extension thrashed, its wicked mouth twisting in a silent rictus, but Elaina had already rolled to her knees and when the head lashed down she whipped her sword up and sliced through its thick yet insubstantial neck. The cry Arby heard this time was only inside his head.

From the archway, where the light of the ward had vanished, the third man came running, this one dressed in a white suit, a snake-necked clown's head riding above him. Alongside him the beast bounded, moving in toadlike leaps.

Elaina cried out. Still on her knees, she had turned to defend herself from the man in gray, but she was too late: her sword came up in time to prevent a skull-crushing blow from his bludgeon, but the weighted club grazed the blade and then clouted her head and knocked her to the ground.

The man stood over her and raised his bludgeon.

Arby was still a dozen feet away. Without a conscious thought, he found himself stooping to pick up a rock as he ran. He threw it, left-handed, and it smacked the man in the side of his head.

The man in gray reeled and cursed in Italian, and his etheric extension whipped about and lashed down at Arby, snapping its jaws, but Arby had ducked down for another rock, and he hurled it from just a few feet away…

This time it hit Elaina in the chest as she struggled to her knees.

The gray man swung his club and smashed Arby in the chest with such force that Arby flew off his feet and skidded along the floor of the tunnel. The beast, now unleashed, raced by, not even pausing, and bounded down the culvert.

There was a long space where breath would not come, where blood would not flow, where Arby believed his heart had been crushed by the blow. His vision went dark, but trembled with erratic light. When at last he succeeded in drawing a breath, it was a whimper.

A dozen feet away, the man in the gray suit had bent down and grasped Elaina's hair, jerking her torso from the floor. His other hand still held his sword. Elaina offered no resistance, as though she were unconscious or dead.

The man in the white suit approached the pair at a run, shouting out a question.

The man in gray responded with a sharp reply.

Arby didn't know who the men were, but he hated them, hated them in a way he'd never hated before, and he felt his aura swell, and then discs of light flew from his eyes toward the two men, imaginary Frisbees of loathing. Neither of the men reacted when their auras absorbed these discs. Whatever dispute the two had seemed to be growing, and the men's voices rose in increasing anger.

Arby pushed himself to his feet, his weight borne by one hand and by the sword he still clutched.

The man in gray pointed at Arby with his sword, shouting in Italian, and the man in white used the opening to whip a dagger upward and slash the gray man's throat.

The man in gray gurgled and clutched at his neck, and his etheric serpent writhed. The yellow glow from the *fornaio* brightened, and in the sudden near-daylight clarity Arby saw Elaina roll to her knees and drive the point of her sword up between the legs of the man in white.

The man stood pierced by a foot of steel, his snake-neck thrashing above his physical body. Elaina steadied the grip with her left hand, lowered her right arm, and slammed the heel of her palm upward into the pommel, driving the sword to the hilt in his crotch, impaling him on three feet of blade.

The man fell without a word or a cry, his etheric neck vanishing. Elaina remained on her knees, her head bowed. The yellow light from the *fornaio* pulsed from behind Arby, illuminating the tunnel in rhythm with some gargantuan pulse.

Then he heard Concetta's sobs from down the tunnel.

He turned. The beast was eating the last scraps of light from the third ward. Concetta was stumbling back toward Arby, but without her flashlight, and Arby realized that she was staggering her way through what for her was total darkness.

The last of the yellow light of the ward vanished, and the beast turned and bounded after Concetta.

Arby glanced back at Elaina. Her eyes blinked their green and red flashes, and she shook her head and pushed up onto her feet.

He ran toward Concetta, his sword in hand, without even a glimmer of a plan. His bruised chest ached with each breath.

In three huge leaps, the beast caught Concetta by the legs. She screamed and fell forward, her calves in the beast's wide mouth. The beast might be translucent, but it was physical; it shook its massive head to the side, and Concetta's legs came free, but torn with a dozen bleeding wounds. Arby saw that the beast still had a dark section of Concetta's aura in its jaws, the light stretching to her physical legs like taffy being pulled.

The beast yanked its head and the aura ripped, weeping dots of light onto the floor.

"Concetta," he shouted, still running, "here!"

A dozen yards from him now, the woman tried to rise and then fell to her knees. The beast took a short hop forward and closed its jaws on the aura behind her back, tugging.

Arby heard footsteps behind him, and Elaina pushed him aside so hard he stumbled and sprawled on the floor. She ran past him and from ten paces she hurled her dagger into Concetta's heart.

Arby stared as Concetta's aura blossomed and then vanished.

He felt Elaina's hands urging him to his feet. "Come on," she said, "get up!"

"You killed her…"

"I saved her, you idiot. Now come!"

The beast squatted, shaking its head side-to-side in bafflement at the sudden disappearance of its prey, apparently unaware of the body that lay before it.

Arby clambered to his feet, watching the beast. Elaina tugged at his arm, and then gave it a hard jerk. "Come!"

Then the beast focused its soccer-ball-sized eyes on him, and Arby turned and ran with Elaina.

Each breath was like a stab in the chest, and over the sound of his labored breathing and the slap of their running footfalls, Arby sensed as much as heard the beast's long leaps.

The most Arby could do was pitch himself sideways to the ground, the force against his bruised ribs bringing tears to his eyes. The beast skidded past him.

Arby regained his feet as the beast turned and faced him, an armslength away.

It opened its froggy mouth and revealed rows of triangular fangs. A bright, restless light glowed from its throat.

Arby drew one achingly painful breath, raised his sword on high with both hands, and slashed down through the center of its head.

It was like chopping the blade through a mountain of pudding.

The course of his blade divided that great head in two, but the edges of the cut flowed back together and sealed themselves into their original form.

The beast shuddered as though it had tasted something unpleasant.

A bright-yellow glow illuminated the tunnel. Elaina's voice shouted, "Ay-yah! Ay-yah!" like a rider goading a horse to a quicker pace.

The beast turned its ungainly body.

Elaina had gathered throbbing light from the *fornaio*, folded in her arms like a bushel of laundry, and the pile she held linked back to the *fornaio* itself by a long banner of yellow illumination.

The black-slit pupils in the beast's eyes widened.

Elaina yelled once more, and then heaved the sheets of light from her arms.

The beast pounced, jaws wide, and began devouring the pile.

Elaina circled wide around it to stand beside Arby.

"How can we kill it?" he asked.

"No need now."

As they watched, the beast finished the piles, and Arby would have sworn that it was growing larger with every bite. It ate its way down the banner of light, and, when it reached the brick wall of the *fornaio*, it reared up onto its hind legs, its lumpen body clasped to the wall as though it sought to mate with the oven within. It had swollen from the size of a hippo to the dimensions of an elephant, and each pulse of light seemed to engorge it further, yet at the same time it seemed to become more shapeless.

"What you eat is what you are, I'm told," she said. "It will keep on gorging until it loses its form."

Arby took a wheezing breath and used his sword as a cane. "Why did one of those—those whatever-they-weres—kill the other?"

She gave an abrupt laugh. "They were arguing over who got to cut my head off, and things got out of hand." The red and green lights of her eyes dimmed. "Your doing, of course."

"I don't understand."

"I know. Help me now, Rain. We need to leave this place."

Elaina wobbled on her feet, and he reached out to steady her. "You should sit down," he said.

She shook her head and pressed her hand to her temple. "We have a dozen things to do first."

Arby took a few steps into Canetti's bedroom. "He's gone."

"Probably ran," Elaina said. "Thought he was warded. Wasn't expecting an ether beast."

Arby started to ask a question, but when he turned to Elaina he saw that she was leaving bloody footprints at every step. Her hands clutched at her head and she stumbled against the wall.

He rushed to wrap his arms around her shoulders from behind. "Elaina?"

"I'm sorry, Rain." Her eyes were already shut tight, but she clamped her palms over them. "I'm sorry. Get me to a chair. Get me something to drink."

He scooped her up in his arms. She was light but solid. He carried her to the drawing room and eased her down onto a couch. He let his pack slide off his arm onto the rug. "What do you need? Water?"

"No! A *drink* drink, a bottle. Whisky, brandy, vodka, something to keep my head from exploding."

He found a small glass-fronted liquor cabinet to the right of the hearth. Among the gleaming inventory sat two bottles of apricot brandy, one half empty. He grabbed them both.

Elaina was sitting upright on the couch, hands still pressed against her eyes. Tears leaked from beneath the heels of her palms. He knelt before her. "I have brandy," he said. "Two bottles."

She pulled her hands from her face, her eyes clenched tight shut, and she reached out like a child seeking her mother. Arby unscrewed the cap of the open bottle and guided her hands around it. Her face was tear-stained, framed in disarrayed blond hair, and starting to show an ugly bruise along the right side, and when her hands clasped the bottle and she nodded her thanks, something caught in his throat.

She slugged down the brandy, gulping it like a runner who had just finished a marathon, and he wanted to tell her to go easy, but instead he said, "Why do you hurt?"

Elaina pulled the bottle from her lips and balanced it on her lap. She panted, and Arby was sure that if he lit a match, blue flames would roar from her mouth.

"Haven't had to open my eyes in ages." A spasm shook her body, and she winced, screwing her eyes even tighter. She laughed, and it came out mixed with a sob. "Why's it hurt? You could see what I see, you wouldn't have to ask."

Arby had no good reply to that, not least because he had no real idea what she meant. As though his mind had risen above the planet, he saw his immediate situation in both detail and context: in a foreign country with a weary blind woman, four murdered people in the sewers beneath the house, and bloody footprints everywhere.

Bloody footprints. He looked at her bare feet and realized the blood wasn't from the dead men in the basement. Blood dripped from her heels and soaked into the carpet, leaving a pair of widening dark stains. "Your feet are bleeding!"

She plowed down a double swallow of brandy. "Used to be tough. Callused. No, wait a minute." She paused. Her free hand dug in the pocket of her blouse and found the sunglasses. "Last body. That was when I was Jenny." She pushed the sunglasses onto her face and took another swallow of brandy. "You woulda *loved* Jenny, they all did.

She was just, *voomp!* out in front, and, *voomp!* out in back, too." She mumbled something else in what sounded like Swedish.

"I'm going to go find bandages."

"'Kay. But first, go upstairs and find that little chien, doggie, hound statue. And a little box to put it in…and a biro, pen, marker, plume, *la plume de ma tante*…"

In the central Rome train station they mailed the hound figurine to the *Museo Archeaologico* in Naples. "S'right city to send it to," Elaina said in a slurred voice. "Maybe the museum'll even want it. Now we need tickets to Milan."

"I thought we were going to Naples," Arby said.

She leaned against him. "Uh-huh. You sure did. Now get me on that train and lemme sleep."

15

Violet Crayfish

In 1945 AD, the most valuable piece of real estate on the planet was the secret city of Los Alamos, New Mexico.

The inhabitants knew it was 1945, but most of them were more concerned with the fact that it was Year Three of the Manhattan Project.

Though the development of The Bomb took place at three secret cities—Hanford, Washington, and Oak Ridge, Tennessee, in addition to Los Alamos—the New Mexican city was the directing mind of the effort, the brain of a far-flung body composed of 150,000 people all laboring toward the same goal.

On the morning of July 16, 1945, when the Trinity test burst open the skies above Alamogordo, Carson Mark, one of the most brilliant minds at Los Alamos, thought that the calculations had somehow gone wrong, that despite the mathematical impossibility, they had unleashed a fission chain reaction that would go on forever, until it consumed all of heaven and earth.

Heaven and earth remained intact. But the power that had been delivered into human hands was unlike anything ever seen before. Power enough to level two Japanese cities with a single bomb apiece; power enough to slay a quarter of a million people with a mass of metal the size of two grapefruit.

That power still weaved its way through the deserted red-rock country of Los Alamos, and reverberated in the thousands of aeolian caves that pocked the cliffs of the ancient river valleys. It was a new power, fresher than the Martial forces that moved beneath Rome; it was Uranian, Plutonian, shining with the ultraviolet of Cerenkov radiation.

Like the power of Rome, though, it was backed with blood and suffering, and the cries of the slaughtered.

On July 30, 1945, the *USS Indianapolis* was sunk by a torpedo. Of the ship's 1,196 men, only 316 survived. Many people know most of the casualties came from the horrific mass shark attacks that followed the sinking: nearly eight hundred men were eaten alive.

What fewer people can tell you is the mission of the *USS Indianapolis*, which was returning from delivering the atomic heart of the Hiroshima bomb for final assembly on the island of Tinian.

Those with ears to hear can still detect the voices of hundreds of American sailors in the Japanese chorus that cries out beneath the red sandstone.

At the end of nearly fifty hours in transit from Rome, Arby felt surprisingly rested. Rome to Milan's international airport via train; then Milan to Athens, Athens to Bangkok, Bangkok to Singapore, Singapore to Houston, and Houston to Albuquerque by air, but all in first class. After the events in Bahrain and Rome, the normally grueling aspect of international air travel had seemed relaxing, and the few times he had grown agitated, Elaina had drained the energy from his body by gripping his wrists.

For her part, Elaina had slept, leaning against him, from Rome to Milan, and had promptly fallen asleep again on the flight to Athens. Once she had awakened, she remained remote and seemed pained, like someone recovering from a migraine. Arby wondered if it were the result of using her eyes, or a companion of the ugly bruise swelling on the right side of her face.

Just before the plane landed in Albuquerque, a female flight attendant had leaned down close to her and whispered, "You can tell me it's none of my business, but whoever he is, honey, you get away from him. Ain't no man worth that kind of shit."

Arby almost laughed, but the woman's hard eyes examined him as though he might be the culprit.

For some time, he had been fretting that Crystal might not have followed his advice to head south and stay with Jilly for a time. When he'd spoken to her at the airport in Rome, he hadn't yet met Canetti or the creatures down in the sewer, so he himself hadn't understood how insane the world had become. She'd promised, but he wasn't sure he'd conveyed the urgency of the situation.

He received no answer at her home so he called her shop. Her assistant Jewel answered and told him that Crystal had been planning on leaving town for a while, and had asked her to take over full-time until she returned. "It was kinda sudden-like, but hey, I can use the extra money."

Arby sighed after he hung up the phone, grateful to Crystal who, for once in her life, had been dependable.

He chose the back road from Albuquerque to Los Alamos—up Highway 44 and then eastward on 4—partly because it was less conspicuous, but mostly because he loved the Jemez Mountains. He discovered that much of his joy in the drive was spoiled by the fact that his companion couldn't see. He attempted to explain the unearthly carbonate dam across Jemez Creek—"Smooth and glossy and white, like stalactites in a cave, but twenty feet high, and the water has tunneled beneath the whole dam and rushes out in this torrent, and…"—but he soon realized that his similes and descriptions were pointless. He drove past a half-dozen overlooks without stopping, and merely glanced at the giant expanse of Valles Caldera as his Jeep zipped by.

"You told me to keep quiet until we were close to Los Alamos," he said. "Are we close enough now?"

She sighed. "Perhaps. What, then?"

"What were they? Those snake-men down in the sewer?"

"Humans. Servants of the *Atrum Arbor*." She paused, apparently searching for a simple explanation. "Cannibals, of a sort. They consume the etheric bodies of their victims and add their own etheric mass."

"Why?"

"To gather power. Gather enough, and they can establish themselves on the Inner Planes, and live on after their human bodies die."

"Live on as what? Ghosts? Souls?"

She touched the bruise on her face, exploring it with her fingertips. "It would be easier to show you than to explain, and now isn't the time to show you. Be patient just a little longer."

Atop the easternmost lip of the crater, the road dove into a steep descent through dry pine country, and Arby began describing junctions. Before they reached the westernmost grounds of the Los Alamos National Labs, Elaina directed him onto a narrow road leading north. From there, her words led him onto a well-maintained dirt road that bore west until it forked at the outlet of two canyons.

"The one with the stream," she said.

The canyon to the left was long dry. Despite the chattering creek pouring from the one to the right, though, it looked unpromising—narrow and steep, and overhung by trees. Arby urged the Jeep into the dark of the canyon mouth, and in a few hundred yards the canyon opened into an escondido, a hidden valley.

The view up the valley was blocked by a long, high stone wall, built of red sandstone. In its center stood two massive wooden doors; the canyon stream flowed from beneath a small stone archway beside the doors.

Five cars stood in the dirt parking area. "Looks like there's a party," Arby said.

"Many people live here," she said. "Park the car and lead me to the gate."

He helped her from the car. A breeze settled some of the dust of their passage into his hair, and Arby reflected that the pair of them looked like vagrants—his clothes rumpled and stained from five days of continuous wear, and Elaina, looking well-pressed as always, but with a bruised face and a skirt slashed open to mid-hip. "I hope you know these folks pretty well," he said.

Elaina paused at the gates and then pushed with both hands, and the giant doors swung inward without a sound.

Behind the doors, the stream had been diverted into a wide pool that stretched the whole length of the wall, but spread only perhaps twenty feet wide from the gateway to the path on the other side. The pool was filled with rushes and sweet flag along its margins, and the pads of water lilies covered the surface.

The path beyond bisected a hundred yards of rolling high-grass meadow and then passed between two crenellated stone towers. Beyond the towers Arby saw a three-story Victorian mansion, swathed in elaborate scroll woodworking at the juncture of every architectural element.

"There seems to be a lake here," he said.

"Aren't there stepping stones?"

There were. Glossy black stones gleamed just above the surface of the water, zig-zagging across to the path opposite. "They must have a tough time getting pizza delivery," he said. "How do we manage this?"

"Just get me to the first stone. The rest of it"—she paused for a sly smile—"I could do blindfolded."

Once she had her foot on the first stone, Elaina walked across as though she were striding down her own hallway. Arby followed, though not so casually. Near the last stone, his eyes were startled by a violet crayfish scuttling up the bank. As a child he'd seen crayfish in hues from pink to red and on toward blue-green, but never violet, and never in a shade of any color so intense.

He shifted the backpack onto his right shoulder and offered Elaina his left arm. "Odd architectural choices," he said as they walked. "Unless it's an unfinished theme park."

"It is the current estate of the Adeptus Exemptus, and it is called La Lune."

Arby resisted the urge to remark on the obvious connection with lunatic.

The tall grass to their left rustled, and a brown dog trotted over and fell into step beside them, its tail wagging. "Hey, boy, how ya doin'?" Arby said. "Dog," he said to Elaina.

"So I gathered."

Another dog loped up from their right, this one larger and covered with grizzled gray fur. This one joined its pace to theirs, but without any tailwagging, and it sniffed Arby's hand with deep suspicion before it relaxed its vigilance. Arby looked into its eyes, and they stared back at him without fear or malice through frosty golden irises. "Umm, Elaina…? This other dog looks a lot like a wolf."

"Must be, then."

The canines escorted them between the two towers and up to the steps of the vast gabled and turreted mansion. Arby paused there, searching the high porch for signs of life. "Do we just go up and knock, or—"

"Back at last!" a child's voice said from above. A dark-haired Caucasian boy—Arby guessed him to be nine or ten—leaned against the rail of the porch. "This our big Hero?"

The boy slouched around to the top of the stairs and studied Arby for a long moment. Then his eyes darted to the two canines, back to Arby, and he began to giggle. "Oh, shit," the kid said, and sat down on the top step, giggling louder, "oh, shit, this is a good one!"

Arby felt his ears and face burning. It's just a kid laughing at you, ignore him. Just a little kid. An astoundingly obnoxious, abrasive, annoying little kid…

"He doesn't know who he is, Jerry," Elaina said, her voice defensive on Arby's behalf, "and I thought it best to keep it a secret lest he let it slip to our enemies…"

"*Still* doesn't know?" Jerry paused as he searched Elaina's face, and then whooped with laughter, lifting his feet up and clutching his hands to his belly, giggling so hard that tears ran down his cheeks.

Arby felt stiff and stupid. "Elaina, let's see the people we came to see, and—"

"Oh! Oh, wow, you really don't know squat? Or wait—maybe squat is exactly what you know!" Jerry gasped for breath, trying to control his giggles.

"Jerry…" Elaina said.

The child wiped tears from his face, still grinning, and stood up. "Well, I'll keep it short. You"—he pointed at Arby—"are The Fool. And *we*…" Jerry opened his young arms wide, encompassing the whole mansion, maybe the whole world. "*We*," he said, "are shit outta luck."

16

Sex Again

The kid named Jerry turned away from them and crossed the porch to the hulking door of the mansion. "Well, hell, you may as well come in." He twisted the doorknob with both hands. "I can see it's gonna be a long fucking day."

Elaina started up the steps but Arby caught her wrist. "What the hell's this about? Is your Adeptus Whoever here?"

Elaina pulled him along with her. "That *is* the Adeptus Exemptus. Gerald Bournemouth Winchester, the Ipsissimus, the Great Mage of the Western World."

They stepped through the door into a wide, oak-floored, Victorian-style entryway. To the right, a burgundy-carpeted stairway ran up to the next floor. A hallway led back past the stairway, and the entryway itself had dark double doors to either side.

"The *kid*?" Arby whispered. He waited for Elaina to step aside and then closed the door. "We flew around the world to see somebody who sleeps with a nightlight?"

"I heard that." Jerry stood by the double doors on the right. He gave an elephant's-foot umbrella stand a petulant kick. "And I'm one-hundred-and-thirty-one years old come October, so you can kiss my baboon-red ass, okay?"

Elaina lowered her voice. "Merlinized. A touchy point."

"Merlinized?"

"You know, the story about how Merlin lived backwards?"

"Yeah, like *half* the story." Jerry opened the double doors. "Round age seventy, you find you're getting younger… Older but younger. Backwards don't enter into it." He stepped through the doorway, and Arby and Elaina followed him into a library.

The room was huge, big enough for indoor tennis. The walls were covered with shelving that stopped just short of the coved moldings on the high ceiling, and those shelves were filled with leather-bound books…and classical busts, and primitive wood carvings, and antique clocks in bell jars, and stacks of rolled scrolls, and sea creatures in jars of formalin, and even more books. In the center of the library, atop a thick Persian carpet, stood a titanic black table that could have seated twenty, and, in a pinch, could have acted as a raft for half-again as many after a shipwreck.

"I don't get the Merlin thing," Arby said to Elaina.

"I understand English as well as she does, you know," Jerry said from across the room, "in fact, better. So you might consider talking to me directly." The kid, or ancient man, depending on your viewpoint, squatted, searching though a cabinet beneath the shelves. "A fuck-up, is why. Life-extension spells don't always go right. This one was from an unpublished Abramelin scroll I copped off that charlatan Aleister Crowley." Jerry set brandy snifters and a crystal decanter at the head of the table. "Should have guessed Crowley wouldn't know Abra-melin from Abra-cadabra."

"He seemed smart enough to me," Elaina said. She crossed over to the head of the table. As Arby followed her, he noticed how confident her movements were. She must have known the house in elaborate detail.

Jerry produced an ashtray from the cabinet. "If Crowley's so damn smart, where is he now, huh? Dead and probably not coming back, and thanks to his effing scroll, I get younger every day."

Arby tried to make what he thought would be an innocuous remark to relax the tension. "Hey—most people wish they were getting younger."

Jerry stood up, a wooden humidor balanced on his child's hand. "Try it sometime, pal," he said. "Oh, it was great for a while. In my thirties again through the 1970s and 1980s. Had a blast. Teenager in the 1990s wasn't bad, either. But now I can't see over the steering wheel to drive." He held up his free hand, made a fist, and wiggled out his pinky finger. "And it's great to watch your dick get smaller every day. One year you're giving some broad the high hard one, next thing you know you barely tickle her. You can see the day coming when she'll be changing your diapers."

"Gerald," Elaina said, "Canetti interrogated Arby and left him sealed."

Jerry thumped the humidor down on the table and blew out a dismissive breath. "Canetti." He strode back around the table to Arby. "Let me see. Here, c'mon, get down, what'm I supposed to do, jump?"

Arby knelt on the thick carpet, bringing himself eye to eye with Jerry. The boy clasped Arby's face between his palms and peered into his eyes like a doctor working up a diagnosis.

Arby saw a spiraling light in Jerry's dark pupils, and found he couldn't look away. The sensation was both captivating and yet slightly nauseating.

"Strictly amateur hour," Jerry said. "Make him talk about it, lady."

Elaina stood behind Arby and said, "Rain, tell Gerald how Canetti made you explain to him our plans for escape from Italy."

Arby said, "Elaina—I've told you, I never—" He felt a choking sensation in his throat, as though something had lodged there. "It wasn't—" He gagged and clutched at his chest.

Jerry backed away, and Arby fell on his hands and knees, dry-heaving. Elaina knelt beside him, her arm across his shoulder, speaking as though to a child: "Go ahead, let it out, let it out…"

"At least cover your mouth," Jerry said, "it's kinda disgusting."

Arby's whole frame heaved, and he felt something long and cylindrical slide up his throat and out of his mouth. His gagging diminished and he stared down at the—the *thing* on the carpet. Something living: a few inches long, the cloudy white color of paraffin wax. Its stubby, flipper-like limbs made it resemble a textbook drawing of an ancient amphibian, like the first creatures to drag themselves out of the sea. The creature wriggled, blinking its nubby eyes, and Arby gagged again at the sight.

"Get up," Elaina said, patting his back, "you're all better now…"

"What—what the hell is it?"

Jerry made an exasperated sound. "Jeez Louise. It's not really there, boyo. Get your head out of Yetzirah." Arby heard the kid scuffing away, muttering under his breath. "Why do I get the remedial cases?"

They sat on the heavy dining room chairs at one corner of the table, Jerry's feet dangling far from the floor. He flipped open the humidor. "Cigar?"

Arby made a polite no-thank-you sound. Elaina said, "I would have thought you'd have abandoned that habit by now."

Jerry shrugged. "Tobacco ain't a habit, it's a sacrament. Ask Showkapeelee." The Adeptus Exemptus busied himself clipping the end of a cigar, but paused long enough to produce a large card, seemingly from nowhere, which he skidded across the tabletop to Arby.

It was the Tarot card The Fool, Key Zero. It showed a young man marching forward, smiling, gazing up at the sky. Suspended from a staff over his shoulder was an oxblood-red satchel with the eye of Horus in the center. A little white dog bounded by his side, looking up adoringly. In another step or two, the pair of them would fall over a high cliff.

"You're telling me I'm a *Tarot card?*"

"Nothing to be ashamed of." Jerry snapped a flame from a lighter and sucked with precision, coaxing the end of his cigar into a perfect cherry. He laid the lighter on the table, inspected the burning end of the cigar, and, apparently satisfied, produced another card and flicked it across the tabletop. "So's she."

On the card, a blond woman in a pageboy haircut sat on a throne, her body robed in green and red. From her left hand hung a small pair of golden scales; in her right, she held an upraised sword. The banner at the bottom of the card announced it to be Key 11. "Justice," Arby read aloud.

"And, wouldn't ya know it? Every body she shows up in, she's blind, just like they say." Jerry pulled on his cigar. "Always has a world-class ass, too." He laughed through the smoke as he exhaled and then coughed, louder and louder, pounding his chest with his free hand.

Elaina said, "Try and act your chronological age."

"Fucking juvenile lungs," Jerry said, resisting another coughing fit. He cleared his throat. "Gimme a break, Elaina. Tell me that derriere ain't part of your Aspect."

"The smaller you get, the more everything is about sex." She felt for the decanter on the table, located the glasses, and with methodical movements poured out three brandies.

"You wouldn't believe it," Jerry said to Arby, "but in her last body, Justice here was a real party girl. This time round, somebody checked the 'prissy' box on her intake form, and we're left with this ice maiden. In the original sense of the word."

"Not that it's any of your business, but this body's been through the motions more than a few times." Elaina lifted her glass. "However, I've come to agree with Lord Chesterfield: 'The pleasure is momentary, the position ridiculous, and the expense damnable.'"

Arby had listened to this exchange with a growing sense of unreality. "Look," he said, "I've been dragged around the world, nearly blown up, attacked by weird occult beasts in some ancient sewer, and every time I've asked a question, I've been told to shut up and wait until I got here. Well, I'm here now. So. *What the fuck is going on?*"

Elaina and Jerry sat silent for a moment. Jerry took a small, cautious inhale of smoke, choked back a cough, and held the cigar up, examining the tobacco-leaf wrapper with an accusing eye. "Okay." He pointed at Key Zero where it lay on the table. "There's a whole lotta metaphysical nonsense based on your little portrait there."

"It isn't nonsense," Elaina said.

"Whatever. What I mean is, you read about The Fool and you get all this academic, metaphoric crap about how it represents the Higher Self of every person, the adventurer about to fall again into manifestation, the satchel as the memories of earlier lives, the little dog as the purified intellect looking to the Master Soul for guidance, and yakety-yakety-yak. May all be true, but it doesn't have all that much to do with *you*, The Fool, the guy sitting here at my table." He flicked the ash from his cigar. "You know much about the history of playing cards?"

Arby shook his head.

"Tarot came first, then degraded into the cards they use in Vegas today, but your poker deck preserves an important truth. The Fool is still there, called the Joker, and he's extra: not in any suit, no rank or number. That's you, my friend. The Wild Card."

Arby rubbed his temple. Something about this sounded true, sounded, in fact, like something he'd always secretly known, and yet it didn't seem to clarify anything. "Is that why things break when I'm around?"

Jerry took a sip of brandy and nodded his head before he swallowed. "Yeah. But it goes the other way, too. Sometimes things go right when they shouldn't. Problem is, people don't notice when their car oughta break down but doesn't."

"They could if they paid any attention," Elaina said.

"Just ignore old Christmas-Eyes here," Jerry said. "She has wild-assed notions about human perfectibility."

"I don't get it," Arby said. "Would a little bit of specificity kill you?"

"Fine. A huge truck-and-trailer is speeding down the road, the driver is scratching his butt and watching for Smokey in the side mirrors, and a little girl runs into the street. It's, say, ninety-nine point nine percent certain that he'll hit her. But you're there, The Fool himself, and this raises your Aspect, arouses your Talent, and you project yourself—"

"I do *what?*"

"Look, what you're doing isn't happening down here in matter, so I don't know what it looks like to you, because it ain't physical. Beams of light from your fingers, arrows, apparent physical proximity—I mean, you're making it all up, it's just a model so you can see something unseeable. Point is, you do the thing you do, and the results are... unpredictable. Maybe the truck tire chooses that moment to blow, the truck skids to the side, leaves everyone unscathed. A miracle."

"Or," Elaina said, "the truck skids to the side, misses the little girl, but smashes into a busload of schoolchildren."

"Or smacks the little girl *and* hits a busload of schoolchildren," Jerry said.

"Or misses the little girl and causes a car to swerve and prevents another accident that was about to happen."

"Wait, wait, hold it." Arby waved his hands, fending off this flow of information. "You're saying that I cause things to go sort of, of... Exactly what *are* you saying?"

Elaina and Jerry exchanged a glance. Elaina said, "If you observed what occurs in Yetzirah, the World of Formation, the sphere of existence just above ours, you would see that any event that occurs in the physical world is at the end of a long branching system of interweaving possibilities, and—"

"Save it," Jerry said. "Look, when a guy throws a pair of dice, in principle the numbers that come up are determined the moment the dice leave his hand, right? Vector math. Momentum, position, angle of incidence, all that, right?" He waited for Arby's nod. "Well, you're the guy who has the power to whack the dice in mid-air."

Arby chewed this over for a moment. "So, can I control the outcome?"

Jerry pulled his feet up onto the chair and perched his chin on his knees. "Not as far as I know."

"Doesn't seem all that useful," Arby said.

Elaina said, "One might feel differently if an axe were swinging toward their neck."

"Yeah," Jerry said, "but something more specific and controlled would be a helluva lot more practical if you're going to go to the trouble to call down a Talent."

"Call down a Talent?" Arby asked.

Jerry grinned. "How much do you know about the metaphysical and etheric sides of sex?"

"Sex again," Elaina said. "I knew you would steer the conversation back there eventually."

The Religious Right may not care to hear about it, but the magnetic, magical, metaphysical force that manifests in sex is the same whether it is man and woman, man and man, woman and woman; whether the physical contact is penile, vaginal, oral, anal, manual, or even mediated by a leather strap.

Sorry. Whether loving and blessed by the Almighty of the local faith, or lustful and furtive in the back of a car, aroused sexual contact is all based on the same juice, and that juice is relentlessly neutral in intent: like electricity, it is equally willing to light a library or a torture chamber.

On the other hand, while the All-Affirming Left may not care to hear about it, there is something fundamentally different about the joining of penis and vagina in terms of etheric consequences.

Sorry again. There's more to the Tab A and Slot B setup than merely bringing together sperm and egg.

Oh, the juice is the same stuff; but the energy in the semen is a centrifugal force involuted, and the power of the womb is a centripetal force evoluted, and when they combine they create an etheric vortex that reaches onto the upper planes and into the inaptly named Well of Souls, and a future Somebody can jump aboard and zip down the vortex like a ten-year-old shooting headfirst down a waterslide.

The vortex-creating properties of Tab A/Slot B, plug/socket, pistil/stamen are a fundamental property of the universe, and they are mighty.

Mighty enough, in fact, that the phenomenon can be reproduced even when transmission of the goods takes place via *Penthouse* magazine at one end and a turkey baster at the other.

When the vortex is not created—when Jeff does John, or Jen does Jessica, or de Sade does von Masoch—then instead of shooting upward on the planes, the sex energy hangs around. Which is why so many magical rites involve sodomy, sadomasochism, homosexuality, or, in the case of talented Tantric practitioners and yogis, male-female penile-vaginal intercourse without ejaculation. There's a ton of etheric energy there if you don't blow it all on a trip to Babyland.

Fine, ignore me. You've already picked out names and a crib and bought IQ-numbing wallpaper for the nursery, and are already trying to have a baby. Jason has stopped furtively whacking off to *People* magazine in the bathroom, and Jocelyn is tracking her temperature and rolling up into a shoulderstand ASAP every time Jason pulls out.

Now, little Connor or Ashley or Samir or LaShonda aren't floating around in the Well of Souls as individual cherubs. Nor are Napoleon or Florence Nightingale hanging about in period costume waiting to be reincarnated.

The Well of Souls is filled with something more like congealing Jell-O-brand gelatin, when it is still in the gloppy, half-liquid state, and some of those globs are shaped like parts of Napoleon, and some of them, in a psychic sense, are shaped a bit like Florence, and—

To hell with it. This simply can't be understood while we are in physical bodies and embedded in time and space.

What is important is that Jason, his wrists tied to the headboard with silk scarves, and Jocelyn, bouncing atop him in her nun outfit, create a vortex, and that whirling tunnel penetrates the Well of Souls, and the glob most congruent to the hyperdimensional mouth of the vortex slides in and vaults down into the physical, and, if all goes well, emerges nine months later, sobbing in pain and anger and fear as it remembers, from the fragments of which it is made, all the drawbacks of the physical plane.

The grass is always greener on the Other Side.

Throw drugs or too much alcohol or a truly twisted relationship into the mix, and the vortex may be so misshapen that it reaches somewhere other than the Well of Souls. It doesn't happen often, but on occasion what may come down the tube is another form of life entirely—an elemental, a husk, or even a being from the Well of Souls in another solar system. The result may be a changeling, or even David Bowie.

With proper preparation and techniques, however, the vortex can be imprinted with a certain shape. Add to this the concentrated sex force of many onlookers or participants, and the vortex can shoot far above the local Well of Souls, reaching high on the Inner Planes to the places where Powers and Talents dwell. Add the right ritual and intent, and the vortex can be steered, and in this way an immortal Power may be called down into physical being.

"I was called down?" Arby asked. "Who called for me, how?"

"No idea," Jerry said. "And, I don't mean this unkindly, buddy-boy, but I seriously doubt they called for *you* in particular."

This was sounding more ridiculous by the moment, but Arby had seen too much in the last few days to deny that something very strange was going on. In fact, although he was loath to admit it, something very strange had gone on throughout his life. "So how did I get here, then?"

"I'm guessing the metaphysical equivalent of a wrong number. I'm sure someone was trying to bring down a Hero." Jerry sipped his brandy and Arby thought the kid tried to hide an expression of mild revulsion as the liquor hit his underdeveloped taste buds. "Apparently, your Talent lets you screw things up at a pretty cosmic scale."

"If I may make a point, however," Elaina said, "unless I am much mistaken, our enemies think a Hero has been brought down. We know the truth and they don't, and in truth there is always some advantage."

"Dream on," Jerry said. "Just means they'll try to crush us sooner, before their hypothetical Hero becomes a real foe." His child's face regarded Arby through timeworn eyes, and Arby sensed that beneath the flippant tone, the child-man felt genuine fear. "Hero Lite: All the extra danger with less than half the capabilities."

"If it is true that our enemies will act sooner, then all the more reason to call the Council now."

"The Seeker only just arrived back from the Middle East." Jerry paused, watching Elaina. "We still haven't heard from Raven. Just our luck—risk three real Heroes on a search for someone who turns out to be no Hero at all." He shot a glance at Arby.

Arby slumped in his chair, mouth tight. He had never claimed to be a hero, had never claimed to be anything, really, and yet he felt disrespected, underestimated, and obscurely shamed and guilty. He hadn't asked for any of this, had made no claims. He half-wanted to leave the room, get in the car and head home, and half-wanted to stand up and shout at the obnoxious cigar-puffing child at the table, but no words came, and he leaned his head back and stared at the ceiling.

On a high shelf one of the clocks, this one shaped like a sailing ship, whirred beneath its wide bell jar. A tiny bronze man doddered across the deck on a track and seized the ship's bell and rang it: once, twice, three times…

Arby counted, and then when it passed twelve, he saw that the others were listening, counting along.

"Thirty-two," Elaina said.

Arby snorted. "I suppose I'm responsible for breaking that, too."

"Actually," Jerry said, "it hasn't moved for about forty years."

They sat silent for a few moments, until Elaina said, "We should bring his mother here, and start training him immediately."

"Whoa, whoa," Arby said, fending off the thought with upraised palms, "training me for what?"

"Helping you recover who you are, so you can protect yourself—and aid us as well."

"Before I decide to aid anybody, I need to know what the different sides are. I'm not sure I'm on anyone's side, yet."

Elaina stiffened. "After the men of the *Atrum Arbor* tried to kill us, you have some doubts which side you support? Perhaps you would like to become as one of them? If you—"

"He's right," Jerry said, "he should have a chance to think it over, meet the others, get some explanations as to who and what…"

"You were the one," she said, "who claimed our foes would now move swiftly."

"Hey—just because *we* know we're on the side of the angels doesn't mean that ace here gets the picture." He addressed Arby. "Get some rest, wander around, meet a few folks—go see Showkapeelee—and we'll call a Council." He picked up his brandy snifter, raised it to his lips, and then put it down without drinking. "You should tell us where to find your mom, though. Elaina's right—she isn't safe out there if our enemies know your name. You have any other near-and-dear types out there?"

Arby began to shake his head, but froze. "Liz." He rubbed his forehead. Liz would never believe any of what he'd been through in the last few days. If he tried to talk to her about this, she'd have a fellow lawyer slap a restraining order on him. "Elizabeth West. But I don't think she'd really like to hear from me."

17

All About Honey

Crystal sat with her back propped against the rear doors of the van. Her wrists were cuffed behind her waist, and a soft cloth gag covered her mouth. All but the front seats had been removed from the van, turning it into an empty can with a carpeted floor.

In principle she ought to be terrified, and she knew it, yet her emotions were subdued, closer to a puzzled uneasiness. Crystal was a believer in the supremacy of intuition, and none of the voices inside her cried out that she was in immediate danger. What she felt most was a sense of strangeness, as though she had stepped out of everyday life and into a movie. Someone else's movie.

She watched the one they had called Rooker, the big man, as the gleam of passing streetlights rolled across him like the scanners of a photocopier. He sat crosslegged by the side doors and watched her without any signs of emotion on his lumpy face.

An odd man—almost inhuman. His stumpy forearms were not only muscled, but the individual muscle strands themselves displayed striations, fibers urging up beneath the skin, like a man made of tight-coiled rope.

His stolid form remained almost motionless on the long drive, a drive that moved from city streets across a bridge, and eventually ascended a ramp onto a long, tire-hissing stretch of freeway. Immobility ruled everything but his eyes, which, in the darting, breaking lights, seemed to be searching her body and her face. That massive frame sat balanced but somehow collapsed, and Crystal was reminded of the sequence of Thai Buddhas she had once seen in a temple: Buddha in the Attitude of Calming the Seas, Buddha in the Attitude of Cautioning Persons Not to Fight With One Another…

Buddha Consumed by Sorrow. His gaze as it roamed across her body could have been resented, but his pupils were the entrance to a well of sadness. It was as though a wounded bear had slumped down across from her, its eyes hostile, suspicious, yet yearning for help.

Poor thing. What have they done to you?

It wasn't a kidnapping, they told her: it was a "rescue'" for her own safety. Crystal knew better. Even in the sixties and seventies you couldn't thumb your way across the country without encountering at least a few threatening situations, and the moment someone started driving you somewhere other than toward your chosen destination, it was a problem, not a rescue.

The first few hours were touch-and-go. They'd made her comfortable enough, but then, in the windowless room, there was a cluster of boring, faceless men, bland as newscasters, with variations on the same questions. What were her movements in 1969? What cults had she joined? Which people had she known? Who was Arby's father?

Right. Like she'd kept notes or something. They were riveted on the whole bit with Anton LaMarr and the Children, and asked endless questions about Arby and Nature Heroes—whatever that was supposed to mean.

Rooker often stood in the corner during the questioning, impassive as a statue. After a time, a trio of different men came, conciliatory, concerned, and false as a politician's handshake. They were worried, they said, that bad people were trying to use her son for evil ends. Could she tell them anything, anything at all, about his contacts?

"Are you guys from the FBI or something?" Crystal asked.

Leaning forward from their straight-backed chairs, two of them began hinting that they were indeed Feds, while the third hastily denied it. Crystal glanced over their shoulders to Rooker and saw him smirking as the men tripped across one another's stories. She sent him a smile and he started like a guilty child before his face resumed its expressionless stare.

The mansion-sized lodge sat somewhere to the east of Mount Hood, because dawn's oysterish light reflected off the mountain's snowy peaks and glowed through the barred window of her bedroom.

As far as she could see, the bars were screwed into the wood frame of the gable windows. If she needed to, she could probably pry the bars loose with…well, with something, and climb onto the roof, but even though her room was only on the second story, the high ceilings of the lower floor left a long drop from the window to the ground.

Worth pondering for a moment, just in case. But for the present, she had no intention of trying to escape. Sure, it was a pisser that they'd snatched her like this, but people do crazy things. So far there was no hint that anyone intended her harm, and their relentless interest in Arby made it clear he was tangled up in something.

Probably something connected to the Middle East, she figured: that place had a bad vibe that ran all the way back to the days when Jehovah told Abraham to sacrifice Isaac, and the old putz had said, okay, whatever you say, boss. Yeah, it was just a test—though in her judgment old Abe had failed it flat out. But now her Rainchild was somehow snarled up in all that madness, and she needed to find out what was going on.

She sighed, and pulled the curtains shut against the increasing morning light. Apart from the wrought-iron bars on the windows, her suite was gorgeous, if incoherent in decor. The expansive but rustic pine-walled bedroom had been furnished in warm, cluttery Victorian elegance, with heavy dressers and chairs sulking in the corners, while the bathroom had a heated tile floor, a claw-footed tub, and enough makeup lights around the mirror to illuminate the Palladium. The cedar-lined closets held a half-dozen outfits that looked as though they ought to fit her.

The whole setup was refined, pleasant, and creepy. In many ways it reminded her of an upmarket version of her garret with LaMarr and the Children—that room, too, had been intended as a cozy prison of sorts. She realized this had to be another nutcase cult.

What a relief: For a while she was afraid she had fallen into the hands of the government.

It had been a long day, and dwelling on the undefined possibilities of the future was pointless. As always, the answer was to be in the now, not in your head. She lounged in a hot bath for a while, calming her nerves with *pranayama* breath. Then she slipped between the sheets of the four-poster bed and watched the weak Northwest sun leak through the gaps in the curtains.

Von Fleischer leaned back on the sofa in the main hall of his lodge, his arms outstretched along the seatback. Cloud-filtered sun streamed through the skylights of the high ceiling, the contrast cloaking the distant walls in shadow.

McMahon stood on the other side of the awkward, overbuilt coffee table, his hands clasped behind him. "She's either a great actress, or she knows nothing at all," McMahon said. "Nothing about Heroes, nothing about her son's powers or alignment, precious near to nothing about LaMarr and the Children. I think she's exactly what she says she is—a young woman who got tangled up in LaMarr's organization and then fled."

Interesting. It was a risk, but if the man had been raised in ignorance of his own identity and powers, it might be possible to make an ally, or even servant of him. It had worked a few times before. "And the son's history?"

"Apart from what we already knew, not much. Some info on girlfriends we can follow up—one lawyer named Elizabeth West who was a long-term romantic connection. Oh, and a history of machines breaking down when he's around. The mother seemed to think that was funny."

Machines breaking down? Von Fleischer nodded to himself. More support for the Nature-Hero theory. The Deer God? The Bull From the Sea? But who was Crystal herself? The odd perfection of her aura suggested something other than simply human. "And the woman? Her parents?"

"We're checking. They're both dead, but so far there's nothing to suggest they were anything but what she claims—a right-wing stockbroker and a housefrau."

Rooker stepped forward from the shadows at the side of the hall. "Let me question her. I'll get you some answers."

Von Fleischer laughed. "I'm sure you would—but would they be true?" He waggled the fingers of one hand without bothering to lift his arm from the seatback, dismissing the discussion. "No. I think I'll have dinner with Miss Keeling this evening, and show her a good time. I'm sure you've heard, Mr. Rooker, that you catch more flies with honey than with vinegar."

"You *attract* more flies with honey. If you want to *catch* 'em—" The man slapped his palms together with such force that the sound made McMahon jump. Rooker's right hand came away in a fist, and he held it up and shook it like a maraca. "*Catch*ing them requires a little force."

It was comforting to be around a personality so consistent— though from the way McMahon always edged away whenever Rooker approached, von Fleischer gathered that not everyone shared this sentiment. "Your position is noted, Mister Rooker." He rose from the couch and stretched. "But tonight…tonight is all about honey."

The windows of the dining hall looked west onto Mount Hood and down the Columbia Gorge. Von Fleischer had chosen sundown to meet with Crystal, and the fickle Northwest weather had favored him by shredding the blanket of clouds so the red of the setting sun reflected on the surface of the wide, slow river far below.

Initially the chef had been baffled by the fact that the guest for the evening was a vegetarian, but then, after dispatching a fast car to Portland, he had outdone himself. Spread on the sideboard before the widest window were enough inscrutable appetizers for a party of a dozen. Von Fleischer had examined a few of the more obscure objects, and decided to stick to the cheese and crackers, perhaps with some bruschetta; foregoing red meat for a night was enough sacrifice without eating things that smelt of soybeans and seaweed.

When he heard Rooker's clumping footsteps enter at the far end of the hall he turned from the window. At the big man's side Crystal strolled along, dressed in a multicolored Indian skirt and a floppy Mexican blouse, apparently at ease. Von Fleischer smiled to himself; of the clothes they'd provided, she'd picked the hippie outfit, and he wondered absently which of the array of panties she'd selected. Well, time enough to ascertain that later this evening.

He widened his smile, and strode down the length of the thirty-seat dining table with his hands reaching out to her. Rooker stopped, and von Fleischer took both of Crystal's hands in his. He let his accent slope into its most elegant, pan-European tones. "I *do* apologize for our…unorthodox way of bringing you here. I can only hope I'll be able to convince you that we acted out of necessity—and that, by the end of the evening, you'll begin to forgive me." A nod, a slight incline of the torso that stopped short of a bow—American women usually went for archaic Continental manners if the movements were kept subtle. "Benedikt von Fleischer." He lifted his gaze to stare into her eyes, and he saw amusement there, but also, perhaps, the beginnings of interest.

She tilted her head a fraction of an inch and one corner of her delectable mouth turned up, and the body math of the motions added up to a minor, uncaring shrug. "Guess you already know who I am."

"Yes." He turned about, keeping hold of her left hand, so he stood beside her as though ready to escort her into a ballroom. As he led her to the sideboard, he heard Rooker's feet retreating from the room.

Crystal glanced back over her shoulder and said, "Catch you later, Charles."

Charles? Von Fleischer had nearly forgotten that Rooker even had a Christian name. At the sideboard he released her hand. "Fraternizing with the help?" he asked, in a light voice.

She studied the spread of appetizers, and then glanced at him with a cockeyed, skeptical expression. "The *help*? So who are you, the Count of Monte-fucking-Cristo?" Her gaze didn't linger, but instead leapt to the bloody skies beyond the window. "*Whoa*," she said, in a long exhalation, "would you look at that?" She shut her eyes and drew in a deep breath, as though she were inhaling the sunset, and when he let his consciousness rise he saw the *prana* flooding into her, and swelling out through her aura.

In most women, the sex chakra was a scanty indigo-red flame set deep in the pelvis, like a tiny pilot light flickering away, unnoticed, and von Fleischer loved watching the moment of arousal when—often unknown to the women themselves at first—that pilot light ignited the flow of desire and the indigo flame bloomed with a suddenness that seemed as though it should be audible, like the burner booming to life on a gas stove. But this woman was different: her whole core glowed indigo-red, like a large pot kept forever simmering. It promised to be a very entertaining night.

He waited for her eyes to open before saying, "I do have some titles, in my native land…" He brushed the issue away with diffident fingers. "I realize such things mean little in the modern world."

She favored him with a smile, and then looked down at the array of hors d'oeuvres. "Amazing layout. When's the party?"

"The two of us are the party. All vegetarian, or so I instructed. A first step toward making some amends."

"All just for us? Hope this stuff keeps."

She accepted the plate he handed her and began sorting through the items, raising each canapé to her face for a thoughtful sniff before adding it to her selection.

Three bottles of *Clos du Mesnil Blanc de blanc* 1995 had been chilling in icebuckets, and he moved one of the stands close to the head of the table, where two places had been set. Crystal turned at the sound of the popping cork. "You do drink champagne, I hope…?" he asked.

"Yeah, sure." She joined him by the table, her plate laden with obscure appetizers, and he drew back a chair at the corner. She kicked off the beaded slippers she wore and climbed onto the seat, adjusting her skirt as she sat crosslegged. Her eyebrows lifted. "So, you going to eat, or just watch me?"

Von Fleischer assembled a hasty plate for himself, and then sat down at the head of the table, scooting his chair to the right so as to sit closer to her. He lifted his glass of champagne, and when she mirrored his movement he clinked rims and said, "To a better understanding in the future."

"I can drink to that," she said, and did.

He twirled the stem of the glass between his fingers. "And again, my apologies. What I have to tell you may strike you as somewhat improbable—"

"Try me." She crunched a seaweed-laden cracker between her teeth, and the tip of her tongue poked out to lick something from her lip.

"Fine." He gathered himself and began, watching her face for signs of disbelief. Her son, he explained, was the incarnation of a god, probably one called down by Anton LaMarr and his followers, but, through mischance, he had been raised in ignorance of his true nature… She drank the champagne and listened with an enigmatic expression, and he refilled their glasses. There were those, he said, who would try to deceive her son, who would turn his powers to their own uses…

"Like what?" she asked.

There was a war, he told her, a war between factions competing for the devotion of human souls. Earth-as-a-battlefield always played well with anyone raised in a Zoroastrian cultural tradition, and the Judeo-Christian-Muslim beliefs were just one variation on that old, tired song. He explained that the old gods still existed—savage beings who had once eagerly accepted human sacrifices. There was enough horror in the bloodstained history of religion that he readily trotted out a few anecdotes, and watched her. Distaste showed on her face, but her aura stayed centered.

"Your son—Rainchild, is it?—has fallen into the hands of such a group. I can't imagine what lies they must be feeding him, but I worry for him—for him, for his soul, for the future—"

"So, what are you?"

"Excuse me?"

"What are you? You some kinda god, too, or what?"

He gave a soft, self-deprecating chuckle. "I can tell you, in all truth, that I am merely the humble servant of a higher power." True enough, as far as it went, except for the humble bit; before he escaped from the Dark Tree, he was the lackey of Asmodeus, and Asmodeus would still love to get his claws on him. "Unlike some, I'm not out to change the world, I'm out to preserve it." Also true enough: the status quo and current trends were just dandy.

"So what do you want from me?"

"I want you to help me convince your son to leave the people he's fallen in with. Or, at a minimum, to convince him to meet with me, hear both sides of the story. Does that seem like too much to ask?"

"Yeah, it does. I mean, I don't really know you, do I?"

He fended off her words with an upraised palm. "Your point is well-taken. And that was part of my purpose in dining with you tonight."

"Look, maybe you've read too many romance novels. I know it happens in books all the time and the chick decides she doesn't mind after all, but I gotta tell you—kidnapping me isn't exactly cool."

"I know, I know, and I apologize yet again. But you must understand. We didn't know who you were, or who you might be in league with, or if you might be using your son as part of some plan—"

"*Using* my son? What kind of whack-job are you?"

"Miss Keeling… Crystal, if I may. Every day parents sell their children into slavery or prostitution. Every day beggars mutilate their newborns to make them better beggars." He assumed a pained expression and shook his head in regret. "I didn't know you then. We had to assume the worst." He put his hand atop hers where it lay on the table. "Please understand. Please take the time to get to know me."

She drew her hand from beneath his, but without apparent rancor, and used it to fetch the champagne from the icebucket that stood near her shoulder. Leaning forward, still sitting crosslegged in the chair, she strained to top up both of their glasses, and then clunked the empty bottle down beside her on the table. "I'm listening," she said.

After three bottles of champagne split two ways, he saw no obvious change in Crystal's behavior or speech, but when she excused herself to go to the hallway bathroom the loosened sashay of her hips told him that she was more than just tipsy.

Four centuries of life provide a wealth of anecdotes, and he'd regaled her with a dozen small tales, each edited to show him in a favorable light, and to update the situations to the twentieth century when needed. He was a philanthropist, a spiritual seeker, and—he let the implications of the stories hint for him—a bit of a ladies' man.

When she returned he led her from the dining hall into the cozy lounge nearby, where the fireplace already blazed. To his delight, she sat down on the couch rather than in an armchair; it made logistics so much easier. He poured glasses of port from the decanter on the coffee table, and used the motion of passing her one to draw attention from the fact that he was easing himself down onto the couch beside her.

He turned toward her, leaning one elbow on the back of the couch. "I've never met anyone like you," he said.

She laughed and rolled her eyes. "I'm fifty, you know," she said, amused rather than offended. "I've heard them all before."

It would have felt good to slap that complacent expression off her face, but now wasn't the time. Someday, though, someday that and more… He gave her a mild, admiring look, the countenance of a misunderstood lover. "You misconstrue my meaning. I sense something about you—a centeredness, a balance…" He gazed into her face and studied her aura.

In general, von Fleischer considered it unsporting to Nudge women during seduction, though he might give them a taste of it later in the affair, when his amusements became a little more demanding; but this was more about business than pleasure. He reached out on the etheric and probed, testing. When he applied force, her aura gave a little, but then rebounded like the skin of a balloon. "What is it about you?" he asked. "This centeredness?"

Crystal gave a slight shrug. "Meditation. And a lot of acid, too, I suppose." Those luscious lips tilted in an unreadable smile.

He gazed into her eyes and at the same moment pressed into the aura that glowed before her pineal gland, keeping a steady, slow pressure. When her pupils widened—*that's right, let me in*—he let a knowing smile appear on his face, and leaned forward and kissed her.

It was planned as a trial run, a gentle touching of the lips, working up to passion by stages, but Crystal's lips opened and when the tip of his tongue touched hers she welcomed it into her mouth.

He knew he had good hands, and he let his right palm caress her face as they kissed. He glided it down her neck and across the lace collar of the peasant blouse until it found her breast, braless. Ah. A true child of the sixties. Now beneath his established pattern of languid, tracing fingers, he let his touch become rougher, with just a hint of a tremble, as though he were barely restraining himself.

With his etheric persona, he continued to play her aura, not only pressing at her, but also coaxing it into expansion, working it like clay. She made a sound low in her throat as they kissed, and his own aura sensed a stirring in her belly. His fingers massaged and stroked their way down onto her hip, and he felt her writhe, felt her soften even more, felt her yield.

Now was the time. He Pushed on her with the full force of his aura.

Crystal's hands slid up his chest and her palms pressed him away, freeing herself to take a deep breath. "Whoo," she said, and then panted for a moment, pantomiming fanning herself with both hands. "Wow, you really know what you're doing, don't you?"

He began to answer with a self-deprecating comment when he caught her look. Her pupils were still wide, and she sounded breathless, but those eyes glittered with an amusement that didn't feel warm. "What is it?"

She stared for a moment longer, and he felt as though she were peering inside him. "Great technique. Just killer." She shook her head with a sad smile. "But not a drop of sincerity. And, hey—that's like a body with no blood."

When his mouth opened to deny her accusation, she pressed fingers against his lips. "Don't bother," she said. "My head doesn't always know, but my body, oh, it knows, it always knows." She shook her head like a disappointed schoolteacher. "You've totally been lying to me all night."

It had been ages since he'd been told no, and even longer since he'd been subjected to such disrespect. Something in her smile repelled him now, and he stood, pushing her away. "Who *are* you?" he asked, his voice thin in his own ears.

Crystal pulled her legs up underneath her, and pushed stray hairs from her face. "Someone who knows when her head's being messed with."

He stepped over to the wall intercom and sent for Rooker and the guards. For the eternal minutes it took them to come, he couldn't bring himself to look at her, and his eyes rested on a knot in varnished wood, a blackish knot with the pattern of a crushed blossom.

They spoke no more until the men arrived, and von Fleischer instructed the guards to escort her back to her room. He turned only when she was gone.

Rooker picked up Crystal's unfinished glass of port and drained it in a single swallow. "So, boss. Not helpful?"

For a moment he almost shouted, and von Fleischer found with surprise that his whole body trembled with anger. "No," he said, controlling his voice, "not helpful at all." He took a few steps and reached out to steady himself on the mantel. His hand clenched at the wood and layers of paint parted in shallow crescents beneath his fingernails.

What was wrong with him? An old body. Age made the heart timid. He ought to bring her back, take her now, with whatever force was needed. With whatever force he happened to enjoy.

In his mind he saw again that penetrating, amused gaze, a look that left him naked, huddling against the cold. Old, old. It might be that he'd have to move into a new body sooner than he'd thought.

But he had nothing to prove to her. With a deliberate effort he calmed himself. "We may need her as a bargaining chip with her son." He swallowed. "Don't cause any permanent damage. Outside of that, she's yours." He began to stride from the room, but paused, and without looking back, said, "Do what you like, but keep her to yourself. I don't want to see her again."

18

The Whole God Gig

Xochipilli sounded like *Showkapeelee*, but before he started out Elaina had explained the spelling to him, as though she'd expected him to care. Great. Between that and *xebec* and *xylophone*, he'd be ready for the *Sunday Times'* crossword puzzle.

Arby left her standing at the rear of the mansion, and he'd felt a wave of weariness from her as she closed the door. A twinge of guilt at her exhaustion was mixed with relief to be away from her for the first time in days.

He trudged up the path in the warm sun, his pack slung over his shoulder, and he listened to the hiss of the tall yellow grass in the breeze, breathed in the baked resin smells from the sparse pine forest on the hills, and felt renewed. The world abided; the hills and the trees and the hum of the insects were always there, waiting for his return.

The ascent was almost imperceptible at first, but after a quarter-mile the trees closed in and the path climbed to surmount the slope at the head of the valley. To either side the steep hills rose, casting the trail into deep shadow. Despite the shade, Arby felt perspiration start on his forehead.

At the low saddle of the hills he stepped into sunlight again, the brightness painful. He shaded his eyes with his palms and panted for breath. After almost two years in Saudi Arabia, at no more than a few feet above sea level, the mile-and-a-half elevation of Los Alamos was a challenge that left him light-headed.

As Elaina had told him, at the saddle the path bifurcated along the ridgetop. To his right the track led along the crest and then clambered up the hill. The hilltop was crowned with an outcrop of red sandstone, the rosy rock pocked with the blackness of a dozen aeolian caves. Unlike most of the barren stone around Los Alamos, though, the red rock was spiderwebbed with green, big-leafed vines that spread and touched again like a diagram of neurons in the brain.

A scrambling sound startled him, and he glanced down to see an animal racing up through the shadows on the path he had just climbed. He felt a grin spread on his face when he recognized the brown dog that had greeted them at the gate. When it gained the saddle it jumped up on him with its front paws, its whole body wagging with delight as it waltzed with him. "Hey, boy," he said, laughing, "hey, hey, I'm glad to see you, too…" He thumped its sturdy torso before he pushed it back onto all fours. "You going to take me to Xochipilli?"

The dog cocked its head and waited, and when Arby didn't move, it sat down, watching his face. He sighed and adjusted his pack. "Not into the whole Lassie thing, huh? Well, let's go."

To the left side of the trail, on the west, huge scallops of earth and rock had eroded from the hillside, leaving the path running atop a barren cliff. Yet the slope to his right remained smooth, and he saw the gray wolf trotting along between the treetrunks, paralleling their path. He made a loud kissing sound with his lips. The wolf glanced in his direction, ears raised, but it neither came closer nor shied away.

Ahead, heat seemed to rise from the dusty path, like the shimmering waves from hot asphalt, and his view of the sandstone outcropping wavered as though the hill lay at the bottom of a mountain stream. Arby trudged ahead, rubbing his eyes with the back of his palm. Perhaps it was the altitude; he felt dizzy. Yet after a dozen paces, all his sensations reversed themselves: his head cleared, and his shifting vision clarified, and even seemed magnified and swollen, as though he gazed through a vast lens.

A young woman stood at the top of the hill, just at the base of the sandstone cap, her long floral-print skirt and blouse fluttering in a breeze that wasn't blowing on him. Her palm shaded her eyes, as though she were searching the mountains, and purple-blue morning glories twined in her cascading blond hair, the vines and leaves as well as the flowers.

Something happened to time. She was a hundred yards away, still high upslope; a moment later he stood beside her, blinking in the sunlight. Arby pulled in a deep breath—oxygen was the sovereign remedy for altitude problems. "I—" Lack of air stopped him. Had he somehow dashed up the slope without realizing it? At last, he managed to say, "*Xochipilli…*"

The woman frowned, her eyes suspicious, and she raised her index finger to her lips to sign for silence. As though they were in a library, she leaned forward and whispered, *"He's working."* She turned and pointed at the sandstone outcropping.

The rock that crowned the hill was larger than it had seemed from below, as high and wide as an old-fashioned two-story apartment building. The vines, he saw now, were also morning glories, and the caves were large—so large that people stood in several of them, peering out in curiosity. Stairways were cut in the stone, running back and forth across the face of the rock, connecting the caves and forming shelf-like landings wherever two stairways crossed.

The woman seemed to be pointing at a statue on one of the landings, carved directly out of the rock. The figure was seated; his legs were crossed at the ankles, but his knees were raised to chest height, as though the sculptor had caught him before he'd settled into a full crosslegged position. The arms were held out beside the knees, the hands forming fists that were not quite clenched. The wide-jawed head was thrown back, its noble Aztec nose aimed above the treetops.

Then the fists clenched tight and the figure emitted a shuddering groan, a sound that might have been pain or ecstasy. Gasps and murmurs came from the surrounding caves, and then, in one quick motion, the figure was on its feet. Short and powerfully muscled, the man also seemed poised to chase down prey, a notion reinforced by the dangling loincloth he wore. He pointed one finger at Arby, and frowned. Even at this distance, when he smiled the flash of white was shocking. He let the extended finger bob up and down like a baton as he said, "Rainchild. Huh. Long time."

The woman darted a look at Arby, and he thought he saw her surprise that the man on the rocks above had deigned to address him. For a moment, she seemed nonplussed, but then, in a practiced move, she turned to face the rock and dropped to her knees, her arms upraised. "*All behold,*" she cried out, her clear voice carrying down the valley, "*The Prince of Flowers.*"

The people in the caves echoed her cadence, but it seemed to Arby that he heard a dozen languages.

Once they were together, seated on the carpeted floor of one of the caves, Arby said, "I remember you, now that I see you up close." Indeed. Even in the dim light of an oil lamp, Xochipilli was unmistakable. Although the man before him was far different from the gangly *Indio* teenager Arby had met, the tattoos were unique.

The tattoos weren't large, but they were scattered across the man's whole body at regular intervals, and they were repetitive, as if he'd been wallpapered. Morning glory blossoms, nicotiana blossoms, two other flowers he didn't recognize, and mushrooms—skinny little geek-necked psilocybes. The pattern continued even across the man's red-bronze face.

Arby tried to remember. Crystal and a few friends had taken ten-year-old Arby on a long drive to somewhere in Southern California, up in the woods—maybe Idyllwild—and they had stayed with some psychedelic commune. There'd been an older kid, sort of spoiled and self-absorbed, who must have grown into this man. "They didn't call you Xochipilli back then, though. I think they called you Two Feathers or something."

Xochipilli laughed, a rumble from that barrel chest. "Man. Their idea of an 'Indian' name, like the Aztecs were Apaches or something, and speaking English on top of it. 'Course, I didn't know what I was back then. Didn't know what you were, either. The people who raised me—well, sweet folks…ut-nay oo-tay ight-bray. Most of them are here with me."

"Your family?"

"My worshippers." Distaste must have shown on Arby's face, because Xochipilli said, "C'mon, man. Call it what it is. What do you call yours, huh?"

"I don't have any. And I'm still not sure exactly who I am." He took a deep breath. "I guess I'd better just tell you what I know."

Arby related the events of the last few days, in as much detail as he could recall, and recapped his conversation with Jerry and Elaina down at the mansion. He found himself relaxing as he talked; at least this person, no matter how odd, was from his own past. Xochipilli listened without interrupting, those black eyes searching Arby's face.

"So now," Arby said at last, "I'm being told I need to choose sides, and I don't even know what the sides are."

Xochipilli nodded his big head. His copper-colored hair had been gathered into tight ringlets that must have been plastered down to his skull with grease, and they glinted in the lamplight. "I hear you. I had to go zero-to-sixty on this in my late teens. Cram course. Find out who I was overnight."

"And how'd you do that?"

"Inner Planes work. Took a walk through my past lives. 'Course, I was so loaded all the time back then, I was spending most days with my head in the noosphere anyhow."

"And you found out you're…well, what exactly are we?"

The man's teeth shone in a smile that was both amused and predatory. "*We* ain't exactly the same. I'm a god. You're an archetype." He clapped his hands twice, and shouted something in another tongue. "I'm some kinda personification of an aspect of the universe. You, you're a personification of an aspect of human nature. In a perfect universe, those'd be the same thing, right—man created in god's image, and all that? Don't hold your breath. The system hasn't evolved that far yet. Hang on—"

A man and a woman, both aging hippies, padded into the room, carrying a short-legged table between them. With their eyes downcast, they positioned the table between Arby and Xochipilli, and then retreated without a sound. On the table sat a crude clay pitcher and two lumpish cups.

Xochipilli lifted the pitcher. "Chicha. My Deadheads do a pretty mean corn beer." He filled the cups. "Cheers."

Arby lifted his cup and drank. Sweeter than beer, and with a disseminated fizz that tickled the mouth. "So where do we come from?"

Xochipilli raised one eyebrow. "Storks?" He grinned and gulped down his chicha. "Okay, sorry. I guess people kind of create us at first, by believing in us. And that belief feeds us. But our being there feeds people, too. It's like two mirrors facing off, anything that happens in one is reflected in the other. Co-evolution."

"I don't get it. What's the purpose?"

"Purpose? You mean everything? The whole enchilada? Got me. This is one little planet in one little corner of the universe. I don't know if there's exactly a *plan*, but I can tell you there sure is a *system*." He lifted the pitcher, offering a refill, but Arby signaled that his cup was still full enough. Xochipilli refilled his own, and drank it down with a grunt of deep satisfaction. "You and me, man, it's like we're part of the machinery of the whole thing. I don't think we get to know what it's all about. Could be that the song's right, the hokey-pokey is what it's all about. But our job is to be us. Grow big and strong. Go Army: Be All You Can Be."

"But *why*?"

"Why lions, why frogs? Why symphonies, burritos, game shows? I'm as confused as you are. More confused, man, 'cause I'm confused on a much higher plane. Don't get all cosmic on me, okay?" He leaned forward and rested his burly forearms on the little table. "Here's what I know. Here's what I re-lived."

The lonely Mexica in their days of wandering already worshipped the Bringer of Visions, at first in his most challenging forms, the devil's trumpet of the datura flower, the crimson beans of the Sophora shrub: harsh and sometimes deadly potions for a people lost in a harsh world. And then they had brought him down for the first time, called him into a physical body, and his role in the tribe had expanded. He helped them find new visionary plants, the Sun-Opener, the Serpent Vine, the little Buttons of the Deer, and these led them south, led them to game and water, and soon he was no longer merely the Bringer of Visions, but Xochipilli, The Prince of the Flowers and ruler of all they bestowed.

He died consciously, carried his memories to the Other Side, and was called down again, and again. The Visions of the Flowers led the Mexica ever south, and at last up the mountains into the high lake and swamp country where they founded their island kingdom, where they found the Little Ones, Teonanacatl, the Divine Flesh, the mushrooms that sprang overnight from the ground. And the Aztec kingdom sprang up almost as fast as the Little Ones, and Xochipilli was worshipped as a living god by thousands in the great rituals—

Arby felt a chill of suspicion crawl across his skin. "You mean human sacrifices?"

Xochipilli sat back from the table. His *Indio* countenance remained impassive, but Arby sensed that he was uncomfortable, perhaps embarrassed. "Yeah, that happened. And I got lots of juice from it, though most of it was for Huitzilopochtli and Tlaloc. The Aztecs were a little vague on some stuff. I mean, I tried to explain that worshipping me in trance floated my boat a lot more than having a stack of human skins dumped on my altar. But what you gonna do? When it comes to worshippers, hey—it's the thought that counts."

He'd been a living god, in his tenth continuous incarnation, when Cortez sacked the city. He sat in trance, his spirit far away, searching for a way to make the invaders disappear, when a Spanish cutlass cleaved through his skull. "No time to prepare to carry my consciousness with me. No followers prepared to rebirth me. Off we go, into the wild blue yonder, a nice long nap of four centuries."

But Hofmann and Huxley and Schultes unearthed the ancient knowledge of entheogens, and the sixties shifted into full gear. "The hippies who decided to call me down didn't know what they were doing, really. They wanted a special child, and they were probably hoping for a peyote spirit or something. What they got was me. Though I didn't know who *me* was for a long time."

Preposterous, but after the last few days, Arby was willing to treat the tale seriously. "And you recovered all this knowledge how?"

"I had a whole lotta allies. 'Shrooms. Mescaline. Ayahuasca, yopo, calea, Sun-Opener, calamus. Even acid—but she's a cold one, she's not trustworthy. Too new, too synthetic."

Arby felt his whole body wilt with disappointment. Psychedelics. Experiences no more verifiable than dreams. "That's it? A bunch of tripping?"

"*Tripping?* A *doorway*, Rainchild. A gate in the castle wall. A bridge across the moat."

"Sorry. I grew up around a bunch of heads, and all their visions ever did was leave them marginalized while the rest of the world moved on."

"While the rest of the world moved backwards, you mean."

"Give me a break, Two Feathers. I can't explain everything that's happened to me lately, but that doesn't mean I've got to throw common sense out the window and explain everything with magic. Especially not the kind you find in a pill."

Xochipilli sat still for a long moment, and Arby half-expected him to erupt in anger, or call his worshippers to throw Arby down the hill. But a slow smile crept onto the man's face. "Magic? No such thing as magic. Only laws of physics you don't understand." Xochipilli rose to his feet. "Come with me."

Outside, on the well-trodden ground that lay before the complex of caves, Arby stared at the view. The valley on the other side of the saddle ran to the west, where the sun now floated. Light danced along the thin line of a creek far below, and he wondered if this set of hills formed part of the Great Divide: surely the creeks in the two valleys ran in opposite directions.

Xochipilli stood at the edge of the hill. "You can see auras, at least. Watch mine."

Jerry had implied that Canetti's selective seal on Arby's speech was a sort of hypnosis, and now Arby wondered, though in a half-hearted way, if hypnosis could somehow explain auras as well. It would be nice to have an explanation he could live with. Nonetheless, he let his awareness rise as Elaina had taught him, and Xochipilli's silhouette began to glow with twining colors. Unlike the rounded auras he had seen before, though, Xochipilli's was ornate; the colors formed ridges, whorls, and striations in patterns that seemed to contain other patterns within them.

Then Arby saw into the hillside, where heaving piles of serpentine energy writhed. "It's like Rome," he said, "big green-and-purple snakes…"

"Another power place, man. That's why we're here—we've attuned ourselves to it. Check out my feet."

Some of the tubes of force beneath the ground had deformed and were bleeding out yellow light into the soles of the man's feet. "I see it."

"You don't see it yet. Wait." He held his arms forward from his sides, bent at the elbows, palms open but relaxed. Arby saw a few tiny threads of golden light leave the man's aura and wiggle their way in various directions, seemingly at random. Minutes passed. Xochipilli seemed to be in a calm trance, apparently willing to wait there forever. A honeybee, its legs heavy laden with pollen, buzzed between them and landed on Xochipilli's thumb, and the man didn't flinch.

After a moment, Xochipilli said, "See it? The bee?"

"Of course I see it."

"Consider it magic? Consider it improbable?"

"What, a bee landing on you?"

"Isn't a big deal, is it?" Xochipilli maintained his perfect stillness as he spoke, only his lips moving; his eyes were heavy lidded, neither open nor closed. "Though honeybees and power plants do have what you'd call a magical affinity…" The bee explored Xochipilli's thumb, and its striped abdomen pumped up and down as it crawled. Arby saw a glow surround the bee, a yellow-orange light. "Cool thing about the Other Side is how distance works. Things that are alike are all close together. All bees are close to all other bees. One bee is every bee. And within shouting distance of all insects—guess that would be obvious— and birds and bats, because of the whole flying thing."

Everything alike was close in space? That made no sense. Freud thought that rockets and flagpoles and bananas were all forms of penises, too, but how could they all be close together in space, especially when bananas would have to be surrounded by other fruit…and for that matter, by butter and sulfur, because they all shared yellowness. He opened his mouth to try and articulate this paradox, when Xochipilli said, "I hope you're seeing this."

In some ways it was still day, yet Arby's eyes saw the blackness of space behind Xochipilli, and in that blackness, a billion tiny pipes of yellow-orange energy running from above to below. Yet they weren't independent lines; like an infinitesimal plumbing system, the pipes interconnected, sprouting arms that tied into other pipes, and the closer he looked the more complicated and interwoven it became, yet the pulsing of the whole all seemed to flow downward. The vision was mesmerizing yet disturbing—like seeing a beating heart within a living chest. "I see something…but I don't know what it is."

An uncountable number of threads of light sprouted from Xochipilli's aura, and shot into the complex of pipes in the black sky. "That's that," he said. "Now just hang out." The man's stance relaxed. "What you're seeing is in Yesod, the Sphere of the Moon, next step up from where our bodies live. And that stuff—whatever it looked like to you—is the Vision of the Machinery of the Universe. Jerry, the old kid down in the house there, probably had to study and meditate twenty years before he got to see that stuff." He studied the bee on his thumb. "Actually, the bee-and-flesh-of-god thing goes way back. There's this place in North Africa—hey you're a geologist, you know the Tassili Plateau, right?—and on the canyon walls there's these pictures from way back in the Ice Age, when the Sahara was like paradise. And it's this shaman, but he has a honeybee's head and a stripy body—and that body is made of itty-bitty, thin-stemmed mushrooms." He grinned. "Goes way back, man. Now you know what the apple in the Garden of Eden really was, right? *My* stuff."

Arby heard a buzzing by his ears, and a honeybee shot past and landed on Xochipilli's shoulder. Another dropped down to land on his forehead, and when Arby looked up he saw that the air above them swarmed with bees, all of them swooping in to land on Xochipilli's skin. Looking down into the western valley, Arby made out tiny black figures flying toward them, as if all the honeybees of the world were converging on this single hilltop. The buzzing rose to a throbbing drone, like a didgeridoo.

Xochipilli's body was buried in crawling, searching bees, layers deep, and every second some fell onto the dust below and then clambered back onto his feet. He grinned, and dozens more fell from his lips. "No laws of physics broken here!" he shouted over the roar. "One bee—no problem, right? This is just one bee—many times. Takes energy. Energy and matter swap, right? Energy and probability, too!"

Arby had never been frightened of bees, but the roiling mass on Xochipilli's body was repellant, and he felt himself back away.

"No, man!" Xochipilli shouted. "Be cool with this! Hey—*bee* cool. Get it?" He aimed one honeybee-covered arm in Arby's direction and thousands of bees took wing and sprayed onto Arby like droplets from a hose.

He fought the impulse to run—hundreds of the insects were already on him—and froze instead. When he blinked his eyes, bees tumbled from his eyelids. His arms, his shirt, his pants: he was clothed in bees. The millions of tiny legs tickled at first, but then the buzz and drone seemed to invade his body, and the boundary between his skin and the bees seemed to vanish. He grew hot beneath that heavy blanket of life.

Xochipilli shambled over, spilling bees with every step, and leaned his head closer to Arby's, speaking loudly over the omnipresent drone. "Feels kinda great, yeah?"

It did, once the fear retreated. Every fiber in his body resonated with that primal buzz and he felt as though he were levitating, incorporeal, his whole being no more solid than a musical note. He opened his mouth, casually blew out the bees that immediately crawled inside, and drew a deep, glorious breath. When had he last felt this alive, this joyous, this…exalted?

"Look behind you!" Xochipilli shouted in his ear. "On the path!"

Arby turned, dripping bees, blinking bees from his eyes. At first he saw nothing, but then he made out the dusky, gray-brown shapes coiled there. Prairie rattlesnakes, six or seven of them.

"Like calls to like!" Xochipilli said. "Bees and rattlers, the whole venom thing! Pick one up!"

"What?"

"Pick one up! You're buried in bees, you're like a brother right now!"

"You're crazy!"

Xochipilli made his way down the path to the closest snake, leaving a trail of bees that crawled after him. "C'mon!" When the man's bee-clad body approached the coiled snake Arby saw its tongue flick out, tasting the air, but it didn't draw its neck into striking position. "C'mon, man! You The Fool, or what?" Xochipilli bent down and reached his honeybee-covered arm toward the snake. It reared, tongue flicking, and he slid his hand under its belly and lifted it.

The snake kept its head up, alert, but coiled its tail along his forearm, dislodging hundreds of bees, most of which flew a moment and landed again, covering the snake. Xochipilli raised his head and lifted his arms to the sky. "Ohhhh…man! Do it! You gotta do it!"

Arby found himself drifting down the path as though weightless, his whole body a-hum. Xochipilli stepped aside to let him pass, and he stopped in front of the fattest prairie rattler he'd ever seen. Without knowing why he felt compelled to do so, he leaned down.

The snake let loose its threatening rattle, and the other snakes took up that buzz-saw warning. A cold fear rushed through Arby but dissipated when it met the warmth flooding from the bees. The rattling of the snakes and the hum of the bees harmonized and melded into one, and without thought Arby gentled the snake into his hand and lifted it, and when it twined itself around his arm it became a part of him. Before he realized it, he had gathered up a second snake in his other hand.

Somehow Xochipilli had gotten below him on the path, and Arby saw that the man now held a pair of snakes in each hand. "Take 'em back up top!" the man shouted.

Standing once more on the hilltop, Arby saw that the inhabitants had come out, two dozen or more, kneeling before the caves, watching.

Xochipilli danced past Arby and then let out a war-whoop, whirling around, a small tornado of bees flinging out from his body and then flying back again. At the edge of the hill, he threw his arms in the air, a pair of snakes writhing in either hand. "Gospel of Mark, chapter sixteen, yeah?" He punctuated his words by thrusting the snakes at the sky: "They shall *take…up…serpents! Yeah!*"

Then the man started to dance again, and sang:

> *Well, gimme that old-time religion*
> *Gimme that old-time religion*
> *Gimme that old-time religion*
> *It's good enough fer me, Oh, Yeah!*

Arby laughed as he recognized the song, laughed louder as he realized that Xochipilli might mean a very much older religion than the songwriter had intended, and then a pair of drums began a beat from deep within the caves, the tunnels channeling and amplifying the pulse until it seemed that the hill itself throbbed beneath his feet, and he found that he too was dancing with Xochipilli, a slow, heavy-footed dance that shed bees into the air with every beat, and the two of them circled as the sun grew red in the west and a soft evening breeze started up from the valley.

"Our friends need to go home now." Xochipilli's soft voice startled Arby out of some distant place. He found that he was standing on the hilltop in the last rays of the sun. Only a few hundred of the bees remained, and they crawled sluggishly. He realized he still held a snake in either hand, or rather that the snakes were coiled around either forearm, apparently content to luxuriate in the warmth of his skin.

Arby moved to the edge of the hill like a sleepwalker and urged the snakes from his arms. The bees continued to take flight and disappear to their distant hives. He had never felt so spent, so at peace. He stood there and watched the snakes crawl off into the rocks.

Xochipilli threw an arm over Arby's shoulder, and the weight of it felt immense. "Not magic. Just unlikely. Now I have more to tell you." He used his arm to steer Arby around toward the caves, and Arby saw that all of the people still knelt there in the twilit shadows. As they walked toward the caves, the man asked, "Say, you need company tonight?"

"Huh?"

He gestured at the row of worshippers. "You know, women, girls. Men or boys, for that matter."

"No, I… No." Arby found it hard to concentrate enough to form sentences. He felt good but lightheaded, and utterly drained. "Not my kind of thing."

"Suit yourself. No wonder they call you The Fool."

Arby stumbled then, and Xochipilli's powerful arms held him up. "You okay, man?"

"Tired." Arby eased out of the man's embrace and focused on putting one foot in front of the other.

"Come on inside for a bit. Get you something to drink, a little food. Talk tomorrow." After a pause, he said, "I'm going to have my people rig up a traveling chair, Inca style, and carry you down to the house. You're in no shape to hike."

"Not necessary."

"Maybe not. But, listen, man—you should take advantage of the perks. Because a lot of this whole god gig? You'll see. It pretty much sucks."

19

People Don't Die from Dreaming

Despite Arby's politically correct misgivings, riding in a chair borne by people felt good. More natural than the motions of a car or plane; more human than riding horseback.

Xochipilli's bearers carried Arby's chair up the stairs and into the mansion. He didn't see Jerry or Elaina, but the cluster of other servants waiting there—more worshippers of somebody or another, he supposed—seemed to know who he was and what arrangements had been made for him.

They deposited him in a suite at the rear of the house and then retreated, bowing and murmuring. He felt like he should reach for his wallet and find a suitable tip, but as he studied their receding faces, he saw something disturbing. Their faces were glowing with excitement, but underneath that there was fear, as if they had just stumbled off the world's most kick-ass rollercoaster.

Arby shut the door. The room had a sense of coziness that erred on the side of padding: plush rugs, overstuffed chairs, a canopy bed piled high with pillows, and a comforter thick as a mattress. He stumbled into the bathroom, turned on the shower, and dropped his clothes on the floor as he waited for the water to warm. The window looked out onto a piney hillside sloping upwards. If he'd decided to exit through the window, the ground was only a few inches below the windowsill.

The thrumming of the hot water against his skin brought back the harmonics of the bees and snakes, but muted now, and when he dried off, he tried to towel the vibration from his limbs. There's a good buzz and even a bad buzz, but this was just too much buzz.

He tossed aside the giant comforter, peeled back the blankets, and climbed naked beneath the bedsheet. There was just enough energy left in his body to let him reach over and switch off the bedside lamp.

He must have slept for hours, because when his eyes opened moonlight gleamed through the west-facing window. Something jostled the bed, and he saw her sitting there on the bedside. Liz. Amazing. Amazing that Jerry and Elaina had found her so fast. Even more amazing that she had agreed to join them.

Arby cleared his throat, wet his lips with his tongue. "You came…" After all the nights dreaming of her in Dhahran, after all the aborted phone calls, it was too much to accept.

She nodded—slow, knowing bobs of her head—and let that sly predator's smile own her lips.

He sat up, reaching for her, asking, "But, how—?" and she pushed him back down with a gentle shove of fingers against his chest.

"First things first," she said, and his body thrilled at the sound of her voice. She stood. She wore only a pale green slip, luminescent in the silver light of the moon. Watching him, she tossed back her shoulder-length blond hair, and removed her little post earrings. It was so Liz to still have them on, so Liz to stop in the middle of things and take them off. "Don't move."

She dropped the earrings on the nightstand and, rather than pulling away the straps and letting the slip fall to the floor, she peeled it up and over her head, and then dangled it between them for a moment before she let it float to the carpet. As always, the only hair on her body was on her head, and there even the eyebrows had been ruthlessly plucked to thin lines. She waited, smiling at Arby with an awareness of her own power, showing him an expression part amused, part contemptuous, part embarrassed…and, what he so desperately wanted to see, part hungry.

Arby swallowed with difficulty and lifted his arms toward her again, but she shook a finger in admonishment. "Hands down. Ladies first." She threw back the sheet. "Well, looky here. Maybe just this once we'll skip the foreplay, okay?"

She straddled him. In the moonglow her small breasts and smooth belly looked sleek and cold, but he felt the heat from her pelvis. Like most night erections, what stood up from his groin was rampant, but accompanied by a full bladder. Arby ran his tongue across his teeth and realized his mouth tasted stale. "I should brush my teeth…"

"Later." She braced herself on one arm and found his stiff cock with her free hand. He watched her face. She frowned as though what she was doing took immense concentration. The tip of her tongue poked out of the corner of her mouth and her gaze turned inward as she fitted him to her. When she leveraged her hips down and he slid partway in they gasped in unison. Arby's vision clouded, and when it cleared he found her eyes focused on his again, but she was biting her lower lip. "Whoa," she said, pausing to catch her breath. "Long time, no see, huh?"

"Just take it slow," he said, though his voice trembled with urgency. "Easy…" He was torn between lust and an urge to weep—it was so good to see her again, to feel her again.

She grinned, but he saw a pulse beating in her slim throat. "No pain, no gain…right?" she asked, and bore down hard.

Arby cried out, a cry as surprised and involuntary as if he'd been flung into an icy river—the sensation was so powerful that the concept of pleasure was banished. To be inside her so swiftly after so long was almost unbearable. He found his hands were clamped on the small of her back, sliding down, and she paused and sat back on her heels while she gathered up his wrists and pinned them down on either side of his head. She leaned down and forward, her nipples tracing twin lines up his chest, and kissed him, sliding her tongue into his mouth and searching.

At last the kiss broke off and she laid her head alongside his and whispered, her lips against his ear as arousing as her body against him.

"My turn, okay? Let me finish this, and then…you can do whatever you want, all right?" She exhaled a long, moist breath onto his ear. "Okay?"

It was all Arby could do to choke out the word okay.

She rocked with painful slowness, grinding down, not letting him slide in or out, just rocking there with all her weight and all her muscles. "You like that?" she whispered. "You like how that feels?"

Arby groaned in response, and she whispered, "Now I'm going to rock your world. Would you like that? Would you like that, baby?"

The question sounded rhetorical, but he managed an affirmative sound. She lifted her face above his and said, "Here…"

It began as a kiss, and her tongue thrust hard into his mouth again. He let his tongue wrestle with hers, aimlessly, but his real awareness was focused a thousand miles south, where they were clamped together so tightly that all boundaries had vanished. Her tongue seemed to swell, to push his aside, to reach for the back of his mouth.

At the same moment, her lips spread wide around his, and then, bizarrely slid wetly up and over his nose, down over his chin. Her mouth covered the whole lower half of Arby's face. Her tongue expanded into a hard, muscular organ that pushed against the back of his throat.

The intrusion was sudden and the cutoff of air was complete. His teeth bit down on her tongue, which was now as stiff as leather, and his frantic eyes saw only the blur of her face pressed against his. Her arms pinned his wrists with terrifying power, and her hips clamped down on his with such force that all he could do was drum his legs against the mattress. She was insanely strong, impossibly massive.

Explosions went off in his eyes, like tiny fireflies igniting and then dying, and his chest heaved and shuddered.

Then that leathery tongue ripped back out of his throat and her lips lost their suction on her face with a wet smacking sound. Through blurred vision he saw Liz sitting atop him, her mouth wide as a soupbowl, a fat tentacle protruding from it. Elaina had her by the hair, and Elaina's sword whistled through the air and chunked into Liz's neck with a horrible meaty sound.

Arby choked and convulsed, half-blind, and felt Liz's weight yanked away from him. There was a thud as Elaina dumped the body onto the floor.

He struggled up against the headboard, still gasping for breath. He shivered, but felt hot tears on his face. "Liz…" he said through a raw throat.

Elaina wore a long white nightgown, sheer enough that he could make out the silhouette of her body against the moonlit window. She leaned forward and wiped her sword on the bed, and he saw the green and red swirl of her eyes. "Not Liz. That was no one. A succubus who took on the form of the one you desired." She glanced down and toed something on the floor. "Attractive enough, I suppose."

He felt sorrow and fear battling inside him, but what came from his mouth was merely childish. "You said I'd be safe here."

"We're not 'here,' though. Look down at the body of the succubus." The idea was sad and revolting, and it must have shown on his face. "Trust me."

Arby rolled onto his side and peered down where Elaina had dumped the body.

The carpet was bare. No blood, no gore. No body.

"You are out of your body, or perhaps 'mostly' out of your body would be more accurate. Your consciousness is here, on the Other Side."

"None of this is real?"

"Oh, to be sure it is real. But real at a different level of existence. My physical body is in a bed at the other side of the mansion. My ethereal body is in this room. If either of us died here, we would die a very real death indeed."

"People don't die from dreaming." He stopped, realizing he didn't know a damned thing. "Uh, do they?"

"Normal dreams don't send your full consciousness to Yetzirah. This trick that some study now, the thing they call 'lucid dreaming?' Yes. You can die."

"Come with me," Elaina said, and turned toward the bathroom.

Really? Well, why not? If what he'd just been through was a sample of dreaming, he'd rather be awake. Arby rolled up to take a seat, and put his feet, if they were really his feet, where Liz's body would have been, if it had been a real body and a real Liz. He stood up and started walking before he realized he was naked. Naked, and still half-erect. What the hell. If it didn't bother Elaina, he wouldn't let it bother him. There was nothing like being raised in a succession of Oregon communes to make you unashamed.

Without turning, Elaina added, "I suggest you resist the urge to look back."

There was no surer way to force him to look. He threw the briefest glance over his shoulder.

In a snap, Arby was there: on his back in the bed, eyes open, limbs heavy, unable to move.

Elaina stared down at him from the bedside. "Fool," she said, without any rancor. It took a moment for him to realize it wasn't an accusation, but his name. "Did I not tell you to not look back?"

Arby had trouble getting his mouth working. "*Did you not tell me to not?* You didn't *tell* me anything. You *suggested.*"

"The vagaries of English. No wonder it is the chief language of lawyers."

He felt his limbs reviving from their paralysis, and hoisted himself onto his elbows. "And aren't you all about law?"

"Rather the opposite. I'm about Justice." For a second, it seemed like she was going to have an emotion, but she recovered. "Now lay down and be asleep again so we can go."

He felt no desire whatsoever to suit up and show up, or don him now his gay apparel, or suck in that gut, soldier, or in fact to do anything that took him out of that bed. With some effort, Arby shook his head. "You know, in the last three days you've dragged me halfway around the world and pushed me through things that make Dali's stuff look like *Dora the Explorer*. What's another day or two? Call me in the morning." He felt an insistent pressure above his pelvis. "Plus, I gotta pee."

Elaina's voice didn't change a nano-iota from its normal flat tone. "If you want another day or two, that means another night or two." Green and red worms chased each other in circles in the irises of her eyes. "A night or two like this one. Or worse."

He knew a threat when he heard one, and this was a damn good one, but he wasn't going to agree. "I just want some explanations."

"You've had many since we arrived here."

"Yeah, right. Kether is the Malkuth of the Unmanifest. Bees call to rattlesnakes. We are all on the Wheel, but some of us abide to let others evolve. I was thinking of explanations that might actually, umm, explain something?"

She studied him, while her eyes continued to put on their lightshow. "Is there not an English proverb, 'Thou shall show, and thou shalt not tell?'"

Didn't sound familiar. "Is that in the Bible somewhere?"

"Perhaps I am mistaken." She shrugged one shoulder. "But that is where we were headed, to show you, when you dashed back into your body. So shall we proceed?"

The best argument he could muster was, "Well, I still need to pee."

She considered. "You are half here and half down there. You can probably accomplish that. I'll tell you if your body is not coming with you."

Following that unenlightening observation, Arby staggered to the bathroom and kicked the door shut with his heel. It rebounded to half-open. To hell with it.

Bladders are willful as housecats, and if they have been too full for too long, they will snub you for a while just to teach you a lesson. When at last he finished, Arby realized yet again that he was unclad.

"Umm, Elaina?" he called out.

"Fool?" she answered from the bedroom, her voice muffled by the half-closed door.

"I'm naked. And you're in a nightgown."

A long pause. "I'm trying to see what you see… Ah. This is not what I sleep in—this is what you *imagine* I sleep in. Just imagine yourself dressed."

He frowned and conjured up pictures of trousers and shirts, shoes and socks, but all he succeeded in doing was increasing his awareness of his nakedness.

Okay. Start at one end and work toward the other. He looked in the bathroom mirror and tried to picture a shirt collar around his neck. To his amazement, something white began to materialize…and then fade. *No!* He concentrated with desperate focus, and it began to manifest—a ring of white cloth around his neck.

Suddenly it popped into clarity: white starched collar, accompanied by a formal black bow tie he hadn't requested.

And no shirt attached. Good evening ladies, and welcome to Chippendale's. "Elaina…!" he said.

"I will do it, then." She appeared in the doorway behind him and favored his outfit with a tiny frown. "Having to dress you is not a promising start."

Arby awaited the abracadabra, or a puff of smoke, or at least a physical sensation. There was no transition. His reflection showed him in a brocade tunic with huge, dangling sleeves; it ought to have been heavy, but wasn't. The fabric itself was green and black, but it was embroidered with myriad symbols—silver moons, yellow suns, and dozens of symbols he didn't recognize. A chain of golden orbs belted the tunic at the waist, creating something of a skirt, and when he glanced down, he saw his legs covered in skintight hose that verged on chartreuse. Pointy yellow slippers finished the ensemble.

Cue the accordion music. He looked like something that had fallen off the cast shuttlebus at Cirque du Soleil.

"Your Aspect," Elaina said. "I thought we could leave the hat and other Attributes for another time."

"No balls to juggle?" he asked. "No unicycle?"

She paused a long moment before saying, "I am not familiar with that term." Her voice was as level as ever, but he sensed her patience had boundaries, and he was nearing the outskirts, where the speed limit would suddenly change.

Arby turned from the mirror to face her. She was dressed in red robes slashed with dark green. The cowl of her hood, thrown back over her shoulders, was the same intense green, so deep you could drown in it. She wasn't just her usual glacial self; in the shadows, with the bedroom lamplight surrounding her robes like a halo, she was now forbidding.

His mouth was dry. Maybe that's why it was so hard to produce the words. "I'm sorry. It's how I talk when I'm confused." He let out a long breath. "And, well, scared."

Her perfect face seemed motionless even though her mouth moved. "I understand. One like you should have been raised with the knowledge of the Inner Planes." The palm of her right hand rested on the pommel of her unsheathed broadsword, the tip of the sword against the floor. That couldn't be good for the floorboards. "I cannot help that," she said. "This is the only way I can help."

"Okay. What now?"

She sniffed. "Return your body to the bed, and step out of your body and come with me."

20

Balance Doesn't Attract Many Zealots

As it turned out, it wasn't hard. Arby sprawled on the bed, closed his eyes, sat up, and stood up. Then made the mistake of looking down at his sleeping body, and, zap, he was back inside it.

Lather, rinse, repeat. It took him a few iterations to learn not to look back at his body, but once he resisted that urge, he could join Elaina in the bathroom, where she waited impassively.

She gestured at the window. It was an old-fashioned affair, with wooden muntins forming a grid between the handswidth individual panes. "This should work well enough. Turn on the light."

He stepped past her and flipped the switch. The harsh light made him flinch.

Elaina said, "Look out the window. See the shadows of the windowpanes on the ground?"

He edged up beside her. The shadow of the window grid showed on the bare ground, widening in the distance where it faded into the trees. "Is there something I'm missing? 'Cause it looks totally normal."

Elaina lifted the lower half of the double-hung window and pushed the screen out onto the high ground. She clambered through, balancing part of her weight on her sword as though it were a cane. When she gained her footing outside, she tugged at the sword, freeing its tip from the floorboards, along with a large chip of wood. She caught Arby staring. "The Sword of Justice is never sheathed," she said. "Which is less than convenient at times. Come along."

"Elaina?"

She turned and squatted to look, a velvety red lump in all those robes. "Yes?"

"Is this real? Or not real?" Even with the little Arby knew, by now he realized that was a meaningless question. "I mean—well, is this just dreaming, or can I, uh, die?"

"It is normal to be able to die." The light from the bathroom was full on her face. "When you face a situation where you cannot die— there is the recipe for real horror."

A snappy caption for a Successories motivational poster. Rather than work through the implications of that cheery insight, Arby crawled through the window.

As he followed Elaina toward the trees, he noticed that what at first appeared to be the shadows of the grid were in truth narrow trenches in the ground, as though a child had dragged a stick to make rectangles in the dirt. Arby kicked them with a yellow-slippered toe. They moved, but they were tenacious, as if the soil particles were magnetized.

Elaina turned right and disappeared behind a tree. When he reached that tree, he saw that the squares continued in a path off to the right; but they were now wide clay tiles, and without the light from the bathroom, they were in the darkness of late twilight.

Farther on, beside another tree—and what was a thick, wide-limbed oak doing in this pine forest?—Elaina glanced back to make sure he was following, and then turned left.

Past the second tree, quite impossibly, the forest ended. The path changed to grayish marble slabs, which ran a dozen yards, ending below the face of a tall stone building that appeared to be a perfect cube. Elaina stood at the foot of a short stairway that led up to double doors; to either side of the doors, light shone from giant stained-glass windows in geometric designs. "Here we are," she said.

Arby hadn't been exerting himself, but he was strangely short of breath. He took a deep inhale and realized how shallow his breathing had been. "Where's here?"

"My temple. The center of my domain. Come." She started up the steps.

"I think I see what you did. Changing stuff bit by bit." He gathered in another deep breath. "What's it called?"

She half-turned. "Most Kabbalists would call it Pathworking. Include that which aligns with the Path, exclude that which does not. But this"—she gestured at the temple with her sword—"isn't part of the Tree. This is a place I created long ago.

"What you see here are abstractions—the math behind the flesh, if you will." She pointed at the doors opposite the ones where they entered. "What do you picture beyond those doors? What do you imagine is out there?"

The image that emerged in his mind's eye was the dark pine forests and stone paths he had seen on his trip in, but with the slope of the land heading downward. As he focused on it, the vision became vivid, specific, almost photographic, and then, at the end, realistic and fully dimensional.

This wasn't so hard. Anybody could do it.

"So," Elaina said, "come and take a look at my little kingdom… or, I suppose, queendom." She crossed to the doors and pushed them wide.

The golden light of spring flooded into the room. Arby joined her in the doorway. It was nothing like his vision. The temple sat atop a green hill in a vale of gently rolling slopes. Black-and-white cows grazed in green pasturelands, the lush fields enclosed by thick, brambly hedgerows; streams meandered into groves of trees. Crows flew cawing high in the sky while a flock of white doves came fluttering down from a tree to the cow-cropped grass. A fox stalking a hare stopped and shot them a startled look before slipping into the bushes. The whole landscape seemed tamed, but as he studied it he realized that it formed a perfect balance of wild and domesticated, of design and chance. "This is yours?"

"In the sense that we own anything, or make anything. I supplied the vision."

"But it's huge."

"In terms of the planet, yes, perhaps the size of, oh…Denmark? But that is not the point. Is it what you imagined?"

"No." Arby tried to recapture his vision, and couldn't. Indeed, he could scarcely remember his steps arriving here. "No. Nothing like it."

"Does this help?" The skies darkened, and gray clouds gathered and paced their solemn way over the hills like an Oregon autumn, and all at once he recognized the gray-green pillars of pines under a crepuscular light, and it started to drift toward what he had seen so clearly before…

But it vanished, replaced by bright light and brambles and cud-chewing cows.

By his side, Elaina said, "You envisioned your version, but you did not *believe* it." For a moment he thought she was done, but she added, "I do not only believe my vision. I *know* it."

Okay, the whole Einstein thing.

The man realized that space and time were dimensions of the same stuff, and that both were expansible or compressible within certain limits. Good call for somebody still enmeshed in the physical plane. If he had realized there were actually eleven dimensions (well, actually ten plus one, which is critically different from eleven), who knows what he might have figured out?

Probably as well he didn't. $E = mc^2$ caused enough trouble on its own.

What he had to say about the "m," about mass, was correct enough, but it only applies Down Here, at the bottom of the pile, where opposites collide. Opposites don't "attract," they lock each other up. As in a bad marriage, each one prevents the other from following their bliss.

Malkuth, our physical world—the Kingdom, of the Kingdom, the Power, and the Glory fame—the Garment of God, the Glittering

World, the Vale of Tears, or even Maya, the Sphere of Illusion: whatever you call this collection of suns and rocks and digital clocks, it exists only because of forces frustrating one another.

The electrons want to go one way, the protons another, and the neutrons want to huddle together so tightly they disappear. None of them want to be locked up as particles, and this was Einstein's real insight: Everything is made of Light.

In the case of matter, very frustrated light.

But that's Down Here. Rise higher on the planes and opposites loosen their reluctant but passionate embrace, electron forsakes proton. The higher one rises, the more like calls to like, and the more antitheses flee.

Down here, baby showers and Superbowl Sunday not only exist in the same world, but can even exist in the same room on different days. Night follows day, and the two even touch at dawn and twilight. Our world is like the surf zone, neither solid ground nor open sea, and we live our lives in the crashing waves where opposites collide.

But travel high enough Up There and things segregate. All bars are gay bars. The local Baskin-Robbins serves Vanilla and Vanilla. At the highest levels of existence, like and unlike exist in separate universes, but between Here and There, things clump up beside their near-clones, like the cliques at junior-high lunch tables.

Which brings us to shortcuts.

The most recent scientific definition of distance is the meter—the distance that light in a vacuum travels in one 299,792,548th of a second. Things are so many meters, or kilometers, or light-years apart. Works well enough in this tiny little slice of the universe. But it gives rise to the belief that the universe is laid out mechanically, that spatial dimensions are the architectural struts of existence.

Believing the universe is mechanical is a grievous error, and if you will please put away that iPod and come here and spit your gum in the wastebasket, teacher will explain. Listen: The architecture of the universe is metaphor. The building blocks of existence are poetry. A woman shedding tears in California is close to a rainstorm in Vermont—closer to that rainstorm than a dry-eyed Vermonter watching it out the window.

It just doesn't look that way from Down Here.

In dreams—when the unconscious wanders the lower etheric—it is apparent. One image calls to another, metric distance melts away, and our dreaming mind stumbles direct from one vision to its close relative. The train becomes a subway becomes a cave becomes a sewer pipe becomes a river becomes a highway.

And Below calls down like from Above. This is why we so often get what we expect or fear—or, poetry being what it is, the opposite of what we expect. Things that are like one another are close together. And so are things that are like each other by being the opposite of each other. Get it?

The point is, at the basic level, the eleven-dimensional map of the universe is a map of metaphor. And we'd reproduce it here, but this isn't *Lord of the Rings*, and there isn't an 11-D printer. And not every map is valid for every user. There are an innumerable number of these maps.

Well, okay, it's not innumerable. It's 258,453 at last count.

The point is, metaphor is a damned handy way of getting around Up There.

Halfway up the hill the trees parted to reveal a cave mouth as regular as a giant cartoon mousehole. Elaina knelt by a fallen treetrunk, thrust her hand into the rotting wood, and ripped out a chunk of woody orange fungus that was whorled and cupped like a human ear.

"Doors, gateways, any kind of portal. These are the—what do you call those small paired wheels on velocipedes?" Red and green swirled in her eyes as she took in Arby's puzzlement. "Velocipedes? Bicycles? The devices installed on them to keep the unskilled from falling?"

"Um—do you mean 'training wheels?'"

"Exactly. Portals are training wheels. Tunnels are most useful of all. Anywhere you can believe in them." She bent over and headed into the darkness. Her voice echoed back at him. "Your current physics would be lost without them. Wormholes, quantum tunneling."

Arby ducked his head as he followed her into the tunnel, avoiding the soggy moss that adorned the cave's mouth. In the dark, the fungus in her hand glowed yellow-green. In a few yards the walls were drier, and the air became less humid. It reminded him of nineteenth-century mines he had visited in the Mojave. Some of them had chambers carved into walls where the old miners had fashioned bedrooms sheltered from the scorching heat.

In fact, around a bend the glow of the fungus showed him a chamber just like the ones he had explored outside Ridgecrest.

"Good. That chamber is yours," Elaina said, walking on without looking back. "Now, what would you expect when we come out the other end of this mine?"

The Spear's Claim, Main shaft. Beyond Old Man Spear's solid rock bedroom, a curve, the growing brilliance of the desert sun reaching in, and a step out onto the platform of tailings that spilled from the mouth of Spear's Main.

He was there, standing beside Elaina. The path to their right wound around an outcrop of fractured rock, and he recalled every detail of how it switchbacked down the steep hillside. He half-expected to see his college field studies group encamped on the desert floor below.

"Is this a place you remember?" Elaina asked. "This path?"

"Perfectly."

"Then let us walk down it."

Easy enough. The path of quartzite sand and rock fragments, the steep fractured rocks of the hillside pushing in on the right.

It seemed familiar, but also not quite right. The fractures in the rocks were too regular, the stacking of one layer above the next too precise. But it was just memory, and memory is always fuzzy.

Around a sharp bend in the path, the hillside sloped away into dunes, and on the sandy valley floor were the Great Pyramids of Giza, the Sphinx sitting apart.

He almost bumped into Elaina, who was waiting, her eyes vortexing red and green. He wished she'd go back to the blind-woman wrap-arounds.

"What the—" He stared at the monuments. They seemed like the real items. But there were no steep hillsides near Giza, and anyway—

"That was too easy, of course," Elaina said. "I only had to imagine the rocks beside the path stacking precisely with more belief than the power of your memory. And once you have squared-off stacked rocks, manifesting the Pyramids almost happens on its own."

She pointed at the Sphinx. "This isn't my envisioning. This place is manifested by millions of minds and millions of photographs, and thousands of books and movies. It is easy to find. It is easy to find many different versions which overlap."

Arby felt queasy. "And, can you change it?"

21

Making Thirteen

He didn't remember falling asleep after Elaina led him back to his bed, but perhaps that only made sense—he had been asleep the entire time. He woke immediately, staggered to the bathroom, and emptied his bladder. He woke again, if waking it was, in the darkness of early morning. Though the moon had long since set, enough light came through the gap in the curtains for him to make out what appeared to be a wad of blankets in front of the bathroom door.

They certainly hadn't been there before. He sat up, rubbing his eyes, and the blankets stretched and shifted. He realized the amorphous shape was in fact a mountain lion reclining on the floor, one hip jutted in feline repose. It lifted its head, and said, in a male voice, "Mmm, hello?" The pale round eyes blinked. "Waking again in his dreams? Once tonight was not enough?" The tone was rich and insinuating, yet calming.

A talking cougar. Fine. "Who are you?"

"A friend. Elaina said the boy would need, as it were, a guardian until morning, and you do, don't you? But now, I propose, why does he not go back to sleep in this dream?"

Arby sighed, and pulled the blankets up to his chin. Why not indeed?

In the morning the cougar had vanished. After Arby's morning shower, a deferential young man had brought him clothes—black trousers and a green polo shirt—and then led him to a patio on the south side of the house for breakfast. Perhaps "brunch" would have been a better term, as the sun was high above the hills that formed the southern wall of the valley. A long-nosed man and a heavyset woman, looking for all the world like the proud owners of a country inn somewhere in Tuscany, stood by the French doors, ready to fetch anything he desired. He'd tried to make friends with them—had even encouraged them to sit down and join him, a prospect that seemed to appall them—but they seemed happiest when he let them keep their distance.

Two giggling girls in sundresses, holding hands, rounded the footpath at the front corner of the mansion and frisked their way up the steps onto the patio, where they stood, openly gawking at him. Not girls, he realized, rather young women, but young women without even hints of wrinkles on their faces. The brown-haired one said, "You ask."

The other, her freckle-face framed in copper-red hair, laughed. "You."

"You'll owe me." She folded her arms over her chest and addressed Arby. "Are you him?"

The redhead shoved her in the shoulder. "That's not asking anything."

"Okay. Sheesh." She looked at Arby again and asked, "Are you the one they went hunting for?" The redhead stood on tiptoe and whispered in the other's ear, and the brunette blew an exasperated breath upward. "And, you're not a Hero after all? You're like The Fool or something?"

They both poked their heads forward a bit, waiting for his answer, and Arby grinned. "I guess so. All I know is what they tell me."

"Can we eat with you?"

They seemed harmless enough. "Sure."

They scampered over to join him. The brunette waved her hand at the couple by the door. "Domenico?" She held up two fingers, and the man nodded. She turned to Arby. "I'm Lacerta. And this one"—she nodded at the redhead—"who is suddenly so shy, is called Selky."

"I'm Arby."

"*Arby?*" Lacerta giggled. "What's that supposed to be?"

"It's a nickname."

Selky said, "I can do it, I'm good at this."

"Can not," Lacerta said.

"Bet?"

"You already owe me. Dig yourself in deeper."

Selky's blue-green eyes scanned his face as though memorizing his features, and then her pale eyelids closed. "Hmm… Fern. Moss. Shadow plants. Moisture plants. Moisture *seeds*…seeds, fetus, baby, infant… Storm. Water, bath, shower, pool, waterfall, *waterfall-baby*…"

"Waterfall-baby?" Lacerta asked. "I don't think so…"

"But something's wet—"

"You, usually."

"Shut *up*! *Storm* was right… No, rain. *Rainman*!"

"Isn't that a movie?"

Selky's eyes opened wide and she stared at Arby. "Got you! Rainchild! Rainchild Abundance!" A blotchy flush rose up her neck onto her face. "Got you, that's you, that's you, that's you."

"That's your *name*?" Lacerta asked.

"Close enough," Arby said. He shifted in his seat and picked up a half-eaten piece of toast. "Rainchild Bounty."

Lacerta shook her head. "Uh-uh, you were wrong about *Abundance*."

"He said *close enough* and it's his name! He decides." Selky held her palms up beside her face, fingers widespread, and tilted them side-to-side, as though miming a minstrel act. "Who's a loser now, huh, huh?"

Lacerta looked as though she were about to launch an appeal to Arby, but Domenico arrived with a tray. He offloaded the breakfasts for Selky and Lacerta—plates of sliced apples, strawberries, glasses of water, and what Arby thought was a small pitcher of syrup. When they poured it on their fruit, though, the slow amber flow told him it was honey.

Arby revised his opinion. No matter what their physical age, these weren't women, these were *girls*. And although he usually didn't care for airheaded femmes, there was something in their easy, aimless banter that made him relax. They were easy to look at, too.

Lacerta lifted a sticky apple slice between thumb and forefinger and slipped it between her lips, then gave a little moan of pleasure. "Mmm. So you're The Fool, huh? What's that about?"

"I'm not sure. I only found out yesterday that's who I'm supposed to be. If it's even true."

"If Elaina says it's true, it's true. Miss Priss couldn't lie if lives depended on it. Who brought you down from the Other Side? Parents?"

"My mom's kind of a hippie. I've never known who my father was."

"Oooo, Darth Vader moment!" She tried to drop her voice by tilting her chin down. "*Luke, Luke…I am your father.* The plot thickens."

"*Guy*, Lacey," Selky said, making the explicative "guy" into a four-syllable word. "You are so effing insensitive sometimes! Who *cares* who his dad is?" She turned to Arby. "I'll make her apologize later."

"Here's my apology now." Lacerta held out an apple slice. "Open wide…"

Arby let her slide it into his mouth, and he crunched down on it. The flood of sugar made him wince. "Sweet," he said, trying to control his grimace.

Lacerta sucked the honey from her fingertips. "Do ya think?"

"Be nice, Lacey," Selky said.

"Look," Arby said, "fair's fair. So I'm The Fool, whatever that means. Who are you two?"

There was a silence as the two girls locked eyes, and for a moment Arby was afraid he'd stumbled across some forbidden boundary. Then the pair erupted into laughter. Selky made a sweeping gesture down at her body. "Am I losing it here?" she asked, still laughing. "Isn't it obvious anymore?"

When Arby looked blank for long enough, Lacerta said, "*Nymphs* mean anything to you? Dryads? The name 'Selky' isn't a clue?"

"Look, it's cute," Selky said. "He's blushing!"

Arby felt the flush on his face, and feeling it made him blush even more. These girls, however old or young they might be, made him feel as though he were barely pubescent. "Never heard of dryads or anything like 'Selky,' except you, of course." He found he couldn't even look at her. "Sorry."

"Skin like a seal," Lacerta said, "she keeps it somewhere…"

Unwilling to look at either of the girls for a moment, Arby let his eyes drift down the valley, toward the gate where he had arrived the day before. The lone figure of a woman came up the path in the distance, wearing clothes that at first seemed black, but flashed in the sun, by turns blue and then deep green. "Who's that?" Arby asked, largely to have something to say.

The nymphs both turned their heads. "Raisa…" Selky said. "Don't see her much anymore."

"You stay away from her," Lacerta said to Arby. "A Rasalka. Don't even talk to her."

Arby used his toast to mop up the last bits of egg yolk on his plate, and the nymphs poured more honey on their fruit. Lacerta was suggesting a sunbathing expedition to a beach along the stream when a young blond man stepped through the doors. The two servants moved far aside and inclined their heads as the man glided between them toward Arby's table. He moved with the grace of a ballet dancer, and had a dancer's build and sinews, powerful yet flexible. "All rested now, fed, ready to meet the day?" The voice was familiar, and Arby remembered the cougar from his dream. "Ladies, should you be bothering him, do you think? Are they being bad?"

The man spun a chair about and sat upon it backward, his legs straddling the chairback, his arms draped atop it. "I am called Helayjah. Perhaps he knows the name? No?" He offered a limp hand, outstretched palm-downward almost as though expecting it to be kissed. "And you are The Fool?"

He shook the proffered hand. "Arby." The languid posture and a hint of underlying alertness and danger made him certain. "You were the one in my room last night."

"In your *dream* last night, guarding. And now perhaps he is restored enough to meet the others?"

The nymphs brought their plates of fruit along when Helayjah led them all into the library. Several of the chairs were already filled, with Jerry and Elaina sitting at the distant head of the table, and all faces but Elaina's turned toward them. The expressions were grave and appraising, and Arby realized that out in the sun, in the company of the nymphs, life had seemed for a time pleasant and almost normal.

"The Seeker is still on the road," Jerry said. He hitched himself up in the chair, trying to sit higher, and it was easy to foresee the day when he'd need a booster chair to run a meeting. "Guess we should start without him."

"Could it be hard to anticipate his votes, ever?" Helayjah asked. He ushered Arby to a chair at the foot of the table.

Arby sat. "Votes on what?"

"On anything whatsoever," Elaina said.

On the right side of the table, a hard-faced man with shoulder-length blond hair said, "And what's wrong with that?"

The nymphs found seats to the right, Selky sitting down beside the blond man. Helayjah slid into a chair to Arby's left, a few seats down the table. "Apart, he means, from the fact anyone can predict his moves, mmm?"

"People, people," Jerry said. "Let's say hi before we let it rip, okay?" There was a murmur of assent. "Allow me to perform some introductions…"

Nearest to the head of the table on the left sat a Hispanic woman in a huge lacy peasant blouse. Her girth more than filled the chair. "This is Zeah," Jerry said. "She's into making things grow." The smile she gave was motherly, but her eyes gleamed with intelligence rather than warmth.

Beside her sat Xochipilli, wearing a T-shirt that emphasized his stocky build. "Xochipilli you know," Jerry said. "I don't think you've met his daughter, Sylvia Divinorum." The dark young woman beside Xochipilli looked like a model from a Visit Enchanting Mexico poster until she glanced at Arby and her eyes glittered like green tinsel.

Between Sylvia and Helayjah sat a man identified as Gareth—"Yet another Mage," Jerry said—who had the mannerisms and clothing of a professor emeritus of dead languages.

On the right side of the table, nearest Elaina, Jerry introduced Raisa, the woman Arby had seen from afar on the path. She was a raven-haired, pale-skinned, slender young woman who would have been the pride of any gathering of modern Goth-girls. The red of her lips was the only color in a study in black and white, and Arby was reminded of the Queen from *Snow White.*

The blond man—though on closer inspection, Arby saw that his yellow hair was woven with gray—was introduced as Hermod. The man gave a curt nod. The acknowledgment showed an element of challenge; add a butch haircut and he could have been a Marine sergeant.

"You already met the Selkie and Lacerta of the Rocks—fast work, ladies—so you're the only one left. Folks: Rainchild Bounty Keeling, Arby, the Jester, the Falling One, The Fool."

Gareth cleared his throat. "And are we assured of his identity? Have the proofs been submitted, the Aspect, the Acts, the Associations, all been examined?"

Jerry and Elaina both made affirmative sounds, and Xochipilli said, "No problem."

"Then I feel I ought to note," Gareth said, "with all due respect to our new guest, that he can't really be described as a Hero, and that we can't really count his arrival here as a step in the right direction, but rather a step backward."

Xochipilli blew out a dismissive puff of air. "C'mon, grandpa. He may not be a big plus, but he ain't a big minus, either. I mean, no offense, but what do those three girls over there bring to the party, other than improving the scenery?"

Selky and Lacerta looked amused, but Raisa glowered across the table.

"I beg to differ," Gareth said. "Your friend here actually is, to use your words, 'a big minus.' Von Fleischer knows we went to some pains to rescue him; ergo, he is valuable; ergo, he is a threat."

Jerry said, "He's right about that. This could be the change that makes him come after us full force."

"So let him." Hermod planted his forearms on the table. "We've played defense too long. Let's kill him, before he kills us all."

"Killing his physical body," Elaina said, "doesn't eliminate him."

"Gets him the hell off this plane," Xochipilli said. "Slows down his growth, too."

"And then what?" Elaina asked. "'Kill him?' You assert that this is a plan?"

"It's a start," Hermod said.

"He says a start, a beginning," Helayjah, said, "but does he say the beginning of what? Beginning of the end, perhaps, mmm?"

"Hermod's right," Selky said, and the whole table stopped short to stare at her, as though her viewpoint were a surprise. She seemed to shrink at the sudden attention, but said, in a smaller voice, "I can't live without the sea forever. It's death here, too. Just a slower one."

Raisa spoke for the first time, and her voice was a smooth velvet thing that stroked the ears of the listeners. "You all have your worshippers and acolytes, but mine come to me one at a time. I honor you for giving me refuge"—she glanced at Jerry, and he nodded—"but I had already set my heart on leaving this place, be the risk what it may. Despite all its comforts, La Lune has become for some of us little more than a prison." Her apple-red lips widened in something that approached a smile. "Though I hate to agree with Selky on any matter, great or small, I think we need to act."

"The girls have all the balls in this outfit," Hermod said. "I say we suck it in and roll the dice. The Fool here may not be a real Hero, but he has powers. Maybe enough to tilt the balance." He turned to Arby. "What do you say, pal? You with me?"

Jerry said, "He's got squat so far. Hasn't recovered his lives, much less learned how to use his Talent."

"All the more reason, I think," Elaina said, "that we should lay out a plan and a schedule, and—"

Sylvia spoke for the first time, and her voice was a small, clear thing. "I can give him his lives back. In less time than a breath, less time than it takes to jump in a pool of water."

"*Icy* water," Jerry said. "If he dips a toe in first, here's betting he backs off."

"Sylvia could take him to his Talents, too," Lacerta said.

"And maybe kill him doing it," Xochipilli said.

Arby leaned forward in his chair and all eyes shifted to him. "Can someone please, please back up and explain? I want to help. And I saw things last night that scared me. But I'd like you to get it into your heads that *I have no idea what you're talking about.*"

There was a brief silence that was broken when Jerry said, "Yeah, okay. When you come back to the world without having prepped for dying in the previous life, the first thing you need to learn is who you've been, everything you've been. That's usually a matter of months to years. And then you need to do work on the Other Side, to sort of, I don't know, *mesh*"—he pointed the splayed fingers of one hand at the other and then locked the two hands together, his child's fingers interdigitating like the teeth of a gear—"the power over there with who you are. Usually takes years. Syl here can make it happen mucho quicko, but..."

"...but it's dangerous," Arby said. "How so?"

"Reliving your lives is just uncomfortable. Regaining your power, well…you could die."

To counter Jerry's grave tone, Arby chuckled, though he didn't feel that amused. "All this talking about dying and being reborn makes that a little less scary, though, doesn't it?"

The room sat silent. Xochipilli said, "You misunderstand, Little Brother." He held up a fist, knuckles toward Arby, and then let it roll open into a flat palm, as if something sat there on display. He pursed his lips and let out a sharp puff of air, blowing an imaginary pile of dust from his hand. "He means the real death. He means forever."

In a distant part of the house, dishes clattered. Selky studied her fingernails. Almost everyone else studied Arby, some openly, some stealing glances.

"I've been getting twangs," Elaina said.

"For some time now," Jerry said. "He's near the gate."

Lacerta pushed her plate of sticky fruit over toward Arby. "Keep your strength up?" she asked. When he shook his head, she displayed the plate to the others. "Anybody need a snack?" Most responded with polite murmurs, but Hermod and Raisa curled their lips in revulsion.

Feet pounded up the steps to the mansion and across the deep porch. The front door opened and slammed, and then the library door flew wide.

The man who stood there was dressed in safari khakis. His figure was spare, almost skeletal, and the sheen of perspiration he wore made his black skin glossy. Wide nostrils flared at each breath. The man pulled the door shut and threw himself into a chair near Arby. "So, you're the man I looked all over the Middle East for, huh?"

"Rainchild Bounty," Jerry said, "meet the Seeker."

The Seeker looked across the table. "Hey, Lace—you mind?" He leaned forward and dragged her plate to him, then stuffed a trio of apples slices into his mouth. "Mmm," he said, crunching away, "sweet stuff." After swallowing, and licking his fingertips, he asked Arby, "So—your mom the type to say she's going somewhere and then not show up?"

Crystal was exactly that type, but Arby felt in his bowels that this wasn't one of the times she'd taken a side trip. "Why?"

"She's not where she said she was going. Nobody saw her leave work, either. I can't find a trace of her anywhere—and I'm good." He grinned at the crowd around the table and then looked back to Arby. "Oh, I know what you're saying—*C'mon, a blind chick found me before you did*. I admit, I am a guilty man, but I gave her the easy duty on that one."

"Where's my mother?" Arby said, trying to keep his voice from trembling.

"If nobody's heard from her yet, then I'm guessing with Mr. Nice."

"And Liz? Where's Elizabeth West?"

"Another good question. Sudden vacation in Cabo, according to her law firm. I don't know where she is—maybe shacked up with some guy down in Mazatlán—but she sure ain't in Cabo San Lucas. I've got her scent so solid I could sniff her out through three feet of concrete, and she wasn't nowhere near Cabo." The Seeker lifted a strawberry to his mouth and crushed it between his teeth. "You're pretty careless with your womenfolk, aren't you?"

"Fuck you," Arby said.

"Just trying to keep it light."

Jerry coughed. "Well, I can see where this is going. The Fool will want us to open negotiations with von Fleischer. And von Fleischer will—"

"No!" Hermod banged the table with a hard fist, and the plate in front of the Seeker jumped. "How far will you let this go? Will you let him go join von Fleischer? Throw another shovel of dirt on our grave? I'll kill him first, and I'll—"

Elaina's voice sliced through his words. "Touch him and it will be you that dies."

Then it seemed that everyone began yelling, until Arby stood up and shouted, "Shut up! Will you *just...all...shut...up?*"

In the silence that followed, Hermod's chair groaned and then the legs snapped in two with a whip-crack, dropping the man onto the floor in a pile of broken wood. Hermod's eyes, now only level with the tabletop, darted back and forth across the faces that stared at him, and as Helayjah and Jerry began to laugh, his face reddened in anger. When Selky and Lacerta joined in, he struggled to his feet and kicked the shattered chair behind him. "This is an example of his mighty powers? Within La Lune we have our vows, but to bait me so is a dangerous venture!" His fists clenched at his sides, he turned to face Arby down the table, and although the others quieted, Helayjah laughed even louder. "Perhaps our new Hero—"

Elaina said, "He has no control over it, Hermod. He doesn't know he did it."

"My honor demands an apology!"

"Back off on the *Beowulf* stuff and I'll give you one," Arby said. "I'm sorry if I insulted you, and I'm sorry that I don't know what's going on here. But I'm willing to do what it takes to find out." He leaned his palms onto the table. "Sylvia? Just tell me what I need to do."

"Regaining his lives is enough for now," Elaina said. "Reintegrating his Talents should be done in the normal fashion, with training, and—"

"—and maybe *I* should make that decision!" Elaina's head turned to his voice as though she were staring at him from behind her sunglasses. "Let me regain, relearn, whatever it is, and then let me decide, okay? Because, I may not know much, but that doesn't mean that I'm going to let my future be determined by committee."

In the astonished pause that followed, Zeah spoke for the first time. "Has anyone noticed," she asked, "that the boy now makes us thirteen?"

"Thirteen," Raisa said, and then added in a greedy voice as though she were ordering her favorite dessert, "Death."

"'Death' of course, seldom means 'death' *per se*," Gareth said, "but more often a fundamental transformation, or the establishment of a directed power circle, as in a traditional coven, or Christ and his twelve disciples—"

"—yeah, and in a lot of cases," Hermod said, "it just means *death*." He pushed more splintered wood away from his feet and backed up to lean against the wall of books with his arms crossed, his biceps bulging. "Well? What now?"

Elaina said, "I suppose that is up to Arby."

22

The Old Asp Business

The thick carpet of Sylvia's chamber, deep in the red-rock caverns of Xochipilli's lair, was strewn with a chaos of cushions. Four sconces, one on each wall, supported terra-cotta lamps, and as Sylvia coaxed each into flame the brightness rose and fell in a slow rhythm that Arby thought might be the pace of her own breath. Dark-green vines twined up the walls almost to the smooth roof of the cave. "Sit," she said, her voice gentle, "get comfortable."

Arby lowered himself to the floor and sat crosslegged on a cushion. He found his hands were shaking. "How do plants grow in here? I mean, no light, and—"

"No matter where you are, there's always light nearby," she said, and joined him on the floor, mirroring him, their knees almost touching. "Give me your hands."

He offered them, and she gathered them up in both of hers and rested them on her crossed calves. Her touch was gentle but confident, a mother's touch, and he wondered how such a young woman could seem so maternal. "I don't see how you can be Xochipilli's daughter. I mean, he's only a little older than me, and when—"

Three of the oil lamps guttered and went dark. Sylvia released his hands and climbed to her feet. "It's natural to be scared—but please don't do that."

As she set about lighting them again, he began to protest that he hadn't done anything, but she said, "This first time, there is no danger. Just truth… But that's scary enough, right?" He heard the puff of her breath as she blew out a match. "Being alive is one long process of denial." She sat and pulled his hands back into hers. "Now relax and let it happen."

Uncle Hawk had often told him that the best way to relax was to overtense first, so Arby tightened all his muscles and then consciously let them go limp. "Let what happen? What is it?"

"First you will see parts of lives of who you have been. When you have passed through those you will see yourself within others—you will see people who have adopted the principle you represent. Because in some sense, you are those people as well."

"And what do I do?"

She smiled, showing her teeth for the first time, and he was startled to see that their whiteness held an unmistakable tint of pale, lunar green. His face must have shown something, because her smile widened and his eyes glittered with amusement. The silver-green of those eyes, he now saw, were veined with darker green, and serrated around the edges, as though her black pupils were wreathed in tiny leaves. "There are many ways," she said, "but the easiest is to kiss me."

Kissing her was easy enough to do—even with green teeth, she was beautiful—though putting mouth to mouth was awkward with both of them sitting crosslegged. Her lips were soft and welcoming, and she opened her mouth and invited him inside. His tongue touched hers for a few moments, and then she eased herself away.

He sat back, dizzy from the sudden kiss, and his tongue seemed to crinkle as if he'd taken a mouthful of salt. The taste was like nothing he'd ever encountered. "Bitter," he said.

"Truth always is, at first. An acquired taste."

He shivered. The taste in his mouth turned to a kind of numbness in his lips and gums and cheeks, and he wanted to poke himself, jab himself, hurt himself, somehow retrieve a normal sensation, even if that sensation were pain. "Cold," he said, and his teeth started chattering.

"Not cold," she said, "*aloneness*. But it isn't true. I'm with you, and will stay with you. In fact, you will be inside me."

She smiled again, and the leaves in those green eyes swelled and then the pupils gaped and merged into one black tunnel. That blackness received him with a terrifying neutrality, and the tunnel twisted sideways and sealed him off from the world of the living.

It was an ancient land, now forgotten, near Sumer, and he had been the son of a successful farmer. When the spreading kingdom nearby demanded tribute, he had protested, but had gone along with the majority who decided to buy off their warlike neighbors. Years of increasing demands, and then a bad harvest: they were left with too little to both eat and pay tribute. The warrior king insisted.

He had raised an army of farmers, and they fought—fought with farm tools and clubs against the armor and arrows and swords and horses of their neighbors. And, against all odds, battles often went their way; for a time, it seemed that the gods favored them. Unexpected rain muddied the battlefield, causing the enemy cavalry lines to stumble and collapse; sudden outbreaks of shitting sickness and fevers rushed through the enemy camps. Yet with time, greater might and better weapons won out, and even the most foolish and battle-hungry saw defeat looming.

The community was split; some argued for capitulation, even if their children would starve, while others planned to load everything they could carry onto wagons and cross the hills to seek a new life in the lands where some of their people had gone before.

A hundred under his command had defended a narrow gorge that led to the pass, guarding the refugees. Men who hadn't shed a tear when their wives and children headed into the hills wept like women as they watched their enemy approach across their farmlands, setting fire to field and homestead, and when the enemy arrived they fought with the fury of final despair.

Him they captured, and took back to their mud-walled, dun-colored capital. Their god-king was merciful; their god-king respected a warrior who fought so long and so hard with so little. He could return to his lands, could rule there as a satrap under the god-king. All he had to do was kneel, to bow his head…

There was a woman he had loved, who had fled with the refugees; he could bring her back. He could repair the damage that had been done to the farms, could help protect his people from the rapacity of these strangers. He could live.

Yet he couldn't do it.

They threw him to the tiled floor of the palace and forced his head down to the floor before the god-king's throne, one of the guards pressing a sandaled foot onto his neck.

An earthquake shook the palace. The god-king and his priests chattered fearfully in some tongue he didn't understand, but in the end the guards dragged him to a deep, dry cistern in an old part of the building and hurled him down the shaft.

His body smashed onto the sharp rocks and he cried out. The circle of light above vanished as he heard the deep-throated screech of the heavy stone cover dragging over the mouth of the well.

No feeling in his feet; no sensation from the waist down. When he tried to move he found he was broken. Each breath gurgled in his chest where shattered ribs had pierced his lungs, and his broken body shuddered with aimless efforts at motion. Alone in the dark, choking on his own blood, at last he surrendered, and mourned his life as it fled: so stupid, so short, so sad, so precious.

She led them to the outriggers at midnight, her followers taking only what they could carry on their backs: dried fish, dried fruits, a few tools, rolls of woven mats and cloths, nets filled with coconuts, some root crops. The boats had been stocked with gourds of fresh water in the twilight, but the piglets that were usually loaded for long sea voyages were absent, as their squeals would have been a sure alarm to the *ali'i* who ruled the island.

On that night as on many the rulers were drunk on *'awa*, soporific on its own, but that evening compounded with a fragment of liver she had cut from the little spotted pufferfish, *o'opu hue*. A larger piece would have killed. The deaths would not have stayed her hand; but a larger piece would have left a telltale scent in the drink.

For two generations the invaders had ruled over the village, taking the best of everything for themselves, slaying or mutilating any who opposed them. That she was a woman was a blessing, for no one noticed that she gathered followers; and she was viewed as touched by the gods, a madwoman, because when she became excited, or angry, the unexpected might happen—nuts might fall from trees, or a fire might spill from its hearth, or a knife might twist in the hands of its user, the obsidian blade springing free from the wooden hilt.

They were accomplished fishermen, her followers, but their way was that of caution and prudence, not fast blue-water sailing. In the dawn light two days out, the boats of the pursuers appeared on the horizon behind them. The wind favored her enemies—from the side it made for a slow, tacking chase, and the pursuers were the better sailors with the better craft.

She prayed for help, but none came; she prayed for a whale to capsize the boats behind them. Yet they gained. She cried out and threw herself to the deck in despair, cursing her gods.

And then the wind shifted round the quarters, blowing cold from the south, and the seas rose. The sky darkened and clouds clawed their way across the sky. Soon her people had to lash themselves to the boat to avoid being tossed into the seething waters.

All through the night it blew, a thrashing rainy storm that tore away all hope of navigation, a storm that left men, women, and children weeping and shivering as they clung to whatever handholds could be found, and in the early morning hours the thunder arrived, the shouts of the gods bellowing in their ears, the crack of lightning blinding.

In the wet gray dawn the storm seemed to pass, but the wind and a heavy following sea chased them onward, and they ran before it without any plan but to keep themselves afloat.

Three more days of hard running, and she knew what her people were thinking: they were far beyond the grasp of the *ali'i* , but also lost in the vastness of the open ocean. The sky cleared to an empty, blazing blue, and the wind deserted them, leaving them drifting on a current that stretched to the horizon on either hand. They were short on rations and conserving their water when a lone, low cloud, flat and thin like a *paki'i* fish, showed to the northwest—a cloud that hovered over an unseen island like a protecting hand.

She died young from childbirth in that life, four years after they made landfall, young but revered by villagers three times her age. The love and devotion of her followers only made it harder to depart.

There were a dozen more lives, and in many he was raised knowing his true identity. In one, as the barbarians approached to sack his city he buried occult wisdom in the designs of decks of playing cards. In another, she broke with an all-powerful Church and established a community based on true Christian principles—a community that was slaughtered. In the Himalayas he taught the act of rising on the planes through alignment of body with spirit, opening a new path bypassing the ritualized worship of the gods. In the highlands of the Andes, she discovered the sacred cactus, and the visions it brought destroyed the authority of the brutal religion that ruled there. In the meager forests of Siberia she allowed herself to be torn apart by demons so that her reconstituted body could return as a healer, and teach others to take the same path.

Yet in other lives he grew up knowing only that he was different, and that "luck," of both good and bad flavors, followed him. He led a people across an opening passage in a wilderness of glaciers, and on to a paradise beyond. She learned, by eating them herself, that the bitter leaves could heal many illnesses, and that there were strong medicines in many of the plants that grew in the wilds of hill and canyon. He buried seeds in the ground outside their camp and stayed behind, tending them, while his tribesmen laughed and moved on with the seasons. He saw the horse in its sea of grass and knew that he could sit astride its mighty back, partake of its speed and strength, and be one with it...

A dozen more lives, a dozen more deaths.

Ah, the whole death thing. Humans have it bad: conscious of death their entire lives, but needing to ignore it to go on. Every man's death is a constant, silent companion, unacknowledged but always taking up space in the room, so that a dinner for ten must seat twenty. Lay down with your lover and there are four in the bed.

The bards lie: there are no good deaths. There are good lives, and there are good moments; there are deaths for good reasons, and there are deaths that offer the good of release from tremendous suffering, yet death itself is still a moment of immense sadness, because to die is to fail.

The problem is, we live in animals, and the animal imperative is to survive. Oh, there is courage and self-sacrifice and a whole host of high and blessed motives, in animals as in us; and in us there are also the miasmas of despair, hopelessness, and uncontainable anger. Any of these can impel us to actions that lead to our death. But in those last moments the animal cries out against what is happening, because it is the job of the animal to go on.

The sadness of that final surrender may be poignant or wrenching or merely regretful, but for its brief time that sadness is the most intense of emotions.

Reliving a death is devastating. Reliving a dozen or more is a kind of hell.

If you want to poke your nose into the muddy waters of past lives, stick to the bits where you are Queen of the May, or Washington crossing the Delaware, or Cleopatra in the early days of Antony.

But try and avoid the old asp business. You won't like it much.

And finally he was Arby. Intelligent but dreamy, vague, and oddly stubborn. The boy who made things break, the child who made plans go awry. And always the reluctant one, refusing to join in the activities of his large, loose family—smiling shyly and refusing to dance, refusing to carry candles into the dark and welcome the solstice, refusing to try the newest massage technique or chanting method or drug or breathwork or evocation process or meditation method. Always the kid with the book on nature or geology or chemistry, off alone or at best around the fringes, smiled at and about by the adults.

Then school, and college, and women, and jobs, and finally Liz and his attempt at a normal, stable life.

A strange life, good in many ways, frustrating in many others, but now, seen as clips from just another life, it seemed rudderless and stupid, aimless and pathetic. He'd spent the last year, no, the last two, wallowing in self-pity over the loss of something he could never have had, and yet he tried to…to what? What had he been thinking?

He awoke sobbing in Sylvia's arms, lying on his back across her lap, and he realized he must have been crying through most of the visions.

"Calm now," she said, and petted him, "you are still here. The matter of dying is never easy, but it is part of regaining your wisdom."

Even in his tears this sounded ridiculous, and he laughed, coughing and snorting. He sat up, wiping his face.

"What is funny?"

"Regaining my wisdom? Where's that going to come from?" He laughed and then had to sniff. "I'm The Fool, remember?"

"Mmm. And as William Blake said, 'If the fool would persist in his folly he would become wise.'"

The quotation seemed too apt and too neat, but he couldn't summon a retort.

"I see now why you have been so confused all of these years," she said. "Your nature is to rebel or move in contrasting ways, but you were raised in the heart of the counterculture with no knowledge of who you are. How to rebel against rebels? So you rebelled by trying to be normal—what the psychologists call reaction-formation against your family system."

He sniffed. "Well, thank you Doctor Freud." He climbed to his feet even though he felt shaky. "I need some air."

"But you aren't done. You didn't even see the parts of yourself that live on in normal people… It would make you feel better, I think."

"Then I'll come back."

He started from the chamber, but her voice stopped him. "A word to the wise—or to The Fool, as it may be. If you happen to encounter

Raisa while you're out there, resist the urge to visit with her. She has poor self-control. She'll take you right to the bottom of her pond, even though she knows better."

Pond? "I promise not to go near the water," he said, and shuffled off down the red sandstone tunnel.

Outside Xochipilli's caverns the day was still bright. A cluster of worshippers on the hilltop saw him and dropped their eyes in deference, and he felt irritated—irritated at them for their behavior, irritated at Xochipilli for encouraging it.

The brown dog sat curled near the slope, and it rose, stretched, and sauntered over to visit, its whole hindquarters wagging with its tail. He roughed its head and slapped its side a few times, and then he headed down the trail with the dog trotting beside him.

Halfway down the trail he sat where the saddle was undermined on its western slope. Another century or two, he thought, with a few decent rainstorms, and the rock would spall away into the western valley, and the saddle would erode quickly. This trail wasn't built to last.

But what was? He felt hollowed out with grieving for his lives, and by the deeper certainty that his life with Liz had been a sham, a retreat, an impossible fantasy. Oh, he'd loved her. But loving someone didn't mean you could have a life with them, and he saw that now, and more tears of self-pity welled in his swollen eyes.

Absently he petted the dog, and its tail thumped in the dust. He glanced down at it and was pierced by what he saw—an animal sprawled by his side, happy to be in the sun, happy to be with his adopted master, happy to be fed and alive and healthy, and apparently not wanting anything more, and Arby felt a deep shame at his own ingratitude to life.

A pair of ravens drifted on the wind high above the valley floor, dipping and gliding, playing with the invisible forces of the air. He rubbed the dog behind its ears. "Time to go back, I suppose."

Heading back up the trail, he saw the gray wolf trotting through the trees down the eastern slope, paralleling their track.

It came easier thereafter, because he encountered only fragments of lives, and those lives were not his own but rather moments Sylvia claimed he had inspired. He hurled rocks at an advancing Chinese tank; she painted pictures no gallery would show. He crossed a cold sea clinging to a log; rose above the ancient Incan plain in a cotton balloon filled with hot air, created a language that never existed for the purpose of writing a story, rowed solo across the Pacific. On a chill coast along the North Sea he became the man who first ate an oyster. Uncountable times he or she set out for a new land, seeking a new home for a family. He wandered jungles in search of rare flowers, or ancient knowledge, or the headwaters of rivers. She created a way of leaching the poisons from acorns, from manioc, from the ancestors of tomatoes. They bred a hundred new animals and a thousand new plants. They made nonsense rhymes and fashioned pointless games and told a million stories. Innumerable inventions that didn't work, and a handful that did…

His mind raced by these images and impressions as though they were boulders he passed as he rushed down a rapids, the experiences solid yet blurred by the speed and commotion, until at last Arby shot past the last of them and found himself floating in a calm place. His lost lives still ached inside him, yet he felt at peace, content merely to drift.

And then he remembered Crystal and the fact that she was missing. And Liz: even if he had been absurd to try and be part of her life, he still couldn't let harm come to her. When he awoke he found himself sitting, gazing at a spring-green field that gradually resolved into Sylvia's botany-laden eyes. He sighed. "What next?"

"Next, you need to stop and think. Because, unlike some, I am reluctant to see you go on to the next stage."

"I agree," Elaina said, and he was startled to see that both she and Helayjah were in the room, sitting on cushions. "It would be far less dangerous to undertake a course of training, no matter how accelerated, than to seek this bridge."

"What bridge?"

"I can't tell you in detail," Sylvia said, "because it is a thing of your own, not mine. But if you choose to travel this road, you begin very far inward, very high on your own interior Tree, on the path that connects Binah to Chokmah, and—"

"I have no idea what you're talking about."

Elaina said, "There is no telling how it will appear in your personal inner space, but it will be the highest, most abstract level of manifestation. Constriction and form will have to contend with infinite space, and you will have to find a path between the two."

"I don't get it."

"You don't need to understand," Sylvia said. "Your challenge will be to find your way back. It might be the matter of a moment. It might be never." She sighed. "I can tell you only this—the path is walked by being your true self, by being you."

"And training instead? How long would that take?"

Elaina and Helayjah exchanged a glance. Helayjah said, "A year, perhaps, should he be lucky? Two, three, or more?"

"I don't have time."

"Arby," Elaina said, "if our enemy has your mother, or your… friend, we can open negotiations, play for time, while you learn your skills—"

"You're the one who showed me his world on the Other Side, took me to see his true nature. And you think I should leave people I love with him?"

"You can't help anyone by killing yourself."

"And apparently I can't help anyone unless I take that risk." He turned to Sylvia. "What do I do?"

"Please…" Elaina said. "Consider for at least a few days. To push ahead like this is foolish."

He laughed. "Did I just hear my name? If the trick is to be myself, then it seems like I should jump on the slide now." To Sylvia, he said, "And—"

She held her palms upward and tilted her head in a display of resignation. "You'd better lie down and make yourself comfortable."

He lay back, and Elaina knelt by his side, opposite Sylvia. "Arby… Rain. Please reconsider."

He sat up, took Elaina's face in his hands and kissed her full on the mouth, taking his time. She didn't resist, and when he released her, her face wore a look of astonishment. "Always wanted to do that," he said, and lay back down. "Off we go."

Sylvia leaned forward. "All you need to do is find your way back here. Another kiss. This one won't be fun." She bent her head down to kiss him and her hair fell like a thick black veil, cutting the two of them off from the world.

As the bitter fluid numbed his mouth, the phrase "kiss of death" occurred to him, but by then there was no one around to share the joke.

23

In Hamster City

The sky above him was a uniform gray, yet somehow distorted, as though he stared up through a bubble. Arby rolled onto one elbow. The sensation of looking through a bubble was not an illusion: he lay on the bottom of a giant transparent sphere, a bubble perhaps five times his own standing height. He tapped at the glossy surface. Glass? Plastic? Cold, whatever it was.

He stood and scanned the surroundings. There was only one view: a caramel-colored plain below and a gray sky above, and both stretched forever until they met at the horizon in any direction. Featureless and homogenous, and after a few moments of gazing, all sense of distance vanished, leaving the impression of two horizontal stripes of paint, gray above dun. After turning about a few times he felt dizzy.

He wasn't sure what he'd been expecting—dragons, maybe?—but it wasn't this. Elaina said the Inner Planes were fluid, and could be manipulated. Fine. How about a tree, a pebble, a blade of grass? Frowning, he concentrated on his wish—just a little rock, the smallest bit of gravel on that plain outside...

Nothing. He knelt to feel the glassy surface again, and then banged on it with a fist. It sat there, inert and infuriating.

How had Elaina done it? By seeking increasing congruency, allowing new elements of what she sought to manifest around a corner, beyond a tree, somewhere just for the moment out of sight.

But there were no corners here, and there was nothing hidden. Nothing visible either, for that matter. In fact, he realized, his throat tightening, there was nothing here but nothing.

Okay. Nothing was happening. Tons of nothing, so there was, what: nothing to be afraid of? Calm down. The bubble was something, not nothing, and a sky and ground existed, even if they looked like something extruded in sheets by DuPont Chemicals.

Could be worse. At least there was no immediate danger. Unless, of course, the oxygen inside this thing were limited. Did he need to breathe in this world?

Really, he ought to have spent a little more time brushing up on the rules before he came here. If there were any rules.

He slapped at his pockets, searching for keys or a comb, something hard to test if the surface of the globe were scratchable. Only then did he realize he was arrayed in the clothing of his Aspect—the black-and-green tunic, the chartreuse hose, the yellow slippers. No pockets there.

Clenching his fists, he tried to summon strong anxiety, or anger, or fear, the kinds of emotions that so often led to things breaking or malfunctioning, but the world around him refused to respond.

He hopped up and down, slamming his feet onto the floor, chanting, "Damn damn damn *damn damn*!" The sound of his own voice echoed in his ears, but the giant bubble encasing him seemed impervious to anything he did—smugly impervious, he thought.

Crosslegged on the bottom of the globe, he pondered. Was this it? If he waited, would something change, or would he just sit here for eternity? Would the sun set and rise, or would it be forever late afternoon? For that matter, was there a sun at all? The illumination seemed to come from everywhere and nowhere, and he cast no shadow.

If this were some test designed to drive him mad, given a little time it would succeed brilliantly. Anything—a junkyard, a horrible slum, a stinking pond filled with diseased fish—anything with variety or texture or irregularity was paradise compared to this bland, complacent smooth infinity.

Perfect homogeneity. Or so it seemed. But was it? Take a common drinking glass, seemingly perfect, and plunge it from hot water into cold. Invisible imperfections would make themselves known as the glass shattered along hidden lines of stress.

On his knees he felt around the base of the globe, searching for even the tiniest variation, and when that was done he began working his way up the walls. What the hell, maybe he'd find a door, an invisible door in the invisible bubble…

Climbing up the side on elbows and knees, he lost traction and slid back down to the bottom. The globe rocked ever so slightly.

At least it was something. He stood and ran partway up the side and hurled himself at the wall, and the bubble rolled.

It took some time to perfect the technique, but once inertia was overcome, he could march along, rolling the ball from the inside like the world's largest hamster globe. The ball could even be steered by stepping toward one side or another, though it required the least effort to move in a straight line.

Now if there were only somewhere to go. There were no coins to flip, so he closed his eyes and spun in circles until he fell down.

Then he stood up and followed his nose.

For the first hour or so it felt good simply to be moving, but eventually he realized that although he was moving, he wasn't really going anywhere. But, then, what were his choices? Rodents on exercise wheels and in globes weren't really going anywhere either. Welcome to Hamster City.

When he first saw a hint of brighter light off on the horizon to his left, he refused to believe in it, and kept moving straight ahead. But soon it was undeniable: he was casting a slight shadow off to his right.

More than the illumination itself, the shadow filled him with a giddy joy. An imperfection on the smooth caramel, a wobble, a bump, a pimple. He kept jogging along, glancing off to the shadow, and the shadow grew in density and texture. He wished it were bigger…and it began to swell.

He guided the globe to the right until the shadow ran off ahead of him rather than alongside, and concentrated on coaxing bits of it into solidity. Glancing behind him, he saw it was working: a thousand blackish lumps trailed the globe's path like droplets of pitch leaking from a hot asphalt truck.

Unbelievable. From out of nothing, form. From monochromatic haze, bulking irregular lumps.

How far could he take this? Was the world his to make?

Let there be…ummm…rocks and stuff.

His shadow widened and ran far out before the rolling globe, and the plain acquired texture, and the caramel became browns and reds and whites, intermingling to make speckled, incoherent ground, then a surface broken and fractured and eroded and torn, and boulders loomed alongside his path, and the globe sped along a dry, sandy streambed, with cliffs rising to the side, the globe rolling on its own now, running downhill faster than his legs could carry him, and he fell forward and was carried up the back wall and dumped on the floor, carried up and dumped again and again before he found that if he lay on his back and lifted his arms and legs he skidded along the bottom rather than being tossed.

Even skidding along was uncomfortable, though, as the streambed became rockier and the globe began to bounce, flinging him high only to thud on the spinning surface once more. "Ow!" he shouted. "What—*oomph!*—does it take—to make you break—*unnhh!*—anyhow?"

A boulder in the path of the globe tossed him high, and just ahead two pillars of stone jutted out from the canyon walls. He was flailing in midair when the globe hit the pillars and shattered. He flew between them with a thousand shards of glass racing alongside him like a flock of birds.

The canyon gaping beneath him could have swallowed the Grand Canyon without a burp.

There was one mad cartoon moment where he hung suspended there, surrounded by motionless daggers of glass, and it seemed that if he only spun his legs fast enough he could gain traction in the air and scramble back to the top of the cliff.

Then cartoons were banished in favor of vector mechanics, and his arc through space turned into an accelerating fall.

The glittering thread at the bottom of the canyon had to be a river, far, far below. But everything worked differently here, right? Maybe he should just wish for, oh, a flying carpet, or a giant eagle, or—

They told you that you could die here. Forever. It isn't a cartoon.

Thirty-two feet per second per second, the acceleration due to gravity. If gravity were the same here. But at some point his wind resistance would slow his fall, and he'd reach his ultimate speed, what the speed engineers aptly called the terminal velocity.

He spread his arms and legs like a skydiver and felt his descent slow. The heavy tunic helped, fighting the air, grappling with the crosscurrents. Reaching down his hands clutched the skirt of his tunic, spreading it like a sail, and his fall slowed even more—but not enough. He remembered being thrown down the dry well in one of his recovered lives, and if he hit even the surface of the water at this speed, he'd end up shattered again, choking on his own blood.

All his fear channeled into a force that swelled in his head and then burst through his eyes like discs of light.

They'd been there before, those discs of light, back when the Tall Boys had attacked Elaina in Rome. Before, they'd been involuntary; now they were urgent, yet he owned them. He knew he was tampering with the fabric of probability as surely as a baby knows it has clutched a desired toy in its chubby fist.

A current of air pushed him hard toward the nearest cliff-face. Yes! He blew more incandescent Frisbees from his eyes. Another current of air seized him like a Pacific breaker and slammed him into the canyon wall.

For a moment he toppled blind, and then he jerked to a stop. Something had hold of his waist, and his arms and legs dangled down like a rag doll. He peered up and to the rear, and saw that the skirt of his tunic had snagged on a protruding tooth of rock.

The irregular walls of the cliff accordioned in and out here, like a rough drapery, and he hung suspended at the forward tip of one fold. Jumbled geology in horizontal stripes—sedimentary beds, no doubt, and he could see that many layers were filled with layers of tumbled rocks embedded there like vast mosaics. Plenty of handholds, but handholds all too likely to pull right out of the sandstone matrix that encased them.

The climb down appeared to traverse the same breed of geology, but it stretched for a mile or two, a distance so great that his vertigo dissipated: the canyon wall no longer seemed vertical, but rather as though it were a jumbled plain. Perhaps that was the trick—turn gravity on its side and just hike down? He played with that notion, but a breeze rocked him where he dangled, and with a lurch his stomach told him that down was still down. Way down. That glittering thread of water at the bottom had to be wide as the Amazon.

There was little hope of climbing up to the rim, but no hope at all of climbing down to the bottom. And there was no point whatsoever in dangling face-down all day.

The protruding rock that had snagged his tunic must have been well-set into the cliff wall, since it had taken his weight plus the full momentum of his fall. So it was the most trustworthy element in his world at the moment. Before he could hesitate and rethink, he groped back above his hip with his left hand, found a solid edge beneath the stiff brocade of his tunic, reached closer to the cliff until he felt bare sun-heated rock, and spun himself hard, lifting with all his strength.

He clawed at the rock face with his right hand, pulling away handfuls of crumbling dirt, while hoisting himself. His feet kicked in empty space. For a moment his right hand clutched a solid rock and he heaved his whole body upward before the rock tore away and fell, but by then he was kneeling on the rock that had caught his tunic.

If he waited there, he knew he would freeze in terror, so he hauled himself to his feet, leaning in against the cliff. He was in a layer of breccia, a mélange of jumbled rocks mortared together by sandstone. About fifteen feet above him the cliff-face curved away from him, and there was no telling what lay above it.

Yes there was. Because that was up to him, right? He was creating this place…or rather co-creating it, or modifying it. Or perhaps changing what place he was in. Whatever the metaphysics of it, he knew there was a ledge up there, something solid, and wide enough to sit or even lie down, because that's what *had* to be there.

Scrambling upward felt like swimming against a current. Rocks tore away beneath his hands and feet, but at every moment he was anchored somewhere, and the speed and forward momentum of his spreadeagled panic took him to the ledge in a cloud of dust and grit that he spit from his mouth as he lay sprawled there gasping from the effort.

A perfect ledge: a layer of black, hard rock. His mind told him that in this environment it ought to be a shale, slick and none-too-hard, but to hell with that; he'd imagined it, and it could be basalt if he wanted it to be. It was his damned rock.

Maybe he should have imagined a subway station while he was at it. The ledge was a mere platform, safe enough, but the size of a typical suburban bathroom. He began to understand the limitations of imagination in this world: what you could create was limited by what you could believe, and his petty, ungenerous ledge was believable in this context.

He wished he was one of those people who could believe in the sudden descent of UFOs or guardian angels, or that he were in the company of someone who could believe in such things. But there was no one here. In fact, he hadn't seen a living thing in this world, not a plant or animal.

As if in answer, a hawk swooped past, carrying a stick in its beak. It vanished around the next fold in the great drapery of the canyon.

The ledge of hard rock disappeared to both sides of where he lay, cut away by erosion. Yet it continued there, a twin to what he stood on, where the hawk had flown.

No. Not a twin. A match as far as he could see, but beyond the next outcropping, he knew with conviction that the ledge continued and even widened, widened into something spectacular, something unimaginable. That old lust rose inside him, that greed for new places, to know what was over the next hill or across that stormy channel. Before he understood what he was doing he was on his feet, wiping the dust from his face. One hand came away muddied with blood and he realized he must have split his scalp when the wind slammed him against the cliff.

A leap of fifteen feet. Or was it twenty? He looked at the cliff-face where it folded inward. No ledge there, but perhaps he could inch across...

And perhaps he could flap his arms and fly across. He laughed, and heard his voice thin out and vanish in the vastness of the canyon. Ridiculous. Elaina hadn't wanted him to come here, and Elaina was perhaps the bravest, most ruthless person he'd ever met. He was already a dead man. Was that so bad? The lives he'd led were extraordinary, but what he remembered most from his time under Sylvia's first spell was the dying, over and over. If he met the final death here and now, would that be an occasion for mourning? Off the wheel and into the long deep emptiness... Maybe he should have listened to Crystal more when she was in her Buddhist phase.

Maybe he should have listened to Crystal more, period. In so many ways he had loved her and yet dismissed her, and now he ached to tell her what a great, erratic, wondrous mother she had been. He knew now that Sylvia was right in her psychobabble—he'd never been himself, only a self shaped by trying to be different from Crystal and her friends.

He'd see her again. He'd see her again or be damned, and he sure as hell intended to see what was around that next corner, to follow that ledge...

He backed up to the very edge of his smooth platform and ran and then leapt into space. The word he cried out was in a tongue dead for two millennia, but the FCC would have bleeped it without bothering to translate first.

Men have died for far less than the scene he found waiting. The ledge narrowed so he had to hug close to the cliff, but beyond the fold the ledge widened into an avenue wide and smooth as an interstate freeway. Black and smooth without being slick, it had been cut into the canyon walls by the hands of titans, and those same hands had sculpted the canyon walls. Dour figures sat there enthroned, a hundred yards high: long-faced, impassive forms like Easter Island icons who had regained their bodies. Rainbows of layered sandstone ran through the first dozen figures but then the colored slashes faded to gray and finally muted to the same black stone of the road.

The road led downward at a gentle slope, curving around the folds in the canyon walls, which now were set at stately distances. He walked a mile or more, marveling at the towering forms, each similar yet distinct. Their gazes were neither threatening nor welcoming: they were further removed from the concerns of individual humans than glaciers.

At last the wall of the canyon thrust out like the hip of an odalisque, and then swerved sharply to Arby's left, the broad road continuing around the curve. But there to the right a giant pillar of stone stood apart from the cliff-face, like a natural skyscraper rising up miles from the canyon floor. An iron bridge wide enough for a chorus line to kick-step their way across spanned the wide gulf and gave access to another black road that curved around the massive pillar and disappeared from sight.

A hawk swooped and cried out, and another followed, its harsh screech piercing the silence of the canyon. Giant egrets, the languorous flap of their white wings slow as the undulations of sea creatures, squawked as they passed. From farther off came another kind of cry, and Arby stopped and listened. It came again, and again, and then in a chorus, and there was no doubt. Somewhere out on that pillar, women were screaming in terror.

There is a thin line between foolish and idiotic.

Sylvia had told him that to find his way back to himself, he had to be himself. These screams smelled of a misstep, an error, a trap, but his heart told him he had to go, even if he had no idea what he was doing…and if that wasn't being himself, what was? He hoped it was merely Foolish.

He ran across the iron bridge. To either side a mighty chain had been strung between a line of jagged spikes, and a few of the spikes wore human skulls.

He reached the black road where it was cut into the side of the pillar of stone, and he realized the pillar was more massive than he had understood: its girth would encircle a few city blocks. A scream came again, where the road curved off to the right, and he jogged in that direction.

Ahead, the road was cluttered with debris, as though rocks had rained down from the cliff above, but when he padded up, panting, he saw the road was covered with battered armor: shields, helms, breastplates and other ironmongery, some smashed beyond recognition. Shattered bones protruded from crumpled metal.

Arby sighed. It seemed like a bad sign.

He gave the medieval junkpile a quick glance, and snatched up a dagger, the only unbroken weapon he saw.

The chorus of screams came once again, and this time one of them cut off in a cry of agony. He ran again, keeping close to the cliff, until the road swerved sharply inward, and there he paused and peered around the edge of the cliff.

The road widened there into a plaza of sorts, and the cliff-face had been smoothed like glass, except for a single, square, ironbound door, perhaps ten feet high, a hard stone's throw from where he stood. The door had been opened against the cliff, and dim light streamed out from the doorway. To the right of the doorway were the women, two of them, clad in white robes, shackled ankle and wrist to the smooth rock. A third set of shackles hung empty.

He took in all this in but a moment's glance, yet he didn't see the monster until it moved, because it was too big.

Its feet were planted at the edge of the black plaza, where the hard surface fell away into the canyon. Clawed three-toed feet bore a spur at the rear, like the slashing razor of a fighting cock, and the legs were yellowish and scaly. The creature stood six stories high, a dumpy, rough green body atop those stilt-like legs, like a titanic avocado supported on straws. Whatever it was, it stank.

Then the women screamed in unison, and its green-black neck snaked up into the sky, recurving into an *S* like a hundred-foot-high heron. The orange spike of a bill, long and squared like an obelisk, quivered for a moment, and then it struck, faster than any serpent.

Arby gasped in horror as it ripped one of the women from her shackles, and blood sprayed out from her wrists and feet. It snapped its bill into the air and caught her as she cartwheeled in the sky, opening its gullet and sucking her down that long throat. It flapped its stubby green wings in excitement, and then collapsed its neck down onto what passed for its shoulders, waiting, its bill compressed against its chest.

For a moment Arby was too stunned to move, but then he heard the remaining woman sobbing. *Now or never: you already stood here and watched one of them die.*

He ran out onto the plaza, waving his arms, shouting, "Hai! Hai!"

One glinting obsidian eye looked down at him and blinked. "Yeah, that's right!" Arby shouted. "You!" Step One: Distract it from its victim.

Only when its neck lifted high into the sky did he realize that he hadn't thought as far ahead as Step Two. So he attacked, charging toward its feet, waving his dagger and yelling, and he let all of the horror and fear he felt pour out through his eyes in yellow disks.

It struck, but its beak hit the ground in front of him, and he slammed into it as though he'd run full-force into a wall. It jerked its bill up, and the force of it sent him skidding across the road until he fetched up against the smooth face of the cliff, not far from the woman. He climbed to his feet. "It's okay," he said between pants, shaking his head to try and clear away the constellations that revolved in front of his eyes, "I'm here now."

High above, the monster shook its own head, and snapped its bill open and closed several times, as though testing for damage. It eyed him with malevolence, but then darted its head down in a strike that ended far short of where he stood, a poke at empty air. "C'mon!" he shouted, and then, some buried part of his brain recalling an exam question in a college botany or nutrition course, added, "C'mon, you, you…monounsaturated oily subtropical tree fruit!"

The bill jabbed down within a few yards of where he stood, and he realized that the next try would most likely nail him. Perhaps there was something through that door—a weapon or tool, or at least a moment to think.

He flooded the air with yellow discs and ran for the door in a cloud of flying emotion, but when he dared to look up he saw that the monster had tracked him and just before he reached the doorway that bill shot down at him like a javelin—

—and Arby, looking up, ran smack into the thick edge of the open door, and sat down hard, too stunned to move.

That cruel orange beak shot by a dozen feet ahead of him, aimed at where he ought to have been.

He clutched his head in his hands, no longer really caring if he were eaten alive: at least it would end the pounding ache in his skull where it had connected with the iron-strapped door. Only after a full minute of rocking in pain did he bother to look for the source of the ponderous thrashing, a commotion he felt as much as heard.

The monster's bill was wedged in the doorway, and it lay prone, struggling with its whole body to extricate its beak.

Cutting its treetrunk-thick throat with only a dagger was an ugly business, one that involved walking beneath its neck and sawing up and down with both upraised arms as its stinking green blood poured down on him. Severing its head would have taken days, like trying to cut an elephant in half with a paring knife, but cleaving through the thigh-diameter veins and arteries and opening the gullet was enough to kill it.

When at last its struggles ceased, the killer avocado bird lost form and evaporated, taking its odorous blood along with it. Although the maiden called out for him to release her from her shackles, Arby was unheroic enough to let her wait there while he sat down and rested his aching body.

He had worried that the shackles would require a key, but they were a simple system of latches. Simple, at any rate, if you could apply two hands to the problem.

The woman—the girl, he supposed, since she looked to be no more than a late teenager, though an overripe example of the species— had the flawless golden-haired beauty of a fairy-tale princess, and despite the wait while he gathered his strength and then fumbled with the rings that bound her to the rock, she behaved with perfect fairy-tale etiquette and swooned into his arms as soon as he freed her.

Laying her out on the ground didn't seem right, so he winced, hoisted her in his bruised arms, and carried her to the doorway. She felt good there in his arms; soft, with a feminine heft, yet not too heavy.

The room inside the cliff appeared to be a massive boudoir, with dressing tables, mirrors, and little gilt chairs, all the furnishings separated into something akin to rooms by silks dangling from the ceiling. The space was illuminated, but he saw no lights or lamps.

To the right, a silk-enclosed alcove held a wide bed, and he lay her down. As he did so, her eyes fluttered open and she reached up to touch his face. "You came," she whispered. "I prayed for someone to come… But look—you're hurt!"

In the space of a single breath she was on her feet and had seated him on the mattress and scurried off, leaving him to reflect on the thousand times he must have heard *But look—you're hurt* in movies. He had stumbled not only into Fairy-Tale Land, but also Cliché-Land, and then he realized that the two were probably one. Hadn't he just vanquished the giant Avocado monster and freed the maiden? Not quite as evocative as a dragon, perhaps, but in his view a hell of a lot scarier.

Plus, she was right. He was hurt.

She returned with a bowl of water, towels, and bandages, and did what was required with exquisite grace, stripping off his tunic and then tending his wounds with delicacy and firmness. His face she saved for last, inspecting every centimeter of his skin as she washed and dabbed, apologizing whenever he winced. Her breath seemed perfumed, and the tight hose he wore suddenly seemed tighter.

He shifted his hips to the side, and she glanced down at him and blushed, but said, "I want you, too." With that, she kissed him, a sweet kiss that grew less chaste as he responded.

He broke away, gasping. "I shouldn't do this. I—I'm on a journey, an important journey—"

"So important you can't rest here a while? So important that you can't—" She seemed as though she were about to cry, and she whispered into his ear, "Please. I want this so much." She opened her robe and led his hands inside. "You saved my life. How else can I ever repay you?"

The clichés were thudding down like coconuts during a tropical storm now, but they were clichés he wanted to hear, and her hot skin under his fingers made him delirious with desire. And, when he tried to think about it, what was wrong with this? He was supposed to be himself, wasn't he, not a monk?

She slipped the robe off her shoulders and rolled onto her back, pulling him alongside her. They kissed, and her hand led his down the taut skin of her belly. She pulled away from the kiss long enough to say, "Be gentle…it's my first time…"

He didn't know if it were the hesitation that came from thinking it might be true, or if it were simple cliché overload, but he eased himself back from her embrace. "We shouldn't…" he said, gasping for breath.

"No!…no, please, I *need* it!" She clutched at his shoulders and tried to pull him back to her, and he tried to push her away with gentle firmness, and she cried out, "No!" and dragged at him and in an instant she was no longer the golden-haired maiden but rather Liz—Liz with a raw red circle around her neck where Elaina's sword had chopped through it.

He shoved himself out of her embrace. Her body fell back and the head toppled from her neck, bounced once on the bed and then rolled onto the floor. Arby jumped to his feet and backed away.

The body—and it was undeniably Liz's body, down to the smallest freckle—pawed about on all fours and eventually groped over the edge of the bed and found her head. The body turned and sat facing him, legs parted and knees raised, and slammed down the head on the mattress like a figleaf. Liz's face glared up at him for a moment from between her own legs before the body hoisted it and ground the head down onto its neck with a horrible squinching sound.

Liz, or rather the succubus, stared, her mouth working as she searched for words, and finally settled on, "Crap."

"But…I saw Elaina kill you!"

"I know. Bitch."

"You aren't dead?"

The succubus's eyes grew wet, and Arby's heart ached; it might be another consciousness within, but those were Liz's eyes. "Would that make you happy?" the succubus asked. "Because it will happen soon enough. That little bit of blood I dabbed off you will keep me going a few more days, but this is the end for me. You rejected me, that bitch cut my head off, and Tanagrim threw me out to die, okay? Happy now?"

"You mean von Fleischer?"

"Whatever."

It might not be Liz inside that body—Liz would never sit unselfconsciously splay-legged like that—but it was disturbing and Arby knew it was affecting his judgment. "Look, you were this virgin princess a little while ago? Would you mind going back to looking like that? Or maybe Herbert Hoover or something?"

"I can't do guys—what do you think I am? And if I had any control, do you think I'd have lost it there when you shoved me a little bit? Do you think I'd have this cut mark around my neck? The princess thing took so much concentration. Probably used up three days of my last few days of life." She clambered to her feet on the bed and stepped down on the floor, and then stomped past him and sat down crosslegged, gazing out the front door onto the plaza. "There, now you don't have to see me. Satisfied?"

Annoyance and uncertainty warred inside him, accompanied by an obscure but rising sense of guilt. "Look. I'm not trying to be mean—"

She didn't turn around. "No? I just offered you everything I have, and you knocked my head off."

"I didn't intend to—"

"And then, back at your place that night, we were having a good time, and just when things were getting good—"

"You were trying to kill me."

"Oh, fine. Typical boy. *It'll only hurt at first. No, really, just relax, you'll learn to like it...*" She lifted her head by the hair and sat it down backward on her neck so it stared at him. "You can dish it out, but when the time comes, you can't take it, can you?"

"I would have been dead!"

"You would have loved it! You and your precious physical bodies." Angry tears ran down her cheeks and spilled onto her backbone. "Like you haven't been around the block a few times. How many times have you incarnated? A dozen? Two dozen?" She stood and spun her body, or Liz's body, in his direction, and then, realizing her head was still on backward, used both hands to jerk her head around to face him. "You see this?" She opened her palms and then slapped her chest to emphasize each word. "*This is it! This is all I get!*" She hunched forward, burying her face in her hands, and sobbed. "I don't even get…my own body…"

He'd always been helpless with crying women, and watching Liz cry was intolerable, even though the Liz he watched wasn't really Liz. He was beside her in a moment, lifting her to her feet. "Hey, hey, c'mon, it's not that bad…"

"It is! I haven't lived long, and now it's all going away…" She pushed him away and waved her hands at her body. "It doesn't have to be *her*, you know. I can be anyone, everyone. How about her?" Her form faded and then twisted into that of Raisa, and though he'd never seen her naked, he was certain that she would look like this, down to the dark pubic hair, the hard, tiny nipples… "Or *her*?" In the next few moments she ran through Selkie, Lacerta, Domenico's wife, Sylvia, Zeah, and he realized she must be riffling through images of every woman he'd seen in the last day, young or old, fit or fat… "Or is it her you want?" Elaina stood there, welcoming him. "Or maybe *her*?" She morphed into Crystal, a young, wet-lipped Crystal—

"Cut it out!"

In a moment she was Liz again, her head tilting on her neck, and she clamped it down with one hand and said, "I could make you so happy, so happy… I could be anyone you wanted me to be, everyone you wanted me to be… I'm dying…"

He carried her to the bed and dragged a sheet over her body. "Look, I don't understand. What can I do?"

She sniffled and wiped tears from her face. "The one you call von Fleischer banished me. Sent me out here to die of hunger." Her eyes, Liz's eyes, were puffy from crying but still beautiful. "I'm fading. In a day or two I won't exist. And I thought if I found you…" With a sudden motion she turned her head away and hid her face behind an upraised forearm.

"What?"

Her voice was tiny and muffled by her awkward position. "It's stupid."

Arby lifted her arm and turned her face back to him. "No. Tell me."

She gazed into his eyes. "I thought you might share." Again she looked away. "And I'm attuned to you, I could find you anywhere, and I felt you coming this way and I swapped with one of the princesses—hey, she was happy to do it, a day off from being bird food—and I thought maybe if I had another chance with you… Oh, I know what you're saying to yourself, she's just a succubus, never amount to anything. But if I only had an opportunity! I mean, all nine of the Muses started out like me, and more devas and demigoddesses than you'd imagine. Oh, sure, they don't talk about it now that they've made it…"

He held her hand. "I know you don't understand this, but I have no idea—no idea whatsoever—what you're talking about." She darted a glance at him as if she thought he might be making fun of her, and he said, "I'm on this journey to acquire my powers. I don't know where I'm going or what I'm doing or how any of this works. Least of all how to help you."

Her eyes widened. "You're telling the truth, aren't you?" She rolled out from under the sheet and knelt there, clutching his hand. "Look— no one worships me. No one even thinks about me. I existed only to find you, to pleasure you…and, yeah, I was supposed to kill you, too, but it's not because I don't like you. I mean, I love you, it's why I was created. But I could be more than that, and it would take so little. If you, you know, cut yourself shaving down on the physical"— she jerked her hand past her own smooth chin—"and thought of me when you did it, just that little sacrifice from down there, why it would keep me alive for months. Or if you"—her face assumed a salacious Liz expression—"if you were fantasizing about me when you, say, spread a little semen on the sheets some night—"

"I think I'm starting to get it, but—"

She held up her palms to forestall whatever she thought he was about to say, and talked rapid-fire, as if a game-show buzzer were about to condemn her to eternal silence. "And I know, it isn't fair to put it all on you and I wouldn't and if I just had a chance I'd earn worshippers, I would, I'd find a way and I'd do what I'm best at already, plus I'd make prophecy or bless their crops or inspire pop songs or something and I'd—"

"Listen!" He cradled her face in his hands, and since she was Liz it felt like the most natural thing in the world. "Listen. I believe you. I even like you. And if I ever get back to my real body, I'll go to the Red Cross and donate five pints of blood, thinking about you the whole time. I'll whack off every day and twice on Sundays and dedicate it to you. But I'm not there. I'm here. And I'm lost."

Her eyes blinked as if she were trying to maintain focus, and then her body fell sideways on the bed, leaving him holding her head in his hands. Her lips moved but no words came.

Awkward as a new father with a newborn, Arby leaned down and tried to fit her head onto her neck. Her own hands came up and helped, but they were weak. "I'm going..." she whispered.

"What can I do?"

"...share?..."

Perhaps it was a test, perhaps this was what he was sent here to do. Or perhaps this was unrelated to his journey, but it had everything to do with what he needed to do now. "Go ahead. Do whatever you need to do."

She reached up with a shaky hand and touched a scratch on his ribs, one she had tended earlier. Her sharp fingernail probed the tacky, immature scab there and then ripped it away, and her arms went around him in an embrace and she clamped her mouth to the wound and suckled like a baby at the breast.

He shivered and then felt a moment's dizziness, a lightheadedness that seemed to rise and fall in unison with his pulse. The succubus released her grip and sprawled back on the bed with a sigh. The cut in her neck healed, and then she grinned at him and transformed from Liz into the virgin princess he had rescued. "Better?" she asked.

"Much better. Though I'd still be more comfortable if you weren't naked." She obliged by magically adding robes. He'd been half-thinking of her as Liz, which seemed unhealthy and slightly nuts, so he asked, "What's your name, anyway?"

"The princess, you mean?"

"No, yours."

She stared as though slightly offended. "I never earned a name. Or an Aspect." She sat up, her expression excited. "You could name me! I mean, if you don't mind…"

"Mind? What kind of name do you want?"

"Something pretty. But solid. Something that really exists, exists forever, like a stone. And unique. My worshippers won't be able to sort out who they mean if I'm called, say, Jessica or something."

He thought of gems and semiprecious stones used as names. Opal, Ruby? No, too country-and-western. Jasper was too male, and Malachite, though a beautiful stone, sounded like an Old Testament prophet with a tangled beard. "Chalcedony—Kal-*sed*-ah-nee. It's a stone, and it can be beautiful, and…"

Her mouth worked as she mumbled the name under her breath. "Chal*ced*ony!" she said, and bounced up onto her knees and kissed him. "I love it!" She sat back on her heels, still whispering the name to herself, and he felt the kind of undiluted pleasure one feels from delighting a child.

"Well, Chalcedony…" She brightened when he said the name and looked at him expectantly. "I need to get back to my body, and I don't know how far it is or how long it will take." He realized that it might be days or even weeks by whatever logic time followed in this place. "Can you help me get home sooner?"

"I can, but I can't take you all the way there. I'm banished from some of the road you would have to travel."

"I'd be grateful if you'd lead me as far as you can. If you're strong enough, now." As he said the words a downcast expression spread on her face. "Even if you aren't, perhaps I could share more…energy… with you, if it would help."

"You'd let me take…more?"

"Whatever's needed."

She instructed him to lie down on the bed and she teased the scab on his side open wider, so a trickle of blood ran down. Her lips were soft around the little wound, and when she suckled a thrill passed through his body and then in an instant he felt too weak to lift his limbs from the bed. He couldn't move his head; it was an effort to turn his eyes toward her face.

She sat there radiant, but with tears running down her cheeks. "I'm so sorry. You're so kind. But I'll never have another chance."

It was all he could do to whisper. "*Me…either.*"

"No. No, listen to me. I took most of your ka, pneuma, ruach, whatever you want to call it. Back down in Malkuth, your body will be dying. But I will stay here and protect your astral body until the end, and when your physical shell dies then you will go back up the ladder until they call you down again someday."

He tried to speak but no words came.

"I'm so sorry," she said again. "I do love you, you know." She leaned over and stroked his face, and her tears fell on him. "I'm so, so sorry, but it's how I'm made. It's my nature."

After his time with Sylvia, he'd learned all about dying, and the wretched darkness that stole across him now was only too familiar and only too sad.

24

Where All the Bananas Went

In 562 AD, the most valuable real estate on the planet was the Mayan Kingdom of Caracol, in what is now the nation of Belize.

Of course, the Mayans didn't know that they lived in Caracol, which is Spanish for "snail shell;" they believed they lived in Oxwitza', which means "Waters of Three Hills."

Neither did they know that they lived in 562 AD. With the most monumental calendar system ever invented, on the most important day of 562 AD they knew they were living in bolon-te' pik uac-te' winikhaab uaxac-te' haab can-te'winik caa-te' k'in, or nine pik six winikhaab eight haab four winik two k'in, which amounts to one million, three-hundred-forty-two thousand, one-hundred-sixty-two days into the present cycle of being (which, incidentally, is slated to end on December 21, 2012).

These folks knew where they stood in the order of things.

The reason Oxwitza' was the most valuable real estate on Earth was that on bolon-te' pik uac-te' winikhaab uaxac-te' haab can-te'winik caa-te' k'in, Oxwitza', reading portents in the sky, conquered its great enemy Tikal, and cemented its alliance with Calakmul in the north.

Of course, the people living in Tikal at the time assumed that they were living in Mutal, the Place of the Pools, while those in Calakmul believed they were living in Kaan, the Kingdom of the Snake, but as Shakespeare was to note about a thousand years later (somewhere around buluc-te' pik uaxaclahun-te' winikhaab hoolahun-te' haab lahun-te'winik uuc-te' k'in or so), the names were beside the point.

Lord Muluc, Lord Water, under whose leadership Tikal was defeated, built up the power of Oxwitza', and his son, Chan Ahau, Lord Luminous Smoke, ruled over a golden age where the reach of their kingdom expanded across the heart of the Yucatan.

Though the Johnny-come-lately Aztecs far to the northwest would later make the Mayans seem like hematophobic pacifists, the kingdoms of the Yucatan were warlike, and shed copious volumes of blood to satiate their gods. Unlike the Aztecs, however, much of the blood the rulers shed was their own. In a classic example of putting their money where their mouth was, the Mayan royalty, male and female, maintained holes through their tongues. When the offering plate was passed around, any good Mayan prince or princess would thread a rough knotted cord through their tongue and drag it back and forth, resulting in a quick-and-easy bowl of blood.

Blood, battle, and a technological prowess that was ahead of its time: the Mayan city-states swelled with power, and their gods grew fat. At its peak, Oxwitza' claimed a population approaching a quarter of a million people, and three times that many paid tribute. Temples rose in the jungle; in observatories built in alignment with the ecliptic, priests studied the night skies.

But the Mayan kingdoms were built, not on sand, but on something far worse: limestone. Thousands of feet of porous, alkaline limestone. Rainfall might be measured in feet per year, but most of that water sank deep into the ground and headed for the sea, wormholing the Yucatan with underground rivers and systems of caverns that extended for miles. The water that collected in pools was too saturated with dissolved alkali to drink.

The Mayans responded with technological sophistication, lining natural sinks with clay so the waters could neither leak away nor leach the limestone, and excavating new pools where needed. The system of reservoirs and irrigation channels formed an interconnected infrastructure that rivaled the aqueduct system of Rome at its peak.

Blessed with year-round sunshine, all that was lacking was a reliable water supply, and once that was established, even in the face of continual warfare the population boomed. Farmers could support not only themselves, but a monarchy, an army, and a priesthood; the wealth and manpower could support not only farmsteads, but giant cities in the heart of the jungle, where temples, pyramids, ballcourts, and ceremonial plazas pushed back the ocean of trees.

As in most of the tropics, part of the year was spent in a monsoon and part of the year in drought. But there came a year where the drought refused to leave, where the rains refused to return. Reservoirs were drawn down; belts were tightened. A better year followed, but then a whole series of dry years came, and famine stalked the land.

The rulers of the Mayan kingdoms redoubled their sacrifices, but rather than turning their treasuries to the expansion and maintenance of the water system, they waged ever-more destructive wars. While chaos spread amongst the starving commoners, warlords pillaged the great temple cities. Disease burned through the countryside. In less than a century, one of the great civilizations of the world had vanished in a miasma of savagery and despair.

By the time that Cortes arrived, bringing a new wave of cruelty, horror, and disease to Mesoamerica, there was no one left who could note the date: buluc-te' pik canlahun-te' winikhaab bolonlahun-te' haab can-te'winik hun-te' k'in. The surviving Mayans had relocated to the coast, their monumental cities in the heartland abandoned to the jungle, and their Long Count forgotten.

Few places that seethe with etheric energy are ever abandoned for long, and sorcerers and incarnated Talents and Powers seek them out—as do artists, composers, writers, and political visionaries (though the non-occult crowd is drawn to such places by subconscious forces rather than by intent). In the 1850s, when von Fleischer came across Catherwood's engravings of the ancient Mayan sites, he knew he was looking at the ultimate prize—an immense power center that lay unclaimed.

Over the next two decades he funded modest expeditions to unexplored parts of the Yucatan, with the antiquities department of the British Museum as the main beneficiary. In the late 1870s, when bananas became the most fashionable dessert on American tables, he began to build his private kingdom in what was then British Honduras.

From the second row of the eight-seater Turbine Bonanza, Miklos threw glances back at the seats where Liz leaned on von Fleischer's shoulder, tossing each look like a tiny grenade. Von Fleischer sent him a conspiratorial wink, but Miklos, unmollified, made a pouty face and twisted forward in his seat. How long would it take to purge those fey mannerisms? For obvious reasons of convenience, most of the bodies von Fleischer had taken over the centuries were those of homosexuals, but he had never before picked someone who was such a, well, flamer. No matter. Once he owned them, those glowering brown eyes and that hurt little mouth would charm men and melt the bones of women.

Liz, already boneless after a few days at the Rancho Bernardo Inn, stretched and snuggled up against him. "I don't know when I've ever been so *relaxed*," she said. "Where are we going? A *banana* plantation?" He worried that she would make the inevitable phallic reference—American women, especially the neurotic ones, were fine in the bedroom, but tiresome outside it—but she peeked out the window and said, "I don't see anything but jungle."

"The bananas are long gone, alas," he said. "My great-granduncle's bananas were the toast of New Orleans in the Gay Nineties, but the Panama Disease, and various hurricanes…" He opened his palm like a magician showing that a coin had vanished. "Our coastal plantations are tourist hotels, and British Honduras is Belize. All that remains is our little inland community."

"Here? There's nothing but trees."

"Nothing but trees? Wait a moment." He raised his voice and shouted to the pilot, "Take us over Caracol."

The plane banked to the right, and in a few minutes the endless green quilt of the forest opened and Liz gasped as she looked down at the gray limestone pyramids and plazas of Oxwitza'. "It's gorgeous."

"Yes. Of course, my little getaway is far more modest."

"My place? What did you say it was called?"

"El Panal. The Honeycomb. You may find it a bit…rustic for your tastes, but I think of it as a step back to a more civilized era."

She wrapped both arms around his elbow and hugged it to herself. "Sounds romantic."

The woman's compliance and agreeability over the last two days had stretched to the point where he was sure that she would do whatever he required of her. That was gratifying, but her surrender had also become so complete that she was in danger of turning very boring indeed. He'd have to find something a bit more…demanding to introduce into their bedroom games.

"You're smiling," she said.

"Yes. It's always good to be back."

Sylvia had sat by Arby's unconscious form for hours now. The tiny quivers and tremblings told no story, but they did show that he had made progress; if he were trapped between Binah and Chokmah, in the Great Contradiction between Form and Space, between the Pillars of Severity and Mercy, then his body would lie still.

Elaina and Helayjah either didn't understand the significance of these tiny motions, or were frustrated by the fact that they could do nothing but look. Early in the process, they had both risen and paced the room as Sylvia waited and watched. They lay back on pillows and stared at the ceiling, or sat crosslegged and stared at the floor.

An hour ago, Helayjah had left the chamber for a time, and returned with a bottle of wine and a bowl of fruit. Sylvia had refused the food, but accepted a glass of wine—alcohol was simpatico with her Talent—and watched.

A shudder ran through Arby's body, and then a core-deep trembling chased it from his limbs and he lay still. Sylvia leaned down close over him.

Elaina must have noticed her movement, because she asked, "What is it?" and a moment later both she and Helayjah were crouched down beside her.

"Shh!" She leaned her ear close to his lips, settled her fingers on his neck. His breath touched her with no more force than thistledown settling on a pond. The pulse in his carotid artery couldn't have been detected by a doctor, and it seemed to fade beneath her fingertips.

She sat back. "He's dying. I don't know what happened."

"He has been attacked, yes, wounded, on the astral plane?" Helayjah asked.

"I can't tell. His vitality has drained away, and there is only the slightest drop remaining."

"What can we do?" Elaina asked.

"Sit with him and wait."

After a long silence, Elaina said, "I should never have let him go." Her voice was smaller, less strident, than Sylvia had ever heard it, and when she looked up she was shocked to see that Elaina had removed her sunglasses, and that tears leaked from the corners of her eyes.

Sylvia reached over and pressed her hand atop Elaina's. "It's not your fault. As surely as the rain seeks the soil, this was his nature."

Elaina turned her face away. Helayjah sat back on his heels and swallowed. "When this matter is done, yes?—I would very much like to kill something? Or, rather, some*one*?"

"Be quiet," Sylvia said, "and wait."

El Panal sat close to the Guatemalan border, and that had pleased three generations of colonial bureaucrats in British Honduras, and continued to bring joy to the hearts of the administrators in independent Belize: Guatemala continued to claim a big swath of the sparely populated Belizean interior, and it was a diplomatic gift to have a village and plantation—especially one owned by an influential foreigner— smack in the middle of the disputed territory. In the interior itself, though, El Panal had an evil reputation among the few villages within hiking distance; there were legends that no curious souls who entered it ever left.

From the sky at first only the airstrip drew the eye, but after a time it became clear that the jungle was pocked with little clearings for agricultural plots and huts—a city with no center.

The little plane glided onto the grass. When the wheel hit a hidden bump and skipped into the air, Liz clenched von Fleischer's hand in hers and he chuckled. "Joy of travel, eh? Relax. We're safer in this than in any jumbo jet."

The co-pilot—von Fleischer didn't believe in flying with only one pilot—hustled back and lowered the stairway, and he led Liz out, while Miklos trailed behind, sulking.

As usual, most of El Panal had turned out to see a plane land, and more than a thousand people stood in the shadows of the high trees that surrounded the airstrip, a line of dark, hawknosed peasants in khaki and olive, enlivened with bright scarves. When they recognized von Fleischer, they dropped to one knee and bowed their heads. Liz gave a little gasp at the sight.

"My family is still quite…respected here." True. This was the fifth generation of villagers to worship Tanagrim, The Ahau, in his various bodies, and he was loved and feared. They believed that to die defending him was to be guaranteed immortality, and he saw to it that they were…after a fashion.

The villagers remained kneeling while he led Liz and Miklos toward them. Liz frowned at the low, grassy mounds that stretched around the perimeter of the field.

"Graves," he said. "The tradition in these parts was to bury the dead under the floor of the home and then abandon the house. I changed that tradition."

"It's *hot*," Miklos said.

"That will be cured soon."

They passed through the line of bowed heads and onto a broad, shady path that led into the jungle. Von Fleischer felt the sweat on his forehead vanish, but Miklos said, "It's shadier here, but it's *still* hot. What is this place, anyway?"

"Part of your inheritance. And, as with most things of value, the best parts are not on the surface." Miklos had become vastly more tiresome since the adoption, and it would be a relief to bid him farewell. "Patience."

A five-minute stroll brought them to the clearing in the trees. The half-dozen guards slouching at the railing around the sinkhole straightened, adjusting the Uzis strapped over their shoulders, and dropped their gazes to the ground but did not kneel. Two of them hustled around to the mighty winch and gearworks where it crouched at the edge of the hole like some predatory insect. One threw the main drive lever, and with a creak and groan the winch began to turn, coiling steel cable onto the big drum.

At the edge of the sinkhole he let them peer over the railing. The mouth was a good thirty feet in diameter, and there was no bottom to be seen: the white limestone walls went down until they grayed out and merged with the darkness. After a moment, the top of the elevator car appeared on the cable, rising toward them, a guy-wire at each corner keeping it from tilting.

"What *is* this?" Liz whispered.

"The main entrance to my little hideaway." He glanced over at Miklos. "And, let me assure you, the climate inside is always perfect."

The elevator car, about the size of a bedroom, lifted out of the hole and locked into place alongside the winch. The car was enclosed on all sides, but except for the structural steel the upper half was covered in heavy mesh. One of the guards slid back the door on the car, flicked on lights, and backed away so they could enter.

"We're going down there?" Miklos asked. "In that?"

"I told you both it was rustic."

"Rust-*ed* would be closer. I think I'll stay up here."

Von Fleischer ushered Liz into the car. "I think you'll find it's worth the ride. It's quite comfy down there."

Miklos followed them in, and grabbed the handrail that ran around the interior of the car. "This looks like it's from some warehouse." The guard shut the door. Von Fleischer pulled the wall switch down, and both Liz and Miklos started as the elevator jerked and began its descent. Miklos's voice trembled. "Are you sure this is safe?"

"It may not look elegant, but it was designed for durability, not glamour. It can handle several tons of weight."

Miklos stared at the four guy wires where they fed through the corners of the car. "This stuff is ancient."

Von Fleischer laughed. "If I'd known you were going to have so much fun, I'd have taken you on this one's older sister, the one they used to build this place. That car is mostly wood. Back during the Cold War, when people talked about fallout shelters, I had to laugh at the idea of people hunkered down in little cubicles, trying to wait out the apocalypse. In the event of a nuclear war, taking shelter here would be like a long vacation."

The lights from the car threw magnified shadows on the uneven walls of the wide shaft, and they seemed to ripple like the surface of an uneasy sea. Miklos asked, "We came all this way to visit a fallout shelter?"

"Only incidentally. This is a private kingdom. And, believe me— after I'm gone and you come into your inheritance, you'll come back here."

Miklos gave him a look that said he'd prefer a trip to the dentist. Liz squeezed von Fleischer's hand and gave it a little shake, as though she were anticipating climbing onto a carnival ride.

Crystal stared out the passenger window of the big SUV they'd rented at the Albuquerque airport and watched the Sandia Mountains roll by. Giant four-wheel drive vehicles weren't her thing at all: they had the aerodynamics of a block of cement, they ruined the environment, and they were ugly to boot.

But for Rooker, she'd make an exception. The oversized clunky car might have been designed for him; all it needed was a few dents and an awkward personality. She glanced over at him and caught him watching her with suspicious eyes. His gaze darted back to the highway. "Hey," she said, "what's up?"

"I must be out of my mind."

"I could go on my own."

"Nope. You need me to protect you."

"Ooh, my own Gary Cooper. If these guys are so bad, who's going to protect you?"

"We got resources in the area if I need 'em. It's just risky. I don't know why the hell I'm doing this." He snorted. "Correction. I'm doing this 'cause you're manipulating me into it." The quick look he gave her was reproachful. "The pisser is, I know you're doing it to me, and I still don't care."

It figured. Guys were like that, most of them, everything linear, all cause-and-effect. Plus, once a boy got a notion about how sex worked settled in his head—usually about age thirteen—nothing short of dynamite could move it. In Rooker's view, it all added up: sex in exchange for what she wanted him to do.

As always, when in doubt, speak truth. She undid her seatbelt and sat on her knees on the seat so she could face him at something like his own seated height. "I know you aren't going to get it, but I need to try and tell you this anyway. You think I'm fucking you so you'll help me get in touch with my son." She sighed. "I can see how it looks like that to you... Look, do you have any kind of spiritual practice?"

He blew out a dismissive puff of air.

"Okay, you don't. I do. And this is synchronicity, all of this. You're in my life to help me with Arby, and I'm in yours for some reason, and whatever is going on with your boss and these people—it's all happening at once, part of some bigger thing."

Rooker put on his blinker and moved into the fast lane to pass a truck hauling a horse-trailer. His gaze fixed on the road ahead, he said, "Just because it's all happening at once doesn't mean it adds up to anything."

Crystal reached over and stroked his hard shoulder. "I wish it *wasn't* all happening at once. I'd be happy to just go off somewhere with you for a few months. This is like being a teenager again, or like the first time I—" She considered, and decided getting specific wouldn't help her case much. "What I'm trying to say is, this all feels *new* to me. And it hasn't felt like that in a long time."

He flipped on his blinker and moved into the right lane, his head facing rigidly forward.

Women from the dawn of time have complained that men listened only to their cocks. Crystal didn't have much of a problem with that—there were worse sources of information—but what made her crazy was when men listened to their cocks, but also refused to believe what they heard. "Charles..." She kneewalked as close to him as the console between the bucket seats would allow, and leaned onto his arm. "When we're fucking, can't you tell that I want it? Can't you feel it?" The pavement changed beneath them as they crossed a bridge, and the zipping whine of the tires dominated the silence. "I'm actually waiting for an answer here, you know."

"Yeah," he said, his voice husky. "Yeah, I feel it. But feelings can lie."

Crystal stood up on her knees and breathed into his ear. "Oh? So, like who's your favorite president?"

"Huh? Of the US? I dunno…Teddy Roosevelt?"

"Really?" She licked his ear and breathed into it. "Mine's George Washington." Her hand roamed across his chest, massaging the knots of muscle that knitted him together. "My body. It cannot tell a lie."

She eased her hips back down onto her heels, reached under his arm to his waist, and unbuttoned his pants.

"Hey—what're you doing?"

"Would have thought it was pretty obvious." She used both hands so she could yank down the zipper, and then laughed as she ran a hand down inside his pants. "Feels to me like you've already got the idea."

"I can't do this—"

"*You* don't need to do anything. Just drive."

"No no no no—" He laughed, but his right arm gently but irresistibly pushed her back onto her side of the car. "I'm serious. If I—I mean, when I'm with you— Look, Crystal. I'd crash this car and kill us both."

"Well, I'd offer to drive, but that wouldn't work either." She realized she was perspiring, and cracked the window. "Hey—still don't believe in synchronicity?"

"Huh?"

"The big sign in the sky at that next off-ramp says *Motel*."

The desk clerk at the Sundown Motel frowned as though he'd never heard of king-sized beds, so they'd settled for a queen, adequate for a sweaty, hour-long bout of sex. With Rooker as her bedmate, though, Crystal found it crowded for napping. She lay on her side next to him, her arms wrapped around his forearm, and one leg thrown high up onto his hip. What had begun as a cuddly post-coital posture had become her only means of staying on the bed as the big man relaxed and spread out.

He had a way, she had discovered, of awakening completely without moving. "We should get a move on," he said, without budging. "Get ready to meet the other team."

"Is that how you think of all this? A kind of game?"

"Yep. You root for one side or root for the other, but it doesn't mean anybody's right or wrong."

"Not even the people who…" She found it hard to say the words. "Not even the people who killed your family?"

"Oh I hate them. But I know why they did what they did. We tried to kill *you* once, you know."

"What?"

"When you were first pregnant. Anton LaMarr and his bunch— we tried to kill them all, and the Hero you brought down."

"Hero?" Crystal giggled, and then laughed louder as she thought about it, and her naked body bounced against Rooker's unyielding mass and that felt good. "He's the world's biggest sweetheart, even if he is kinda serious, but—oh, wow!"

"Your son and the bitch he hangs out with now—Elaina Svärdfors—killed three astral assassins and an ether beast only a few days ago. No typical mortal could do that. Your son is a warrior."

"Oh, man—you've really got the wrong guy." She dearly loved Arby, loved him with the whole of her heart, loved him more than all of her lovers rolled together, but the idea of him as Action Hero was the silliest thing she'd ever heard. "Charles. Arby shot a bird with a pellet gun when he was eight, and I thought we'd have to send him to a shrink. You're all, like, really confused. He's one of the good guys."

"There aren't any good guys. Except maybe you." His gargantuan paw cupped her face and he looked at her. "And maybe you're fooling me. I don't care anymore, because I—" He stopped and swallowed. "You could really fuck me up if you wanted to."

His pupils widened and it seemed as if she could see into his head, and she laughed with surprise. "That's some big risk? *I* could hurt *you*? What do you think it's like every time I get naked with you?"

"Yeah, but that's—"

"Shut up, okay? I'm not complaining. You feel like I have the power here?" She tried to peer into his head again, but he looked down at his own arm where it wrapped around her shoulder, his gaze unfocused. "That kind of power is called *surrender*."

His mouth worked through a few abortive words before he said, "I just don't—"

"Shh. I know. It's scary at first. That's part of the turn-on."

He rolled his massive head down and kissed her. "I just hope you're right about your son." The bed groaned as he disentangled himself and sat up. He retrieved a cell phone from the tangle of clothes on the floor and flipped it open. With a motel pen from the nightstand he poked at the numbers, and she realized his fingers were too thick to work the dialpad. "We're going to get a chance to see here soon. But I'm warning you—if he attacks me, I'm gonna defend myself."

Sylvia didn't turn her head from watching Arby, but she sensed Xochipilli striding into the chamber; her father's aura could never be mistaken. He squatted where she and Elaina and Helayjah knelt, making a rectangle around Arby's unmoving body. "Anything?" he asked.

"He still lives," she said.

Xochipilli wrapped his muscular arms around his knees, clasping his wrist to brace himself solid. "There is a problem. His mother has been taken by Tanagrim."

"I thought as much before," Elaina said.

"That's not all. One of his men, one called Rooker, has called. He and the mother wish to meet with us, and The Fool, for a parley."

"Oh?" asked Helayjah. "And they have, I suppose, a purpose, a plan, a proposal?"

"I'll bet they do, but they didn't tell me about it. Just a meet. Claim the mother wants it."

"And what does Jerry say?"

"He thinks someone needs to go, to discover their thinking, even if…" Xochipilli inclined his head toward Arby's still form.

"I'll go," Elaina said. "I've had some dealings with Rooker. What are the terms?"

"Only The Fool and one other from our side. Only the mother and Rooker from theirs." He nodded to himself for a moment before adding, "We must assume they are lying, of course."

25

The Plighting-Ring

Chalcedony the succubus leaned down toward Arby's face. "I can't hear you."

"Can't die," he said, and though he put all the force he could muster into his words, they came out as a feathery whisper. "…people." He breathed before saying, "…stop von Fleischer."

She exhaled a sad little sniff. "Don't be silly. You can't."

"Have to try." He blinked. The world around him was made of viscous liquid, swirling slowly, and darkening by the moment. He consciously moved his lips into a weak smile. "My nature."

The succubus breathed onto his face and his vision cleared. "You mean that? You plan to attack him? He'll destroy you."

His body still lay paralyzed, but he heard his voice grow stronger. "Probably."

Chalcedony studied him, and for a moment she lost control of her face and Liz, Elaina, and several other women appeared there before she steadied back into the princess again. "I wish I could trust you."

"I trusted you."

She gave a bark of laughter. "Yes, and look at you now." He felt her weight rise from the bed and he heard her footfalls move away and pace, but he was still too weak to turn his head. At last she came back and sat down beside him again. "Why would you do this? Why not ally yourself with him?"

"I've seen his realm. Not something I want to own a piece of."

"You're a very stupid boy." She sighed. "I'm stupid, too, I suppose. Do you swear you won't take vengeance on me?"

He wasn't sure what she meant, but it seemed safe enough to swear.

"I'll help you, then." She shook her head and looked as though she were going to cry again. "Oh, please, don't make me regret this..." She breathed down onto him again, and as he inhaled he felt as though he were inflating, growing larger, swelling with life.

With a grunt of effort, Arby sat up. Chalcedony stood several feet away, watching him with wary eyes, as though she might have to flee. He could move but he still felt weak. "I'm keeping half, okay?" she asked. "That way, if anything happens to you, I'll have some time."

"Thank you," he said, and meant it, though he wondered how he could complete his journey in this exhausted state. "Maybe I should sleep for a bit..."

"Sleep here won't refresh you," she said. "This isn't Malkuth."

The thought of heaving himself to his feet almost made him regret not dying. "I don't even know where I'm going."

"Back, of course." She reached out her hand. "I can guide you part of the way...and show you a place where you may be able to renew your energy."

Chalcedony made him put on a dented helm and breastplate from the junkheap on the plaza. "Your tunic attracts too much attention. Try to look like a warrior." Despite the added weight, he obeyed.

As she cinched the leather straps of the breastplate across his chest, he looked across the plaza to where she and the other maidens had been chained. "What is this place, anyway?"

"A place where this particular thing happens. It will happen again in a matter of time."

"But why?"

"Everything has to happen somewhere."

She led him back though the maiden's chamber and lifted a hanging tapestry on the rear wall, revealing a spiral stairway leading up. Like the chamber itself, the stairs were illuminated without any apparent source of light.

In only a few minutes he was panting, and, despite her warnings that rest did no good on the astral plane, he sat down three times before they emerged on a mountaintop. The scenery was far different from the barren canyon they had left; although they stood far above the treeline, the valley below was forested. Chalcedony gestured for him to follow, and he staggered behind her on a rocky path leading down.

When at last they entered the pine forest, he felt safer and somewhat refreshed. This was familiar territory, a damp evergreen wood like those from his childhood on the Oregon coast. In fact, the familiarity segued smoothly into recognition—a lightning-blasted Doug fir stood at the intersection of two paths. "Wait a minute," he said. "I know this place."

"We are closer to Malkuth. Things ought to be more similar."

"No. I mean I know this exact place." He rounded the blackened fir and headed down a side path beneath the trees, where rain-soaked ferns bowed down on both sides, wetting his hose as he passed.

From behind she called, "That's not the way back…"

The path led up, and two moss-covered boulders of black basalt pushed through the earth ahead. Almost running, he turned sideways to slide between the rocks, and heard the crash of the surf.

There was no doubt. He stood high on a cliff, the Pacific surging through jagged haystack rocks far below. To his right, a twisted cypress sprawled its limbs like a mighty octopus. He turned left on the path that led along the cliff's edge.

Chalcedony leaned between the rocks, and said, "This isn't the way!"

"It's the way to where I need to go! This is home!"

"This isn't your home! It's only *like* your home!"

A spindly grove of hemlocks stood before him, their droopy branches interlocking, and he bent down to find the hidden child's path that led through them. Branches snagged at him—he was no longer eight years old, and when he had last passed through here, he hadn't been wearing a helm or breastplate—but he stumbled at last into the clearing beyond.

The red cedar that waited in the clearing was ancient. Its top had been taken off by centuries of lightning and storm, but the girth of its base made it seem like a sequoia. He ducked under the big branch that thrust toward him, and stepped around to find the hollow heart.

The space within was smaller than he remembered, but big enough for a grown man to stand inside. The pungent cedar smell welcomed him home.

Propped against the wall were his hiking stick and his red leather backpack. Yet both were transformed: the backpack was actually a satchel, though still embossed with a hundred sigils, and the stick was a smooth staff surmounted by a golden knob. He knelt and opened the satchel, expecting to find his keepsakes, and instead he found knowledge.

The bag was filled with memories. Not the memories of lives he'd lived, but memories of things he had learned. In the space of a single breath, he knew once more how to shield himself in his sleep, how to hold his consciousness down in Malkuth, how to cross over into Yetzirah, and how to wield his Talent—insofar as his Talent could be directed, that was.

He stepped out of the hollowed tree. Chalcedony crashed through the hemlocks, making sounds of exasperation as the branches snatched at her robes. "What are you *doing*?" she asked.

"Finding things I'd lost," he said. "We can go now."

When they stepped out of the tunnel entrance and saw the black boulder, he knew the place at once. "I've been here before. This is the edge of von Fleischer's world."

"This is as close as I can go to the lower worlds, now that he has cast me out."

Was it always twilight here? The clouded sky still moved uneasily, and shadowy figures stalked across the plain. A relatively easy walk back to La Lune from here, if he remembered correctly, though it would be the first time he had navigated the etheric plane alone in this incarnation. "I think I remember the way." He hesitated, feeling an odd affection for the succubus, and a gratitude for the fact that she hadn't left him sucked dry. "Chalcedony…when I get back, I promise you—"

"No. You shouldn't head back yet. I brought you here for a purpose." She pointed at the plain. "Down there. Those things…" Her pointing hand revolved and she closed it into a half-fist and then wiggled her fingers upward, mimicking the undulating anemone-like creatures below. "Those are fountains of energy. Slice one with your dagger, drink deep, and then run back here. You'll regain all the energy you had, and more."

The suggestion unsettled him. Was it a trick? But if she wanted to destroy him, why not leave him drained back in the chamber of the maidens? "Will you come with me?"

"I am banished. If I so much as set foot in his kingdom, he will find me…and what he does to me then will be far worse than turning me out to die."

Arby tried to think it through, but Machiavellian reasoning had never been one of his strengths. She had no reason to restore his energy rather than letting him die; she had led him this far, faithfully; and she seemed to be anticipating his return to the physical plane, where he would send her energy and let her build her own life on the Inner Planes. But perhaps it was all a ruse to make him trust her, to deliver him here and have him walk into von Fleischer's world willingly. He rubbed his forehead. It might not be within his power to follow all the twists and turns of possibilities, like some chess master, but he now knew his own nature and his own heart. "Isn't it guarded?"

"Of course. That's why I said to drink and run." Chalcedony's maiden princess face showed not the slightest trace of guile, but that meant nothing.

An involuntary sigh heaved from his chest. So tired, so weary in every cell, it seemed he would never feel anything but this drooping lethargy again, even if he knew for a fact that Chalcedony had drained half of his life force. Like a penitent shambling toward Lourdes, if a cure lay ahead, he was willing to go there, even if he had to crawl the final distance.

He dropped his staff and satchel beside the woman and then half-slid, half-staggered through the talus that sloped down from the mouth of the tunnel. At the base of the steep hill, he saw a demarcation, clear as a boundary on a map, between the smooth plain of von Fleischer's world and the rocky hillside, and unless memory deceived him, the boundary had crept toward the hillside since he was last here. When had that been? A day ago? A week?

When he reached the boundary he stepped across without pausing. The nearest of the anemones stood perhaps a hundred yards away, insofar as he could judge distance in this impossible world. He fixed his eyes on it and lurched forward, the breastplate and helm weightier than ever. The turbid skies that formed a backdrop made him queasy, and he tried to concentrate on the undulating, fat purple tentacles.

The plant, or whatever it was, stood a bit taller than him. He dropped to his knees, pulled out his dagger, and slashed a slit into the purple skin. Wine-dark liquid, viscous as cold syrup, welled from the wound.

One deep breath, and then he leaned forward and wrapped his lips around the wound and sucked. A new taste, neither sweet, nor sour, nor salty; a humming, crackling, nose-wrinkling taste like the smell of ozone translated to the tongue. Everything about his body seemed to swell and grow. He gulped the sticky fluid, the plant pumping it into his eager mouth, and he paused to gasp for breath and then began feeding again, the archaic sucking of the infant mammal at the mother's nipple.

An instant later, Arby was full, and the idea of swallowing another drop was revolting. Sitting back on his heels, he wiped his mouth, and then felt a vague but growing unease in his gut, as though he had eaten spoiled food. His body vibrated with energy, a vivaciousness he hadn't felt since childhood, but he was simultaneously nauseated. He gagged, but nothing came up from his throat. Bending forward, he made a deliberate effort to vomit. In response the phosphenes of his optic nerve exploded in a tiny fireworks show, but nothing came up.

When his vision cleared he saw he was surrounded by a hundred fat rodent-like creatures, some as big as possums, most of them bearing humanoid faces, both male and female, but those faces were framed in fur. They jostled one another, fighting to get at drops of fluid that had fallen from the cut he'd made; many of them stared up at the drooling slit in the plant with yearning.

One of the creatures addressed him in what sounded like stilted German, and then another said, "Prithee, share thy bounty. A small matter to reach forth thy blade…" A hundred faces looked up at him from atop hunched rat-like bodies, and a woman's voice said, "Please… *please.*"

What the hell. He slashed the tentacle in a dozen places, and then slashed two more of the nearby arms.

The feeding frenzy was abrupt, but short-lived. For a few moments the lumpy brown-haired bodies rolled across one another like a muddy stream tumbling across stones, but then the whole crowd settled down, satiated, though not apparently nauseated. A few groomed themselves like rodents and others hunkered down like contented dogs.

"Why d'you come here, Master?" The voice had an English accent. Arby saw a bulbous-nosed little human face looking up from a rat's body. "Do you come to cast him down?"

"I'm tired. I won't be casting anyone down—not this evening, at any rate."

"Then flee! For, if it is a bargain you seek, you will be cheated. His right hand I was for twenty-five years, back when George sat his throne, and no man had ever a servant more loyal. Immortality, he promised me, and immortality I have—after the fashion you see here. If you do not come to offer battle, leave now!"

Run, Chalcedony had said, but the nausea had driven it from his mind. He clambered to his feet. An impossible combination: still sickened, his body vibrated with energy, a perverse arousal like some unwanted and disgusting sexual desire. Turning, he headed back toward the hillside.

The clouds had lowered during the time he had been in von Fleischer's world, and one had reached a long vaporous arm down to the ground between him and the slope. The mists spread and rolled, tickling the ground, and then the plain trembled and split open. From the chasm, a rider and his steed burst forth and galloped up the arm of cloud as though it were a road. The cloud road wrapped into a wide horseshoe, and the rider spurred his mount up to the apex of the horseshoe and then sped down the other side, battle-lance ready, and onto the flat ground not a dozen feet from Arby.

The man wore a green-black helm with a grille that hid his face, and he wore green-black armor that glistened like the wings of a beetle. His horse wasn't quite a horse: its softball-sized eyes glowed with a knowing light, and its flaring nostrils were sticky muscular holes that clamped shut between each breath. Its lips curled as those huge eyes stared at him, and then a fat humanoid tongue protruded and waggled at him before licking side-to-side.

The rider lifted the helm from his head and cinched it down onto the pommel before him. His locks were blond and his face was as beautiful as a woman's, but cold. "Declare yourself. None pass this border without warrant, and no man has been given license."

"I'm Arby." His voice sounded small and thready in his ears, but then he felt a surge of energy. "I'm only a passing traveler—and I didn't see any *No Trespassing* signs."

"You are a liar or a fool, or perhaps both. Your helm and armor are dented, and you venture to feed at the fountains of Tanagrim. A vagrant Hero, I say, and I name you coward for not owning your true name. Once more I demand: Declare yourself." The steed's nostril's widened, and Arby glimpsed fangs inside them. Great. Nose teeth.

"As I said, I'm Arby, and I'm leaving."

"You will bend the knee, and you will stay until the lord of this land chooses to wait upon you."

"Appreciate the offer of being waited on, but I need to be moving along. Don't bother to see me out." Arby stepped to the left, as though to make a wide circle around the rider.

The rider closed his steely eyes and drew a hand down across his face as if wiping condensation from a windowpane. His palm passed by to reveal another face—this one scarred and hawklike, made of sharp planes as if welded together. He spurred his mount and lifted his lance, jerking the reins in the direction Arby had headed.

Arby darted to the right, running toward the chasm in the plain. He heard hooves pound and wheel about behind him, and then take up pursuit.

The fissure was about ten feet wide, and he jumped it and then fell and rolled. The rider came on behind him. Still on the ground, Arby looked back and focused. He threw discs of light from his hand, aiming them now—aiming for the steed's hooves, for its eyes, for the rider's eyes, for his hands, for the lance, for the chasm itself…

The steed leapt but stumbled. The chasm widened and then slammed closed around the mount's body, crushing its legs. But the rider was thrown from his saddle and hurtled toward Arby, and by chance or by skill the tip of the lance was still aimed at him.

Arby began to roll. The lance embedded in the ground beneath his armpit and then slung the rider though the air to crash on the ground beyond.

The steed bellowed in agony. Arby tried to move, but realized that the lance had pinned one of the straps of his breastplate to the earth. He struggled, trying to pull it away or break it, but to no avail.

The rider clambered to his feet and shed his armor in a few practiced moves, but instead of moving toward Arby, he ran to his steed, and then, after embracing its neck, stood back and slashed its throat with his sword. The animal gurgled horribly and then died.

Arby had come to his senses and was scrabbling for the dagger in his belt to cut the strap when the rider turned and marched toward him. "That beast was worth the lives of a thousand like you. An honorable death you might have had. But now I will gut you and leave you for those rats you were feeding."

Lying there, Arby abandoned any attempt to cut the strap, and threw probability discs with all his might. But walking forward with intent doesn't leave much room for error, and if the rider's steps faltered a little, it didn't slow his advance.

The only chance was to throw the dagger—a low-probability chance in the first place. He lifted the dagger by its blade, concentrated all his power, and then hurled it with a sharp snap of his wrist.

The rider slapped the flying dagger aside with an unconcerned swipe of his sword and then strode up until he stood over Arby. That evil face closed its eyes, the head spun, and the beautiful young man regarded him through icy eyes. "I gave you a chance of honorable surrender, but you showed your nature. You ran, you attacked my beast, and at the last you cowered down and tried to magick me." He poked his sword down between Arby's thighs. "Your manhood I shall take first—since you seem to hold it so cheap."

The man drew the sword back and then wobbled and collapsed. Chalcedony stood behind him. In her hands she clutched a heavy black rock from the hillside, and it dripped blood onto the ground. Even before she dropped it, the human-faced rodents were gathering at her feet.

"Up, up. Hurry!" Chalcedony knelt by his side and sawed through the strap. He needed little encouragement. At the moment he was free, he stood, and, making sure she was beside him, ran for the boundary.

They were only a few feet from the boundary when he heard her gasp as though she had been gut-punched. She hunched forward, then stood upright and arched back as if heading for a seizure. "Chalcedony!" he said, and reached for her.

She straightened, and a man's voice came from her mouth. Rich and distinguished, with a pan-European accent, it said, "*Chalcedony?* You've named the little chippy? Better working conditions in your union shop than mine, it might seem."

"What... Who are you?"

"That might seem to be my question to ask, but I am Tanagrim, known below as Benedikt von Fleischer, and this is my realm. And you?"

"Arby. Arby Keeling."

"I had guessed as much, but I meant your higher identity. You come dressed as a Hero, if a battered one, and stride into my lands as though by right." The eyes that stared from the face of the princess maiden were keen, watching Arby the way a sea captain studies the dawn horizon. "How are you called, and where is your stronghold?"

"I'm only a traveler. Not a Hero."

"Oh? And yet you seem to have slain one of my guardians. Come now: How are you called, and where is your stronghold?"

How was he called indeed? Based on the debates back at La Lune, confessing to being the Fool seemed to offer no advantages. Well, he *had* killed the giant avocado bird… "I'm the Monster Slayer, the Defender of Chained Women, and my stronghold is in the Heart of the Wood."

Chalcedony's lips worked as the man inhabiting her muttered under his breath. At last, she shook her head. "Riddles. Perseus or a dozen others might have worked for the first two; any number of itinerant knights for the latter. But the combination makes no sense." Chalcedony stroked her chin in a very masculine gesture. "Let us be frank with one another, shall we? I know you have taken up with that rabble at La Lune. But why join the losing side?" Chalcedony's hand swept back at the vastness behind her. "The day will come when the whole noosphere around the human world will be under my dominion. Why not ally yourself with me?"

Arby considered carefully before he spoke, and took the time to step closer to the boundary. "You haven't given me reasons to trust you, and you've given me several reasons not to."

"What, a few paltry attempts on your life? The normal course of events."

"And…you're threatening people who matter to me."

"Threatening?" Chalcedony's features slithered into Crystal's. "My guest? I'm protecting her. Your mother is an obvious target for those who would exploit you. You may think you're cooperating freely with those at La Lune, but I assure you, if they had seized her, you'd be doing their bidding with her as a hostage."

With a shiver of realization, Arby saw that what von Fleischer said was plausible, even possible. But then he gazed out across the man's blasted realm and compared it with Elaina's world, and knew that what he heard was a lie. He looked into Crystal's eyes, where another intelligence peered out, and asked, "Then my mother is free to leave?"

She shrugged. "Come and claim her any time you wish." Crystal reshaped herself into Liz. "As to this one, she is my guest of her own free will. And, although I understand you two had a parting of the ways, I can assure you she's had a change of heart. Meet with me. Meet with her. I'm sure she can convince you that an alliance with me would… fulfill everyone's desires."

If there was one thing Liz had never been, it was malleable, so either von Fleischer was lying or something had happened to her. "Meet with you? Aren't we meeting now?"

"In Malkuth, in the physical, where things are more…certain."

In an instant, Arby understood the searching gaze that had looked out of all of the women's faces: absurd as it might seem, the man was frightened of him, or at least frightened of the fact that Arby was an unknown quantity, and he wanted him back down in the world where the rules were more clean-cut. "I'll consider it. Right now, I have other things to do." He turned and walked across the border, saying over his shoulder, "Come on, Chalcedony."

"You, of course, may go. But I have unfinished business with this one, whom I banished. I showed mercy before, but…"

Chalcedony's appearance shifted back to the princess maiden, and her own voice said, "*No, please…*" Her hands lifted up, clawlike, and she screamed as she raked her nails down her own face, digging bloody trenches in her skin. One hand clenched into her cheek and ripped away a handful of her own flesh. Her sobs and cries were interrupted by von Fleischer's voice saying, "Bit by bit…we'll make a fine example of you…"

"Stop it!" Arby shouted.

Chalcedony's body stopped still. Blood poured from her face and soaked the front of her robe. The humanoid rodents gathered around her feet, licking up the droplets of blood and squabbling over the gobbet of flesh she had tossed down. "Do you give orders here?" von Fleischer's voice asked.

"Don't hurt her any more. Please."

There was a pause, and then the man gave a surprised laugh that rang with genuine amusement. "This one? You care about *this*? She's nothing."

"Then let her go."

"As a favor? I might." In a ludicrous parody of thoughtfulness, Chalcedony's hand scratched her scalp above the bloody ruin of her face. "And in return, you agree to meet with me? To hear me out?"

Arby tasted blood and realized he was gnawing the inside of his cheek. Chalcedony casually took the little finger of her left hand and bent it backward until the bone snapped. Her body jerked in pain, but she made no sound. "Come now," von Fleischer said. She broke her ring finger.

"All right, I'll meet with you. Stop it now."

"Ah. And not that I doubt your word as a gentleman, but..." Chalcedony knelt and used her unbroken hand to scoop up a bit of soil. Making a fist, she squeezed the dirt, and then opened her palm to display a golden ring. "Give me your vow, and swear it on this."

"What's that?"

"A plighting-ring. As though you don't know." Cupping the ring in her hand by pressing it between her palm and her two smallest fingers, Chalcedony used her other digits to bend back the thumb on her other hand and break it with a sickening crack. "Stop stalling. Swear to meet me before the moon is full again."

"I'll meet you before the moon is full again, I swear. Now leave her alone."

Chalcedony tossed the ring toward him, and he reached out to catch it, but somehow it ended up on the ring finger of his left hand. "She's yours, then, though why you want her is a bafflement to me. A vicious and willful little bitch; spare the strap on her and you'll regret it."

"I don't know where to find you."

"All you need to do is stop hiding. Leave La Lune and my people will bring you to me." Chalcedony raised her hand to her forehead in mock salute. "By the next moon, then."

Chalcedony's voice wailed in pain and she stumbled into Arby's arms. The army of rodents hurried along behind her, lapping at the trail of blood, but stopped short in milling confusion at the border.

He knelt, still holding her. "Can you heal yourself? Take energy from me if you need to."

She nodded, still weeping, and slashed his forearm with a fingernail. Her mouth clamped there, nursing, and he felt the strength flowing out of him, but this time it felt healthy; the energy he had consumed in von Fleischer's realm was leaving him. When she sat up, the bleeding had stopped and her cheek was restored, but thin white scars ran down her face where she had raked herself.

"I can't believe you did that for me," she said. Then her expression changed as she read something in his eyes. "I'm scarred, aren't I?"

"Yes. But maybe more beautiful." It was true: her beauty before had been perfect and a little insipid; now she had the look of some strange goddess, lovely and terrible.

"The bastard. When you kill him, make him suffer."

"I doubt I'll have the chance." He stared at the ring on his hand. What had he committed himself to? "I need to go home now. Are you sure you won't come with me?"

"My access to your world was through him. I can't go further."

"Take *me* with you, Master!" The little bulbous-nosed rodent stood at the very boundary.

Chalcedony glanced at the rodent and then looked back at Arby. "Ignore him. He's nothing."

"Ah, and you're a fine one to talk! You're naught but a creature of the ether. At least I was a human once."

Chalcedony tossed her head. "And look at you now."

"Why should I take you?" Arby asked. "And why should I trust you?"

"Why take me? So that I may die, climb back on the old wheel of life and death." The little face looked up at him, beseeching. "As to why you can trust me—because I hate him. Served him for decades, I did, and you see my reward?"

Arby stood and helped Chalcedony to her feet. "Can you go somewhere safe? Can you live for a while until I send you more energy?"

She nodded. "I can survive now. But don't forget me." She kissed him. "I'll never forget you."

"And don't forget Bert, either!" the rodent said. "Take me with you, Master!"

Arby leaned down and picked up the plump rodent, letting it rest in his hand. Chalcedony wrinkled her nose in disgust, but leaned her lips close to Arby's ear and whispered, "If you run out of energy on the journey home—eat him."

26

Ipsissimus

Crystal watched the two men who had shadowed them from the parking lot slip off into the trees as she and Rooker arrived at the path. "So, this is like an ambush or something?" she asked.

"Protection," he said. "Who knows what these guys'll try?" He reached down awkwardly and clasped her hand in his huge paw as though they were teen lovers out for a stroll. "If anything goes wrong, you get behind me, okay?"

"Can we check out the park after we get Arby?" She'd never been to Bandalier National Monument before, and the wild dry air reminded her of Sedona before the big hotels arrived. Rooker sighed, and she could tell he thought she was naïve and a little ditzy. The violent see violence everywhere, and it was sweet, if corny, how he wanted to protect her from the hardness of the world.

Ahead on the path the pinyon pines and scrub oaks opened into a meadow of tawny knee-high grasses, and a few redwood picnic benches were scattered along the margin. At the nearest bench sat a svelte blond woman in a dark suit, wrap-around sunglasses perched above high cheekbones. Crystal wanted to laugh: the woman waited in pert composure with her hands folded on the tabletop, as though she were there for a board meeting, and Crystal began to say as much to Rooker when he said, "That's her."

"Her who?"

"Elaina Svärdfors. Don't be fooled. She looks cute, but she's deadly."

Ridiculous. The woman looked a bit cold—not unlike that poor Liz Arby had been so infatuated with—but she was no more deadly than your average deputy director of human resources. "So I see," Crystal said, but she could tell her tone was lost on Rooker.

He crunched forward on the path, leaving Crystal trailing behind. He halted a half-dozen paces away and said, "Where is he? One of you, plus him, that was the deal." Crystal heard his voice flatten and diminish as he spoke, and the sensation was one of power gathering itself, like the sea drawing back before a crushing wave. "So where is he?"

"I was party to no agreement," Elaina said, her voice clear and even, "and circumstances prevent him from attending at the moment."

Crystal realized she had been standing still and hurried to catch up with Rooker, but he stomped forward to the bench and seemed to swell even larger; she could see energy surround his body, bending the light of the blue sky around his silhouette. "How can you?" he asked. "How, how, *how*—" The words changed into deep huffing sounds as though he had lost the power of speech.

"Is the mother here?" Elaina asked. "Something important has happened."

Rooker raised a fist over his head, his whole body trembling. "I said *where is he?*"

"Charles!" Crystal reached up and grabbed his shoulder. "Stop it!"

He shook as though he might explode, and then slammed his fist down onto the picnic bench, and the nearest two-by-eight splintered and burst under the blow. He roared, and the sound was so shocking that Crystal staggered back.

Elaina sat unmoving, but Crystal saw pulses of light flying from the woman's forehead into Rooker's chest. He stood with both hands clenched, bent forward as though he might drop onto all fours like a beast.

"Utamatzi?" a man's voice called out from somewhere in the meadow, but Crystal saw no one. Rooker didn't seem to hear at first, but when the voice asked, "Utamatzi, yes? It is you?" Rooker turned his head and stared.

Then Crystal saw a slender man, his hair, clothes, and skin all the same shifting gold-brown shades of the dry grass. He stood in the field thirty yards distant, in plain sight, but if she let her eyes drift just a bit he blended back into the weeds.

His voice shocked into a whisper, Rooker said, "*Helly?*"

Crystal's eyes were even more bewildered when the man leapt forward. She saw a tan blur, as though the world were a wet painting and a child dragged a dirty finger across the canvas, and a second later the man vaulted over the tabletop and wrapped his arms and legs around Rooker's torso. "The roar, yes? The man, the voice, I never would have known, but the roar? Utamatzi!"

"Utamatzi?" Crystal asked.

"My brother. The bear god, yes?"

"God?" Rooker asked, his arms still frozen at his side. "Wait a minute." He raised his arms and eased Helayjah's arms and legs away until the man stood on the seat of the picnic bench. "Where the hell did you go that night? They always told us, down the tunnel and—"

With Helayjah standing on the bench, the two men were the same height. "Trapped in my room, yes?" Helayjah said. "They were already in the house, the killers, so out the window, hmm?"

"I waited by the tunnel exit. You never came."

"Yes? And where?"

"In a tree."

"Well. And you thought, hmm, you would see me? Into the tunnel I went, and more times than one, yes? While you sat in your tree…?" Helayjah shrugged, a movement as natural on him as a bird fluffing its feathers. "Oh, I hid, I searched, and then hid and searched more, yes, and wept, too. But no Utamatzi, no."

"This is not the best place to talk," Elaina said, "and I need to attend to Arby. May I suggest we continue this discussion at La Lune?"

Rooker laughed, but the initial sound of amusement tapered off into a tone of uncertainty. "You think I'm walking into Winchester's place with you to have a chat?"

"No. But I think you might walk in with your brother. Don't you trust him?"

Crystal saw conflict and suspicion flood across Rooker's face. He turned and looked at her with his brows raised high on his lumpy forehead. "I think it's safe," she said.

He waited, his hands clenching and loosening. "Okay. Let me go call off my guards."

Helayjah smiled. "I hope they were not friends? As I already took care of them, yes?"

Rooker and Helayjah led the way in the big SUV, and Crystal followed them in the Jeep. From the passenger seat, Elaina said, "I have to warn you that your son is in…in a sort of trance. And he seems to be weakening."

Crystal kept her gaze on the road. "I guess I don't understand. But I tell you, in here…" She lifted one hand from the steering wheel and touched her heart. "In here, it feels better than when he was in the Middle East. Now *that* felt spooky."

"He's somewhere far more risky than that now." Elaina smoothed her skirt, as though an orderly world might be a shield against danger. "I blame myself for allowing him to go."

"I've got no clue what you're talking about. Did he want to go?"

"He thought he had to."

"Well, then," she said, as though that settled the matter. Sweetest little boy in the world, her Rainchild, but at times the stubbornest, too. "Are you two making it?"

"Pardon?"

"You and Rain. Are you, like, doing each other?"

"Are you asking me if I'm having sex with your son?"

"Just curious."

"No, I'm not." Elaina straightened in her seat, as if she weren't flagpole-upright already, and Crystal saw a flush bloom in the woman's cheeks. "And I wonder why you'd even think such a thing."

"You seem like his type, is all." Pale, beautiful, and a little icy.

"I've seen 'his type,' and I'm not sure I'm flattered."

"Liz? Is she here, too?"

"No." Elaina paused, clearly searching her mind for what to say. "We assume she's probably with von Fleischer, as you were."

"She's probably having the time of her life, then. No offense to Arby's ex and all, but von Fleischer's gotta be her dream date." Crystal slid open the window of the Jeep and let the late-afternoon smell of hot pine resin swirl into the car.

"I know a little of what they do to women. It must have been terrible for you."

"Not so bad. Von Fleischer came on like Casanova, but he's a big phony. Had no idea what to do with a real woman. So he dropped me like a hot frying pan, and left Rooker to catch me."

"You don't need to fear Rooker any more. At La Lune we can keep him away from you, and—"

"What?" Crystal burst into laughter and the Jeep swerved side to side. "No, no, no, you don't get the picture, here. We're an item. Best time I've had in ages. He's like no guy I've ever done before—he's like, well—"

"He's a god."

"An animal, I was going to say. A big animal."

"He's both. Literally. And as such, don't be surprised if his moral code is not like your own." Elaina turned her face toward her, as if studying her, a strange move for a blind woman, and then she frowned. "Your aura is unusual. Very balanced—like mine, I might say—but of a very different composition."

"I get that all the time, most recently from your pal von Fleischer, who didn't seem to dig it much. It ain't balance. I just don't mess myself up trying to be somebody else any more."

"Ipsissimus."

"Come again?"

"Ipsissimus. One of the highest grades in the old occult lodges. He—or she—who is most himself." Under her breath, Elaina added, "Or herself."

"Cool. I'll have to write that down. Last time I talked it over with somebody, they suggested 'self-centered slut' was a better word for it."

Ahead, the SUV pulled over toward the shoulder. Something about the car's body language was wrong, and it braked to a sudden stop. "Uh-oh."

"What?"

"I don't know." Crystal began pulling to the side of the road.

The driver's door crashed open, rebounded, and then Rooker straight-armed it open again. He climbed out of the car, head down, and staggered off toward the side of the road, clambering over the dirt embankment and then disappearing down the slope into the trees. Helayjah followed from the passenger side, but halted after a few steps, calling out something Crystal couldn't understand.

Crystal jerked on the parking brake and opened her own door, but Elaina said, "Wait. Tell me what's happening."

She stepped one foot down onto the asphalt. "Rooker's gone off into the trees. I think he's upset."

"He probably finally understood it all—that he's been working for the man who killed his parents, that he's done more evil in one lifetime than most manage in a hundred. Let him confront it."

"He'll hurt himself!"

"I doubt it…but he might hurt you. Learn to let some of the justice of the universe take its course. I'd advise you to sit back down."

"And I'd advise you to go get fucked before you dry up." Crystal jumped out and slammed the door and ran over to the spot where Rooker's feet had plowed through the crusted dirt piled along the edge of the roadway.

"Perhaps you should leave him for a bit, yes?" Helayjah said.

"Perhaps you should mind your own business, yes?" Crystal said, and jumped onto the soft pine duff on the downslope.

He wasn't hard to find. Not only were his staggering tracks through the pine needles as clear as an interstate, but she heard the crashing and cracking sounds in the woods below, and the inhuman roars of anguish made her heart ache. She passed the tatters of his shirt, and then she ran, skating on the loose bed of needles, until she entered a clearing on the slope.

A manmade clearing, that is. The pine saplings, many thicker than her arm, had been snapped and thrown down, and the sparse undergrowth had been uprooted and then trampled flat. Twenty feet downslope an old pine had its bark ripped away on one side, exposing the hard white bones of its wood, and Rooker stood beside it, stripped to the waist, his hard-breathing torso knotted like some ancient snag. In the shadows of late afternoon she saw a twisted light around him, stretching up a dozen feet, the silhouette of his true being, too huge to fit even in that oversized body.

She picked her way through the ruined forest, and at first he only stood there. Blood dripped from both fists. He growled, a low, throaty sound that made the hairs on her arms stand, and when he tilted his face to stare at her she saw glistening raw flesh on his forehead where he had hammered it against a tree. Flat eyes stared at her as though she were a thing, but then those eyes focused and saw her. His face flushed, and he turned and stumbled away.

"Charles…" She ran after him. "Charles, dammit…!"

The slope leveled and the trees disappeared as the ground beneath her feet became red sandstone. Perhaps thirty yards ahead Rooker stood, panting, before a wall of boulders. To her left she saw the opening of a deep slickrock canyon, a black gash through the red plateau, and something told her she needed to get there before Rooker realized it existed.

Crystal kicked off her sandals and sprinted, the ground hot under her feet. Toward the crevasse pebbles and rocks became more common and they hurt like hell; the teenage toughness of her feet had apparently faded away.

There is a perverse satisfaction when someone behaves as predicted, even if the behavior is frustrating, and Crystal spun about a few yards from the edge and saw that she had been right—once Rooker noticed the crevasse he had run for it, but she'd arrived first. She knelt, grabbed a rock, and threw it, smacking him in the forehead from a dozen feet away.

Rooker slowed, blinking away the blood that ran into his eyes, and came to a full halt when she hit him in the nose with a second stone. "Unh!" he said, and rubbed his face.

"You want to hurt yourself?" she yelled, and smacked another rock into his shoulder. "Here. Let me help!" This time he held up his hand to protect his face, and the rock smacked into his raw knuckles.

"Ow! Will you cut that out?"

"Will *you?*" Crystal cocked her throwing arm, another stone at the ready.

Rooker stared at her in disbelief and then started laughing and raised his hands as though she were pointing a gun at him. "I give," he said, and sat on the ground, wincing as his wounded hands helped him down. "I give." Then he began to sob, covering his bloody face with his raw hands.

Crystal knelt by him and pulled him to her breast. The sobs echoed in the hollow of her chest and seemed to shake the world, and she wanted to sweep him up in her arms and dandle him until he fell asleep or drag him to a bed and pull him on top of her, but the one was impossible and the other ill-timed, so she cradled his head and petted him.

Mingled with his sobs were words, and at last she made out, "…*terrible things*…" She made motherly, reassuring sounds, but he said, "You don't understand…" He pulled his hands from his face and looked at her, his whole countenance smeared in a shiny blend of blood and tears and snot. "I've done *awful* things, *unforgivable* things…"

"Nothing's unforgivable," she said, wondering at the same time if that were true.

"…and I helped him, helped him with everything, helped *make* him…" He buried his face in her chest, and she felt the hot wetness seep through her thin blouse.

At last his breathing calmed. "We can't change what has been," she said, "but we can always make amends. And if you made him, maybe part of your job now is to help unmake him." She patted his rocky shoulders. "Meanwhile, if you need to be hurt, come to me. I was never much into the dominatrix scene, always more of a bottom than a top, but for you…"

She waited through a long pause until, in a tone that was part hurt and part wondering, he said, "You're making fun of me…"

"Get used to it, big guy," she said.

By the time they pulled into the parking lot of La Lune, the only evidence of the sun was a raw pinkness in the clouds to the west. It had been a long, weird, quiet ride, and Crystal wanted to break that silence before they climbed out of the car and passed through those imposing gates. "I'm sorry about what I yelled at you back there," she said.

"What?" Elaina asked.

"The whole 'go get fucked' thing? Not only because it was messed up, but because I hate it so much when guys say that—you know, that 'Oh, she just needs a good fuck' stuff."

Elaina showed no obvious emotion. "Well, perhaps sometimes it's true."

Crystal laughed. "Hey, I hate it even *more* when it's true. So what? Who doesn't? Like they don't?" Elaina's lips spread into a wide smile, and Crystal decided that maybe Arby's taste wasn't so strange after all. That smile was like a ray of sunshine in a long Northwest winter, and all the sweeter for its unexpectedness.

"I will share something with you," Elaina said, "only because I think that you, with your big, balanced aura, might understand. People think I am passionless. I think sometimes my passions may be bigger than those of others, but they come up against other, equally large passions, and then they are locked up. So people think I am cold, that I am frozen, but frozen and motionless are different. Don't you think?"

"I'm not like that, but I believe you." Crystal climbed out of the Jeep and went around to help Elaina, but by the time she rounded the rear bumper Elaina had slammed her door and stood there smoothing her skirt. She took the woman's hand, which initially lay unmoving in her own, so she interwove their fingers and squeezed. "Sounds like a bummer." Over at the open gates, Rooker and Helayjah waited in the shadows, but she and Elaina walked several steps on the dusty ground before she felt a squeeze in response.

It had been a very strange day, and it was still only dinnertime.

27

Where All Things Are Possible

He knew that Miklos would require some handling, so von Fleischer had installed him in the most lavish bedroom El Panal could offer. In size it was closer to a ballroom, the ceiling twenty feet high to accommodate the twin crystal chandeliers. The walls were plush with velvet, the floor so thick with piled carpets that it amounted to one endless mattress, and though the carpets and low, soft furniture made a bed superfluous, the canopied bed at the far end of the room was draped by hangings that extended down from the ceiling, giving it the look of a modernist cathedral.

The marble tub at the other end of the room could accommodate a dozen, and sometimes did, as von Fleischer used this exercise in excess every few years to stage little orgies. These were amusing in themselves, but their main purpose was to convince his worshippers in the village above that they'd had a taste of the afterlife—and that it was worth the price of admission.

Miklos was harder to please, of course, but he was a great lover of excess, and by the time von Fleischer had Elizabeth West settled in her quarters, Miklos was already bathed and lolling on the bed in a silken robe. Von Fleischer carried two goblets on a round silver tray, and Miklos raised an eyebrow. "Servant's day off?"

"Something special," von Fleischer said, "something private." He set the tray on the low nightstand and kicked off his slippers before climbing onto the bed.

"Private? The little blond thing can spare you for a while?"

"You know I have to keep up appearances. And, despite what you think, women have their charms."

Miklos reached one arm high, stretching, and then fell onto his back with the arm sprawled above his head, as though the very concept had exhausted him. "You'll never convince me it is better to give than to receive. And if your little toys are so satisfying to you, why do you need so many of them…?" He pulled his arm down and cocked his elbow, his hand behind his head, vamping. "And yet only one of me?"

"Stop being bitchy."

"Come on over here and make me."

Von Fleischer smiled. "An inviting prospect. But first, a little surprise." He lifted one of the goblets and passed it to Miklos, who grudgingly supported himself on one elbow to take it.

The boy sniffed at the drink. "What is it?"

"Something like you've never tried before. Something that will take you to a whole new world."

Miklos wrinkled his nose. "Smells funny. What's it do?"

"At first it will make you sleepy—"

"Like 'ludes?"

"A bit. But it will also, um, relax you in a very special way—"

"Like poppers?"

"Better."

Miklos arched an eyebrow and took a gulp of the drink. His face showed puzzlement at the flavor. "Sweet. But weird, weird…" He drained the goblet in two more swallows and handed it to von Fleischer as though he were a waiter. "Aren't you having any?"

"I have a glass of wine, and I'm planning on being companionable until you're completely relaxed. At the risk of committing an Americanism, you can't pitch and catch at the same time."

Miklos sent back a lazy, dopey smile. "Can I do anything for you while we wait?"

Von Fleischer put down the empty goblet and picked up his own wine. "Just look decorative."

The boy—von Fleischer couldn't help but think of him as a boy, even though he was now twenty-one—undid the sash on his robe and let it fall open. "Mmmmm." Miklos laid his hands on his own smooth chest and ran them both down across his taut abs. "Like this, you mean...?" His cock was as engorged as it could be without actually standing at attention, and he gave it a lazy swat that lolled it over onto his thigh. "Oh... What is this stuff? Are you sure I didn't take too much? I don't know if I'm going to be able to do anything..."

"Let it happen. If you want to sleep for a few moments, go on. I promise you, when the time comes, we'll do something together you never dreamed possible."

Miklos gave a hum of anticipation that ended in a great yawn. For a moment, von Fleischer thought he had fallen asleep, but then the boy murmured, "Benedikt? I know I've been a bitch lately." A long pause. "I do love you..."

Von Fleischer leaned over and brushed his knuckles down that perfect, sculpted face. "I know. And I mean it when I say I consider you to be my own flesh and blood."

The labyrinth of delights von Fleischer had constructed on the Other Side followed a principle of the old-fashioned cards that displayed the Twelve Days of Christmas: each time you entered, a new little door would open. The architecture was von Fleischer's, but the delights would be from Miklos's own mind, for the mirrors in this funhouse reflected his own desires. Each time he entered, a new door would open, and he would be drawn into increasingly deep and childlike rapture of his own creation, until there was no need to return.

He waited until the boy had drifted into the world of dreams, and then he raised his own mind into Yetzirah. Miklos wasn't hard to find Up There, and von Fleischer spoke to him and led his logy consciousness to the entrance to the funhouse. There was no way to determine what Miklos saw on the featureless doors of that drab building, but his sensual mouth curled out of its typical pouty expression and into a wise smile.

Down on the bed in El Panal, von Fleischer let his consciousness creep into Miklos's body. As always, the sensation of being inside a new body was vertiginous: on the physical plane, until consciousness was anchored in the brain the underlying sensation was dizziness. Before he could fully inhabit his new body, a week or more would be needed to adjust the hormones and neurotransmitters to a tolerable replica of his own system, and fine-tuning it often took months…

Von Fleischer wiggled the fingers on Miklos's right hand, and was gratified when they responded. Now a fist, and now each finger alone.

This little piggy went to market…this little piggy stayed home…

Liz had insisted on the grand tour, so he'd given it to her. From the base of the pit, where the elevator had dropped them, the lower, more primitive tunnels—some of them no more than the natural channels of the river—branched out. He led her to the great steel gate and made her touch the cold metal and feel the hum of the river that thundered just behind it. Her eyes widened as the vibrations of all that power quivered under her palms, and he gave her his most knowing smile.

From the labyrinth below, they returned to where the elevator waited, and entered one of the staircase tunnels that climbed to the first part of the honeycomb. Here were the storage rooms—the granaries, the vast freezers, the wine cellars—the machine shop, the woodworking shop, and the armory. "It's like a city…" she said. Dark-eyed villagers, men and women alike, dropped to one knee wherever von Fleischer appeared.

"A modest city…but an effective one. I flatter myself that one could live in comfort here for at least a century, were the world outside to be overcome by some disaster."

Another long flight of stairs led to the living quarters of the servants and the armed guards, a series of big rooms off two long corridors. Again, everyone knelt, and he watched Liz take in the instant deference. He could tell she liked it.

In a few of the downcast faces he detected hints of his own features, but in even more he recognized the descendants of bodies he had worn decades before. One woman in her twenties let her gaze sneak a glance at him, and he suspected he must have slept with her on some previous trip. Certainly she was pretty enough.

Liz stopped and peered into one of the rooms. "Wow. Fancy accommodations."

"Yes. Like heaven compared to the jungle outside, isn't it?"

She lowered her voice. "Are they just going to stay bowed down like this the whole time we're standing here?"

"Unless I tell them to do something else. Do you speak Spanish?"

"Enough to talk to my gardener."

"That should do. Pick, say, three of them."

"Huh? What for?"

"For whatever you like. To be your personal servants while we're here."

Like most closet submissives, she relished submission in others, and she strolled through the kneeling figures, taking her time. "Men, or women?"

"Well, I suppose that depends on what you plan on using them for." He watched her color a little as she took in this remark. She picked three young women, all pretty. He snapped out a few words in modern Mayan, and the women rose and followed them, a few paces behind, as he led Liz up to the palatial third floor of El Panal.

They were engaged in some lazy foreplay when he raised the subject, and Liz said, "You're crazy." But he felt her body warm even more as she thought about the idea. "Are you just trying to get rid of me?"

"No. I'm trying to help you keep your word. Does the phrase 'anything you want' sound familiar?" He slid his hand down onto her bottom and squeezed, too hard, grinning at her squeak of protest. "You've said it often enough. Time to show me you mean what you say." He squeezed again, harder.

"Ow. That hurt."

"I imagine. Are you going to do what I tell you to?"

She snuggled up against his chest. "You know I will." Her breath felt moist on his face. "Did you have someone in mind?"

"Suppose I asked you to have sex with Miklos?"

She laughed and wrapped her legs around his thigh. "It takes two, you know. If I climbed into his bed, he'd run screaming."

"Perhaps he just hasn't found the right woman."

"More like he wants to *be* the right woman."

"Will you do it?"

"Of course. Will you do me?"

In reply, he rolled her onto her back and she wrapped her legs around his hips. He gazed down into her eyes. "Good girl. This time I'm going to take you someplace you've never been before." As his body entered hers he Nudged her aura, and then Pushed in with force, and felt her will retreat before him.

"Oh my god…"

He worked her on the etheric along with the physical, until her subtler bodies were nearly disconnected from her flesh. "Say that again."

"Oh my god…"

"Indeed."

Until now, their sex had been physical, with some strong Nudges, but she had now surrendered to him enough that it was time to give her a taste of the Other Side, where all things were possible.

Two days later, von Fleischer lay in bed alongside Miklos's sleeping form. Each day Miklos had drunk the potion; each day he had come back a little less; each day von Fleischer had taken more permanent control of his new body.

Von Fleischer was never satisfied with life—satisfaction was the first step toward complacency, and complacency led to erosion. To paraphrase the American singer Bob Dylan, he not busy expanding is busy shrinking. Nonetheless, things were going well. The previous night had shown that his new body worked superbly. And the girl: Liz West barely had a will left to call her own, and now that he had shown her that he held the keys to eternal life, she'd knife her own grandmother if he demanded it.

Arby Keeling remained his only real concern—Arby and his inscrutable mother. There was something he was missing there. Who were these people? Crystal was maddening, a woman with none of the normal buttons of a human, and her Hero son remained unidentified despite hours poring over books of lore. No matter. Soon Arby Keeling would have to come in response to his silly acceptance of the plighting-ring. By then, von Fleischer would have a new, vibrant body, and Arby's former lover would be von Fleischer's slave. Perhaps he'd simply kill Arby—it would be the safest move—but the Hero had shown himself to be so sentimental over a succubus, of all things, that binding him as a servant in exchange for Liz wasn't out of the question…

Beside him on the bed, Miklos stirred. Time to dose him again. Von Fleischer made sure that the body was fed and went through all the necessary biological motions during the hours that he wore it, so there was no reason that Miklos shouldn't tumble back to slumberland immediately.

"Mmm. Benedikt?"

Von Fleischer pushed back the hair from Miklos's forehead, and already it felt as if her were touching his own skin. "Yes?"

"This stuff is brilliant… God, it feels like I've been tripping for *days*."

"You like it? Time for more?"

"Oh. Definitely. This is…" The boy hugged himself lazily. "Have I been out of bed, doing things?"

"No. Why?"

"I had the strangest dreams." He laughed, a relaxed, stoned laugh. "You'd be proud of me. I dreamed I fucked your little blond thing."

Von Fleischer leaned over and fetched the goblet from the nightstand. "Oh? And how was that for you?"

"Well, just as bizarre as it sounds." The boy's mouth angled into a smile that was half-puzzled, half-malicious. "I was pretty rough with her, but she liked it. Who knew I was so butch?"

"Who indeed?"

He helped Miklos sit up enough to drink the potion, and the boy drained the glass eagerly. "Yum. Grows on you, doesn't it? I could do this forever."

Von Fleischer eased the boy's head back onto the pillow and stroked his beautiful face as he left the physical yet again. Then he ascended on the planes, eased into this new flesh that fit him better with each passing day, and dressed. It was time for the people of El Panal to meet their latest Master.

28

A Lovecraftian-Enough Mood

Arby awoke on cushions, staring at the smooth sandstone ceiling of Sylvia's chamber. He glanced down his right side and saw that Bert's fat body still lay draped in his hand.

"Come back further," Sylvia's voice said. "Much of your mind is still in Yetzirah." Arby pulled his consciousness downward, and she leaned forward over him. "For a time, we thought we had lost you." She glanced down. "What's that?"

Bert's voice answered, "Just a visitor, come here to die and start over." Bert's form was now half-transparent, like a thick clear gelatin.

Arby laid Bert's near-weightless body on a nearby pillow and groaned as he sat up. "I understand who I am now." He shook his head. "I've wasted so much of this life. I don't know what I could have been thinking."

"Thinking is the problem. In the tarot card that represents you, the little white dog that bounds along beside you represents intellect. That is the proper relationship between self and intellect—intellect is a fine servant but a poor master."

Arby's body felt tired, still drained of energy, but his mind felt as though he stood on a mountaintop, at once peaceful and energized. "If I recall, the dog in that picture is about to follow its owner right over a cliff. Looks like a warning to me."

"If you look at the cliff as sure death, then you might think taking the next few steps would be madness. But mortal life by definition ends in death. Is it madness to march happily forward rather than cowering?" His hands lay folded on his lap, and she pressed her own hand atop his. "At a deeper level, your Aspect represents all of us—we choose to fall back into manifestation, to answer the call of life's journey. We are all of us on a fool's errand in mortal life. Now, let me tell you what has been happening while you were gone."

Crystal hugged him again and said, "I knew you were okay. I can tell when my boy's safe and when he's not."

"From now on," Arby said, "I'll pay more attention to your intuition."

She held him back at armslength and smiled. "Oh, I sorta doubt that."

The giant who had followed Crystal into Sylvia's chamber cleared his throat. "So, do I get to meet the Hero now?"

"Oh." Crystal stepped aside, and edged toward the big man. "Arby. This is Charles Rooker, Utamatzi, the Bear God of the Miwoks. You remember the Miwoks, don't you—used to live around Harbin Hot Springs? Anyway, Charles used to work for that weirdo von Fleischer, but now..." She sidled up next to him, and Arby got the picture immediately, having seen it a hundred times before. Uncle Utamatzi, no doubt.

A little voice piped up from the floor. "Von Fleischer?" From the entrance to the chamber, Xochipilli and Helayjah craned their necks to see who spoke, and everyone in the room except for Elaina jostled around until they formed a semicircle around Bert's ghostly form on the pillow below. "Did he promise you eternal life? Give you a few tastes of heaven? Don't believe it. Thirty years I served him, and this is the eternal life he gave me—a little rat, scuttling around his kingdom."

"What are you saying?" Rooker asked.

"You work for him? Remember a guy named Williams, died just a while ago? Joined us recently. What did he promise you? A Portal to the

Other Side, your own world? We live at the edge of his kingdom, on his scraps, and he feeds on our pain as well as the pain of the world." The human-faced rodent wheezed, and lay panting, as though his tirade had emptied him. "I came here to die. You'd do better to die now, too, than see what he has in store for you."

"I ain't going to see nothing," Rooker said, "because I'm going to kill the sonofabitch."

Arby held up his hand, displaying the ring on his finger. "You may need to take me with you," he said. "I seem to have gotten into something I don't quite understand."

"That would be novel," Elaina said.

It was a joy to sleep through the night confident that he knew how to shield his consciousness, but it seemed he had no sooner climbed into bed that he was summoned to the next morning's council meeting. He snatched some food on the porch, where Domenico and his wife fussed at how rapidly he ate. From there he wandered into the library, where the inhabitants of La Lune were once again assembled in their customary places, this time with Rooker and Crystal at Arby's end of the table.

The discussions were slow going for the first hour, with interminable questions to Rooker about von Fleischer's operations, many of them relating to past decades. Rooker himself seemed tolerant enough, but eventually stood up and leaned his hands onto the table. "Look," he said, "there's no time like the present. Von Fleischer is distracted. He's changing bodies. Get down there and get him now."

"Hear, hear!" said Hermod from the other end of the table. "It's about time somebody with balls joined the party."

"Excuse me for slowing down the war dance," Jerry said, "but won't this be the time that he's most cautious?"

"Most nervous, anyhow," Rooker said. "He's been feeling old for a while. Your boy here"—he nodded at Arby—"and even his mom, are making him crazy, because he knows they're somebody, but he can't figure out who. Especially Crystal."

"The Powers and Talents," Gareth said, in his most academic manner, "invariably forget how far humans may evolve through their own efforts."

Jerry nodded his head and Crystal smiled, but Rooker said, "Whatever. There's one other thing that may make a difference to you. Anybody here ever heard of OCX-27?"

The faces around the room showed not the slightest sign of comprehension, so he explained in a few short sentences.

"There's toxic wastes all over the world nowadays," Arby said. "Plenty of them cause cancer or birth defects. So?"

"So, you don't get the picture. Von Fleischer has sold this stuff to about two dozen different flavors of terrorist and paramilitary groups in as many different countries. And he's convinced them that this stuff'll let them walk in and do whatever they want to whoever they want to. But he hasn't mentioned that anyone who breathes it will have freaks for kids. We're talking tens of millions of people, maybe more."

"What's the point of that?" Hermod asked. "Destroying your enemy's descendants does nothing to win a victory."

"It is perfect for his purposes," Elaina said. "Long-lasting grief and hatred and misery. Hatred for America for creating such a substance. I can think of nothing more horrible than mutilating people's children."

"I always knew you were a smart lady," Rooker said.

"And I always assumed that you were capable of being a party to such things."

"Hey, we been over this ground already. You want my help, I want yours, so let's cut it out." Rooker stood up, lifting his palms from the table and perching them on his hips. "My business is with him, but I'm not sure whether you guys are all fired up to save the world, too. Because about a hundred tons of this stuff has already made it into Mexico—he's going to hold a little auction down there later this month—and the other two hundred tons of it ought to be loading onto a freighter in Chesapeake Bay right about now."

"I'm not sure whether such things are part of our immediate concern," Gareth said.

"If we stand by and let such a thing happen," Elaina said, "then we're no better than him."

A minor hubbub broke out, and Jerry quelled it by climbing onto his chair and forcing a piercing whistle through his fingers. "Hey! Shit, I thought I was the only one in grade school here. Getting emotional is only going to make it worse." Still standing on the chair, he addressed Rooker. "How do we get at him in El Panal? From your description, it sounds like the place is loaded with old power. First time one of us steps into the place, it's going to shake his web like crazy."

"It's no different anyplace else he goes. When he travels, there's at least a dozen guards hidden around him somewhere. He saturates the ground for a mile in any direction with the stuff he pulls down from Up There." About half of the table drew in breaths of surprise at this last statement. "Hey, it's nothing to him. He pulls in enough juice every day of his life that he can throw it away like that. No matter where he is, he's got a web around him."

Jerry sat down. "But in El Panal, it sounds like he's got an army, too."

"About a hundred and fifty guys, give or take. And maybe fifty of them are trained for etheric combat, so they can make snake heads and bite at you—if you're dumb enough to stick your head out on the etheric plane in the first place. But shoot 'em and they die. Hasn't anyone here got any followers?"

"I can give you thirty," Hermod said. "But my thirty are the equal of three times their number."

"Don't bet on it," Rooker said. "I've seen his guys. Their training probably ain't up to your standard, but they're suicide-bomber-crazy devoted to him."

"We'll smash them."

"Don't let me interfere with your shock-and-awe moment here, guys," Jerry said, "but you call this a plan? Go attack and hope for the best?"

"Look, once he's in a new bod, you can bet wiping this place out will be his first order of business. You've always been a pain in the butt, and now you're guarding these folks"—he glanced at Arby and then Crystal—"you're top priority, because he *hates* stuff he doesn't understand." Rooker shook his head and sat down in his chair, which creaked under his weight. "As to a plan, I'd tell you more, but I keep getting interrupted. I was explaining how the underground stuff is organized there? Well, distract everybody with a direct attack, and then let a bunch of us creep in through one of the blocked-off underground river channels while he's fighting a war on the surface."

"You know where those are?"

"Sure. Four or five different entrances."

"But it makes little sense, yes," Helayjah asked, "to leave entrances, lines of attack so, hmm, unguarded?"

"Oh, they're guarded," Rooker said. "With the best he's got. But, as far as he's concerned, they aren't entrances. He thinks they're exits, like the tunnel Mom and Dad used to have."

For the first time that morning, Selky spoke up. "And are there others you don't know about?"

Rooker nodded. "Bet on it. I think he trusted me more than anyone, but he didn't trust nobody one hundred percent. There's probably all kinds of surprises in El Panal. But if you guys just sit here, you're dead. One of the uses of OCX-27 would be to spray this joint and then just stroll in and chop off heads."

There was silence in the room until Hermod said, "Men, guns, trucks. How do we get all of that to Belize?"

"I can get anything into that country within three days," Rooker said. "What the folks in the business call porous borders. Believe me, I've done it before."

"Guns?" Arby said. "I thought everything you guys did was with swords and Renaissance Faire crap."

"If we want to kill the soul of another," Elaina said, "and they will meet us in etheric combat, then only handheld weapons will do. But I'm certain that everyone here will settle for merely dispatching Tanagrim's physical body."

"I'm taking my axe just in case," Hermod said.

"But I don't get it," Arby said. "I just came back from a long trip on the Other Side, and it all seemed pretty medieval to me."

Xochipilli said, "The parts you visited, man. But there's World War I trenches up there, and Neanderthal caves, and even a bunch of digital crap."

"The noosphere," Gareth said, "seems to reflect the history of human imagination. One shouldn't be too surprised if it errs slightly on the side of the romantic."

Zeah shifted in her chair and leaned forward, and she so seldom did anything apart from sending her gaze from face to face that every head turned toward her. "I don't always understand what I hear only once. Perhaps I don't understand what I have heard today. And I am not a War Goddess. But it seems to me that if we are to attack our enemy, that these two—Utamatzi and The Fool—these two must stay behind." There was a murmur of voices and she held up her hand. "Unless my understanding is wrong, these two have no temples on the Other Side, no followers to call them back."

"I don't give a damn," Rooker said.

Questions had been nibbling at Arby like a horde of minnows on a crust of floating bread. "I'm not sure I have much choice." He held up his hand. "Some of you know about this plighting-ring gadget. I swore I'd come to von Fleischer before the next moon, whenever that is—"

"Thirteen days," Gareth, Selky, and Zeah said all at once.

"—and I'm not sure what will happen if I don't."

"It depends on the conditions laid down, but if you fail to meet your vow, there will certainly be adverse consequences," Gareth said. "Often it might involve dominion over your will, or other times it might produce tentacles that burrow into your heart. If the one who fashioned it were in a Lovecraftian-enough mood, it might strip your flesh from your bones and leave your soul gibbering in the cold darkness at the edge of the universe..." Gareth frowned. "Didn't you *ask*?"

"I was in a hurry."

"Yes, but still, you—"

"Spare me, okay? So it looks like I have to go. Second question: Can von Fleischer be in two places at once?"

Judging from the sounds around the room, the question was confusing, and Jerry said, "Come again? We all exist on all planes at once, and—"

"Yeah, yeah," Arby said, "and nothing truly exists but the Now. What I mean is, can he have his consciousness in multiple places at once? Can he be, say, holding an intelligent conversation down here and also be playing chess Up There?"

"In a word," Jerry said, "no."

"Then it seems pretty obvious what we need to do. Attack his kingdom Up There, and then go after him down here."

Helayjah's smooth tone cut through the rising stir of voices. "But Up There, his superiority over us is far greater than it is on this plane, yes?"

"The kid's right," Hermod said. "We don't have to win up there. Just keep him occupied for a little while."

"Like defending Pyrrhus," Gareth said. "But where are we going to find our band of Spartans?"

A moment of silence was broken when Hermod said, "If I brought out all my forces on the Other Side and wedged them into the little pass where he's expanding toward my kingdom—"

"Then he'd mash you flat in less time that it takes to pop a stick of gum in your mouth." Rooker raised his hand to forestall Hermod's reply. "I ain't saying you don't have the right stuff. I'm just doing the math."

"I couldn't fight him and win," Arby said, "but I'll bet I could keep him occupied for a while. He's cautious about how he comes after me because he can't figure out what I am. Silly as it sounds, I think he's afraid of me."

"He is," Rooker said. "But don't count on him staying that way once he realizes he's stronger than you."

"Are you seriously proposing," Gareth asked, "that you assault the largest kingdom in the noosphere by yourself? Because the idea is—"

"Foolish?" Arby asked. "Uh-huh. Of course, you're welcome to tag along."

Helayjah said, "Perhaps he would like to explain, hmm, how he will both attack von Fleischer's kingdom on the Other Side, and also arrive to present himself in Belize."

"That part," Arby said, "will require a little help from my friends."

After a private talk, Arby convinced Xochipilli to have two of his worshippers become devotees of the new goddess Chalcedony, the Scarred Beauty, and then Arby and Sylvia sat together in her chamber and watched Bert breathe his last and vanish from the pillow.

When he opened the door to his room, he found Crystal sitting crosslegged on his bed with his backpack on her lap. "So long ago," she said, her fingertip tracing the embossed designs in the red leather. "I saw Hawk a while back. He's old now, but he looks good. You should go see him."

"Maybe when I get back."

He sat down beside her, and when she looked up he could see she'd been crying. "I don't want you to go. I don't want you to do this. You said that next time you'd pay attention to my intuition."

He held her. "I know I said that." He chuckled. "And, if I recall, you said I probably wouldn't."

"It's because of her, isn't it?"

"Liz? No. But I suppose I owe her something for getting her into this mess."

Crystal eased out of his embrace. "Rooker tells me that she'll probably be completely under his control now. She never was strong. That's why she couldn't love you." She gazed into his eyes, her own red-rimmed. "Stay here."

"I have to go. There's the plighting-ring…"

"If they kill him, the ring won't matter. Gareth said."

He pulled her into his arms again. "I have to do this. This is what I was made for."

29

The Complete Woman

Despite forty years at sea, Captain Ole Ankerssen was tempted to ignore the SOS when it came across the international distress channel. They had loaded a single cargo the previous night high up the Chesapeake, and though US Army personnel had supervised the winching of the containers into the hold, Ankerssen had the distinct feeling that whatever was in those containers might not be legal. Two hundred tons net, but six hundred deadweight tons gross: whatever was inside was wrapped up in a lot of metal. It had a familiar feel about it, a familiar feel of wrongness. After years of running arms, contraband, and even a few cargoes of human traffic, he trusted his intuition, and he'd prefer to avoid any contact with the authorities.

His course was set for Tunisia, where he would offload the first of the containers, and his heart sank as he triangulated on the beacon: the distress call was from nearby, and no other ship was half as close. In fact, the vessel was almost dead ahead, no more than three nautical miles.

He sighed, called for Akaba, his first mate, to join him on the bridge, and pushed the *Jenny Lind* up three knots to her top speed.

A major tropical storm was cartwheeling its way across the Caribbean, trying to work itself into a hurricane, so the gray sea ran a little rough even this far north. Nonetheless, Ankerssen was surprised when he made out the white hull of a capsized sailboat in the twilight; even an amateur should have been able to ride these seas and winds with confidence.

He called all hands to the starboard rail, forward, and saw his crew of twenty scramble across the damp gangway below. A motley bunch; *Jenny Lind* was registered in Liberia, and a good half of the crew was West African, with the rest divided between Malaysia, Hong Kong, and Scandinavia. Through the loudspeaker, he ordered, "Ready a boat for survivors! Get a winch over the side and stand by to make fast to that vessel! Emergency flotation! And, Wong, get your damn lifejacket on!"

He slowed and steered slightly to port, but he could already see that they were too late. The hull of the sailboat already rode with its prow tilted above the water, but aft it was submerged, and in an instant it slipped away, a glimmering light vanishing into the gray waters.

He raised his binoculars to scan the sea; at the same time a half-dozen of the crew cried out and pointed. A small white figure floated near where the boat had disappeared, and now it swam toward the *Jenny Lind*, plunging forward through the waters like a sea creature. The entire crew watched in amazement as the pale woman glided toward them, diving through the crests of the waves and bursting out the other side. Everyone, including Ankerssen, was so transfixed by the sight that she was nearly alongside before anyone recalled that they should be throwing her a lifesaver and line.

She had come aboard wearing nothing but white shorts and a spaghetti-strap top, but Wong, the smallest of the crew, fetched her a set of dry whites from his cabin, and a half-hour later they were underway. The woman sat on the bridge, wrapped in a blanket, sipping a mug of hot tea that she had sweetened with what Akaba thought was a revolting quantity of sugar. He listened as the captain gently questioned her. There had only been the two of them, she said, she and her friend, and a freak blow had taken them far out to sea. One sudden squall, and her friend had been knocked unconscious. She had only managed to figure out how to trigger the distress beacon when the second squall capsized them, and she had barely been able to get to the surface.

She seemed at ease with her situation and unfazed by the loss of her friend. The captain told her that he'd put her aboard the next US-bound vessel, and offered to call ship-to-shore so she could contact relatives or friends. At this, she shrugged, and Akaba decided she was in shock.

"What's your name?" Ankerssen asked.

"Selky," she said, and watched them both as though they might react.

"A pretty name."

"It's Irish."

That at least made sense—milky-white skin scattered with orange freckles, and coppery hair still damp from the sea. A pretty girl—no, a stunning, beautiful, girl, who seemed curiously unshaken by her near-death. He didn't have a penchant for white women as a rule, as they always appeared to be undercooked, but he'd be willing to bend the rules for this one; and he had no doubt that every mind on this ship was fixated on her.

He excused himself to go check on the crew. Belowdecks he stepped through a hatchway and was shocked to see two figures embracing in the dim-lit hall. At first it seemed to be Anders and Motando, but when they saw him they moved apart and he saw that they had been mutually wrapped around a small, slender woman. Dark eyes stared at him from a pale face framed by damp black hair. Her lips were impossibly full and red against the pallor of her skin, and they panted slightly with what seemed like passion but might have been fear.

"What the fuck is going on here?" Akaba asked, walking up. "What the hell are you doing to her?"

"I was cold…" she said. "Lonely, too."

"When did she come aboard?" He looked at her. "Where did you come from?"

"Maybe I'm a stowaway. What you want to do about it?" She sauntered up to him as she said this, her black shift plastered to her slender body, and he felt what must have been a visible stirring in his pants. "Are you the captain?"

"First mate," he said, his voice hoarse.

She slid her hands across his chest and undid the top of his shirt. "Good idea. You boys have some place private around here?" Anders and Motando crowded in behind her, their hands searching her body. "Slow, down, slow down. I'm a one-at-a-time kind of girl. But I promise everybody will get a turn."

Perhaps he was turning into an old fool, but Ankerssen had never met a woman as fascinating, as complete, as the one who called herself Selky. It seemed that every virtue of the female sex was combined in her. She was charming in a naïve, girlish way that made him feel paternal, yet at the same time she seemed knowing and seductive, a compassionate tease, sympathetic but distant. For the first time in his life he was seized with the urge to write a poem, because there was no way to express the complexity of what he felt. Every time she shifted position and he saw a new bit of her—the curve of her calf when she idly kicked her leg, the swoop of delicate flesh below her ear when she brushed aside her drying hair, the uplift of her shoulder as she shrugged back into the sagging blanket—with every motion she made his heart break for the fact he hadn't met her years before, that he hadn't known she existed.

And she listened like no woman he'd ever met, patient, fascinated, interrupting only to ask questions that made it clear she wanted to know everything about him. It seemed as though he had talked for hours about every facet of his life: his voyages, his years in the Navy, his family, his childhood, even his hopes and fears about retirement. From time to time he wondered why Akaba hadn't returned yet, but a part of him prayed that Akaba would never return.

Without warning, the ship ran hard aground, hurling him against the console and throwing Selky to the floor. He felt blood trickling down his temple from where it had smashed against a sharp edge, and he scrambled to help Selky up.

The girl appeared unhurt and calm. Outside the fore window of the bridge he saw a low barrier island, hardly more than a sandbar, with low brush snaking down the island's higher ground. He felt the impact of breakers on the ship's hull, but she didn't shift; her keel had wedged deep into the sand. Impossibly, a gray dawn just showed itself to what must have been the east, but the ship had run hard aground heading north-northeast. It was insane—there was nothing to be found in the deep Atlantic at this latitude.

He glanced at the GPS readout, then forced himself to look again: 37 degrees 6 minutes North, 75 degrees 55 minutes West... He leaned down and rapped at the digital display, as though it were a needle that might have become stuck. 37° 06' 39.96" N, 75° 55' 16.13" W...

Madness. That would put him near the mouth of the Chesapeake. And then, as clouds shifted, he saw the light of the Cape Charles lighthouse to the north.

He sounded the alarm, but no one came. He mumbled something reassuring to Selky, and then hurtled belowdecks, shouting for Akaba, or Anders, or anyone. Running through the steel corridors, his voice echoing, it began to feel nightmarish, as though he were alone in the bowels of an endless ship.

He fought his way up the stairs onto the starboard gangway and stood blinking in the growing light. Far aft, Selky stood on the rail, still wearing Wong's whites, and he cried out to her as, in a perfect dive, she flew out far from the ship and cut into the angry gray sea. He scanned the surface, but her head didn't emerge again.

A motion near where she had stood drew his eye. Another girl, a naked girl, had climbed onto the rail, a handful of soggy black clothes clutched in her hand. She stared down the gangway at him, a perfect, shapely, dark-eyed waif, and for a moment it seemed as though she might climb back down and come to him, but she only waved a reluctant wave and then followed Selky's dive into the waters below, leaving Ankerssen on his deserted, beached ship.

30

A Walk in the Storm

A few minutes before, rain had drummed on the corrugated metal roof with such fury that talking became useless, but it departed as quickly as it had come. The metal hut offered little in the way of comfort—a trio of canvas camp chairs, a table built from a wooden box and a few slats, and a mattress on the floor—but in the candlelight, Arby thought Elaina looked as composed and elegant as ever. Unlike his own crumpled outfit, her green battle fatigues looked freshly pressed, and her bare feet beside the heavy boots she had kicked off might have just come from a pedicure. "You were asking?" she said.

"What his 'Talent' is? I mean, is he going to throw fireballs from his fingertips or something?"

"On the Other Side, maybe. Down here, he can corrupt hearts and minds, urging them toward certain kinds of desires, yet even then he does not create those desires." She leaned forward and unerringly found the mug of tea where it waited on the table, next to the walkie-talkie.

"That's all?"

"Poor Arby. The boy who didn't believe in magic becomes a believer, and then finds that magic is but a small thing." She sipped her tea. "Hitler built an empire out of such small things."

Arby stood, restless, and then realized there was nowhere to pace in the small room. He backed up and leaned against the wall, which gave a metallic groan, and Elaina frowned at the noise. "And once corrupted," he asked, "do they stay corrupted?"

"As well to ask how much people can change." Her expression softened. "You are wondering about *her*, aren't you, whether you can rescue her? I will not say to give up hope, but neither would I advise to let all of your other hopes rest on that one."

He sighed. "I need to take a walk."

"A walk? In the storm? Why?"

"It isn't storming right now, and I need to think. Don't you ever go for a walk when you need to think?"

"Being blind, going for a walk is perhaps not as relaxing for me as it might be for you." She seemed ready to argue, but then shrugged. "Be cautious, then, and don't travel far. Remember that many lives are depending upon you come the dawn."

"It would be hard to forget."

He pulled up the latch on the crude door, but her voice stopped him before he opened it. "Arby? Back in Sylvia's chamber, before you went up the planes? You kissed me."

He looked and saw what seemed to be genuine puzzlement on her face. "I did."

"Why?"

"Because I wanted to, and wasn't sure I'd ever get a chance again. Are you annoyed?"

"No. Just trying to understand."

He surprised himself with his laugh. "To understand, I suppose you'd have to be me." Wind pushed at the door and he stepped back and let it open. "I'll be back in a few minutes."

Once the door to the shack was closed, the darkness of the night seemed absolute, and the gusting wind clutched and released him like groping hands. As his eyes adjusted, he saw the trampled mud of the large clearing, and, far across the mud, a second corrugated-metal hut, and the larger open-fronted building that housed a tractor and some jumbled machinery. What was this place before Rooker acquired its use, and where were the people?

Breaks had appeared in the clouds, showing the hard gleam of stars in the sky, but the clouds ran so fast before the east wind that a star was no sooner glimpsed than it was hidden again. He had been apprehensive about sending Selky and Raisa onto the Atlantic with a hurricane mounting in the Caribbean, but the others at La Lune had laughed at him, so he supposed the women knew what they were doing on the water.

Arby walked down the three wooden steps and picked his way around the edges of the muddy clearing. The hurricane wasn't expected to come aground in Belize, but the edges of the storm were spectacular. Hermod had seemed thrilled—"Couldn't ask for better cover!"—and his green-clad soldiers had grinned through their warpaint as they climbed into the backs of the transport trucks. Rooker, Xochipilli, and the Seeker had all seemed grimly elated, and even Helayjah's constant expression of bored skepticism was belied by the glitter of satisfaction in his eyes.

What would it be like to be dead? He'd never had a temple to retreat to, and though he'd recovered many memories, they were all of dying—which was invariably unpleasant—but never of what came after. And, as he understood it, if von Fleischer killed him on the Other Side, he would not only be dead, but would no longer exist—whatever that meant.

Oh, well. It was metaphysically impossible to be aware of not existing, so it probably wasn't unpleasant. In fact, it probably wasn't anything.

The wind gusted with such force that he almost skated backward on the slick mud. A splash of droplets on his face made him aware of a wall of trees to his left. The ground had been littered with coconuts that still remained when La Lune's little army had arrived that afternoon, and a pair had come down like bombs as everyone watched. He glanced up. Nothing seemed ready to fall, but the pale trunks of the coconut palms lashed in the wind like the legs of an overturned beetle.

The ominous, unsettled weather fit his mood and the occasion to perfection. There had been a time when he would have cried coincidence, but now he felt fully his mother's son: this was synchronicity.

The wooden latch on the door of the second hut had swollen with the rain. He forced it up by butting it with the base of his palm. As far as he could tell in the darkness, it was a clone of the shack where he had left, nothing more than a mattress and a few chairs.

The wind yanked the door from his grip and smashed it against the outside wall, the whole clanging like a deformed bell. He struggled to keep his footing on the steps, slipped, and finally crouched down.

A splash of near-horizontal rain hit him in the back, followed by a flash of lightning in the sky. In the roar of the wind the boom of the thunder felt small. Time to get back inside. The wind came in powerful bursts followed by dead lulls, and he took a moment to slam and secure the door.

As he struggled back along the edge of the clearing something slammed into his back and knocked him flat onto the mud. A tree branch rolled along in front of him and then took wing once again, vaulting into the sky. In another flash of lightning, he saw trees near Elaina's hut thrash and bend, and then one of them cracked.

He shouted but at the same moment he threw his Talent with all the force he possessed, and the discs of light flew at the hut, the trees, the sky, the mud. A mighty branch fell, but toppled off-center and smashed down on the corner of the shack.

Elaina struggled to open the door against the wind and he fought his way to his feet. In a flash of lightning he saw the door rip from its hinges and hurtle around the edge of the shack, and for a moment it looked as though Elaina would fly after it, but he saw her balanced in the air for a second before she fell down the steps.

Half-blind from the flashes of lightning, Arby ran across the clearing toward the hut. His boots grew heavy with mud, so that each step felt like running in a dream, and he ran crossways to the wind so that the gusts tried to throw him on his side.

In the next flash of lightning he saw Elaina crawling away from the shack. The trees bent low. He ran with all his might, yanking his feet from the sucking mud, and he flung discs of light at Elaina, at the trees, at the sky, spraying the world before him with prayers that things would be different.

In the blackness the thunder boomed close at hand. He stumbled against something and realized it had to be Elaina on hands and knees. The sky above the hut exploded, bright as daylight, and lightning crackled down and hit the trees, and this time the boom came before the light faded. He dragged Elaina to her feet and ran back the way he had come, half-carrying her, and he felt rather than heard massive objects slapping down to either side of them.

Arby had seen Elaina be cold, be courageous, or even floundering in drunken pain, but he had never seen her shaken before. In the safety of the second hut, Arby dropped his boots, now carrying a good twenty pounds of clayey mud, and peeled down to his boxers and did his best to clean up. Her sunglasses had been lost, but Elaina stripped off her mud-laden clothes with her usual matter-of-factness, and once Arby managed to light a candle, she stood in her practical white cotton underwear as he tried to wipe the mud from her feet and hands with one of the rough blankets he'd found folded on the bed. With no water it was a long and unsatisfactory task that left her looking as though she wore brown gloves and socks, and he was working at another smear on her face when he realized she was trembling. "Are you cold?"

"Yes. No. I don't know. I need to sit down. Is there a chair? Or maybe a bed?"

A sudden gust made the hut shake, but the storm's fury was either dying, or had taken a coffee break. He wrapped one of the other blankets around her shoulders, led her to the mattress and helped her sit down. She tugged him down to sit beside her.

"I'd make some more tea," he said, "but everything's back in the other hut. If it calms down a little, I can go back there and—"

"No." She lifted his arm and put it around her shoulders and snuggled up against him. "Just stay here." Her whole body shook so hard he expected her teeth to begin chattering, but instead she reached up, turned his face toward hers, and kissed him, a long, passionate kiss that pulled his tongue into her mouth.

When she broke away for breath she said, "Because I wanted to." Her hand dragged his free arm under the blanket and although he felt wrong about touching her with his mud-stained hands, any qualms he felt were banished when she pushed his hand up under her bra. She swallowed, her mouth still close to his, and said, "I know this is sudden, but I haven't been good to this body, and tomorrow it may die, and you may die, and it might be we'll never be together again, and you don't have to if you don't want to but—"

He cut off her words with a kiss.

For all her usual poise and elegance, she was a clumsy lover, struggling out of her underclothes, fumbling into position, jabbing him with knees and elbows. When at last he was atop her, she stopped him to whisper, "Be careful…it's been years and years and years…"

She made love with a desperate, maladroit passion, clutching at him, and whenever he lifted himself up to gaze at her blind face, she pulled his head down into another kiss and pinned him there with an elbow looped around his neck.

"Well, I got to say this is a big surprise!"

The voice woke Arby, and he sat up, blinking. The Seeker stood in the doorway. The dull gray of a stormy predawn shone around him. Elaina awoke with a start and pulled the blanket up to her chin.

The Seeker spoke into his walkie-talkie. "Yeah, they're here, and plenty alive by the looks of it. I'm guessing their walkie was in the hut when the trees came down. Gimme a minute. Out." He glanced down at the clothes on the floor. "You two do mud-wrasslin' as foreplay? You need to haul up now. It's almost morning." He left the door standing part-open as he clumped down the steps.

The candle had long since burnt away. Arby reached over to touch Elaina, but she squirmed away. "What happened last night?" she asked, her tone verging on accusatory. "What did you do to me?"

"What do you mean?"

"You know what I mean. You hit me with your Talent, and that made me—"

"Elaina!" He turned her head to face him. "Don't talk like that."

Something in his expression made the coldness on her face melt away, and she said, "God, I'm sorry. I'm sorry, I didn't mean that, I was just so surprised to find myself here like this…" She pulled him down and kissed him. "I'm sorry. I wanted that to happen."

As they dragged on their clothes, she said, almost to herself, "Still, it probably wouldn't have happened if I hadn't gotten in the way of your Talent. I mean, I'm glad that it did, but I wouldn't have had the, the impetus, the momentum, the—"

"Courage?" he asked.

"As good a word as any." She hugged up against him and the mud smeared on their fatigues squished between them.

Outside the Seeker stood with his hands on his hips, looking at the pair of trees that had flattened the other hut. Arby saw the tracks of feet where he and Elaina had run, parallel lines of oversized footprints right between the bodies of the trees. "Rough night back here," the Seeker said, "though it looks as though you two made the best of it."

"How's the squad?" Elaina asked.

"Hunkered down, but intact. Hermod's people are tough as nails. It's us god-types as might need a nap and a hot bath."

Even standing in the mud with the sky dark-gray above, the world looked beautiful to Arby. "Let's go," he said, and wrapped his arm around Elaina's waist. She resisted a moment and then acquiesced, and they splooshed forward through the puddles to the waiting truck.

31

A Polite Way of Saying "No"

Elaina waited on the mattress in the rear of the big transport truck, and Arby crawled on beside her. The Seeker gave Arby a thumbs-up and a pair of questioning eyebrows, and Arby nodded. The Seeker said, "You take care, now," and dropped down the green canvas flap and cinched it down over the tailgate.

Arby lay back alongside Elaina. Once the truck started rumbling down the road, his hand sought hers. "You ready?" he asked.

"The question would be more a matter of whether you are ready."

The truck slowed and then crawled up and over a bump, jolting hard when the wheels landed. "He must be driving over treetrunks," Arby said. "Am I going to be able to stay asleep?"

"Strictly speaking, it isn't sleep. You will feel your body, vaguely, but you can ignore it."

He stared up at the canopy of dark canvas overhead and reflected that this might be his last glimpse of the world. Sad, really, that it couldn't be the view from a mountaintop; but, on reflection, most Americans' last views of physical life were the sterile walls of a hospital or the shattered windshield of their cars, and this seemed nice by comparison.

He closed his eyes, relaxed with a few deep breaths, and stood up out of his body, taking care not to glance down at his own sleeping form. His hand patted for the long dagger sheathed on his belt. With a sudden jab, he drove the dagger through the canvas on the side of the truck. The fabric cried like an angry cat as he dragged the blade down to open a wide gash. He balanced one foot on the bench along the side of the truckbed and then pushed himself through the opening in the canvas.

Inside the old-fashioned tent were three rolled sleeping bags, a sack of food, and a child's plastic bucket filled with seashells.

He turned to help Elaina through the gash in the rear of the tent, and her eyes were wide open and swirling with crimson against green. She took in the scene. "Unusual move."

"Childhood scene." He unzipped the front of the tent.

The tent sat at the edge of a heaped pile of driftwood logs, and beyond them the sea crashed on a rocky shoreline. They worked their way past the driftwood, across the sand, and down to the rocks. He led her toward a jutting point of black rock, wending his way past tidepools filled with scuttling green crabs and swollen purple anemones.

The path climbed up toward the rocky point, and there the anemones were stranded, waving their arms in the air. When they rounded the point, the rocks plunged down into a small ravine, and here the anemones were wide-spaced but waist-high, and now resembled rubbery purple candelabras rather than tentacled powder puffs. On the other side of the ravine stood the remains of a motel, the roof long caved-in, the *Vacancy* sign pocked with bulletholes. "You have an agile imagination," she said.

"I figure there aren't tunnels and caves every place I might want to go," he said, and they started their scramble down the rocks toward the old streambed.

Around a bend in the ravine, the ground dried and the black rock gave way to a brown desert varnish. Only one purple anemone stood there, head-high, with no more than a half-dozen fat tentacles, a plant that might have escaped directly from von Fleischer's world. Nearby lay a broken, weathered wheelbarrow, its white paint peeling in scales. Where the ravine widened for a moment, someone had constructed the furrows and ring-hillocks of a vegetable garden, but there were no signs of plants. The clay soil had dried under the sun into something hard and brittle as pottery.

Near a high boulder another anemone stood, and they paused in the shadow of the rock before stepping around the rock. On the other side of the rock the shadow remained with them, because there it was twilight, and the ravine opened into a broad alluvial fan that led down to the boundary of Tanagrim's kingdom. Arby pointed to the barren hills that marched off to the right side of the ravine. "I think the mine you led us through is over there."

"You're a talented navigator."

He shrugged. "Free association. Can you find your way back easily?"

"Of course. And the Seeker will give the go as soon as I get there, so you shouldn't waste time getting started. Remember, stay close to the edge of his kingdom—the deeper you go, the more solidified his world is, and the less you can affect anything."

"Believe me, I don't plan on getting far from the edge."

"Rain…don't play for *too* much time. We want you to come back to us." She hesitated. "I want you to come back to me." She kissed him, wrapping her arms around him and pulling him close. When she released him, he saw she was blushing, but above those rosy cheeks all the lights of Las Vegas swirled in her eyes.

As he stepped across the boundary of von Fleischer's kingdom, he felt small and alone, and he laughed aloud at the thought. Small and alone weren't so much feelings as facts, and he had done it to himself. He had convinced everyone he ought to come alone: he was the only unknown of the inhabitants of La Lune, and bringing others would make their enemy suspicious immediately. And, what could the rest of them do? Would Elaina gentle Tanagrim back to balance? Could Hermod axe him into submission, might Xochipilli intoxicate him into bliss? He'd made these arguments with some force, and now here he was. BYOP Hoisting Party tonight: Bring Your Own Petard.

The first anemone across the border seemed as though it were a mile off, and he jogged toward it, his army boots clumping on the bare ground. The dry air made the mud on his fatigues harden and fall.

He looked over his shoulder and saw a trail of dirt flakes following his footprints.

When he drew close to the anemone, he slowed and pondered, trying to see beneath its rubbery surface. Complex lines of force pumped up from below; he sensed a slow but steady engorgement. He flicked a few discs of his Talent at it, and the whole plant quivered. One fat tendril swelled to stiffness, but two others withered and sprawled on the ground like burst balloons.

Delicate mechanism.

Time to get to work. He pulled his dagger from his hip and jabbed the stiff tendril, and it sprayed a stream of purple syrup twenty feet. From nowhere, the human-faced rodents appeared, a mob of them licking up the droplets where they fell, while even more clustered around the base of the plant, clamoring for his attention. "Bert sends his regards," he said, "and asked me to give you this." He slashed his dagger through two more tendrils, and the syrup gushed out.

A sudden wind came up, stirring dust, and the dust gathered and shaped itself into a blunt-featured humanoid ten feet tall. Its arms and legs were stumpy, unarticulated clubs, its mouth a lipless hole, and where its eyes ought to have been there were no more than indentations. Its voice echoed as though it were shouting into a metal trashcan. "By what right come you here?"

"I want to talk to your boss."

"You will treat with me first."

"Nope. Who are you supposed to be, anyhow, the Gingerbread Man? Last time I came here, I had to break one of your colleagues— and the horse he rode in on."

"My pleasure would be to crush you where you stand." The creature took a step forward, and where its foot should have been its blunt leg thudded into the ground with terrific force.

"Look," Arby said, wondering if the creature could move any faster, "I want to talk to your boss, your boss wants to talk to me. If I destroy you, that'd be bad news for you, but if you destroy me and your boss wanted to talk to me, that'd be bad news, too, right? So either way, you lose. *Unless you do what I say and get me Tanagrim.*"

The creature stopped still as a sculpture, and then collapsed into a pile of dust, a few wisps floating off on some unfelt breeze. In the sky above the clouds moved in an impossible pattern that coalesced into a giant face—the face of von Fleischer Arby recognized from photos. His voice boomed down like the voice of God. "Yes?"

"Arby again. I want to talk terms and conditions."

"Terms and conditions?"

"You said you wanted an alliance. What's on offer? And can you come down out of the sky? I don't like feeling like I'm negotiating with God Almighty."

"Here, I *am* God Almighty."

"And in my version of the yearbook I'm Homecoming Queen. My neck's getting a crick in it from looking up. Come on down, okay?"

"No. We already have an appointment. Time enough to talk then." The face began to dissolve.

"You won't mind if I stay here and amuse myself, then?" Arby turned and threw his Talent at one of the anemones. It absorbed all of the luminous discs and writhed before bursting open and collapsing.

"Stop that!" The voice rolled like thunder, and then von Fleischer appeared in his human form a dozen feet away. In a normal speaking voice, he said, "Some gods have lived for years on less nourishment than one of those produces each day. Each one of those plants is valuable beyond belief."

"Not to me, they aren't." Arby crossed his arms on his chest, and then, deciding that looked too defensive, put his hands on his hips instead. "So, whatcha got?"

"Don't be vulgar." Von Fleischer gestured and an overstuffed armchair appeared behind him. "Won't you sit?"

Arby glanced back and saw that a chair had been provided for him as well. "I'd rather stand."

Von Fleischer shrugged one shoulder in a suit-yourself fashion and dropped into his own chair. "I'd need to see what you have to offer me, first. Which is rather hard to determine when you won't even tell me your immortal identity, or where your kingdom lies. To use an analogy that ought to make sense to an American, you're asking me to bid on a car without giving me a hint of the make or model."

Arby felt a pair of thudding sensations in his back and realized that back in Belize the truck must have ridden over another treetrunk. Von Fleischer noticed his discomfiture, and asked, "Is there a problem?"

"Old war wound," Arby said. "I see your point. But to use an analogy that ought to make sense to a guy, you're asking me to leave my wife before I've even seen you in a swimsuit." Von Fleischer made a moue of distaste at the analogy, and Arby said, "Hey, you started it."

"Are you telling me that you're already involved in an alliance? Good, that sweetens the pot. We can sort out details when we meet later"—Von Fleischer threw a meaningful glance at Arby's hand that wore the plighting-ring—"as I trust you have not forgotten you promised to do. On my side…" Von Fleischer gestured vaguely behind him. "The largest kingdom and the most power in the noosphere, and much more besides. Do you mind my noting that you seem a little, perhaps, medieval in outlook? I'm more of a Renaissance type myself."

"Medieval?"

"Notions of chivalry, and other sentimental concepts. Not that these are devoid of charm. But in that line, as I mentioned before, I can offer you a prize no one else can provide: the return of your mother, and your former…companion, Elizabeth West." He leaned back in the chair and steepled his fingers. "There's little point in pretending that I did this out of concern for their welfare or for the thrill of their company. You want them. I have them."

Arby turned away to guard his reaction. Apparently von Fleischer didn't know that Rooker and Crystal had fled, and the man's searching eyes seemed able to read too much. He composed his face and turned back. "How do I know you have them?"

"It ought to be easy enough to ascertain they've gone missing. And I can arrange for you to visit with them when you come see me— say, in a week? Your mother—a difficult woman, by the way—I can return unharmed. And Miss West…well, I can return our little Liz much improved. I think you'll find her much more agreeable, much more compliant, than when you knew her in the past." Von Fleischer stood and brushed non-existent dust from his sharply creased slacks. "And now, please cease and desist, head yourself back Down There, and prepare to visit me a week from now."

"No," Arby said. "I'm not done."

Von Fleischer stared at him. "Don't make me leave my own house before my guest…I do so hate discourtesy. We have a deal. There's nothing more to be said."

He turned away and his shape began to glimmer when Arby said, "So you wouldn't mind it if I made myself at home, here? Maybe carved a few highways through this annoying brush?"

When von Fleischer turned, Arby hurled his Talent at a yet-untouched anemone a football-field away and watched it wither and collapse. Nice that it worked every time; von Fleischer's crop must be so improbable that any deviation was lethal.

"Stop that! Stop it now!" Unguarded anger showed on the man's face. "You saw what I did to the succubus? It is nothing compared to what I will do to your women! Toy with me and you condemn them both to living hell!" Von Fleischer seemed to swell with each word, until at last he stood tall as a house.

Arby tried not to glance to the side to gauge his distance from the border. He already knew how far it was. Too far. "Oh, bullshit. You're not going to do anything to anyone. Because I'm going to destroy your so-called kingdom right now." He hurled his Talent at a half-dozen other plants, and before he could look to assess the damage he had done, von Fleischer roared, an ear-shattering bellow that made Arby stumble back and fall to the ground.

Von Fleischer grew a hundred feet tall, and as he grew he changed. His nose retreated to a pair of punctures in his face, his eyes grew beady and piglike, and his mouth widened until it stretched across his broad, flat face. His skin turned a wet, blotchy black and red, like the weeping flesh of a burn victim, and when his crimson mouth opened it revealed rows of fangs, every serrated triangle the height of a man.

Without taking his eyes off Tanagrim in his full Aspect, Arby scrambled to his feet and began backing away. Tanagrim raised his left hand and his fingers turned into the lashes of a giant whip.

Arby threw his Talent at Tanagrim with all his might, and discs flew toward the figure's giant chest like a swarm of fireflies. Tanagrim whipped his hand down at Arby, the lashes whistled through the air, and one of them, thick as a treetrunk, bashed Arby in the ribs and sent him flying through the air. He crashed to the ground and fought to get his wind back.

"Is that it?" Tanagrim asked, his words clear despite his deformed mouth. "Is *that* your Talent? I felt nothing!" He lifted his whip-hand again, and Arby threw discs with desperation. The lashes hit the ground to either side of him, slapping the earth so hard that Arby bounced, but the tip of one recoiled and snapped Tanagrim in his swinish eye.

The giant wailed in pain and clamped both hands over the injury, the lashes of his left hand dangling down over his face. Arby forced himself to get up and run for the border despite the fiery pain in his diaphragm, and he tried to think of some way to change the ground in front of him, to transport himself somewhere else, but the plain was too featureless and empty to imagine anything in its place, and there were no corners to hide other realities.

A wall of boulders burst through the ground ahead of him, blocking his escape. Yet this might give him something to work with, given a moment's time… The boulders rose higher, in piles, like the stacks of fragmented rocks at Joshua Tree National Park in the California desert, but they were moving, jostling one another like a herd of animals.

He turned to look at Tanagrim, far behind him. The giant had recovered now—witness the squirming wall of rocks between Arby and the border—and his mouth opened in what might have been a smile. Tanagrim's hands were hands again, and he swept them into the air as though conducting a symphony. A cube of earth ripped out of the ground near Tanagrim's feet and flew through the air in a beautiful arc toward where Arby stood.

There was no room to run toward the boulders, so he ran back toward Tanagrim, and as he did so he saw other cubes of stone take flight, ripping from the earth. The first cube slammed down behind him like an earthquake but he kept running, trying to dodge right and left like a rabbit, so his moves couldn't be anticipated.

Rabbit blood ran thin in his genetic heritage. A huge block fell behind him, and when he dodged to the left another fell, and when he dodged to the right he slammed into one that had landed when he hadn't been watching. The block he hit stood shoulder-high, and he clutched his right hand on its edge and tried to drag himself upright…

He sensed rather than saw the next block hurtling down, and tried to snatch his hand away, but too late. Arby screamed when the cube crashed down to stack itself perfectly atop the cube he clutched.

For a moment the pain was so intense he couldn't see, but then he focused and forced himself to look. His ring and pinky fingers were crushed between the two cubes. He groaned in despair, and tried to tug his arm away, and the pain made him cry out. He was bound there just as surely as if he'd been shackled.

A hundred yards distant, Tanagrim laughed. "I owe you a debt. I'd become old, timid, querulous. You've made me feel young again. And I promise you, your death here won't go unsung." Tanagrim held up one palm, and Crystal appeared there, no taller than one of his fingers. He lifted her squirming figure by its legs, grabbed her head and torso with his other hand, and then twisted as though wringing out a washcloth. The crumpled thing that was left he tossed aside as he strode toward the place where Arby was pinned. "No, your impotence and cringing will be recorded in the ether for all time. This one…" Liz appeared naked in his hand. "By tomorrow night, I'll have her masturbating as she watches you die. I assure you, it will give her a thrill." He lifted Liz by one ankle, and, as if she were a wishbone, ripped her in half. "I'll feed on their pain for years. Not that nutritious, perhaps, but spicy."

This isn't real, this isn't physical, Arby told himself. *This isn't Malkuth. You can do this.* He pulled his dagger from his belt with his left hand and slashed at his crushed fingers and then howled in pain.

"Oh, setting yourself free? All the better. Say, did you ever hear the one about the retarded coyote…?"

This time Arby screamed in advance of the pain, and this allowed him to saw through his fingers in two hard strokes.

"…Seems he chewed off three of his legs but was still caught in the trap! Fine, don't laugh…but you must admit, it's droll in its way…"

Arby forced the dagger back into its sheath and clamped his bleeding, three-fingered hand under his opposite armpit. He staggered from the chamber of blocks, toward Tanagrim, the only way out.

A stadium-length to his right, where there had been nothing before, was a carven cliff-face covered with a bewildering array of interlinking staircases. The perspectives seemed to shift, so that a staircase that at one moment seemed upright at the next seemed upside-down.

"You like fine art, boy? Come in further, I'll show you a few things."

Arby staggered to the right, and tried to imagine what might lie around the far corner of this stone cube, something far outside von Fleischer's realm.

"Are you sure you won't beg for a bit? I *can* be merciful. And don't forget Liz. She's going to get her jollies on this for the next fifty years. No? Ah, well."

Arby glanced back over his shoulder. Something huge dragged itself around the cube far to his back. At first it seemed to be the wall of boulders that had blocked his path, but the boulders resolved into the scales of something stone-colored but reptilian…

It opened its long snout and showed its jagged teeth. Reptilian, yes, specifically crocodilian, with long front legs and tiny stumps of legs at the rear. Wonderful. A crocodile monster the length of three buses.

Arby began to run, his right hand still clutched under his left armpit. When he glanced back, he saw the crocodilian press the tip of its long snout to the ground, and then roll itself into a wheel like a thin strip of carpet.

It all became clear—the cliff covered with staircases, the creature in the shape of a wheel, Tanagrim's fine art reference: Escher. The creature behind him began to roll, its legs working in pairs to speed it along, and he pulled his bleeding hand from beneath his armpit and ran in earnest.

When he was close to the base of the cliff, he risked a glance backward, and at that moment the wheel-creature vaulted forward, uncoiling like a striking snake, and he threw discs and ran for the nearest stairway. The jaws of the monster slammed shut behind him, and its snout rammed against the cliff.

At the top of the first stair, perhaps twenty feet up, the stairs forked at a landing and he doubled back and up, panting for breath. Below, the creature had rolled itself into a wheel once more. Its bulging eyes peered out from the side of its coil, peeking around its stumpy legs. A second landing, and he zigzagged back, throwing his Talent at the creature with the briefest glance, but at the landing above him a cube of stone crashed down, and he heard Tanagrim's laughter. He stumbled backward to the previous landing, and the jaws of the creature snapped shut above the staircase.

He charged up the other staircase, but he began to feel it was hopeless: he would be exhausted before he could get beyond the reach of those jaws. He reached that landing and continued in the same direction, but another cube fell to the landing above.

Arby stopped on the stairway and tried to catch his breath. He wouldn't keep running aimlessly, running only to die, panicked and hunted. Blood dripped from his hand and splattered by his boots.

Down below, the monster was coiling itself for another leap. He prepared to hurl his Talent, but that probably constituted a losing strategy: it was as likely to work against him as for him. Now was the time for something unexpected. He glanced side-to-side, trying to find a hidden spot where he could imagine an escape. Nothing hidden here; he was exposed as the centerpiece on a huge killing display, and if the creature didn't swallow him, Tanagrim would drop a cube of stone and squash him flat.

As if in response, a cube of stone crashed down onto the landing he had left. Tanagrim was closing off both his retreats and his exits. He could jump down to a lower landing, maybe…or wait here on the stairs until the rolling crocodile perfected its leap. Better to be swallowed than crushed like an ant.

Better to be swallowed. A crazy idea, but one he could believe.

Here was hoping belief was enough.

He pulled his dagger from its sheath with his left hand and looked down. The monster's eyes blinked once from the coils and then it struck, hurling itself upward. When that rubbery snout unfurled and gaped open, he stared for a moment at the black gullet beyond those teeth, raised the dagger above his head in both hands, took a deep breath, and then jumped from the landing, feet first, plunging into its open mouth.

The teeth flashed by to either side like white rungs on a vast ladder, and then his feet hit the throat and his whole body slid into a slick channel that first admitted him, and then tightened, squeezing him down into darkness.

With all the strength left in his arms, he jabbed the dagger forward into the surrounding flesh. The muscles of that throat held him stretched out for a moment, but he pulled his knees up toward fetal position, and that bracing dragged his arms down, slicing through more flesh…

In the desperation born of suffocation he dragged the dagger up and down, burying his arms in wet, bleeding flesh. The creature's body around him thrashed in torment, but he blanked his mind to the sensation, concentrating only on one place, on the place he knew lay just beyond the gash he had created in that throat, and he felt his hands and the dagger rip through the skin into open air.

Other hands seized his wrists and hauled, and without warning it all became easy, as though a door had opened before him.

The Seeker dragged him through the slit in the canvas and onto the mattress in the back of the truck. Elaina's ethereal form stood there with a knife, apparently having just slashed the canvas open even wider.

Arby coughed and sputtered. His body was covered with slime, but the humid air of the Belize jungle tasted like champagne.

"I take it you didn't come back the way we went there?" Elaina asked.

Between gulps of air, he managed to say, "Shortcut."

"We thought you were gone, man," The Seeker said. "You were out there three, four times longer than we expected."

"Great," Arby said, still gasping for breath.

"When you are recovered, would you mind not laying on me?" Elaina asked. "It makes it hard to get back in."

Arby glanced side-to-side and saw that his ethereal form lay crisscrossed over Elaina's body and his own. No, not over: he lay through their bodies. It is disconcerting to see one's own body, but even more disconcerting to interpenetrate it at a random angle. He scooted himself sideways, out of Elaina and into himself, and sat up in his body.

His ring and pinky fingers were numb, and when he tried to flex them, they didn't move. Elaina sat up beside him. He waved his hand at her. "A couple of my fingers got cut off Up There, and now I can't feel anything with them or move them. Will they come back?"

The Seeker said, "Stranger things have happened."

Elaina said, "That's his polite way of saying *no*."

From far off, Arby heard gunfire. The Seeker tossed back the canvas at the rear of the truck, and kicked open the tailgate. "C'mon, folks," he said, "let's join the party." He leant Arby a hand, and helped him down onto the muddy road. The sky was still dark-gray above, but the earthy smells of the jungle were so delicious it felt as if his head might explode with pleasure.

"Umm, boys?" Elaina said. "Can you give me a little guidance here? Down on this plane, I'm still blind, you know."

Arby helped her out of the truck. Without her sunglasses—her eyes held shut—she seemed naked. He said, "You know, I'd feel better about all of this if you stayed here."

She laughed. "That's quite touching, and thoroughly out of the question. Has anyone noted that you have old-fashioned notions of chivalry?"

"Yes. You-know-who said something along those lines just a little while ago."

The Seeker said, "You-know-who is probably back at you-know-where by now, so I suggest we put on a little hustle, okay?" He hefted the walkie-talkie. "Hey, Vikings. We're late but we're still coming. Over." He frowned as he listened to the reply.

Arby grabbed one of the Uzis from the crate in the truck. His total of five hours practice back at La Lune hadn't been enough, and its weight felt clumsy when he slung it over his shoulder. When he handed Elaina one, her hands ran across it with swift competence, her thumb testing the safety catch, and she tossed it onto her shoulder as though she were grabbing her purse. Arby strapped the headband with the little lamp around his head, began to offer Elaina one, and then realized there was no point.

"Sounds like Arby let us catch the man napping," The Seeker said. "Xochipilli says the folks aboveground didn't see it coming, and Hermod's guys chewed right through 'em."

"What about below ground?"

"Below ground, radios don't work. But if we don't shake 'em hard, it'll all be over by the time we get there."

"One could only wish," Elaina said.

32

Having It All

Uzis slung from their shoulders, the three of them marched down the road with Elaina in the center, their arms interlinked. The rapid and coordinated trudge of their feet had echoes of a children's game rather than grim purpose, and Arby felt a giddy urge to whistle "We're Off to See the Wizard."

The Seeker's eyes scanned the ground. Arby let his consciousness rise a bit, and he saw the green-and-purple coils of old power, and, a few steps farther on, glimmers of a fine silver webbing. Another ten yards and the webbing was clear: they were within the reach of von Fleischer's consciousness, and had crossed the border of his stronghold.

Up to this point, they had trudged down the road, but now the Seeker said, "We need to head over this way." He gestured with his head off into the trees to their left.

"How can you tell?" Arby asked.

"You're joking, right?" The Seeker steered them off into the trees.

The gaps between the trees narrowed. They had to hold hands and travel single-file, Arby at the rear. Elaina stumbled over fallen branches, but kept on plodding forward, her expression showing only a hint of irritation when she almost fell. From time to time there were bursts of gunfire in the distance, but they now sounded very indistinct. The way widened again into a flat path carpeted with decomposing leaves, and they linked arms once again. Glancing at her flawless profile, Arby was struck again by how beautiful and yet how self-contained she was, and he realized any fantasy he had about them becoming lovers in more than a physical sense of the word was just that, fantasy. Elaina might have her passions—deep and well-governed passions—but her soul needed no one. The thought was sad yet liberating.

The ground rose. The Seeker whispered for them to wait and disappeared into the trees ahead.

Elaina stood at his side, calm and waiting, and he marveled at her composure; if anything went wrong out here in the early daylight, she would be blind to her attackers. Yet he felt some of the same disregard for consequences, and he understood that deep inside he hadn't expected to return from his confrontation with Tanagrim. Everything that happened from here on in his life was a lagniappe thrown in by fate. He hugged Elaina's arm where it was linked through his, and she smiled.

The Seeker reappeared. "They went in up here. Helayjah's little pawprints are all over this."

At the base of a jungle-covered hillock, they found two shacks camouflaged beneath living vines. The Seeker parted the vines, and Arby saw the bodies of four of von Fleischer's soldiers seated against the back wall, their heads dangling at improbable angles from their necks.

The Seeker stepped around the corner of the shack and walked to the steepest part of the hill. "And here's where our boys went." He pushed aside a wall of vines to show the entrance to a limestone cave.

"Help me get inside," Elaina said from behind them. In the darkness of the cave mouth, she rubbed her eyes, parted her eyelids, and then winced. "I'm going to regret this." Her pupils stared at Arby from the center of red-and-green swirls. "Either let me go first, and you can use your lights, or—"

"I'm good to go without light," the Seeker said.

Arby's consciousness was already on the lower etheric, and he could see the cavern, smoothed by years of waterflow, stretching away through twining ropes of ancient purple-green power. "Me, too," Arby said.

"Get your head out of Yetzirah if anybody comes for you on the etheric," she said to Arby. "Better a dead body than a dead soul." She unslung her Uzi from her shoulder and turned and jogged into the cavern, ducking her head. Arby and the Seeker followed.

Thousands of years of waterflow had buffed the limestone tunnel into unnatural smoothness, and only seldom did it meander from its course. In a few spots some freak of geology had created wide chambers. In the areas where some more resistant outcropping narrowed the way or lowered the ceiling, the hand of man could be seen where the rock had been chiseled wider. Smaller, rougher channels entered or left at times, but these were few and far apart.

From the growing tightness in his diaphragm, Arby knew they had jogged a half-mile or more when Elaina stopped. "Light," she whispered, her eyes clenched shut.

The Seeker steered her up against a wall and signaled with a jerk of his head for Arby to follow him. The Seeker ran ahead in a crouch, his feet touching down with a near-imperceptible padding sound, and Arby tried to imitate him but managed nothing better than a half-hearted thud.

For some distance Arby saw no light, but then he became aware of a glow. The tunnel curved, and beyond the bend a doorway had been chiseled into the tunnel wall, with the glow of a bare bulb blazing from the opening. The Seeker crept up, the Uzi cradled in his arms, and peeked around the edge of the doorway. The tension left his shoulders and he stood and signaled for Arby to come.

Two guards sat at a card table, their heads both thrown back in dead upward gazes. A third lay on the floor. They were von Fleischer's men, no doubt, but for a moment Arby wondered who they were, what they had cared about and loved, and he was startled to realize how easily he had come to accept killing and mayhem. He began to say something of the sort to the Seeker, but the man said, "Shh!" and switched off the lights.

Out in the tunnel they could now make out a hint of more light far away. The Seeker leaned close. "You get Elaina this far, have her stay here. I'm gonna go looky-loo."

Arby hurried back and fetched Elaina, explaining as they ran, but a little short of the doorway, when Elaina was already beginning to squint her eyes against the trace of light that could be seen afar, the whole tunnel boomed with sound.

At Niagara Falls there is a tunnel deep in the rock that leads to an opening behind the thundering curtain of water, and Arby thought this sound was the same—a powerful, undifferentiated roar. Yet, as he listened, the sound broke up, and he understood he was hearing storms of automatic gunfire.

He urged Elaina into the guard room and ran in the direction the Seeker had gone, keeping close to the left wall of the tunnel. The whole watercourse entered a long leftward curve, the lights brightened, and he saw the Seeker crouched down at the edge of a wide opening.

The gunfire came now in harsh belches, separated by long, ringing silences. As if sensing his approach, the Seeker glanced over his shoulder and signaled for Arby to join him.

Arby's first reaction was to gasp with wonder. Around that rough corner lay a warehouse-sized limestone cavern filled with all the white glories of the finest caves: glistening wasp-waisted pillars and wide smooth shields, massive draperies and delicate tubes. The whole was lit by dozens of hanging industrial lamps in rusted iron cages.

A soldier popped up from behind a magnificent drapery and fired a burst aimed far off to Arby's right. The soldier ducked back down as a few answering shots zipped above his head, and Arby's whole body vibrated with anger. Vandals! How the hell could anybody shoot at one another in this natural cathedral?

The Seeker jerked at his sleeve and nodded his head to the right. "Our guys. You cover me."

Cover me? Arby had heard it in a thousand movies, but he had no idea what it meant in practical terms. Before he could ask, the Seeker had jumped into the cavern and dodged to the right. Arby saw someone stand up from behind a thick shield, and so he leaned around the corner and fired three bursts, groaning to himself as he sprayed the room with bullets. A burst came back in reply and he remembered to jump back behind the shelter of the wall.

The Seeker leaned around a pillar and fired off a long burst, and Arby jumped right to do the same, but almost immediately he was pulling on a dead trigger. He dove back. To his amazement, the clip was already empty. He snapped it off and felt for one of the three spares on his belt—no one had told him you ran out of bullets that fast. His hand brushed the barrel and he swore and sucked at his finger—the damn thing was hot!

He had only gotten the new clip engaged when the Seeker fired again, and Arby saw a shadowy figure run from the grove of stalagmites on his right and dive down beside him. Arby scrambled back, trying to position his gun, but then he saw it was Helayjah.

"Until moments ago, all was calm, hmm? And now we are pinned there, running out of bullets, yes?" Helayjah rolled to his knees and patted Arby's shoulder. "You must have done well, yes? Only now has our enemy awakened..." He held up his dagger and pointed at the grip. "Is this rubber, hmm, or plastic, or what?"

Staring at the handle, Arby frowned at the apparent non sequitur. "*I* don't know."

"We'll find out, hmm?" Helayjah eased into a low squat. "When I run, you will stand and fire, yes, draw attention, keep heads down?" He slapped Arby's back and then leapt back into the cavern and dodged toward the left, a gray-and-tan shadow in the stark black and white of the room.

Arby shook his head and then remembered to step out and fire. He tried to space out his bursts to conserve ammo, but still ran dry on the fifth pass.

He dropped to his knees just before the first responding fire, but the response was cut short when the Seeker bobbed up and shot off a few short bursts. At first he couldn't find Helayjah, but then he saw him—the man had climbed ten feet up the wall and clung there, sawing at something… Sparks crackled and the cavern went dark.

Arby squinted and blinked into the blackness. There were cries of confusion from around the room, and a few shots went off. When the dazzle of the light had gone his etheric vision showed the Seeker running off between the pillars, and distant figures stumbling in what to them was the dark.

He was fumbling to attach his third clip when he saw four figures vault over a low shield twenty yards away and run his direction. Long etheric necks protruded from their fleshy shoulders.

They saw him when he pushed himself to his feet. Tall Boys, or something like them, but dressed in von Fleischer's soldier gear. He tried to smack the clip home and dropped it, and four demon faces lifted high in the sky atop those snaky necks as they ran toward him. They carried automatics in their arms, but from the way their mouths gaped he guessed they would rather eat him.

Arby dropped down again and grabbed his clip, trying to snap it in place, unable to take his eyes off the advancing figures. If they were going to try and kill him at close quarters he needed to drop down into normal consciousness, but then he would be blind—

An immense figure rushed them from the side, and the yellowish ursine figure of Utamatzi swelled out from Rooker's body. Arby recoiled from the bear-god's roar as that colossal figure shoved all four of the Tall Boys to the ground, then knelt, and, seizing one by the ankles, snapped him to the side like a boy cracking a wet towel. The man's head exploded, and the mocking demon face atop the whipping neck vanished.

Rooker turned, snarling, ready for more, but as he snatched down at the nearest, one of the others rolled onto his knees and aimed his gun.

A long spray of fire came from behind Arby, and all three of the remaining Tall Boys died.

Elaina stepped forward. "Why didn't you shoot them?" she asked Rooker. "It's no time to indulge your Aspect."

The big man stood panting, etheric edges of his true form expanding and contracting around his flesh with each breath. "No more bullets," he said. "Left the empty gun wrapped around some guy's neck." Two more bursts of gunfire came from across the cavern, along with a cry, and then there was silence.

"I make it twenty in this room," the Seeker said, as they jogged down a path toward another tunnel. "And he called out the A team."

"Ten more minutes," Rooker said. "Ten more minutes and we would have caught the boss flat on his back."

"I tried," Arby said.

"Hey, man, no criticism from me." He gave Arby what was probably intended to be a light slap on the back, and almost sent Arby face-first onto the ground. "We're farther than I thought we'd make it down here."

The tunnel they entered ran perhaps a hundred yards, and then the Seeker held up a hand. "Whoa. Machinery's moving in there."

Rooker edged up beside him. "This is the main Pit. Somebody's coming down the elevator."

The Seeker, Rooker, Helayjah, and Arby all edged their way inside, but Elaina held back. Arby followed all the other gazes up, a hundred feet, two hundred feet—the height was staggering, but he couldn't judge the distance because the light from a descending industrial elevator, an elevator the size of a bedroom, blocked the view, and he understood that Elaina's sensitivity to light had held her back.

The Pit itself was enormous, thirty feet across, with a half-dozen tunnels leading into it. The feature itself must have begun as a natural sinkhole, probably one that had enlarged by a small river thundering into it, but it had obviously been smoothed and enlarged by human labor also. Four cables were bolted into a wide cement pad in the center, and Arby saw that these were guides to keep the elevator from tilting.

To the other side, a heavy steel door like the entrance to a bank vault was embedded in the limestone, and around it Arby made out huge concrete reinforcements. Rooker followed his gaze and said, "The river. Hydroelectric runs the whole joint." The man glanced up at the elevator and said, "You folks might want to get ready to blow somebody away, here."

"No." The Seeker shook his head. "It's Hermod. Can almost smell him."

Fifty feet up, the elevator light flickered and went out, and Arby guessed someone had unscrewed the bulb. Arby studied the shaft of the Pit, but couldn't see the top.

The elevator, a ramshackle affair mostly walled with heavy steel mesh, clunked down on the pad, and a big door on the side opposite slid open. The Seeker was right, of course. Hermod stepped around the corner of the elevator and raised his battleaxe. He wore no shirt, and his muscular chest was hairless. With his blond-and-gray hair draped onto his shoulders and his customary grim expression, he looked like a poster for a barbarian movie…except for the drab pants and the army boots.

"Victory is ours," Hermod said, as they approached, "though Xochipilli may not live. Surprise was total, and without our enemy to guide them, they fought bravely, but foolishly."

"And the boss?" Rooker asked.

Hermod shrugged. "No sign."

The Seeker nodded and pointed at a staircase inside a doorway. "That's 'cause he's still in there."

Hermod patted his axe. "He's mine."

"I don't give a damn who kills him," Rooker said, "so long as we make him dead." Hermod grinned and started toward the doorway the Seeker had indicated. "Not that way," Rooker said.

"Why not?" the Seeker asked.

"That's the way in. But he knows we're here now. He just doesn't know *I'm* here now."

They left Helayjah and Elaina to watch the tunnels entering and leaving the Pit, and Rooker led Hermod, the Seeker, and Arby to a wide crack in the wall far away from the elevator pad. The entrance was narrow, and the walls hadn't been smoothed. The whole tunnel, if something so ragged could be called by that name, seemed to dwindle after a dozen yards, but Rooker stretched out prone and dragged himself on his belly beneath a downthrusting section of limestone that snagged his shirt and ripped it open.

Beyond that the tunnel opened and then reached a narrow stairway. The rough-hewn stairs climbed without doubling back, and Arby guessed that they had climbed five stories before they reached a landing. There, Rooker paused, a finger pressed to his lips for silence, and gestured at the flat wall before them. After squinting for a moment, Arby saw the outline of a door.

Rooker mimed pushing the door, and then pointed to the Seeker and Arby in turn, and mimed spraying bullets from an Uzi. Arby shook his head and threw up his hands, trying to suggest his incompetence. He unslung the gun from his shoulder and handed it to Rooker.

Rooker made a gesture of acquiescence and took the Uzi. He then mimed pushing the door, and, with an open palm, gestured diving flat.

Arby nodded, and stepped between the men and leaned his left shoulder against the door. Hermod backed away, his axe hefted above one shoulder. Rooker and the Seeker readied themselves, and then Rooker smiled and jerked the tip of the gun's barrel at the door.

Arby shoved with all his might, and the wall swung away so easily that he crashed to the floor. A dozen soldiers stood there with their backs to them, staring down a stairway opposite, and though a few spun and fired as they died, bullets from Rooker and the Seeker cut them down.

A well-lit passage to the right had a dozen doors, all closed. Rooker helped Arby to his feet with a meaty hand. "You got more clips?" he asked.

Arby's ears rang from the recent gunfire, but he understood. "None."

Hermod was bent over the the Seeker, who had pulled himself up against the wall and clutched at his shoulder. The Seeker grimaced, but said, "Go on, I've had worse just getting to the corner market. He's up here, he's close, man, he's so close…"

Rooker had started down the hallway and Arby and Hermod followed a dozen paces behind, trusting to Rooker's knowledge of El Panal.

On the right a door flung open behind Rooker, and two women brandishing butcher knives leapt into the hallway and ran at Rooker's back, but Hermod shoved Arby aside and took off their heads before Rooker even turned around.

Hermod leaned on his axe, trembling with emotion. "I hate killing women."

Rooker looked down at the two decapitated bodies, their unattached heads still rocking. "Meat's meat," he said. He stepped over them and looked into the room the two women had left, his gun at the ready.

Arby glanced into the room, had the brief impression of something palatially appointed, and then edged past the bodies. Whatever was to happen here lay in front of them, not behind them, something inside him knew it. His hand felt for the knife on his belt, an etheric version of which had so recently carved off two of his fingers, and he tried to wiggle those same fingers. No luck. Their fleshly counterparts still stuck off the end of his hand when he looked down, but as far as his mind was concerned, they weren't really there. The Seeker had said they might come back, but Elaina had scoffed, and—

Twenty feet ahead the last door or the right flew open, and von Fleischer jumped out, a sword strapped at his side. Arby almost laughed—he'd accused Arby of having romantic notions?—but von Fleischer's hand reached out the way he had come, and Liz, wearing a diaphanous ivory gown, pulled herself along it and ended up in his arms facing Arby, a maneuver Astaire and Rogers couldn't have down more smoothly.

He froze, staring at Liz, searching her face for signs of recognition, but she turned her head to look at von Fleischer, and, with a roar of anger Rooker shoved Arby aside and ran forward, leveling the Uzi.

"No!" Arby shouted. Von Fleischer's eyes widened as he recognized Rooker, but without hesitation he lifted a pistol and fired at Rooker, once, twice, three times, and Rooker stumbled. Von Fleischer pumped out round after round and Rooker staggered back and fell, his twitching trigger finger blasting bullets into the ceiling until the clip ran dry. Hermod kicked Rooker's Uzi to the side and jumped past him, bellowing a war cry that made Arby quiver in fear, but von Fleischer fired another shot and Hermod fell.

He swung the pistol toward Arby, but nothing happened, and he threw the pistol at Arby's head. Arby ducked, and the pistol smacked the wall with such force that chips of limestone showered down.

Hermod heaved himself upright with a cry of frustration, but von Fleischer had already pulled open the door across the hall, and he ran in, Liz following. Hermod hoisted his axe and pursued, hopping on one leg.

Arby ran after them, and when he reached the open door he saw a magnificent carpeted room filled with plush furniture and surrounded by tapestries on every wall—one of which Hermod ripped down to reveal a hidden doorway. Hermod charged into the opening, still favoring one leg, and Arby decided to follow, but Rooker's voice stopped him.

"No." The big man was on his feet, staggering toward Arby. "There." Rooker pointed to the end of the hall. "The other elevator. Keep him there." Rooker coughed and spat up a glob of bloody mucus. "I'm coming. Go, goddamn you!"

At the end of the hall a wide, well-lit stairway ran down to the left. Arby ran and jumped down the stairs, praying that no more of von Fleischer's soldiers would be waiting. One landing by another long hallway, and the stairs doubled back; another landing, and at the far end of that hallway men and women, but not soldiers, milled about. A woman saw him and screamed, pointing, and he ran down the next set of stairs. What the hell was he going to do if he caught von Fleischer, anyway? Offer a dagger-sword duel?

Stall, he supposed. He'd gotten good at that.

The final landing held a doorway on the right, and Arby tottered through it, gasping for breath. It was the second Pit that Rooker had briefed them on, and the elevator was already winching skyward. Hermod had tossed his axe to the ground and charged that direction in a limping run, but when he leapt for it the elevator was already beyond his reach. The warrior stumbled and let out a cry of frustration that echoed across the Pit. His Aspect swelled out of his body, a trembling giant.

He turned and saw Arby and yelled, "Hurry." The man scrambled to his feet, ran forward a few paces, and held his clasped hands down before him as though offering a boost. Arby hesitated—the thing was impossible—but Hermod shouted, "Now!" and Arby ran and jumped and the warrior caught the soles of Arby's feet and hurled him into the air.

There was just time enough to flail his arms and worry about the problem of landing before he slammed down atop the roof of the rising elevator.

He pulled himself to his hands and knees, trying to pull in a breath; the fall had knocked the wind out of him as surely as a sucker-punch to the belly. There was another shout from Hermod, and then a loud thunk. The blade of the battleaxe was embedded in a side timber of the roof, the long handle humming like a tuning fork.

When he had caught his breath, Arby stood and worked the axe out of the wood—no easy task, as Hermod had thrown it with preternatural force.

Then he set himself to chopping a wide hole in the ceiling.

This elevator was far smaller than the one on the main Pit, about the size of a large bathroom. The hole turned out to be an easy job: the timbers of the frame around the elevator were stout, but the boards between them were no thicker than flooring. When he had bashed out a hole the size of a shoebox, von Fleischer's voice said from below, "This is an old structure. I wouldn't feel too free about chopping on it."

"Nonsense." Arby let the axe bite into the wood again and the hole lengthened to shoulder-width.

"It's you," von Fleischer said. "Well, better you than one of the La Lune fanatics."

Arby ignored him, chopping away until there was a hole the size of a desktop. What next? Jump down and challenge him? But the man had a sword and presumably knew how to use it, while Arby's battleaxe skills were limited to chopping wood.

Perhaps it was enough to wait. Hermod's men would be guarding all the exits including the top of the Pits...but they might slaughter Liz along with von Fleischer. He glanced over the edge toward the bottom of the Pit. The elevator traveled slowly, but he guessed they were already a hundred feet in the air. He backed up and hung onto the winch cable for support.

"Arby?" Liz looked up at him through the hole. "I can't believe you came for me. It's so...brave. I've missed you so much." She flashed him her best crooked smile. "But you're on the wrong side, baby. Those people you're with are crazy, they're murderers and worse." She seemed to blink back tears, and looked down for a moment before she raised her eyes. "I've wanted you so much. I've ached for you. I never knew what I had when you were with me, and I'm so sorry now, so sorry… but we have another chance. We can have it all, baby—not just each other, but anything we want."

It was hard to watch Liz's face look up at him and plead without being tempted, and he looked away, watching the light from the elevator crawl up the far wall of the Pit. "I'm sorry, Liz. But it can't work like that. No matter what I do, people are waiting up above. Your friend has already lost."

Von Fleischer's tall form stepped up behind Liz and the motion drew Arby's eyes. "So you'd consider a proposal?"

"Didn't I come to you on the Other Side and ask for one? Net result, you tried to kill me."

Von Fleischer dismissed this with a toss of his hand and an apologetic smile. "I'm not used to disrespect in my own kingdom. I admit, I overreacted—but you might have, too, were our situations reversed. If I entered your realm and began smashing, oh, your precious heirlooms, mightn't you fly into a fury?"

What the man said seemed sensible in its own way, and Arby could easily imagine Xochipilli or Hermod reacting as wildly as Tanagrim had. Liz leaned back against von Fleischer's chest in a companionable fashion, wholly at ease, and it was hard to believe that there weren't two sides to the story of the Talents and Powers. "Maybe you're right. But it doesn't matter."

Liz's delicate shoulders relaxed in the embrace of von Fleischer's long hands. "Don't decide I am vanquished so soon." He squeezed her shoulders. "She *is* yours, you know. You can have her, and more—more than you can imagine…"

"Like I could trust you."

"There are inviolable contracts, like that ring you wear on your finger; contracts hooked deep into our basic essence."

Arby shrugged. "But it's over. Go up, go down, La Lune is waiting."

"No, no, today is the day that La Lune has defeated itself. Because there is a stop we will make on the way up, and from there I can let the river have its way with the lower levels of El Panal." He smiled. "I'm sure the two of us allied could clean up any who remain on the surface."

Both faces stared up at him from below, waiting. Liz lolled her head back on von Fleischer's chest, snuggling there, but an internal flash in Arby's mind conjured up another vision of von Fleischer and Liz: Monstrous Tanagrim lifting her by her leg and ripping her in half.

Arby let his consciousness creep onto the etheric, and he saw big fronds of purple-black power reaching up from von Fleischer, their tips pressing at Arby's own aura. He was being Pushed, Pushed with everything von Fleischer had, and once he realized what was happening, he shook away those intruding fronds from his consciousness like a dog shaking off water. "No, I don't think so. You've lived a long time. I think today is your day to say goodbye."

The smile didn't leave von Fleischer's face, but his eyes hardened. "And how will you manage that?" The man drew his sword. "*Mano a mano*, is that the plan? Dramatic perhaps, though I doubt you'd win—but I don't think you'll have the chance." He murmured something into Liz's ear.

"*You fucking loser*," she said to Arby. Her face went blotchy and as he watched it contorted into an expression more angry and hateful than any he'd seen in their worst quarrels. "Every time you had a chance you walked away from it. You're a coward! You're…you're an idiot! I should kill you myself!" Von Fleischer slipped a dagger into her hand, and she turned and began climbing the steel mesh siding. "I had more pleasure in ten minutes with him than in my years with you. What did you ever give me?" Her hands, one still holding the dagger between thumb and palm, reached through the hole and onto the roof, and below Arby saw von Fleischer grinning with satisfaction. Arby backed away when her contorted face showed itself. "Eternal life! He's shown me a whole world out there that lasts forever! And *you*—you want to throw it all away!"

At the words *eternal life*, Arby saw Liz's face on a possum's body, fighting her way through a mob of other rodents to lick up drops of blood from an anemone.

He stomped on her fingers and she cried out and fell back into the elevator cabin. He knew now what he had to do.

"Not very chivalrous," von Fleischer called out. "Let's try that again."

Arby found the spot where the winch cable was bolted into the central timber of the frame. He raised the axe and chopped down into the adjacent wood with all his might, and a wedge of wood flew out. The blade was buried deep, and he booted it out of the wood and raised the axe again.

"What are you doing?" von Fleischer asked, an edge of panic in his voice.

Arby chopped down, yanked the axe out, chopped again.

"You fool! What are you doing up there?"

Liz had dragged her head and shoulders through the hole and was pulling her weight up out of the cabin on her elbows. "I'm sorry," Arby said to her, and chopped down at the timber one more time.

There was a crack, and the whole elevator lurched. For a moment it seemed to stabilize, but then the timber gave a long splintering cry and they fell.

Arby tried not to cry out on the way down, but as he knew well, dying is always an unpleasant business, and before the end he let his voice join in with the screams from Liz and von Fleischer.

33

Chapter Thirty-Two Plus One

It was a month before Rooker was willing to travel, but as soon as he consented, Crystal had left La Lune. There was no way to avoid the black valley of grief over Arby, but La Lune and its populace only made things worse.

She sold the shop in Portland and dragged Rooker off to a remote cabin in the rainy islands of British Columbia. The life she built was simple and repetitive: a little cooking, household chores, some reading before the fire in the evenings, and, as Rooker recovered, some nice, satisfying sex lessons. But an invariable event of her day was a midafternoon meditation, where she tried to contact Arby's spirit. The crowd at La Lune had assured her that his essence still lived on out there somewhere, and she believed with all her heart that someday she would find him again.

Rooker spent most days out prowling through the forest, and as she had suspected, this not only hastened his healing, but made him ever-more himself. No wonder his parents had wanted to raise him and Helayjah in Montana: he was a creature of the wilderness, and though he was at first reluctant to admit it, the forest resonated with his soul.

Much later that year, when they drove to a village to buy supplies, there was a letter waiting at General Delivery behind the counter at the store.

Crystal had spent a little time in Elaina's suite at La Lune during her previous stay there, and had found it luxurious but overly organized. Yet from the moment she and Rooker stepped in the door this time, it was obvious something had changed. The same elegant violin sonatas played on the sound system, and the furnishings were still like something from a museum but everything was, by Elaina standards, disarrayed. Piles of towels sat on the bed, and several cloths were strewn on the floor.

Elaina sat in a peacock chair in the wide-windowed dayroom that opened out from her main chambers. "It's us," Crystal said, and, as so often happened, those sunglasses turned toward them as though the woman could see. She held a bundle in her arms, and as they approached Crystal saw that, no matter how improbable, Elaina was nursing a baby. Elaina held the finger of her free hand to her lips to sign for silence, and they crept across the padded carpet, even Rooker's heavy footfalls muffled.

The baby's head lolled back from Elaina's swollen breast, trailing long threads of saliva, and it was obvious the baby had been asleep at the nipple for some time. Elaina did up the flap on her nursing bra. "I'm glad you came."

"I didn't know you were pregnant," Crystal said.

"Neither did I, for a long time. And when I found out, I thought about telling you, but I wanted to be sure of—well, what I believed." Elaina's austere white skin had been invaded by the glow of pregnancy and nursing, but now Crystal thought she detected a blush rising on those cheeks. "Once, if you recall, you asked me if Arby and I were—'an item' is how you put it. We were, just once, the night before he died."

"This is Arby's kid?" Rooker asked. "How do you know?"

The baby awoke at the sound of the loud voice and screwed its little face into a look of displeasure that Elaina swiftly dandled away.

"Not that it's any of your business, but I haven't been with anyone else in ages."

"This is my grandson?" Crystal asked. She leaned forward. She'd never thought infants were cute, apart from Arby of course, but when this one closed its eyes and yawned, she was willing to make another exception.

"Sort of," Elaina said. "I mean, yes, but there's more. This isn't just Arby's son. This is Arby."

"What?" Crystal asked.

"Doesn't make sense," Rooker said, and both of the women shushed him. In a whisper, he added, "You can't get a woman knocked up with yourself. You'd have to be in two places at the same time."

"No you wouldn't," Elaina said. "He was alive when we…made love, obviously. And that creates the vortex. But conception isn't complete for hours after that, sometimes not for two days. And only a few hours later…"

"He died," Crystal said. "What's the baby's name?"

"Rainchild Bounty. You named him, not I."

"This is crazy," Crystal said, and then she realized Elaina was holding the baby up for her to take.

She gathered the bundle into her arms and strolled around the room, dandling him and gazing down at his face. Even if it weren't Arby, it had to be Arby's son—she could see it in the way his mouth worked in his sleep, in a hundred other elusive details, even somehow in the smell of his skin. Crystal rubbed her nose against his, breathing him in, and his eyes and mouth popped open in surprise. For a moment it seemed as though he might cry, but then his lips drew sideways into a toothless grin, and she saw it in his eyes. Her breasts ached in a little flash, as though she were engorged with milk and heard her child cry. "My god, it *is* him."

"Yes." Elaina had risen from her chair, and walked toward Crystal with all the confidence of a sighted person. "For some time I have had no doubt. And we find ourselves in a situation he once described to me on a walk in Bahrain: Arby has two mommies. He's as much your child as mine. More, perhaps. Would you consider raising him together with me?"

Rooker leaned in between the two women to look at Arby. "Raise him in this loony bin? Take him somewhere real. Alaska, maybe." He reached a big finger down and poked the baby in the chest. "Sound good, little guy? Want to go live with the bears?"

Arby stared at Rooker in astonishment, with the same stunned expression a baby might have if someone clashed a pair of cymbals by his ear. Then he twisted his face to the side and wailed.

The two women edged together, their shoulders closing Rooker out, and held the baby at the same time, bouncing him and cooing.

The disc-changer on the stereo cut off in the middle of a Mozart string quartet and spun to the ending chords of Beethoven's *Moonlight Sonata*, then spun again to a Bach fugue, and then shut itself off. The FM receiver powered on, and early Pearl Jam blared into the room.

The baby looked alarmed for a moment, but when the women began to laugh his mouth grew wide and he gurgled with joy, watching their faces.

"We'll stay," Crystal said.

THE END

About The Author

David T. Isaak (1954-2021) was an American author of both fiction and nonfiction.

Dr. Isaak held a BA in Physics and MA and PhD degrees in resource systems. His professional work spanned the globe, taking him to over forty countries. He co-authored three technical, nonfiction books on oil and international politics, and wrote numerous papers, monographs, and multiclient studies.

David had an eclectic life. His first major in college was music, and he played piano and flute. He was a certified Bikram yoga instructor, an accomplished vegetarian cook, a creative mixologist, and an avid reader of fiction and nonfiction alike. He was driven by great characters and story, original voices, and especially by his love of the craft of writing, all of which are reflected in his own writing.

David passed away in April 2021. The five novels he left behind are as diverse as his life. These novels form ***The Isaak Collection***.

Sign up here to stay in touch and receive regular updates about ***The Isaak Collection***:

https://theisaakcollection.co/IWillFollowYou

If you enjoyed this book, please consider leaving a review wherever you purchased the book. Thank you.

Keep reading, for the first chapter of book 5 in
The Isaak Collection

SMITE THE WATERS

THE ISAAK COLLECTION
DAVID T. ISAAK

1

CARLA

Phil ran a classy place—the cleanest, most spacious porn shop in downtown Portland, Oregon—but you didn't see many unaccompanied ladies there, so when the woman pushed through the frosted-glass door, jangling the overhead bell, he stood up behind the register and put on what he hoped was an open, nonjudgmental expression, the face you'd want your doctor to wear.

She was bundled into a massive Gore-Tex jacket with the hood pulled up, as though she'd come in from mushing huskies rather than a wet Northwest evening. He didn't get a clear glimpse of her shadowed features before she turned and shambled across the store. In the middle of the shop she paused at the Valentine's-Day display of lingerie, the dangling scraps of red and pink lace insubstantial as mist beside her shapeless olive-green coat.

There'd been a time, a brief time, back in the early 1990s, when as many women as men had visited the shop, the ladies usually arriving in giddy twos and threes. They seldom bought anything on the first visit, but they'd slip back to the store a day or two later, solo, and snap up the goodies they'd been embarrassed to buy in front of their friends. He'd liked it, women in the place; it made the whole enterprise feel happier, goofier, less, well, *dirty*…but the Internet had put an end to all that. Sure, women were buying more sex toys and more porn, if you could believe the surveys, but they were doing it on the sly with a click and a credit-card number, delivery in UPS brown; which left Phil with the raincoat crowd, and squirrels like the trio of frat boys who were sniggering their way through the video section in the front of the store.

He settled back onto the high stool behind the counter and picked up his book of crossword puzzles.

The woman was across the room now, her back to him, studying the wall that displayed vibrators and dildos in all their latex and glitter-jelly glory. She tossed back her hood and he saw short blond hair. Short, but not dykey-short.

Phil was chewing his lip over the clue *Source of Nobel's fortune* when a burst of strangled laughter from the guys in the video section jerked his head upright.

All three were talking in loud whispers, looking toward the woman in the rear of the store. The biggest guy, the one with the mullet haircut—a mullet, for Chrissakes—said, "Psst! Wanna save some money?" His friends giggled.

The woman ignored them, but Phil slid off the stool and onto his feet. "Hey."

Only one of the trio, a boy in an orange windbreaker, looked over at him. "Cool it, Jake," the kid said to the guy in the mullet.

"Yo." Jake leaned back, still watching the woman, and clasped his hand over his crotch, hefting. "Yo, *Eskimo Pie*. Got the real thing here, no batteries required…"

The woman turned and looked over at the boys. Something about her stance made Phil stare. She hadn't recoiled, hadn't backed away; she stood with her legs braced, her face hidden from him by the thrown-back hood.

After a long moment she went back to her browsing, and one of the boys giggled again.

Phil roused himself and slapped the counter. "Hey, goddammit!" This time the whole trio looked at him. "Out." He gestured at the door with his thumb. "Now."

Jake swayed, and Phil realized the boy was drunk. "Look, man," Jake said, "it's a free country…" He started toward the counter. Another boy, the one in camo fatigues, put a restraining hand on his arm, but Jake shook it off and kept coming. "Why doncha mind your own fuckin' business, huh?"

Phil held up the receiver of the phone. "See the phone?" He held up his other hand, index finger raised. "See the finger? Want to see it dial 9-1-1?"

"Wanta see that phone shoved up your ass?" Jake stumbled into a rack of discount videos but kept coming, his fists shaking.

Phil dropped the receiver into its cradle and hoisted the 12-gauge from beneath the counter. "Want a couple pounds of lead up *your* ass?" He didn't point it, just held it in one hand like a sceptre, letting the boys see it. He tilted his head at the door. "Out."

Jake raised his hands, palms forward and even with his shoulders, somewhere between *slow down* and *I surrender*, but he didn't move until his pals crossed the room and led him out the front door. As he stepped out into the night his courage revived enough for him to kick the doorframe and shout, "And fuck you, man!" over his shoulder.

The bell ding-a-linged as the door shut.

The woman had gone back to her browsing. "I'm really sorry about that," Phil said. She shrugged without turning. "Seriously. We're"—he searched for words—"grateful for your business." *Grateful for your business. Christ. What a putz.*

He sat down, realized he was still holding the shotgun, and stowed it back under the counter. It wasn't until he let loose of the gun that his hands started trembling, and for some reason it seemed that the thing to do was sit on them, palms down on the stool, the pressure of his weight strangely calming.

He sat like that until the woman headed toward the door. As she passed the counter, he stood again. "I really do want to apologize…"

She stopped and regarded him with an indifferent frown, as though he were an unfamiliar television show: a little puzzling but not of any real consequence. He guessed she was about thirty; a good face, strong bones, but one with red-rimmed, bloodshot eyes and skin that turned sallow under the shop's fluorescent lights. He smelled the alcohol on her—not the smell on her breath, though that was there, too, but the stale odor that emanates from the pores after a few days of hard drinking.

"We don't—" he began, and swallowed. "Things like that don't happen here much." She continued to stare. "Maybe I should call the police anyway, huh? Or, maybe I could get you a cab?"

It could have turned into a shrug, but she only tipped one shoulder forward a half-inch before she turned away and pulled the door open.

Out on the darkened sidewalk Carla tilted her head back, eyes closed, letting the cold stroke her face. She should have taken off the jacket when she was inside, but it'd seemed like too much trouble, and besides, it was so damn bulky she'd have knocked things over. She straightened up and unzipped it halfway, shivering with relief as the chilly night air searched out the perspiration on her blouse.

She checked her watch. A little after 10:30. Maybe time for one more vodka-tonic before catching the 11:02 bus across the river to the East Side. She headed north, wishing, not for the first time, that she still had a car. And, hell, as long as she was wishing, a license, too.

The store was well south of Burnside, below the restaurant district, and at night cars passed infrequently, their tires making the sound of ripping paper as they rolled by on the wet asphalt. Typical Portland weather: you had to look at the puddles to tell whether it was raining or just misting. The streets, sidewalks, and buildings glistened like hard candies beneath the streetlights.

The slapping sounds of footsteps came from a dozen yards behind her. She glanced back, and saw, without much surprise, the boys from the porn shop. "Need some company?" one of them yelled.

She kept walking, but unzipped her jacket and pulled it off, hanging it over her right shoulder by hooking her thumb in the hood. A catcall from the rear, and then a voice urging her to take it all off.

Her eyes scanned the sidewalk ahead. No open businesses, and nothing handy in the way of bricks or clubs.

Another voice: "Guys, this is *not* cool." She stopped and glanced back. The kid in the orange windbreaker backed away and headed across the empty street, putting distance between himself and the other two.

Jake and the kid in camo stopped for a moment. Then Jake made a gesture of acquiescence, tilting his head and revolving his thumbs outward—hey, what can I say?—and the two of them turned into an alley on their right and vanished.

She didn't believe it, not for a minute.

Sure, it might be the adrenaline talking, but when adrenaline talked, Carla paid attention.

She shifted the jacket to her left shoulder as she walked, tried to get out of her head and into her body. Too much to drink. One drink, that could actually loosen you up, speed your reflexes, but she'd been knocking them back since, what, noon? She drifted to the left, toward the curb; if they came back it would have to be from the right, and the main thing with males was to keep them from getting a grip, prevent them from using that unfair upper-body strength.

She reached the corner, glanced around it, crossed the street. Her face was wet from the continual drifting drizzle. Seemed sometimes like she'd been damp her whole life: Oregon, Georgia, and then, when she thought she'd left water behind for a while, even in the Middle East. Who would have thought it: a godforsaken *humid* desert. Jeddah, Dhahran, Bahrain, Abu Dhabi, even stinking Karachi. Wet but barren.

Arizona. I'm going to move to Arizona. Air so dry your skin cracks.

They stepped out from a building ten feet ahead of her. How the hell had they gotten there without her seeing them?

Because you're drunk, you silly bitch.

The two boys stood there, hands on their hips, fingers forward, lords of the universe. Girls could put their hands on their hips either direction, thumbs forward or thumbs back, but there was something wrong with boys, they always did it thumbs-back. She kept walking toward them.

A hunnert men and a hunnert women, Jill had said, take a hunnert men and a hunnert women, and pick the hunnert strongest out of the whole bunch, and you know what you get, girls? Three women and ninety-fucking-seven men. Ninety-fucking-seven.

Jill slapped her hands down on her hips, thumbs backward, like a boy. You girls think you're strong? You let him get aholda you and your average outta-shape fat-ass heart-attack banker will wrestle you down and pin you in a fair fight. Never close with a man. Never. Use our secret weapon. And you know what our secret is? Anybody?

Jolene had piped up from the back row. *We're smarter than they are, Lieutenant.*

Chuckles.

Jill smiled, sweat glistening on her face in the Georgia sunshine, but shook her head. *Since when's that a secret?* Laughter. *Anybody?*

Silence.

Killer Jill grinned. The secret is, we're meaner than they are. Way meaner. So you do this: Hurt 'em bad and hurt 'em fast, before they get aholda you.

Before.

Where was Killer now? Probably a fucking general. And here was Carla, out of shape and out of work and plastered, stumbling down the sidewalks...

Jake had said something, but Carla hadn't heard it, and now he was only a few feet away, and he said, "Hey, come on, we've got a room, we'll show you what a real one feels like, no charge for the first thirty minutes," and he reached out a hand and snatched at her arm and Carla grabbed his thumb with her right hand and torqued with her whole upper body and there was a crack and he screamed, but she twisted harder and the pain hurled him to the ground and as soon as Jake hit the pavement she whipped her jacket over Camo-boy's head.

She booted Jake in the face with her imitation Doc Martens, not combat boots but damn near as heavy, and when Camo-boy finally threw the jacket from his head he left a beautiful opening, his arms upstretched and his neck tilted back and she punched him in the throat, hard, not a killing blow, well, probably not, but his hands scrabbled at his neck as he choked. She took the time to glance at Jake, who clutched his hands to his bleeding face, before she stomped down hard, her full hundred-thirty pounds on Camo-boy's instep, which brought him crashing to the sidewalk alongside his pal.

Carla waited, knees slightly bent, poised on the balls of her feet, deciding what to do next, tuning out the sounds the boys were making. *Breathe. Don't use energy you don't need. Scan the body. Relax the face. Shake it out of the shoulders and let 'em hang. The perineum, those complex, subtle, layers of muscles between the anus and the genitals, let them go, you don't need them.*

Unclench. Unclench everywhere. Breathe.

She turned her head away, almost ready to leave, shivering with the post-adrenaline letdown, but looked back. Camo-boy was still fighting for breath. Jake's hands covered his face, his broken thumb out at a cockeyed angle, and he might have been crying.

For a moment she felt a quiver of guilt, as though someone had plucked a tendon in her body like a guitar string; but then she pulled in a breath and thought about what Jake might have done if she were helpless, if he were the one making the decisions.

She shook her head to clear it, centered her balance on her booze-addled left leg. She kicked him in the knee with all the force and precision she could muster, and drove his kneecap out of its socket and up onto his thigh.

Carla was contemplating whether that was enough when the patrol car pulled up.

She worried that Lydia might still be out, but Lyddie picked up on the fourth ring, her voice filled with sleep. "Yeah?"

"Lydia, it's Carla. I need a favor."

A long pause. "What is it this time?"

"I'm downtown. In County. I need to swing bail somehow. It's too late for tonight, but in the morning—"

A deep exhale across the phone line. "Why didn't you call in the morning, then?"

"Wanted to be sure I got you." Carla glanced at the deputy waiting stolidly by the door, a big woman whose broad hips were exaggerated by a belt carrying a half-ton of cop crap. "I—" She stopped. "Look, they're charging me with assault"—she heard Lydia's intake of breath, and hurried to forestall her—"wasn't my fault, it wasn't, these guys jumped me, and I have a witness who'll tell 'em how they were hassling me, and probably the DA will just drop the whole thing, but that's what the police have booked me for right now, and—"

"How much, Carla?"

"It's… They tell me it's three thousand dollars." She braced herself for the explosion, but there was a long silence. "Look, I know I already owe you some back rent, and I know I been fucking up a lot lately—"

"That's not it." Lydia's voice was mild. "Hon, short of mortgaging this house, there's no way I can lay my hands on that kind of cash. Can't you go to one of those bail bonds guys or something?"

"They don't have those in Oregon. Besides, what could I give them as collateral?" The after-booze headache announced its arrival in her skull, strolling right in without knocking and making itself at home. "Lyddie—I'm going to get a job real soon, I really am. I'll pay you back, with interest."

"You're not getting it, are you? It's not that I don't want to help you, it's that I can't, okay? I can't." The sounds of a cigarette being lit came across the phone, and Carla pictured smoke rolling out of Lydia's lips as she added, "And I don't think you're going to get a job anyway. That LRI company that keeps calling—"

"Lyddie, they won't let me take a job as a rent-a-cop."

"—and you just brush 'em off. Is that how you act if you really want a job?"

"Lyddie, it's not a matter of *want*. They can't bond me."

"Well, the guy who owns that company was by here just before dinner—in person—and he seemed pretty anxious to meet you, and I tell you, he looked like he had serious money. Maybe he'd offer you some other kind of job, something else with his company—"

"Yeah, what? You think I know how to type?" The visiting headache, having spent some time lolling on the couch up in the frontal lobes, found the stereo hidden in Carla's brainstem and cranked the volume so high that all you could hear was the pulse of the rhythm section. She pushed the heel of her free hand against her temple. *It's got a beat, you can dance to it.*

"—but you're not even interested in trying, are you?"

"I'm trying." Right now she needed aspirin more than she needed a get-out-of-jail-free card. "I'm trying. But I need help."

"Carla. Pay attention. By the time I could raise that much cash, you'd already have had your first court thingie. And if you're as innocent as they say, they'll turn you loose, right? And..." Lydia hesitated, and Carla heard her take a drag on her cigarette. "And, hon? I know this is gonna piss you off, but it wouldn't hurt you none to stay there and dry out for a couple of days."

The night could have been worse. Being booked on a violent felony kicked her to a cell of her own, skipping right past the drunk tank, and once she'd begged a couple of Excedrin from the deputy she lay on her mattress and covered her eyes with one arm, trying to calm the throbbing in her head.

There was no thinking, not even any dreaming, before the door to the cell buzzed open. "Smukowski?"

"Huh?" Carla uncovered her eyes and struggled to sit up.

A fat black woman stood in the doorway, ready to explode right out of her Multnomah-County-deputy costume. She checked her clipboard. "You Carla Smukowski, right?"

"Yeah, sure." Carla's stomach rumbled. "Breakfast already?"

"Uh-uh. Morning. But no breakfast for you. Your bail's posted and you on your way out."

Lyddie, God bless her. She'd found a way.

It took an hour to get through the formalities and climb back into civvies. When she finally walked out into the lobby of the Justice Center, Lydia was nowhere to be seen. She glanced around the room, turning slowly with the big coat draped over her arm, but all she saw was streams of what seemed to be lawyers, heading to and from the elevators.

"Ms. Smukowski?" The man's voice was southern but elegant, and the figure she saw when she turned matched the voice perfectly—a tall, slender man whose gray suit made his hair shine silver by contrast. His hand was outstretched to shake hers, and as she took it he said, "Lamont Richter, LRI Security. You're a mighty difficult woman to find."

She realized he was done shaking hands and that she ought to release her grip. "Where's Lydia?"

"Your landlady? When I called on her this morning, she was kind enough to let me know where you were. I was hoping you'd have a little breakfast with me." His eyebrows lifted, and he gave the slightest sweep of his hand toward the entrance.

"You stood my bail?"

"Might have been hard for me to join you for breakfast if I hadn't. Short of getting myself arrested."

He began ambling toward the doors, and Carla found herself keeping pace. "I've told your office before, Mister—?" *Ricktah?* Was that what he'd said?

"Rich*er*. Like the way they measure earthquakes." He opened the glass door and ushered her through.

"I've told your office before, there's no bonding agency that'll cover me on a security gig..."

He swished the problem away with a languid toss of his long fingers, and headed down toward the sidewalk. In the southeast a break in the ceiling of clouds let through the weak glow of the February sun, and up and down the street Oregonians craned their necks, seeking the source of this unexpected light. Richter stopped at the curb and raised a hand as if hailing a cab. "Truth be told, Carla—you don't mind if I call you Carla, do you?—truth be told, we're not in quite the line of work you might think."

No, she didn't mind being called *Cahlah*, but she doubted that he really understood the situation. "I just don't want you spending money thinking that—"

"Don't you worry about it. Either way, I assure you, I'll write it off on my taxes."

A hulking blue-green Mercedes pulled up in the street, and the chauffeur jumped out and ran around the car to open the doors. No, not a chauffeur, Carla decided, assessing his build and watching his moves. Bodyguard.

Once they were settled into the back seat, Richter asked where they should go for breakfast, and Carla protested that it was up to him. "I don't know my way around this town," he said. "It's your breakfast. Pick anywhere you like."

"Let's go to Sam's then." The driver glanced back. "Over in Hollywood?" Richter and the driver both blinked in that out-of-towner way that said the only Hollywood they knew about was in LA. "Across the river, over by where I live. Just head for my place—you were just over there, right?—and I'll give directions when we get close."

After profuse apologies, Richter immersed himself in a series of cell-phone calls, discussing some sort of contract in terms that were meaningless to Carla. The Mercedes ran smooth but heavy, and it wallowed a little on corners, like an oil tanker changing course. Armored. Had to be. She reached up and rapped the window with a knuckle, then swiveled her hand and tapped with a fingernail. Sure as hell not glass. Probably one of the new Lexan derivatives.

The driver caught her assessing the car and grinned.

Sam's Billiards was a venerable neighborhood institution, one that was open to all kinds, but once the two of them were seated at a table, she regretted her choice. She watched Richter's eyes wander to the scarred L-shaped bar to the right of the door, and then back across the rows of pool tables on the left, tables that queued up far behind where they were seated. It was 9:30, too late for the weekday breakfast crush and too early for the lunch crowd. Far in the rear, a pair of hardcore pool pros practiced, and the sharp cracks and the rumble of balls running down the throats of the pockets provided the only background noise. Sam's must have been there since the forties, and even with the windows that had recently been punched into the front wall, it felt dark and smoky inside, as though the ghosts of hustlers long dead still controlled the lighting.

The old guy behind the bar came out to take their order— poached eggs on toast with coffee for Richter, two over easy, bacon, hash browns, wheat toast, and a Bloody Mary for Carla. In the silence after the waiter left, Carla said, "Probably not your kind of place, huh?"

"It's"—Richter managed a small, graceful smile—"colorful." He leaned forward onto his elbows and clasped his hands. "So. That *rara avis* in the flesh, a female Ranger."

Carla snorted. "Ain't any women in the Rangers. Never will be, either."

He elevated his fingers and unclasped them, dismissing her words, and then interwove them again. "A quibble. Same sort of training…"

"Not really. There were a couple of squads. My bunch got a lot of diplomatic training. K Force."

"Ah, yes, Special K."

Carla put her palms flat on the table and studied him. "Where'd you hear that?" Their drinks came, and Richter went through an elaborate ritual with his cream and sugar. Carla lifted her Bloody Mary, careful not to seem too anxious, and took a long swallow, letting her eyes close as the heat moved into her core and then radiated out. It was all she could do not to give a sigh of relief, the same sweet outlet of breath that came to your lips when you emptied a painfully full bladder.

He watched her as she sat the glass down and doctored it with pepper. "Why the Army?"

"Family tradition. Plus, hey, I grew up in Eastern Oregon. Short of swimming down the Columbia, military's about the only road out of there." She made a sound she intended as a laugh. "And here I am back in Oregon. Least I'm still on this side of the mountains." She took a long drink and then sniffled as the pepper oils raced up the back of her nostrils. Her hand moved to set the glass down, but, on reflection, she lifted it again and drained it first instead. The clack of the tumbler on the table had the intended effect: the bartender looked over and she tapped the rim.

"Perhaps you'd be so kind as to give me a little background on your time in the Forces? An informal resume, as it were?"

"Why? You seem to know everything." She wasn't sure why she was being obstreperous; something about the man made her want to disrupt his smooth manner.

He smiled. "Maybe I'd just like to hear *your* perspective on things."

Carla's tongue sought out one of the cracked fillings in an upper molar while she considered. Why not?

K Force had been a product of typical Army thinking: Unless you want to fuck them, women are invisible.

Damned if the jackasses weren't right. Women bodyguards, women security forces, women counterterrorist squads—it's like they weren't there. Has the target got anybody with him? Nah—just some girls.

There'd been some turf battles with the Marines at first—the Marines had always supplied the security for US embassies, and they didn't see why they should hand over security details for traveling politicos to some newfangled pussy parade—but after 9/11, there'd been more unofficial diplomatic visits than ever before, and if you needed to stay beneath the radar of the press, and sometimes beneath the radar of your so-called allies, then a Marine escort wasn't a buttload of help in staying inconspicuous.

Carla'd been in the right place at the right time; she'd already been through two years of weapons training, hand-to-hand, explosives, and clandestine ops; they'd already had three years to load her down with Arabic—though she had a hard time making her accent understood west of Suez—plus good Urdu, decent Hindi, and even enough Pushtun to negotiate a surrender or order roast lamb. Once the Twin Towers hit the ground, and low-key envoys—the ones the American public never knew about—started slithering around the Mideast and Pakistan, Carla was a hot property.

Her second Bloody Mary came. "You probably know what happened after that." She tossed the celery stalk onto the table and shook pepper into the glass until less red than black showed on the surface.

Richter sipped his coffee, his pinky finger extended as though he were at an afternoon tea party. He set the cup down in the saucer and raised his eyebrows politely.

She exhaled. "Okay. It's like a month after Bush Junior goes into Iraq. We were in Amman, in Jordan, when we weren't supposed to be, at least according to the official Washington rap. We came in on tourist visas—yeah, right, tourists in Jordan, in the middle of Gulf War Two, the sequel—and we don't even drop through our embassy. My guy is set up there for a few weeks to talk to the Palestinians, off the record, without the Israelis knowing. Or maybe Mossad was supposed to know—maybe the whole point was that they were supposed to find out. Who effing knows, right?"

Sometimes a drink before breakfast can go straight to your head. She looked at Richter to see if he was following. He nodded, so she went on. "So we're there in this half-assed Jordanian international hotel, typical overpriced boring fucking Arab hotel, when some raghead sonofabitch slams a car-bomb into an Army checkpoint in Iraq. One of the first attacks, right after Baghdad goes down. And…" Carla lifted the glass, took a long drink, and then blinked, tears rushing to her eyes as the pepper rushed to her sinuses. "My brother Kevin. Three other guys."

He reached across the table and settled his fingers on her free hand, but she shook them off. "Don't," she said. "Army was decent about it. Promised to fly me home right away, just as soon as they could rotate one of my cohort in, couple three days at the most, a month's compassionate leave. Month's leave. I woulda rather they sent me into Iraq with an M60 and unlimited ammo belts, but, hey, they were being decent. And it all woulda worked out, except the next morning there's these fuckers, these fuckers right on the front steps of my hotel, *celebrating*, celebrating the fucking car-bomb that killed Kev, waving around this fucking poster of Osama, and worst of all I can understand what the fuckers are shouting, and… Shit. No excuses. I lost it. Totally effing lost it. Completely fucked the dog." A sad smile. "Course, the weaseldick with the poster turns out to be the son of the Saudi ambassador…but you knew all that, didn't you?"

"Not the part about your brother."

"Hmmph." She took a big swallow of her drink and put the tumbler down, put it down so hard that even though it was only half-full the drink nearly sloshed out. "So the brass had to waste me to keep the Saudis happy; but they couldn't totally fuck me without drawing attention to the whole Special K, which is low-profile city. So they double-dissed me—dishon discharge. And here's Smukowski, back in the gray and the green."

He waited for a moment. "Tell me, Carla. You sorry now you did it?"

She started to answer, but their breakfast orders arrived, and she sat silent until the waiter left. "Sorry I fucked up the guys out on the steps? No. Sorry I got kicked out of the service? Of course. Why wouldn't I be?"

"I surely don't know." He picked up his knife and fork and used the knife to slice through the yolks of his poached eggs, letting the startling gold liquid spill out across the whites. "Exactly how *do* you feel about those fellows who were out on the steps?"

Carla tried to drop her shoulders and relax. Breathe. Out of your head and into your body. Unclench it. "How do I feel? About them?" Part of her said this is no way to get a job, babes, but a bigger part of her said, just say it, just for once in your fucking life really say it. "Fuck 'em, that's how I feel. I'm sorry they're still fucking alive." She tried to relax, just let it ride, but it felt too damn good to say it right out loud. "In fact, you wanta know the truth, I'd like to see toe-tags on all of 'em, men, women, and children, from Afgagisburg all the way over to fucking Morocco. Fuck 'em. They hate us? Fine. I hate them, too." She sat back and folded her arms, staring at him.

"Well." His voice was mild. He had sliced off a piece of yolk-saturated toast, and he forked it into his mouth. He chewed, swallowed, and dabbed his lips with a napkin before he asked, "And what about Nigeria? Or Is-rai-el?"

Carla's arms tightened. "Fuck them, too. And Somalia. And Sudan."

"Hmm. You know…" He folded the flimsy paper napkin as though it were top-class linen before he put it down beside his plate. "You know, I might be able to offer you a position you'd appreciate. One that uses your real skills." He flagged the bartender as the man passed. "I believe the young lady needs another one of your fine cocktails."

Carla unfolded her arms and leaned forward. "What do you mean?"

"I think—just think, mind you—that I'm prepared to offer you a job. A job, I might add, that seems to mesh almost perfectly with your…attitudes." He pointed with his fork. "Your eggs are getting cold."

She killed the last of her second drink, and then forked up a mass of egg and hash browns. The tastes in her mouth—greasy starch, fatty yolk, rubbery proteins—coaxed forth a rush of saliva, and in its train followed a low, demanding hunger that she hadn't felt in ages. She began to eat in earnest, chasing sloppy, egg-drenched potatoes with crunchy bites of toast, until her third Bloody Mary arrived.

She peppered it and raised it to her lips, but before she sipped it, Richter said, "You savor that one, okay, Carla? Because that's likely the last drink you're going to have in quite some time." He stared at her.

She took a sip, rolled it on her tongue, and then swallowed.

It felt good to be hungry again.